Praise for novels by Allison Pittman

The Seamstress

"Allison Pittman has taken a minor but memorable Dickens character and created a whole world for her, thoroughly researched and beautifully detailed. The seamstress's rags-to-riches-to-rags story is an endlessly fascinating and touching one. You'll find yourself caring deeply not just about her, but also about everyone she cares for."

GINA DALFONZO, founder and editor of Dickensblog

"I finished reading *The Seamstress* three days ago and can't stop thinking about it. Well-drawn characters inspired by Dickens's *A Tale of Two Cities*, and exquisite writing in the spirit of Victor Hugo's *Les Misérables*, combine in Pittman's latest novel of life and faith amid the upheaval of the French Revolution. Researched in great detail, a brilliant and ingenious work, not to be missed."

CATHY GOHLKE, Christy Award–winning author of *Until We Find Home* and *Secrets She Kept*

"Destined to be a classic in its own right, *The Seamstress* is everything I love about historical fiction. The robust characters not only interact with real and pivotal events, but they embody the attitudes of the day in ways that are accessible for the modern reader. Pittman's power of language drew me deep into revolutionary France, and her accurate and sensitive portrayal of the turmoil earned my undying respect. *The Seamstress* is an intricate tapestry hemmed in truth and gracc. A masterpiece."

JOCELYN GREEN, Christy Award–winning author of *A Refuge Assured*

"Set amid the tumultuous French Revolution, *The Seamstress* is unabashedly profound and yet crafted with such care that I relished every heartrending word until the very last one. Through the lives of vibrant and genuine characters, notes of love, faith, and loyalty rise from its pages—all striking with one unanimous chord of *courage*. Allison Pittman has woven a novel that fortifies the spirit brick by brick so that as a nation is broken and transformed, so takes new shape yet another landscape: the reader's heart. *The Seamstress* is an absolute masterpiece with all the makings of a classic, and is one of the finest novels I have ever read."

JOANNE BISCHOF, Christy and Carol Award–winning author of *Sons of Blackbird Mountain*

"In *The Seamstress*, Allison Pittman has given us a novel of revolutionary France sweeping in its scope, a story of hope and despair, strength and frailty, courage and cowardice seamlessly stitched. With its pages filled with characters who will haunt the heart long after the last is turned, it is a story hemmed in triumph—of the human spirit in the midst of national chaos, but even more of Christ's infinite love, transcending ideology, reaching alike into palaces and poverty. I finished this novel with a holy hush in my soul."

LORI BENTON, author of *Burning Sky* and *Many Sparrows*

"In the midst of revolution and royalty, Pittman weaves a captivating tale of two cousins whose humble beginnings birth remarkable journeys. A beautiful, rich tale of love, loss, and amazing faith, *The Seamstress* is a book that haunts, satisfies, and inspires all at once. I loved this book!"

HEIDI CHIAVAROLI, author of *Freedom's Ring* and *The Hidden Side*

"*The Seamstress* is a study in nostalgia: carefully evoking a classic while establishing itself as a classic in its own right. Deftly and intelligently nodding to its magnanimous source material, *A Tale of Two Cities*, it remains confident as its own entity. Appealing equally to Dickensian readers and the uninitiated, *The Seamstress* is a lush, moving, and brilliantly sewn world. The thinking reader's inspirational read, it is at once rich, beguiling, and accessibly readable. Its aftertaste will spoil you for any other story for a long, long while."

RACHEL McMILLAN, author of the Van Buren and DeLuca series

Loving Luther

"Accessible writing infused with romantic tension creates a provocative and heartwarming read."

LIBRARY JOURNAL

"*Loving Luther* is a sophisticated, provocative novel . . . with depth, and it is unexpectedly touching."

FOREWORD MAGAZINE

"Pittman pens an exquisite tale based on the limited historical sources about Katharina von Bora, capturing the emotions of a nun grappling with the idea of bondage to the church versus a new and unfamiliar freedom in faith."

BOOKLIST

"Although Pittman's previous novels have been set in the United States, she feels quite at home in 16th-century Wittenberg. This novel should be of interest not only to readers of Christian fiction, but to readers of general historical fiction as well."

HISTORICAL NOVEL SOCIETY REVIEWS

"*Loving Luther* showcases author Allison Pittman's genuine flair for compelling and memorable storytelling."

MIDWEST BOOK REVIEW

On Shifting Sand

"Pittman manages to . . . satisfy readers' thirst for drama, deceit, and deliverance."

BOOKLIST

"Demonstrating her versatility as a novelist, Pittman has written a moving tale of temptation, surrender, guilt, and redemption."

LIBRARY JOURNAL

"Pittman effectively contrasts the repercussions of forgiveness when it is withheld and granted."

PUBLISHERS WEEKLY

"Pittman makes a departure from her usual genre with an elegantly written novel. . . . The tale is so well told it will stay with you."

ROMANTIC TIMES

The Roaring Twenties Series

"Deftly intertwining the 1920s plotline with diary entries, Pittman's third series outing is filled with family drama, suspense, and enough twists and turns to keep readers engrossed until the very end. This tale of truth and forgiveness will attract fans of Francine Rivers, Rosamunde Pilcher, and those who enjoy family sagas."

LIBRARY JOURNAL on *All for a Sister*

"Pittman handily captures the societal extremes during the Jazz Age, and her focus on the roles of women, from demure traditionalists to the influential McPherson and the 'modern' woman, adds a nuanced level of conflict to this entertaining novel."

BOOKLIST on *All for a Story*

"Pittman skillfully paints the complete picture of this bold female character. Readers of inspirational fiction will be stirred as this story of longing unfolds, revealing testimony to true contentment."

BOOKLIST on *All for a Song*

"Mesmerizing. . . . Allison Pittman's latest novel is a delight to read, having been woven together with beautiful narrative, stirring faith, and characters you will connect with. . . . *All for a Song* is a book that will not only entertain you, but will leave you thinking about why we make the choices we do, and even how we use the gifts God has given us. I award this book my highest recommendation, and a rating of 5 out of 5 stars."

CHRISTIAN FICTION ADDICT on *All for a Song*

"*All for a Song* proves Allison Pittman is not only one of the most talented and literary writers in the CBA but also an author with a tremendous writing range. Never afraid to confront subjects that have a bit of edge, Pittman sets the coming-of-age story of innocent Dorothy Lynn against the Evangelical fervor strummed up by charismatic speaker Aimee Semple McPherson. The result is an engaging and unique experience that reads like a breath of fresh air in a market filled with many similar historically influenced tales."

NOVEL CROSSING on *All for a Song*

The Sister Wife Series

"Once again Pittman tells an engaging story in which the characters are moved to examine their faith and make difficult decisions. Readers who enjoy CF dealing with family relationships and crises of faith will appreciate it."

LIBRARY JOURNAL on *For Time and Eternity*

"In the second book of the Sister Wife series (*Forsaking All Others*), the characters are unforgettable. Pittman pulls the reader into her stories and gives them a glimpse of the values the Mormons believe in."

ROMANTIC TIMES, 4½ stars

the Seamstress

a novel

ALLISON PITTMAN

Tyndale House Publishers, Inc.
Carol Stream, Illinois

Visit Tyndale online at www.tyndale.com.

Visit Allison Pittman at www.allisonkpittman.com.

TYNDALE and Tyndale's quill logo are registered trademarks of Tyndale House Publishers, Inc.

The Seamstress

Designed by Jennifer Phelps

Edited by Kathryn S. Olson

Published in association with William K. Jensen Literary Agency, 119 Bampton Court, Eugene, Oregon 97404.

Library of Congress Cataloging-in-Publication Data
Names: Pittman, Allison, author.
Title: The seamstress / Allison Pittman.
Description: Carol Stream, Illinois : Tyndale House Publishers, Inc., [2019]
Identifiers: LCCN 2018027835 | ISBN 9781414390468 (sc)
Subjects: | GSAFD: Christian fiction.
Classification: LCC PS3616.I885 S43 2019 | DDC 813/.6—dc23 LC record available at https://lccn.loc.gov/2018027835

ISBN 978-1-4964-4018-1 (HC)

Printed in the United States of America

25 24 23 22 21 20 19
7 6 5 4 3 2 1

I have a heart full of grateful memories for all those students who climbed into the tumbrils and rolled along with me through all the reading, the analysis, the journaling, the experiencing of the beloved novel, A Tale of Two Cities*—with special thanks to:*

SS—who pulled a cardboard ship through the aisles of my classroom to capture the ominous journey toward the Loadstone Rock . . .

GG—who donned a puffy shirt and transported a classroom of high school sophomores to a place of harrowing, dark confession . . .

AC—who met my eyes one afternoon when he discerned Carton's plan and the world became a place where we two shared a secret . . .

And now I share with you a few secrets of my own invention.

A Prayer

God of heaven, see me now
'Neath stars and moon and darkest cloud.
Grant me dreams to sleep in peace,
And with the sunrise in the East,
Wake me to a glorious day.
Father, Son, and Holy Spirit—I pray,
Amen.

Une Prière

Dieu des cieux voyez-moi maintenant,
Sous les étoiles et la lune et les nuages gris,
Accordez-moi le sommeil de rêves tranquilles.
Et au lever du soleil à l'est,
Réveillez-moi pour voir un jour glorieux.
Au nom de Dieu le Père, le Fils, et le Saint-Esprit—je prie,
Amen.

Part I

Le Printemps (Spring) 1788

Dieu des cieux voyez-moi maintenant . . .

L'épisode 1

Renée

MOUTON BLANC, LA VALLÉE

My first and last memories are my cousin Laurette. She wasn't quite three years old when I came into the world, but her arms were sturdy enough to hold me, and my mother never missed an opportunity to thrust me upon her. Laurette's was the breath on my cheek as we slept, curled together on the tiny mat in the corner of our tattered house. She spoke the nightmares away, softened my bread with milk, entertained me for hours on end with a knotted string and games of cat's cradle.

Our mothers were sisters, sharing a house on the fringe of our village—Mouton Blanc, named for the white sheep that produced fine, prized wool. Our family never owned any sheep of their own. We had no farm, no land. Only two rooms and a fire, but subsisted on the prosperity of the town. Laurette and I grew up smelling their roasting meat, and shared tiny portions cooked in stew. We walked through the bustling market square, past baskets overflowing with harvest, watching our mothers trade small coins for the remnants hidden behind the merchants. The yeasty smell of the baker's shop meant a fresh, hot loaf of bread, and a crossed bun handed over the counter for the two of us to share, bite by bite.

My father was unknown to me, and if my mother knew his name, she never uttered it. I was given no fanciful tale about a dashing stranger, or a wandering minstrel, or a farmer's son overtaken by desire. I asked once if I could call Laurette's father my own, as we shared the same roof and table, but was delivered a slap to my face that left the mark of my mother's hand for nearly a week. I never asked again. At the time (I was probably six years old) I assumed my mother reacted so harshly because she wouldn't want such a man for my father. My uncle was short-tempered and often drunk, quick to violence and raging. But then, as I grew older, I noticed the way he looked at my mother—she was the more beautiful of the two sisters—and having learned a bit about the workings of men and women, I wondered if I hadn't come close to guessing the truth.

Though our household was never prosperous, it was, for the most part, quiet. Content. Laurette's father worked for different farmers, hiring himself out during the shearing season and throughout the year, mending fences and whatever day labor he could get. Always, it was enough to feed us and allow him nights at the tavern to drink up the rest. Our mothers did village work, too, carding great sacks of wool, teaching both of us the art as soon as our hands were big enough to fit the wooden paddles. Laurette never mastered the skill, but I loved any moment my hands were occupied with creating. Mother would barter old clothes from the rag man, and spend winter evenings cutting and mending, turning women's skirts into boys' breeches and old nightshirts into christening gowns, edged with lace tatted from spinners' scraps.

I was too young to take note of all the changes as they happened. Realization dawned that we had less money. Less food.

Less everything. I understood the years of drought and the toll they took on the local harvests, but I had no concept of the role the king played in the slow death of our town. I didn't know he took good grazing land and gave it to the Church. I didn't know he imposed taxes beyond what my neighbors could pay. Therefore, I didn't understand the hopelessness that would drive Laurette's father to kill her mother in a drunken rage, nor the hanging that left us equally fatherless. Even more, I could not fathom a grief that would cause my mother to simply walk away one night, leaving us equally orphaned. I was ten, Laurette was twelve, and we lived for nearly two months on the scraps of neighbors' charity before anyone else even knew she'd gone.

But Émile Gagnon found us. Rather, we found him. I would guess that his flock still numbered five hundred head at the time, and Laurette hoped we would find work—in his kitchen, in his fields. Winter was coming and we had nothing to fill our bellies or warm our hearth. We'd heard him one day at the inn, Le Cochon Gros, the same place that slaked my uncle's thirst and nourished his anger. Gagnon was lifting a toast to the fine price he'd fetched for his wool, wishing a blessing on the carders and spinners, the weavers and tailors who take the humble offerings of his sheep and make clothing fit for the king.

"Think of it, spun fine and stretched over the queen's legs . . . ," one of his fellow drinkers said, the rest of his comment spoken low and drowned out by raucous laughter.

It was Laurette who approached Gagnon. Looking back now, I realize what a young man he was. Everybody in town spoke of him with such glowing reverence, he might have been a founder. But he was only twenty-two—old enough to laugh at an off-color joke, but young enough to be embarrassed by it. He, too, was an orphan, if a grown man could be called such, having inherited his farm when his parents died in quick succession of a fever. Not a year later, he became a widower, losing his young wife and newborn child within an hour of each other. While some men might have turned bitter in the wake of so much loss, Émile Gagnon grew stronger.

He had turned away, a blush on his cheek, when Laurette walked right up to him.

"It's a fine thing," she said, "to ship everything away and leave nothing for your poor neighbors who are facing a winter with our dresses worn clean through."

That very evening we had a new home in Gagnon's barn. The small one, meant only to house his milk cows and dogs. It smelled of sweet hay and felt warm, with straw-stuffed ticks and feather pillows waiting in the loft. The walls were thick, the roof solid shingles, and while Gagnon said he wouldn't risk the danger of a stove to heat the room as we slept, we had the promise of hot irons during the coldest of winter nights.

For six years we have lived here. His sheep, our sheep, and this spring afternoon, Laurette and I lie next to each other, two shepherdesses stretched out on a carpet of green grass as they graze nearby.

⚜

"Your turn, Renée."

Laurette's voice is slow, the words almost slurred to a stop. I look over to see her arm flung across her eyes, blocking out the piercing sun.

"You're not even looking."

"I trust you." There's a hook of a smile at the corner of her mouth.

"All right." I turn my attention back to the vast sky above, dotted with clouds. "I see your rabbit." Pointing, the tip of my finger traces what could be a long, floppy ear. "But I'm afraid he's done for." I rise on one elbow and describe the mass of dark-gray clouds newly formed to the east. "Three dogs—or maybe one, like Cerberus."

"Cerberus?" Laurette never did pay as much attention to Gagnon's stories as I did.

"Cerberus, the three-headed dog that guards the gates of the underworld. Your little rabbit doesn't have a chance."

"Let them have it. They're probably hungry. I know I am."

I am, too, but I don't say so. Complaining about hunger is like complaining about being alive. It seems ungrateful, knowing we had our fill of bread and butter early this morning, and would find a good, filling bowl of soup upon our return. In between, we'd shared a flask of water and a boiled egg each.

"If only we could catch it," I say. "We could eat it ourselves, or most of it, anyway. And give the scraps to the dogs. Everyone, happy happy."

She lifts her arm enough to show me one open eye. "Even in fantasy you are practical."

I lie back down. "And even when there's nothing to be done you are lazy." She laughs, short and hearty, and I grin beside her. "Your turn."

"Non." She hums the word. "Why waste our time finding stories in the sky when we can drift off and find them in a dream?"

"Because we have to bring the sheep in."

"There's at least an hour before sunset." She settles in for comfort. "Do what you want with your time; I'll do what I want with mine."

Soft snores come within minutes, and I sit up, then stand up, brushing the dry grass from the back of my skirt. Looking out to the east, the same direction where my doglike pack of rain clouds seems to be gathering strength, I can just make out the white, woolly flock grazing on the horizon. More and more the air smells like rain, and I think it's best not to wait. Rain makes the sheep sluggish. Given the chance, they would stand still and turn into soggy statues.

Not far, a massive stone offers a better view, and I climb up, my bare feet gripping the smooth surface. Once standing, I bring two fingers to my mouth and whistle a distinct five-note command. Within seconds there is movement on the horizon. Two small, quick forms. Cossette and Copine, the dogs I helped train since their birth, are running in circles around the herd to gather it.

The herd is small now, little more than one hundred, and they move at a purposeful trot. The dogs flank them, taking on a pose that makes them look like two wolves stalking prey rather than beloved companions bringing them to safety. Thus, the sheep obey. I feel a certain pity, knowing that they live in a constant state of fear. Always feeling chased, hunted, watched. Ever alert and uneasy, their rest coming only when they are safely stabled in the yard. Or, better, in the barn, where the dogs sit as sentries outside, out of sight.

"You think they'd learn," I told Gagnon one afternoon when the sheep, grazing on the new, lush grass, shifted and startled with each movement of the dogs.

"Learn what?"

"That the dogs mean no harm. That they are champions, protectors."

"They're safer to keep their guard up," Gagnon said. "The dogs feel nothing for the sheep. They act in obedience to us. They run circles because it's a game, because we feed them. Their loyalty is to their own survival. If we ever stopped feeding them, left them to their own instincts, be certain they'd feed themselves somehow. The sheep are the smart ones. Better to live by the instinct God gave you than to be fooled by tricks and manners."

Now my instincts tell me to get ourselves home quickly, where we can have our hunger sated by whatever waits in the pot before tucking ourselves safely up in our room. I blow another signal, and the dogs break, double back, and begin to run. The sheep run with them, their woolly heads filled with fear at the chase. When they are close enough, I whistle again. Cossette and Copine drop to the ground, and the sheep come to a dead stop, their hooves rooted in place.

There's a rumble of thunder in the distance, and by the time I return to Laurette, she is sitting up and waiting.

"We'll have to hurry," I say. "To beat the rain."

She waves me off. "Afraid you'll melt? Like you're made of sugar?"

I want to say something back, but hold my tongue. This has been characteristic of my cousin of late—short, barbed remarks that make me feel my status with her has changed. Not really an enemy, but a rival of sorts. For all of our lives we have occupied the same space in the world, but there are moments like this one where I feel her nudging me away.

And so we walk. A brisk pace, but comfortable, the sheep behind and then beside us, responding to the pace set by the dogs, who seem much more eager to reach shelter than we do. The drops begin when we are in sight of the farm. It's nestled in a valley, bordered by a stream. There's a large, fenced corral for the sheep, as well as a long, flat building to house them in the winter and on nights like tonight. Gagnon's own house is a simple stone structure, and I can see smoke coming from the chimney promising a good fire and supper. By the time we arrive at the gate, the storm has broken out in earnest and Gagnon, wearing a waxed wool coat and broad-brimmed hat, meets us on the path.

"Go in!" he shouts above the storm. "I'll get them settled."

We obey, breaking into a run, new, soft mud beneath our toes. Every hour of a day spent beneath the sun washes away, our sweat replaced by sweet, fresh rivulets, our skin cooled.

We take off our sodden caps and unfasten our hair, raking our fingers through to distribute the wet. How disheveled we must look when we finally burst through Gagnon's door, thoroughly soaked, teeth chattering.

"W-we have to ch-change," Laurette says. "Or we'll catch our death."

"Change into what?" I have one other dress—same as she—and it is across the yard hanging on a hook next to my bed.

"Here."

I follow her into the great room, where a long trunk sits beneath a window, its lid a cushioned seat. Inside, Gagnon keeps blankets and linens. With the authority of a mistress, Laurette opens it, rummages through, and takes out an old, yellowed shirt and two blankets.

"Strip down and put this on." I obey, comforted by her maternal tone, but feel a new onslaught of cold when my skin is bare. She strips, too, and I'm struck—not for the first time—how much more of a woman she is than I. True, she's almost three years older, but she'd already developed the soft curves of her body when she was my age. While I'm rolling up the shirt-sleeves, I'm aware of the thinness of the material that falls past my knees. Such a garment would not suit Laurette. She might as well wear nothing.

In fact, she seems prepared to do just that, wrapping the thin blanket around her shoulders, holding the ends tight against her as she shivers by the fire. With her back to me, I notice a small hole right in the middle of the fabric, just atop her back-side. Moths, I suspect, eating right where the blanket had been folded in the trunk.

"Let me see that," I say. "Take it off. I have an idea. Bend down." This, because I barely reach her chin, and I slip the blanket over her head.

While rifling through the contents of the trunk, Laurette

had tossed a long strip of linen to the side. Picking it up now, I place it across her stomach, thread it through a smaller moth-hole near the small of her back, and wrap it back around, securing the loose blanket with a knot at her waist. The result is a dress, its hem long past her knees, the sleeves wide like tulips at her elbows. There's a clean line of color across her chest, outlining the bodice of her daily dress. Here, the fabric takes a sharp plunge beneath it, creating a soft V shape and an unprecedented view of the figure beneath.

"Aren't you the clever one, *Cousine*?" She puts her hands on her hips and parades around the room.

"It'll do to keep you warm, at least."

We gather our wet clothes and spread them out on the floor in front of the fire. Laurette steps carefully between our garments and ladles out a bowl of soup for herself, then one for me.

"Shouldn't we wait for Gagnon?"

"He'd want us to be warm on the inside and out. He's good that way, *non*?"

"He is." I accept the bowl, my hands gradually growing warm through the wood, and blow on its contents. There are large chunks of vegetables—carrots and turnips and onion—but no traces of meat. Still, the soup is flavorful and filling, and in my hunger I slurp it from the wooden spoon so quickly it burns the roof of my mouth. It's not long before I am full. Or, at least, full enough. Before either of us can be tempted to ladle a second portion, I take my bowl—and Laurette's—and dunk them in the bucket of wash water before returning them to the cupboard.

Outside, the storm rages so loudly it takes a while to distinguish a pounding on the door from the sound of thunder.

"You locked the door?" I cross the room to open it, as Laurette shows no sign of getting up from her comfortable slouch by the fire.

"Couldn't very well have him coming in while we were changing, could we?"

Scowling over my shoulder, I lift the heavy latch and let the wind push the door. Gagnon enters, rain pouring off his cloak creating a puddle on the floor. He hangs it on a spike and I fetch a bowl to place underneath it, all while he feigns irritation, saying, "That's a fine thing, to lock a man out of his own home on such a night."

"Come, sit," I invite, "and warm up. I'll fetch you a bowl."

He waves me off, but comes to his high-backed chair by the hearth, staring not into the flames, but at the empty dresses stretched across the floor. His is a handsome face, with broad features that give him an appeal much younger than his years. Though Laurette and I are nothing like the girls we were when we first arrived, he remains unchanged. True, he is our patron, but the years between us seem compressed. On evenings like this, I can easily make the mistake of thinking we are peers.

He wears his hair cropped close, joking that it gives him a sense of camaraderie with his sheep during shearing season, and a thin beard stretches across his cheeks and chin. He rubs it now, absently, and I know in this very moment he is lost in the memory of the woman who wore one of those dresses before. My own means nothing, as it was handed down to me two years ago when Laurette could no longer fit into it. But the other, the blue, once belonged to Gagnon's wife, dead since the year before Laurette and I came to live here. The dress looks like an empty life rumpled on the floor, and I don't doubt Gagnon is remembering the sight of his wife within it.

A clap of thunder startles all of us, and the room is lit white by lightning. We all laugh nervously.

"Doesn't seem to be letting up anytime soon," Gagnon says. "Short walk to the barn will soak you to the bone. Best plan to stay in the house tonight."

"If you think so," Laurette says, stretching her arms and legs, arching her back like a cat on a cushion. "I could curl up right here and go to sleep. I already have my blanket."

"I see that." Gagnon squints and takes on a teasing tone. "You look like a monk."

I am quick to defend my work. "She doesn't, either!"

But lazy Laurette finds the energy to join the joke. She gets up from the chair and adopts a posture of piety, folding her hands on an imaginary belly, and chanting nonsense syllables meant to sound like Latin in the deepest voice she can muster.

"There's no hood," I protest, though the two ignore me. "And it's the wrong color. Since when have you ever seen a monk in anything other than black? Except maybe brown. But never anything quite so—"

"Fashionable?" In an instant, Laurette changes everything, becoming a woman of the queen's court, one hand held aloft, the other fitted nicely at her waist.

I am not at all amused by the spectacle. "What do you know about fashion?" It's a mean comment, and I'm instantly sorry for the awkward way Gagnon leans back into his chair, avoiding the inevitable conflict.

"As much as you, I imagine."

"Girls." With a single, soft word, Gagnon has choked our argument, and Laurette falls back into her chair, sullen. I take up a spot on the trunk bench under the window, my elbows propped on the sill, and watch the rain. It is thick, pouring down the glass in rivulets, distorting the reflected image of Gagnon behind me.

⚜

We've slept on the floor, trading the comfort of our straw ticking and feather pillows for that of a fire, and my bones—young as they are—pay the price in the morning. Sharp pain between my narrow shoulders, a hard chestnut at the base of my spine. There's little light in the room, and I've been awakened by the silent crow of my own mind telling me to rise and begin the day, though the sounds of sleep all around me make me wonder what type of beginning this day may have. The only movement I perceive in Laurette is the steady risc and fall of her breast, and the door to Gagnon's room is closed without the thinnest ribbon of light showing through its seams.

Outside, the rain still falls, but without the drama of the night before. Just a steady pour, a single sound, impossible to imagine it is made of so many millions of singular drops.

Creaking like an old woman, I stand and patter my bare feet to the door, opening it to find the gray outside only a few shades lighter than that within. The yard is a great, brown sea, and somewhere across it waits a cow and five goats to be milked, along with dogs to be let loose after a night's confinement.

My dress is on the drier side of damp, so I put it on over Gagnon's old shirt and, taking a liberty I know he would have granted, put his coat on over that. Holding the coat to keep the hem out of the mud, I slosh across the yard—quick enough to keep my toes from getting mired, but not so quick as to risk slipping. Once at the barn, I reach for the latch, high up so the dogs won't open it for the cow's escape, and find it has already been dislodged. That's when I peer through and notice the interior is warm with lamplight, and when I press my ear to a tiny crack in the door, I hear the steady *vsh, vsh, vsh* of the cow's milk above the steady hum of rain.

"Qui est-ce?" I know it might be Gagnon. He would not bother with his coat for such a short trek across the yard, but I'd heard nothing of his leaving the house. Heart clenched with the fear that it might be some vagabond escaping the rain, I inch the door open, prepared to bolt back to the house for safety.

"*Tiens*, Renée." The voice is familiar, masculine. Comforting. "*C'est moi.*"

Marcel.

Immediately, my fear is alleviated. Marcel Moreau is anything but a stranger. Not to us, not to anyone in Mouton Blanc. As far as we know, he has no family, and can claim no roof as his own, yet he has no problems finding shelter. Our little barn is a favorite of his, and I regularly climb down from our loft to find him sleeping on a bed of straw. This morning my only surprise is to find him industrious as he works the cow's udder, extracting streams of sweet, warm milk.

"It's you," I say, thankful to have the cow's flank between us so he will not know what a pleasant surprise he really is.

A few more squirts and the rough horse blanket falls from his shoulders, leaving him naked to his breeches. His shirt, like our dresses, lies flat on a hay bale, drying. After a moment, I avert my eyes.

"Has Gagnon finally put you to work, then?" I slip out of the greatcoat and hang it next to the rake.

"You're a fine one to talk. All of you lazing abed in the castle there, while this poor old girl is about to burst. I couldn't sleep with her groaning."

"Well, for that I thank you. On her behalf as well."

My thought had been to change into my second dress, but not with Marcel within eyesight below. To me he is a man, though I know him to be nineteen—just a year older than Laurette, but in possession of a mysterious charm that keeps him often at the edge of my thoughts, and my person nearly frays with nerves. He is, simply, more handsome than anything I could conjure from my imagination. Gagnon likes to tease and say he is "pretty," with delicate features, perfect teeth, and hair that springs in an explosion of curls reaching to his shoulders. Usually he corrals them into a tail at the nape of his neck, tied with whatever ribbon has lately been given to him by a village girl. But now—like mine—his locks have been left free to dry.

"So, you were caught in the rain?"

"Yes." He continues to milk with perfect rhythm. "Rather, thrust out into it. The accommodations I'd secured for myself became, shall we say, stormy? But I knew here I would find a welcome spot on the floor and a good solid roof, if nothing else."

I've only the faintest notion of what *nothing else* implies, but enough to make my cheeks burn despite the chill, and my legs feel like they've turned to mud beneath my skirt. Gagnon always speaks about Marcel in a cautionary tone, saying any man who loves that many women can only truly love himself. Always, Marcel is welcome at our table, welcome to a spot by Gagnon's hearth, even welcome to shelter in our barn, but Laurette and I have been warned, with absolute clarity of intent, that we are to be on guard in his presence, lest we fall as so many other girls before us.

Cossette and Copine had escaped out into the rain the minute I opened the door, and I spy them now, waiting for a command to come back in. This I give, then hold up my hands against the spattering of water as they shake their coats dry.

"Well," I say once my own laughter dies down, "it doesn't look like it's going to let up anytime soon. Bring the milk in when you've finished. I'll ask Laurette to make us a batch of bread porridge for breakfast. And there's tea."

"*Merci.* I'll be in directly."

I think of Laurette, lounging on the floor in her makeshift blanket dress and decide I'd better move quickly. Without further conversation, I climb up to our cozy loft and find my basket. Knowing today will be largely spent indoors, I might as well take advantage of the time. I look around, briefly, for anything Laurette might want for a day of leisure. Finding nothing, I grab my comb and two pair of warm stockings and head back down the ladder, pausing at the bottom rung to enjoy the sound newly added to the morning. Marcel, just under his breath, sings an unfamiliar tune. Its lyrics are nothing more than the hiss of soft consonants, and I want to ask him to sing louder, clearer, but something tells me it is a song I'm not meant to hear at all.

L'épisode 2

Renée

MOUTON BLANC, CHEZ GAGNON

Two days, and we have experienced no more than a few hours' respite from the rain.

At any other time, such a deluge would be welcome, farmers out in their fields, faces upturned to catch what glorious drops they could. But our field is empty. Everybody's field is empty. The ground has yielded less and less for two seasons now, and what it has provided has been harvested, sold, and given over to pay taxes on the very land that bore it.

"We grow hungrier and hungrier," Marcel says, the candlelight making great slabs of shadow on his face. He is bent low over a pamphlet, moving it this way and that to fit within the light. "And they are too fat to fit through their doorways to see."

Laurette giggles at the image, but I know better than to laugh. I occupy myself with my needle and the skein of yarn I've managed to card and spin from scraps left in the bins after Gagnon returns from market. It's been dyed a rich berry hue, and I'm working it into a thick lace—something I hope to stitch over the cuffs of my dress after adding mismatched length to the sleeve.

"I don't know how you can complain of hunger when you've been eating at my table for two nights," Gagnon says without malice.

"Well, I've no means to my own table, have I? No land of my own to work—as if any of us can claim our own land."

"I can," Gagnon says. He, too, has taken up a fireside chore, whittling thick pegs to mend the sheep's pen that will surely be flattened by the time the rain stops. "My grandfather was born in this house, and every man in my family until . . ."

His voice fades, because the last of his line to be born in this house never took a breath.

"Until the day they decide to take it." I'm silently grateful to Marcel for steering the conversation back to his rant. The grayness of the day needs no ghosts.

"No one's taking my land. It isn't mine to lose."

"Exactly my point."

"No." Gagnon never looks up from his knife blade. "Not your point, I don't think. This, and all that I have, belongs to God. I work it at his pleasure. When he withholds the rain, I let my fields go fallow. He grows the grass that feeds my sheep."

"And for all that, you give more than half what you earn to those who care no more for your life than they would the life of one of your precious sheep."

"You're wrong, Marcel," Laurette says. Of all of us, only she sits with idle hands. "Any one of Gagnon's sheep has far more value than any of us. They have wool, we have only flesh."

"And some of us not much of that." I feel Marcel's eyes on me as he says it, his voice tinged with worry.

"And some of us too much," I say, lifting nothing but my eyebrow in Laurette's direction.

"No such thing," she says. Gagnon makes a chastising sound,

but Marcel laughs, whether at my comment or hers, I cannot say, but the sound dissipates the festering anger in the room.

Later that evening we have supper—a pie Laurette has made from a sodden grouse Marcel found taking shelter under the eaves. We join hands and bow our heads for Gagnon to ask God's blessing on the meal. Rather, Laurette and I do, for a moment, looking up at the thinly veiled harshness of his voice.

"We are bowed in prayer, *mon ami*."

Marcel sits, one hand gripping Laurette's, the other mine, plank-straight in his chair. "By all means, proceed." He gives my hand a little squeeze. It feels like a wink, and I wonder if he's done the same to Laurette.

"The Gospel says that he who will confess Christ before men, him will Christ confess before the Father in heaven. We shall *all* acknowledge God at my table, and give him thanks for his provision."

"Ah—" Marcel uses our joined hands to point to the pie—"but *I* found the grouse for the pie. Do you not think I am owed some thanks as well?"

Laurette unsuccessfully stifles a laugh, bringing *their* joined hands to cover her mouth. To my shame, I also find Marcel's reasoning amusing, but when I witness the glare Gagnon sends across the table, I fight for a stoic expression.

Once again, Gagnon bows his head, and I follow suit once I see Laurette has, too.

"For the food on our table, and the friends at hand, we thank thee, our Father." His words are simple. Humorless, but gentle. I open my eyes to find Marcel's dark eyes still open and the slightest furrow between his brow. He must not know I'm watching, because he looks at Gagnon with unveiled affection. For all his bluster, for all he would deny God's hand in his life, it is clear at this moment that he is awash in gratitude. Not only for the food at the table, I suspect, but for his place among us.

When Gagnon says, "Amen," I must tug my hand from Marcel's grip to sign the cross.

There are parsnips and peas and a fine, thick gravy saturating the crust. Marcel drags his spoon along the edge of his portion and attempts to transfer it to mine.

"Do you not like it?" Laurette asks, her attention captured by the sound of the scraping spoon.

"She's too thin," Marcel says. He sits next to me, and I lay my hand upon his to stop him.

"I'm fine, really. This is enough."

"She doesn't eat much," Laurette says, assuming the authority of the table.

"By choice?"

"Please." Wanting nothing more than peace and giving no thought to manners, I reach over and pluck a tantalizing piece of meat from Marcel's offered portion. I chew and smile, my lips slick with grease. Once I swallow, I say, "Thank you," and glance across the table to Gagnon and Laurette to see if they, too, are pleased to see the end of the discussion. For his part, Gagnon has not looked up from his meal to register an opinion, but Laurette looks on with unabashed hunger. Not for the lingering gravy on my fingers, nor the uneaten food on Marcel's spoon, but for Marcel himself. And, I suspect, for the ease the two of us have together.

"You may as well finish, since you've taken the choicest part." With no further ado, he empties his spoon onto my plate.

If not for the fact that, as our guest, he's been given the lion's share, I might have protested more. In one aspect he is right—I *am* hungry. It is a constant state with me, a low buzzing at the base of my head, a cord that cinches my stomach at the thought of food when I know there won't be enough. Perhaps that's why I often am satisfied with so little. I take the few bites with gratitude, ignoring Laurette's glare.

When darkness falls on this second day of rain, it is Marcel who will sleep in front of the fire while Laurette and I make our way to our loft.

"Wouldn't have to if Gagnon would open that second room," Laurette says once we make it through the door. "The woman has been dead for seven years. It's a waste of an empty bed." We've covered our feet with a double layer of burlap to protect us from the mud, and I kneel beside her, untying the cords.

"You shouldn't say such things. A man's grief is his own."

"Can I tell you a secret?" She kneels and releases my feet from their mud-caked slippers. "When I'm here by myself, I go in there. All the time."

"Laurette! That's terrible! That's . . . dishonest."

"Just to check, and tidy up. What if there were a leak in there, ready to flood the whole house? Or mildew growing in the corners? If nothing else, sometimes I'll open a window to let out the spirit."

I shudder and cross myself at the thought, then follow her up the ladder, noticing the width of her calf. How is it she maintains such nourishment when the rest of the world around her suffers such pangs of hunger?

When I've stripped my dress and settled beneath my blanket, there's just enough light through the slit in the lantern to allow me to see my needle. Working to complete one last row, I'm too distracted to suppress a sigh.

"What is it?" Laurette asks from the darkness.

"What is what?"

"What is it that has you breathing like a bear?"

I giggle, and relay the story. Marcel, the hole-ridden blanket on his shoulders, then dropping to reveal so much of him.

"What a waste," Laurette says.

"How so, a waste?"

"Your attraction. He feels nothing for you other than that

any man would for a little sister. Or a starving dog. Makes me sick how you ate off his plate. We don't even allow Cossette and Copine to beg at the table."

"I wasn't begging." I steady my hands not to drop a stitch.

"But you took it."

"I tried—"

"With those skinny little fingers. Took it right off his spoon."

"You're just jealous."

Her laugh pierces, sharper for the shadows that encase it. "Why would I be jealous of a child?"

"I'm not a child."

"You're younger than he is."

"As are you." *If only a year.*

I've finished the row and put my project in the basket beside my bed. The lamp hangs on a pole jutting out between our beds, and I take a stretching step to blow it out. On very cold nights, Laurette and I will huddle together on one mattress, keeping each other warm, though I doubt how much I contribute. Tonight is it almost chilly enough to warrant such closeness, but I can tell by the edge of her voice I would not be welcome.

Before getting into bed, I kneel beside it to say our prayer—the one Gagnon taught us. Laurette does not stir.

"Prayers," I remind her, and can sense the irritation in the way she throws back her covers and comes beside me.

"God of heaven, see me now,
'Neath stars and moon and darkest cloud,
Grant me dreams to sleep in peace,
And with the sunrise in the East,
Wake me to a glorious day.
Father, Son, and Holy Spirit—I pray,
Amen."

The rain hits steadily, like whispers, and my ear strains to the occasional heavy droplet. To think, being in such a small space, every drop of it is splashing only inches above our heads.

"You wouldn't understand," Laurette speaks as if nothing has interrupted our conversation.

"Understand what?"

"Marcel. And just how wonderful he is. You only think he is handsome because you are silly. You could never know what it is to truly love a man."

"Marie Antoinette was younger than me when she got married." Other than reports of her beautiful dresses, it is one of the few facts I know about our queen.

"Yes, well, since your blood has no value, you'll be spared that fate."

I laugh, and she does, too, knowing that we both live lives of little value to anybody but each other. "It's a good thing, too," I say. "Otherwise, Marcel wouldn't want to have anything to do with either of us. You know how much he hates the monarchy—"

"And the government—"

"And the Church—"

"And so," Laurette says with giggling declaration, "if I present myself as nothing more than a poor, classless heathen, I should be the perfect woman for him."

"You're not a heathen," I say, sobering, with just a hint of uncertainty. "You were baptized into the Church, same as me. And you believe in God—I know you do."

"Just because I believe in him doesn't mean I trust him. Marcel says we have to take our lives into our own hands. Like I did when I brought us to Gagnon."

"I think God brought us to Gagnon."

"Think what you want, Renée."

Silence again, except for the rain.

"Would you really want to marry Marcel?" I ask. "And leave me here alone?"

"Oui . . . et non." There is a pleasant sigh in between.

⚜

The next morning Marcel is gone, and we are given the run of the house, as Gagnon has gone to a neighbor's to confer with other farmers. In his estimation, the rain has been nothing short of a miracle, soaking the ground while the few seeds for this year's scant garden nestle inside. Too deep to be washed away. Too soon to have sprung up with new, fragile growth.

I prop open the windows, allowing sweet, fresh air to chase out the dank of the house. The stone floor must be swept and washed, as our muddy tracks have made it indistinguishable from the yard. Neither of us has the energy to wash our linens, but we hang them out just the same, letting them soak and be cleansed in sunshine. Through it all, Laurette works half as hard as I do, and grumbles twice as much, but I don't mind. It feels good to work after two restless, rainy days. Not that I've been idle. I've mended every stocking in the household, patched breeches, repaired pockets, reinforced seams. I've cut scraps into quilting squares, and used the trimmed-off strips to braid into belts, and tied bits of thread end-to-end to wrap around my spool.

So when, midmorning, it seems that the sun will hold for the day, I offer to take the sheep out to the southern field. Laurette begs off. I suspect her reason has to do with what we talked about the night before, the second bedroom locked away and her propensity to open it. But when I confront her, she just laughs.

"Don't be stupid. I just don't want to tramp around with a bunch of dirty sheep is all. Going to toil like a Turk and then—"

She could never stop herself from her own secrets. "Then, what?"

"Go into the town, maybe. That's all."

A blush has risen up, bursting into roses on her cheeks, and blotches of uneven color spread across the ample chest bared by her bodice.

"What for, in town? You haven't got any money."

"What do you know what I've got? Plenty to stop in with some friends and have a cup of wine to the rain."

"I suppose Marcel will be there, too?"

The deepening of her flushed state answers long before her assenting nod.

"Did he invite you?"

"I don't need to be invited to a public house, Renée."

"Gagnon won't approve."

"I don't need permission, either. Besides, I'll be home long before he is. And more sober, too, I'll wager."

I touch my tongue to the back of my teeth and call the dogs to my side. "Maybe you should take Cossette with you? For the walk there and back. You shouldn't go all alone."

"I'll be fine. Besides, if all goes as planned, I won't be walking home alone."

Pushing my uneasiness aside, I go to the corral, open the gate, and give the dogs the command to run the sheep through it. I stand, staff firmly planted as they tear past me. In years past, I would pull my skirt up and tuck it into its waist, creating a pair of rough, ratty bloomers. Recently, though, I've devised something infinitely more clever. My skirt has been cut into panels, and these panels wrap around my waist, creating a thick belt into which I can tuck a bit of needlework to pass the time. Today, though, I've vowed to give myself respite from my crochet hook and simply bask in the beauty of the day. Underneath the skirt wound around my waist, I've fashioned breeches that fall just below my knees. In an instant (meaning, at Gagnon's approach), I can unwind the belt and button up the panels, creating a dress as convincing as any other. Until then, I opt for comfort and function, even if—as Laurette says—my knobby knees make me look like a malnourished peasant boy. An image I'm sure is complete with the addition of Gagnon's wide-brimmed leather hat.

The grass is cool and wet beneath my feet; more than once I have to use my staff to keep from slipping. The flock moves as a single meandering mass, and I whistle one command after another, steering them to the left or right, sometimes because I feel they are traveling too far from the promising field, other times just to amuse myself at their obedience. I think about Laurette's comment—how common we are. Peasants, even. I may not have royal blood, but I have power. With a whistle and a click I command the dogs that command the sheep. I will decide where they eat, and how much. In a few weeks' time I'll help shear their wool, keep remnants to card and spin and dye at my pleasure. These sheep live so my feet will be warm in winter. One of their lambs will be my supper this Easter. Another, a stew.

How could any queen have more power?

And yet, as far as I can tell, our sheep do not despise me. Not the way our country has grown to hate Queen Marie Antoinette. Gagnon refuses to speak of her, claiming no good can come of vile gossip, but Laurette takes great pleasure in showing me the vulgar drawings circulated in newspapers and political pamphlets. I don't always understand what I see, and Laurette is sometimes incomprehensible through her giggles.

"She's a whore," Laurette says, among other things. "And they say she reeks of rotting flesh from having too much sex. She's diseased. A monster."

I don't want to think of my queen as a monster. I don't think of myself as one, even though I gladly steal the flesh of my sheep. I have seen—not in real life, of course, but in drawings, the ones that aren't so vulgar—that she is still young, and beautiful. She wears her hair in a powdered white tower. And though she's criticized for the excess, I hear that her gowns are stupendous. Imagine, a new one each day. Sometimes more than two a day. I like to think that she is a queen like I am in this moment, bringing my sheep to the greenest grass I can provide. Caring for them the best I can. Did our queen diminish our harvest? Does she make the laws that keep us impoverished? Or, would she, on a day like today, want to tuck her skirt up and spend it in a cool, lush field, smelling the sweet refreshment of rain?

I send the dogs and the flock down into a valley and stay up on the ridge where I can sit on large, smooth, dry stones. The brim of my hat shades my face, but my bare legs are warm in the sun. Ever-present hunger gnaws at me, and I think about the drawstring pouch at my side. In it, a dry crust of bread and a small pot of milk. By now the sun is past full noon, and I tell myself I will wait one more hour, eat half the bread, drink half the milk, and finish both after one more hour. If I'd brought my needlework with me, I could have measured the time in stitches. Instead, I create stitches in my imagination, envisioning the patterns I would make given an unlimited skein. And when my mind wanders from that, I think about Laurette, walking into the village pub, eyes searching hungrily for Marcel. And then I think about Marcel. I've seen him with all kinds of girls around the village, shamelessly parading them at his side. One in particular, Francine, his current favorite, even let him kiss her right out in the open street. Not two weeks ago, Laurette and I came out from Madame Ledard's bakery and there they were, his face buried in the curve of Francine's neck. Her eyes closed to all of us who watched.

Laurette said that Marcel meant to share Francine's bed the rainy night he came to sleep in our barn. And that they must be done with each other if she sent him away. But I remember the look on Francine's face. Like she'd died in the street and Marcel's lips were somehow poised to breathe life back in. Francine is beautiful in a way neither Laurette nor I can ever hope to be. Delicate of feature, proportioned in figure. On that day, when I looked over at Laurette, she looked like she had died, too, and the poor thing had only my tug on her sleeve to revive her.

I know I shouldn't think such things about Marcel. Shouldn't dwell on the memory of his gaze at the table. Shouldn't touch the curve of my neck and imagine his kiss.

But I do. Alone on a rock, a monarchy of my making, I indulge my mind, bringing together Marcel, and what I know of his lovemaking, and what I've seen of his body, and what I infer from the images I've seen of our queen—all of this I imagine with my own awkward, half-starved self. For a while, I feel no hunger.

A sound catches my attention, and in the distance I see a carriage emerging where the road cuts through a corner of forest. It's a road that winds to Mouton Blanc, but is longer and less-traveled than the one we usually take. Once free of the trees, the driver whips at the horses and sets them at a fast pace—too fast for the road that is still stained dark with rain.

The sheep sense the intruder, though they are nowhere near its path. Still, I whistle for the dogs to bring them closer to the ridge to be sure. Once they've cleared, I see a dark rut in the road, and from this angle, I can imagine its depth. The driver, though, I'm sure, cannot. But the horses can. They balk at the ridge of it, rear up, veer, and turn the carriage on its side, throwing the driver clear from his seat. His wig flies from his head, landing like a tiny lamb in the grass.

It takes the last of my wits and my breath to give the dogs the signal to take the flock home, praying I remembered to leave the gate to the corral open. If not, they'll just have to congregate in the muddy yard. I run through a sea of fast-moving sheep, making my way toward the man lying prone next to the carriage and the woman screaming from within.

L'épisode 3

Laurette

MOUTON BLANC, LE COCHON GROS

Laurette watched until Renée was well out of sight before strolling back into the house. Even though she knew she was alone, she glanced over her shoulder before lifting the key for the second bedroom from its place on the ledge above the door and turning it in the lock. The room was no mystery to her as she ran a cloth across the surface of the dressing table, along the door of the armoire, and round the bedposts. She bent close and smelled the ticking, worried that it might have absorbed the dampness of the past few days, but found the stuffing to smell nearly as sweet as it did that day months ago when she'd stolen in with a sack of straw to freshen that which had gone flat. For good measure, she livened the fallow feathers in the pillows.

She worked with both the speed of a thief and the ease of a mistress, humming a cheerful tune, talking out loud to the furniture. "Such a shame," she said to the tall, narrow bachelor, running her cloth over each brass handle, "to lock you away. Fine bit of craftsmanship you are."

By now she'd memorized the contents of the drawers. Handkerchiefs, mostly, and garters. A few ladies' stockings that must have been tucked away in here for some sentimental purpose, because everything else was decidedly masculine. Gagnon's refuge for his meager belongings. There were coins in the top drawer which Laurette had carefully re-scattered after counting them on the day of her discovery. She had the exact amount memorized, ready to jog Gagnon's memory should their finances reach that desperation. There were notes, too, bundled together and tied with a strong red string. These Laurette left unmolested, not because she would never be able to replicate the intricate knot, but because she was utterly unable to read them.

Every bit of Laurette's housewifery was a prayer of thanks. To Gagnon. She took the folded linens from the armoire, snapped them free, and refolded them, saying, "Thank you, Gagnon, for the bed you provide for me." She never spoke any of this aloud, knowing Renée would chastise her for thanking Gagnon rather than God himself. Gagnon would, too, as he was never slow to give thanks for every bit of their meager existence. In this, her perception of the world and her place in it, Laurette felt utterly alone. Cared for, but not belonging. Fed, but not nourished. Covered, not held. And so she saw in Marcel a kindred spirit, he too having nothing from God to call his own. They could run off together and leave nothing behind.

Having finished her secretive task, Laurette turned the key in the lock and found its place above the door, marked with a tiny notch in the wood. She brought in the linens now crisp and dry, and made up Gagnon's narrow bed. This she did without tune or conversation, simply performing the task, tucking the corners, and leaving with a turn of the heel. She took the others up to the loft, made her bed, leaving Reneé's bare with the sheet folded at the foot.

Humming resumed, she stepped out of her work dress, took off her cap, and released her hair from the pins that held it in place. Unlike her cousin, Laurette had no trouble indulging in personal vanity. Her hair was the color of red oak leaves in autumn, and almost too thick to be contained in her encircled hand. Once loose, she brushed it, doubling the volume before smoothing it back and replaiting it. Now, she pinned it without thought to convenience, expertly drawing out a few strands to frame her face.

"Where are you when I need you, *Cousine*?" she said before taking a deep breath and pulling the strings of her stays, bringing a new flatness to her torso and pushing her ample bosom just a little higher. Breathless and satisfied, she wrapped the cords and tied them around her waist. She donned a new, clean vest, deep green and embellished with stitching of peacock feathers—Reneé's gift to her last winter—and tied a bright-red kerchief around her shoulders.

This was Laurette as nobody had ever seen her, and without a glass, she could not see herself. Instead, she judged her appearance by the swelling pride she felt within. The strength behind the breath that filled her figure, the curling tendrils at the corner of her sight. Surely she hadn't imagined the hooded glances Marcel sent those past two evenings by the fire. She jangled the few coins in her small purse. Enough, as she'd said, for a first drink.

The village of Mouton Blanc was laid out as a single, large square, with a raised platform at its center. In better times, times that formed her childhood memories, farmers would parade the finest of their flocks for auction. Now, the shops surrounding the square were largely abandoned, their owners having realized the futility of trying to wring blood from the stone-empty pockets of their customers. The once-thriving commercial community had been reduced to a struggling bakery, a few rag shops, a shabby apothecary, a one-eyed tailor, and a near-empty dry goods.

Even the church, l'église du Mouton Perdu, offered less to the lost sheep of its congregation. When the girls were little, Father Pietro always gave them slices of bread and cups of milk while they endured his catechism along with the other children in the front pews of the chapel. Endured, because the priest's French was so thickly accented with his native Spanish as to be barely intelligible.

Laurette gave her first Confession wondering if the man on the other side of the screen had as much difficulty understanding *her*, secretly hoping that he did. She had much to confess. How a secret part of her was glad to see her father hang. How she hated her mother for being too weak to throw him out, and her aunt for being too selfish in her grief to care for them properly.

Laurette took her first Communion understanding nothing, as Father Pietro spoke in Latin. She knew that the bread was the broken body of Christ and the wine his blood, but felt no change after consuming it. Just as she'd felt no change having confessed her sins, or speaking the prayer of contrition that followed. Thus, her first Communion was her last, which explained why, when the starving girls presented themselves at the church in need of permanent shelter, Father Pietro sent them away with suspicion and prayers. In spite, Laurette took them straight to the pub, and straight to Gagnon.

Le Cochon Gros. The Fat Pig. The pub remained the only unchanged, thriving life in Mouton Blanc. Though the establishment was as old as the town itself, it created a home for a new idleness, brought on by poverty, and given over to a population still uncomfortable with empty days and emptier stomachs.

Laurette was well aware of the attention she sparked as she

walked through the wide, sparsely populated street. A few scraggly chickens scattered out of her way, and more than one skinny dog engaged in a hopeful gait beside her, but it was the gaze of the men that brought a flush to her cheeks. She was no stranger to the village, but even these wastrels seemed to sense her renewed purpose. She walked through their comments as she would a familiar forest, their words fluttering behind her like dry, dead leaves. Her bright face, her fine figure. Crude insinuations and unflattering propositions. Gagnon was a well-enough respected man in the community to keep any of them from getting too close or speaking too loud. They murmured and whispered and buoyed her along with laughter that scratched like straw at the back of her neck. Uncomfortable, but not unwelcome.

Le Cochon Gros sat on the northeast corner of the square. A moment's hesitation, a final deep breath, and she stepped over the threshold into the darkness. A hush of a moment fell. She was far from the only woman in the room; in fact, each of the long, warped tables hosted at least one on its bench. Dressed in stained shifts, open at the front, with frizzled curls springing from beneath dirty caps, these women emitted the first cooing noise at Laurette's arrival. Not a noise of affection, but a warning to the fresh young face that dared show itself in their nest.

"What do you want here, *mademoiselle*?" The question came from a tall, bird-thin man, Alain Saumon, proprietor. He spoke from behind the bar, his question tinged with deference and warning.

"I'm looking for a friend," Laurette said with a touch more confidence than she actually felt.

"You won't find a friend in here," Saumon said, followed by an immediate squelching of the comments that suggested she was welcome to be a friend to one and all. "There's business to attend to. Best you go take your refreshment someplace more suited."

No doubt he knew who she was, and that knowledge gave her some status.

"I'll choose for myself what suits me," she said, eliciting a cackling approval from the women.

"Now, listen, girl—" A new man stood up, taller than the proprietor. Jacques Dubois, trusted to monitor the scales when the bundles of wool were brought to market. He'd personally held the fortune or loss of nearly every family in the community in his hands and had been revered for his unfailing honesty and precision. "Do as the man says before—"

"Let her in. She's here to see me." An undeserved pride gripped Laurette's heart when she saw how the room responded, all heads turning, leaving both Saumon and Dubois listless and silent. Marcel's words propelled Laurette through the maze of tables, and when she reached him, he gripped her shoulders and pecked two kisses—one on each cheek—whispering, "What in all of heaven are you doing here?" between each embrace.

"I came to find you," she said, despite the myriad of excuses she had rehearsed on the road. "When you were gone this morning, I was afraid, somehow, that we'd offended you. That Gagnon had made you feel unwelcome."

"Since when have I ever felt the need to feel welcome?" His smile wrapped her even closer than the arm that drew her to him. "My fellows, let me introduce you to Mademoiselle Laurette Janvier. Is she not a bloom of beauty?"

Laurette felt pure joy churn upon itself within her, and even more so when one of his fellows asked, "Is this the one you were talking about?"

Then all was swept away when Marcel replied, "*Mais non!* Does she look like she is starving? No, it is her little cousin, Renée, who embodies the health and vigor of our people being ripped away. This one—" he tightened his grip, and she could feel his fingers splayed against her waist—"she is our *résistance*.

Our resilience. Our refusal to die under the yoke of the oppression of the monarchy. Or to waste away in the void of its neglect."

The crowd, or at least those gathered at the nearest tables, roared in appreciation and raised their pewter mugs in her direction. Marcel stepped away, until only his fingertips touched hers, and he curled them in a grip. "Look at her. Like a goddess who abandoned the empty promise of eternity. I know her to work miracles, my friends. Miracles that have filled my stomach. And how? Not because she waits." He spit the word like an action despised. "And not because she begs. But because she *takes.*" At this, he gripped her wrist, pulled her close, and kissed her full on the mouth.

A goddess. That's what he'd called her, never mind that she understood little of the rest. As he opened her mouth and breathed life into her, she felt immortality take its hold. She closed her eyes against the darkness of the room and felt only the lightning of Marcel's touch. And then, with the same unexpected swiftness, it was over.

"Stay close to me," he whispered before pulling away. "And speak to no one else, understand?"

She nodded, bringing the back of her hand to her lips as a gesture of promise.

"And you will tell no one of what you hear in this place today. *Oui?* Not even Gagnon. Above all, not Gagnon. *Entends?*"

"*Oui*, Marcel."

He drew her close again, pressing his lips to her brow, and she wondered that he did not pull away at her fever.

Marcel possessed her in this place, always keeping a hand on her shoulder, her waist, her arm. She didn't know if he meant to claim her, or protect her, or remind her that she remained only at his behest. Her ears roared with the rushing of her own blood, the echo of her very pulse, drowning out most of the surrounding conversation. Bits and pieces seeped through—the weakness of King Louis, the inexcusable waste at court, the odiousness of the queen, and the questionable paternity of her children. All of this she'd heard before, even in talk at Gagnon's table. But here, there was no voice to interject reason. No opinions to temper the flaring anger. They spoke in circles, each accusation igniting a new, more heinous one.

Marcel had summoned the tavern keeper to bring Laurette one cup of wine after another, and though even her uneducated palate could taste the water, the excitement of the surroundings heightened its effect. She felt herself growing warm, flushed from beneath her skin. Soon she contributed her own witticisms, and was rewarded not only with laughter, but with Marcel drawing her even closer. He buried his face in the curve of her neck, and she inclined her head to hold him until a deep, sneering laughter tore him away.

"Do you see, Moreau, why you could never be fit to lead us? How easily you are distracted from our cause?" Jacques Dubois had returned, scattering Marcel's audience.

"I am distracted by nothing," Marcel said. Already Laurette's flesh had cooled.

"I don't blame you entirely. You are too young to be decisive. Quick to temper but slow to action, as much as you seem to admire that very trait in this girl. Weakness can only hide behind words for so long, my boy. Revolutions might begin with the tongue, but they live in our arms. Our fists. We lost a great opportunity today."

"We lost nothing." He moved away from Laurette—just an inch—but she felt a new valley of distance between them.

"A carriage with a royal crest? Nothing?"

"Without so much as a single guard." Marcel stood, and though Dubois was the taller by far, Marcel's confidence bridged the distance. "What good would it have done for us to waylay a member of the court too insignificant to warrant protection?"

"They could have had money," Dubois said, garnering tepid support from those gathered at the table.

"They are the thieves," Marcel said, "not us." He sounded much like Gagnon in his reasoning, as if our countless hours of talking by the fire had seeped in without his knowledge.

"There might have been food." This from a scrap of a man at the end of the table.

Marcel's voice softened. "Nor are we beggars. Trust me, *mon vieux*, the time will come when we will want no more. We will take all that is due to us, and we will feast on bread and victory. But we have to be smart." He began a slow pace around the table, and every greasy head turned to follow. "When you want to kill your prey, do you cut off a foot? Do you aim your shot at the hind's hoof and hope it will trip and fall into your snare? No. You wait, you track, you follow. And when you strike, you strike at the heart."

He'd come full circle and stood directly behind Laurette, his hands on her shoulders. Her own heart stopped.

"They will hang us if we hunt," Dubois said with disgust.

"No more than if we steal. Be more patient, *mon ami*. There will be time for a better shot."

Marcel's final proclamation diffused the tension in the room, and all those who had been paying rapt attention to his words turned to their private, petty business. Her awe at his power to command the room sent a shiver through Laurette's being, which Marcel took for cold, as he bent low to speak an invitation to sit with him in the corner where a fire burned low.

"Two more drinks," he said en route, gesturing to Saumon with one hand, and clutching hers with the other. "And whatever you have to eat."

"I should tell you," Laurette said, keeping her voice low to save both of their pride, "I don't have much money. Not nearly enough to pay for—"

He squeezed her hand. "Even here, I am a kept man. My presence brings in others. And today? A fresh, pretty girl."

"You shouldn't say such things." Though Laurette's smile belied her disapproval.

The small table and two chairs were occupied at their arrival, but a dismissive glance from Marcel soon emptied them. Once Laurette sat, Marcel pulled the second chair closer and leaned in to speak.

"Why are you here, Laurette?"

"I told you—I came to see you. To be sure—"

"Tell me the truth."

"Because . . ." The idea formed as she spoke. "I wanted to see where you go. Who you are when you're not at home."

"I have no *home*."

"You do, always. With us."

"That's not your home to offer, is it?"

Chastened, she sat back and stared into the fire until the keeper came with a tray of wine and plate of paté and bread.

"Merci, *mon ami*," Marcel said, and began to serve himself before the man walked away. He portioned the same for Laurette, who took it gratefully and forced herself to eat slowly, not only to savor the deliciousness, but to keep the delicacy down in her swirling stomach. Meanwhile, Marcel wolfed down his first slice, and set about immediately dressing another. "Do you know what I think?" The firelight sent a devilish cast to his complexion, his loose curls doubled in shadows on his brow.

Laurette forced a swallow. "The whole room knows what you think, Marcel."

"They do, indeed. And all would agree—I don't think you came here to see me at all. You came so that I could see you."

"But you see me nearly every day."

"Not like this. I see you on that wretched farm. Always with sheep and mud. Some ridiculous cap on your head, your sleeves rolled up to your elbows so you can scrub something clean. Until that night, that first night that it rained, remember? And you were wearing that garment Renée fashioned for you. I got just a glimpse as you ran back to change." He closed his eyes, and Laurette would have, too, but he was too beautiful to shroud in darkness. "I can see you now. Every bit."

Her bread went slack in her hand and fell to the floor, forgotten. Marcel opened his eyes, reached for her, and pulled her into his lap.

"What do you mean?" she asked, though she knew. "What do you see?"

In response, he buried a hand in her hair and pulled her down for a kiss that left their previous one in its shadow. His arm encircled her waist and she wrapped hers around his neck. Certainly, she thought, they would melt into a single being, like two wax figures left too close to the fire. Perhaps sensing that he need not urge her to kiss him, Marcel took his hand from her hair, dislodging its loose gathering as he did so. She felt a grazing across the fabric of her vest, briefly tracing the stitching of the peacock feathers, and finally a very surprising, but not unwelcome, grip to her bare calf. A protective instinct roared to life.

"You mustn't," she said, breaking their kiss to look at the others in the room. If she and Marcel had attracted any of the patrons' attention, they knew enough to glance away at that moment.

"Do not mind them." He continued his touch. "You are not the first woman to be seen in such a position. Our times are too desperate for modesty."

"I may not be the *first* woman. For you. But I've . . . I've never—"

He kissed her again, irrevocably erasing the word *never* from her mind, drawing away only when distracted by a commotion at the door.

"Mes amis! Mes amis!" He was a small, wiry man, and he jumped about with flailing arms, like a featherless bird. "You would not believe! A royal carriage, just on the other side of the trees. You know, that little valley? Overturned! Wheels spinning in the air!"

As the man spoke, Marcel carefully dislodged Laurette, returning her to her chair, and stood, moving closer as if to catch every detail.

"You see?" Dubois said. "Look, we are given another chance."

"So we are," Marcel said thoughtfully. Then, to the newcomer, "You can find this again, Gerard?"

"I think a cup of wine might aid my memory, but since this has interrupted my business, I'm afraid I don't have . . ."

Marcel summoned the patron. "Saumon! A glass for our friend here, who will lead us to great fortune!" Then, to Gerard, "Drink it down fast."

"Oh," said Dubois. "Quite a change of tune, eh, Moreau? What was all that earlier? That we are not thieves? Why chase down now what we could have taken hours ago when they drove through our streets? So fast any of us could have been killed by their golden spokes?"

"Perhaps," Marcel said darkly, "circumstances have changed that they will not put up as much of a fight. If any at all."

His words elicited a grisly cheer, and Laurette, as unimaginable as it seemed given her state just moments ago, felt herself grow cold. Perhaps he sensed as much, because he turned away from the crowd and drew her up into his arms again.

"You will come with us, *ma belle*?"

"Non."

"Laurette . . ."

"You just said—Marcel, what about not being a thief? And hanging. You wouldn't—I know you couldn't kill . . ."

He gripped her arms, his eyes hypnotic. "It is known that even the greatest predators will chase their prey, waiting for it to tire and become weak. You wanted to see who I am, Laurette? This, this is who I am. I am a lion, and my prey has fallen. Show me that you have a lion's heart to match my own."

L'épisode 4

Renée

MOUTON BLANC, LA VALLÉE

By the time I arrive the driver is on his feet, covered in mud and swearing the way Gagnon does when he thinks we're not around.

"Are you all right?" I ask, still running. "And the horses?"

He either doesn't hear me, or doesn't find my concern worth his while. Instead, he makes his way around and stops the still-spinning wheel, then hoists himself up to pound on the carriage door. Now I hear the sound of whimpering coming from within.

"Madame!" he shouts, as he cannot reach to the window. "Are you hurt?"

More sounds come, the volume intensified to a degree that I am satisfied whoever is inside the carriage feels more anger than pain. There is a loud banging sound, and the door bursts open—straight up, like that of a cellar.

"Very good, *madame*. Very good. I shall—"

By now I am close enough to be within reach of the carriage, and I make myself known to the driver. He is not a young man, his face thin and jowled and speckled with gray whiskers. He looks at me and makes it clear that I am to stay quiet. Not to make myself known to the passenger inside. Hopping down from his perch on the useless wheel, he holds the back of his hand to his mouth and whispers, "*Garçon.* Go, fetch help. Two strong men, at least."

I only balk for a second at the realization that he thinks I am a boy.

"There's no one," I say, because there isn't. Not at home, anyway. I could go to the village, catch up with Laurette on the road. Or, maybe, if I run fast enough, find Marcel and bring him here. But the sting of *garçon* takes on new life. I'm scratched and muddy, I'd be breathless and red-faced from the run.

"Are you stupid, boy! *Allez!*"

"Oui, monsieur." I turn obediently, and rather than heading north toward home, following the sheep, I veer when I get to the cross path. Gagnon said this morning he was going to meet with other farmers in our area, to see if they suffered any damage from the rain. But I know that is not the true nature of this meeting. What farmer could suffer damage from the merciful, blessed soaking God sent to us? There'd been no wind, no hail, nothing that could have blown off a roof. Nothing to beat down a crop, if there had been a crop to beat down.

No, he and others would be gathered around the table at the Girard place, not quite a mile from ours. I see Madame Girard in the market from time to time, and she always looks at Laurette and me with the most accusatory, suspicious glare, then says that she doesn't trust a man who doesn't have the decency to take a wife. She and Monsieur Girard have a grown-up daughter, Elianne, somewhat simple in the head with pock scars scattered on one cheek. I know it is their greatest wish to find her a home and a husband, and Gagnon is their greatest hope of all.

So when he says that he is going to "meet with the neighbors," they gather at the Girards', not at our house. At least, not anymore. The last time they did, I hovered at the edge, a pitcher of sweet water in hand, listening, waiting for them to talk about crops, or flocks, or anything to do with land or livestock. Instead, they spoke of taxes. Of their land being parceled away from beneath them.

"It's not right that we produce food we cannot afford to buy," Monsieur Girard said that day, slamming his meaty fist on the table. "They take and they take and they take—until we have nothing. And it will only get worse until we become men of action."

Gagnon put a calming hand on Girard's shoulder. "Leave that talk to younger men."

"*You* are a young man," Girard said, eliciting sounds of agreement from around the table. "But you'll die under the weight of your labor soon enough. Think of your father—"

"My father would have me place my faith in God, for in his hand the heart of a king is like a stream of water."

"Perhaps we need a stream of rebellion," Girard said.

At that moment, Gagnon registered my presence and bade the men to silence. Thereafter, they moved their meetings to the Girards', and I was strictly forbidden to accompany him, even when Madame Girard was to pay me a thin copper for the dress I mended for Elianne, or when she promised me a whole bag of scrap wool for carding.

"Tell me what she's promised and I'll bring it to you," Gagnon would say. "Stay put until I get home."

Until today I've obeyed without question. When I come in sight of the clearing and see Girard's house, larger than ours by far, I stop and take a few deep breaths, then push myself to run faster than before.

"Allô! Allô!" I pound on the door until the sallow face of Elianne appears. "I—I need to see—"

"Renée!" Gagnon pushes Elianne aside and grabs me by my shoulders. "You know you're not to come—"

I point, vaguely, behind me. "I had the sheep in the south pasture, and there was a carriage. And it—there was a hole. Washed out from the rain. And the horses . . ."

My thoughts are as fast and shallow as my breath.

"It's overturned, then?" His face fills all of my vision, his gray eyes wide with concern for me. For what I may have seen.

"I think—" and now it comes to me, what I saw in the flash of the carriage door opening—"there's a crest on the door. And—" I remember the blinding—"it's gold, and *mon Dieu*, Gagnon."

"Hush, now."

He pulls me close and stops my words with the coarse-spun fabric of his shirt. My head fills with the unspoken possibility. *Royal.* And when I do pull back for a bit of breath, he must sense I'm about to speak again, because he puts his hand to the back of my head and brings me closer. It's now I realize that somewhere along the way, I've lost the broad-brimmed hat.

"Say nothing more, Renée. I'll make some excuse to leave, and then you can take me to the place."

"He said to bring two strong men," I whisper when released.

"That's because whoever it is assumes he has two friends in this place."

Gagnon leaves my side and I overhear him tell Girard that one of the sheep is caught in a bramble and he must go to free it. It is the only time I have ever known Gagnon to lie, reinforcing the power of this secret. What follows is a chortling conversation about the uselessness of such a young girl to tend a flock, and the strength and agility of Elianne, who is offered up to accompany us. I hold no grudge against Gagnon, for I know he was only participating in a ruse, but I match Elianne glower for glower before the door is shut behind me.

By now I've caught my breath somewhat, and while I can't maintain the pace with which I ran to fetch Gagnon, we walk at a quick gait and reach the scene of the overturned carriage in good time. From a distance I can see a tall woman—the bright silk of her dress a stunning contrast to the rich brown and green of the land around her. I can hear her high-pitched wailing carrying across the distance.

"Surely that's not—"

"No," Gagnon says. "Not her, not the queen. But the crest on the coach is that of the palace." He says it with an air of confidence. "Speak to no one. Do you understand? I'll answer for you, should the need arise. But I can't think of anything a member of the royal household would have to say to a shepherd girl."

"Boy."

"What?"

"They thought I was a boy." Here I see the hat on the ground where it must have fallen shortly after I took flight. I pick it up and pull it down over my ears, but not soon enough to drown out Gagnon's laughter, as if he's just noticed my attire.

"Even better. What could be more useless than another poor, starving boy?"

I fall back as Gagnon sprints ahead, and witness an immediate change in the woman's posture. Where she had been pacing, arms flailing in accompaniment to her tirade, she now stands still. Stiff, really, with her chest thrust out and one hand perched at the thinnest part of her waist. It is a pose I've seen many times whenever Gagnon comes into a woman's presence. He is a handsome man, after all. Usually, though, it is the lower class of woman who will so blatantly display herself—the kind of woman who loiters at the pub or preens in the alleys at the edge of the market. But this is obviously a woman of substance and wealth. No doubt the only hunger she knows is that which is apparent in her eyes as she takes in the vision of my guardian.

"What's happened here?" Gagnon asks, ignoring the woman completely and heading straight for the driver.

"Nothing that wouldn't have if you people could properly maintain your roads," the woman says, physically inserting herself between them.

"I beg your forgiveness, *madame*." Gagnon removes his cap and bows his head, speaking to the ground at the hem of her skirt. I bristle at his subservience. "God saw fit to bless us with rain. We've grown so unaccustomed to any good thing, the very dirt on our paths was taken unaware."

I stifle my giggle a little too late and the woman scowls at me. "Impudent boy."

Gagnon doesn't correct her, so neither do I, but I scowl right back from under the hat's brim. When he notices, he says, "Renée," in a tone fraught with enough warning for me to settle my features back into something like respect.

While Gagnon and the driver examine the underside of the overturned carriage, I take an opportunity to examine the gown of the woman standing beside me. It is the color of a hearty red wine, the bodice trimmed in a dark-blue velvet, and the sleeves edged with lace. Never have I seen such finery up close. The silk of her skirt glistens, like it has been poured from her waist and somehow suspended in motion around her. She's pacing—short, angry steps—and I can hear the rustle of petticoats. Like the sound of dry leaves on a flat stone. My own clothes, and those of everybody I know, are too worn and soft to call attention to themselves. This woman's dress would announce her presence long before she turned a corner. It speaks.

Now she speaks too. "What are you staring at, boy?"

"Your dress is torn." I point to a place where the flounce has ripped clear away from the skirt. "I imagine it happened when you were climbing out of the carriage."

She lets out a yelp of exasperation, and makes herself look silly turning and twisting in all directions to try to see the damage. "It's ruined. Utterly ruined. And loaned to me by the queen herself."

I gasp. "The queen? Herself?"

"Hush," she says. "Your mouth's not fit to say the word."

It's meant, I'm sure, to be a stinging blow, but I laugh instead. "There's no such hierarchy. I can say what I please and she'd be none the wiser. You, on the other hand, I assume will have to return the dress?"

She wrinkles her nose and bends down, bringing it close to mine beneath the hat's brim. Her face is pale, narrow, and pinched. "You're not a boy at all, are you? No boy's mind is so shrewd."

I grin at her assertion. "I can fix your dress for you."

"Don't be ridiculous." She stands straight again. "Of course you can't. I've none of my things with me. Not even a needle and thread."

"*I* have a needle. And thread. Not so fine as what's been used here, but it will do."

"Oh, will it? Will it *do*?" She turns her attention to the task at hand behind her. "*Attention, messieurs.* How long will I be kept here in the blazing sun? I'm to be in Paris tonight."

"You won't be in Paris tonight," Gagnon says before, bracing his shoulder against the wheel, he lets out a grunt and turns the carriage upright. To be fair, the driver aided in the process, but showed nowhere near the strain of effort.

"And why not? Given we're right side up again?"

"One of the wheels is broken, *madame*. It would be far too

dangerous to drive at the pace necessary to get you to Paris tonight. I can see to scaring up a saddle for the horses should you wish to ride; but—"

"Give care, man." This from the driver, whose interruption made clear Gagnon's place. "You are speaking to Madame Gisela Poitiers, a high-ranking friend of the court, and not one to be the target of such disrespect."

"My apologies," Gagnon says, without any hint of an apology at all. "I only wished to convey my desire for the lady's safe travel."

"And you'll speak not to her if she has not addressed you."

"But she *did*," I say. "She asked him—"

"Assez." Madame Gisela punctuates her command with a thwack of her walking stick against a nearby stump, leaving no doubt that she'd prefer to strike my person. "Enough of this bickering. What, then, *messieurs*, is to be our course?"

"Re-hitch the horses," Gagnon says. "If we walk them slowly enough, we can get the carriage back to my farm, and I'll see what I have to repair the wheel. At least to secure it enough that it will see you home."

"Would it not be better to return to—what is the name of that village? Mouton Blanc?" The driver asks. "Is there not a blacksmith? A proper inn for my lady?"

At this, Madame Gisela holds a lace-trimmed handkerchief to her nose, as if already fending off the noisome atmosphere of any inn Mouton Blanc could offer.

"Did you stop there?" Gagnon asks. "On your way through?" Neither respond. "I thought not. Wise of you. You have my word that you'll be comfortable and safe in my home. But I cannot guarantee as much should you go into town. We don't get many like you here as flesh amongst our flesh. And to be so helpless, with no means of escape . . ."

As he speaks, he moves closer and closer to Madame Gisela

with mock menace, and I can tell she is equally terrified and delighted.

"I haven't been to a farm since I was a child," she says, lowering her handkerchief to reveal a thin-lipped smile. "I'm sure to find the prospect charming."

"Take her, Renée. See that she is settled, and fix us a supper fit for a special companion of the court and her driver."

Madame Gisela bristles, clearly unwilling to be so closely associated with a servant, but desperation begets necessity, and she turns on her heel to follow me.

Never before would I have considered the walk back home to be in any way arduous, but on this afternoon I experience it through the steps of another. Every tiny spot of mud reminds me that my walking companion is wearing silk shoes that will lose all of their beautiful stitchery before we reach home. Not only that, but the chill of the remaining damp must be seeping through, as my own bare feet are nearly numb with it.

"Tell me," she says, "now that we are away from the prying ears of men, what is it exactly that you are wearing? You can imagine why I thought you to be a boy, as I mistook your garment for breeches, but now I can see that it isn't, quite."

"No, *madame*." Nobody ever asks about my clothing, and I feel a stirring of pride at the chance to share my ideas with this woman. "I've taken my skirt and rigged some fastenings, especially good for when I'm out walking with the sheep when the ground is wet. It keeps the hem of my skirt dry."

At this, she looks down to where she's carrying her own skirt aloft, gripped in an attempt to rescue the poor, torn flounce. "What do you care if your skirt gets wet? Doesn't look like it would be ruinous to the fabric."

"No, *madame*. But the wet, then, it . . . well, it chafes against the skin." I stop there, as it feels unseemly to discuss the raw flesh created by the constant friction.

"And I don't suppose you have stockings."

"No, *madame*."

"Nor shoes?"

"Not at the moment, *madame*. But there's time before winter." There's no hint of compassion in her voice, and I hope she hears no petition for charity in mine.

"Show me."

"Pardonnez, madame?"

"Your skirt."

We are standing in the middle of a meadow, a shallow valley that I always call the saucer. Whenever I crossed it, I delighted in the momentum of running down the edge, holding my arms out to keep my balance, and maintaining the speed until I was up on the lip on the opposite side.

"Why do you want to see?"

"Because I do. Because you intrigue me."

My pride has now become pure determination, and I transform the garment, unraveling the panels and fastening them to each other, disguising the breeches with a skirt.

Madame Gisela does not seem impressed. "With buttons all exposed."

"Yes." I stare down at the plain wooden nubs, feeling both deflated and defensive. "But if I had a print material I could hide them, or if I had the means to paint the buttons, they could be equally embellishments and function. And see how they angle? I've never had a chance to see, but I feel like the line could create the illusion of movement. Like the skirt is swaying even if I'm standing still. Tell me, does it seem so?"

Forgetting my station, I take a few steps away and give a slight twist under her scrutiny. Countless times I have asked Laurette this very question, but she merely rolls her eyes at me and asks how a skirt can move if the girl inside it doesn't. Madame Gisela feels no such confusion.

"*Oui.* I can see. Quite a genius. But tell me. Living out here, why do you not simply wear breeches if you wish?"

I laugh. "I don't think Gagnon would ever allow such a thing."

"Gagnon? That man? Your father?"

"He is not my father." I start walking again, and she joins me.

"What is he to you, then? Is he married to your mother?"

I'm glad for the brim of the hat and the distance to hide my face. "He is my guardian." I'll not invite this woman into the tragedy of my mother. And she'll learn soon enough that Gagnon is not married to anybody.

"Is he good to you?" Here, I can almost hear true concern.

"Very. He is a good man."

We walk a little farther before she tells me to take off my *ridiculous* hat, and I obey because deep down I am hoping that she will look at me and tell me I am far too pretty to cover my face, but she doesn't.

"Can you do nothing with your hair?"

I reach my hand back to finger the strands caught in the ribbon at the nape of my neck. "What else should I do?"

"You're right. It's thin, isn't it? I can see your scalp at the part. But you're almost blonde, and fair, so I suppose you do well to wear this." She waves a dismissive finger at the hat, which I take as her dispensation to put it back on.

"I'm working on a better one."

"A better hat?" She sounds amused.

"We have a tanner in the village. He saves scraps for me. . . ." And I tell her how I treat them, and soften and braid them. "To make something more like for a lady. Like a straw hat from leather."

"And why not straw?"

"Because it has to last. And be strong."

The farm comes into view, and I want to run ahead, grab

my unfinished hat—still little more than a coil of soft, plaited leather in a basket—and come back to present it for her approval.

"Tell me your name again, girl."

"Renée."

"And your guardian? Monsieur Gagnon?"

"*Oui.* Émile Gagnon."

"Your house, from here it looks quite small." There is an accusation in her voice I know well.

"I don't sleep in the house." *With him.* "My cousin and I, we have a loft in the barn. It is quite cozy. A bit warm in summer, but there is a window, and since we're up high it is safe to sleep with it open."

She laughs outright. "How is it that an orphan shepherd girl who sleeps in a barn would have such fine sartorial sense?"

"Why do you say I am an orphan?"

"You sleep in a barn. It is the kindest word I have for you."

It is the first thing she has said to me in which I sense no hint of derision. So, trusting, I ask, "What did you mean when you said I had a *fine sartorial sense*?"

"*La mode.* Fashion, clothing, and the like. You have ideas."

"I can fix your dress." The idea has been working in my head since noticing its tear.

"And why would I let such dirty little hands touch my dress?"

"I can wash my hands. You can't fix your dress."

She stops again and touches a long, white finger beneath my chin, raising my face to see her. "How do you know I cannot fix it?"

"You said you don't have needle and thread. You'll have to rely on mine." That is the polite answer, but we both know that the tools of mending would be useless in her hands.

The sheep are gathered in their pen, as I knew they would be. The dogs function as a barrier, lying nose to nose in the open space. I make a clicking sound, releasing them, and close and latch the gate. When we step inside the house, I'm overwhelmed with a sense of fierce pride. Yes, it is small, but it is decently furnished and neat. Many of our neighbors' homes have been allowed to fall into disrepair, as if poverty were an excuse to disregard the comfort of the home God provided. Gagnon would let us all go cold before he would sacrifice his furniture to the fire. Our meals might be meager, but we have a table upon which to serve them, and a hearth to call home.

Madame Gisela takes a deep breath upon entering, at last dropping her grip on her wounded skirt and clasping her hands to the flattened point of her bodice. "I grew up in a home much like this. Very simple. Very—small."

"Wait here." I offer her our most comfortable seat. "I'll fetch some water for the basin. If you want to wash up."

"I believe you are the one who needs to wash up. Especially if I am to allow you to touch my dress."

"I will."

And I do, straight from the well bucket, scrubbing and rinsing my hands until they are two full shades lighter than the skin above my wrists. The water is cold and we have no soap, so it is only by harsh friction that I get them clean, and by that time I need to dump the bucket of gray water and haul up a fresh one for Madame Gisela. I clean my face, too, and smooth the loose tendrils of my hair. When I walk back into the house, I find her reclined on the seat, sodden shoes beside the stool, ornate hat in her lap. Seeing her in repose, her face is softer, and I can almost imagine her growing up in such modest means.

Moving as quietly as possible, I pour the water into the washbasin and examine the larder to see what I can offer for supper. This is Laurette's strength, the ability to create a meal when it seems there's no food to prepare it. I find only the remainder of a loaf of bread and a crock of stew grown cold. Its texture would be unappealing after another heating over the fire, and there isn't enough for all of us. I take a pinch of bread and dip it in the cold stew so I can say with complete honesty that I ate while she slept, and I trust that Gagnon has eaten with Girard. Laurette will no doubt sup at the inn, leaving only Madame Gisela and the driver to feed.

It will be enough for tonight.

Tonight.

The house is small.

This is not a woman who can sleep in a barn loft, no matter how cozy. Nor could she spend the night in Gagnon's room, even if he sacrificed his bed to sleep in the barn, as he has done on other occasions of an overnight visitor. She needs a proper chamber, and though I've been obedient to Gagnon's request and haven't taken so much as a peek through the keyhole, I must assume that proper lodgings wait behind the closed door. Closed, and locked, making me run for the kitchen stool to get the key down from the jamb.

I cannot say what I expected to find on the other side. It's late afternoon and the light is dimming. The shutters closed tight over the single window make the room almost completely dark. It smells of musty linen, but nothing rank, and as my eyes adjust, I'm pleased to find it as tidy and neat as any other room in the house. The bed is large, set with a full, bare ticking. There'd be no shame in offering this as a place of sleep to our guest.

"Renée."

His voice, soft as shadows, hits me like ice. I don't want to turn to face him, but I do. He's nothing but silhouette.

"I'm sorry, Gagnon. I only thought—"

"Who asked you to think?" I can hear the grief in his voice. It sounds fresh, as if this room had been vacated yesterday rather than years ago. It is such a rare thing to ever hear him speak with anything other than indulgent humor that I don't know how to respond, so I repeat my apology.

"What is this?" Madame Gisela appears behind him. The broadness of Gagnon's shoulders don't permit her to peer inside. "Is this to be my lodging for the night? Can the carriage not be repaired before evening?"

Wordlessly, he enters, walking straight to a trunk at the foot of the bed. With heart-stopping reverence, he kneels, opens it, and takes out a short stack of folded blankets, and when he walks toward me, I stretch out my arms to take them. Instinctively, I bring them to my face and inhale the scent. Though I know them to have been stored for my lifetime here, I can still smell the sun of a happier time. Gagnon opens the shutter, flooding the room with light. All of this he accomplishes with his eyes downcast, his shoulders coiled like a spring, and I'm afraid any sound or gesture will bring him to explode. So I whisper, "Thank you, Monsieur Gagnon," hoping Madame Gisela will be prompted to echo my gratitude, but she merely sniffs.

Say nothing, I plead in silence. *Not now, not in his presence. Do us the honor of a modicum of grace.*

"It will do," she says, and I exhale.

L'épisode 5

Laurette

MOUTON BLANC, LES BOIS

The party was five in all. Jacques Dubois, Marcel, Laurette, and Le Rocher—a man who looked strong enough to hoist the carriage on his shoulders and bring it back to the village in triumph—followed Gerard, who wasted no opportunity to regale them with details of his chase.

"On my way into town, a few rabbit pelts to trade if I could, and I see this thundering chariot coming over the horizon. I'll tell you when we get to the place where I saw it."

"It's not a chariot," Dubois said humorlessly. "Nothing more than a painted cart, the same as we use to take pigs to market."

"Oh, and painted it was," continued Gerard undeterred. "Black like silk, sun bouncing off the shine like a lake of ice."

"Never mind trading the rabbit pelts," Marcel said. "Sounds to me like you could go in and sing tales for your supper."

Everybody laughed, including Laurette. The sound drew Marcel's attention, and he turned to take her hand.

It was dusk when they came to the clearing, and if there was any doubt they'd arrived at the appointed place, Gerard boldly gestured, saying, "There. Right there, as sure as I live."

The little party stood at the lip of the meadow, staring at the emptiness below. Dubois spoke first. "Broken to pieces, was it?"

"As I breathe, *messieurs*. Shattered. Bits of it scattered a quarter mile or so."

The man who looked strong enough to transport the carriage wasted no time displaying his strength on the hapless Gerard, leveling him with a single blow to the man's slack jaw.

"Enough," Marcel said, moving bodily to block any further attack. He looked down at the cowering Gerard. "Are you positive, my man, that the carriage wasn't simply mired?"

"It was more than that," Gerard replied after taking a moment to be sure he retained his power of speech. "Else I would have put my own shoulder to it to help. Earn a coin or so."

But nobody believed the man had the strength—neither physical nor of character—to accomplish such a task, no matter if doing so would have resulted in a story grand enough to earn a night's worth of wine.

"Do you see now?" Dubois towered over Marcel, one long, dirt-crusted finger an inch away from the younger man's nose. His presence was so imposing, Laurette backed away, lest she be caught up in the whirlwind of his anger. "This, *this* is why we strike in the moment. That carriage drove through our street with no regard for us, or for the hungry children with caps in hand. I had to pull my own son out of its path or he'd been trampled under the horses."

"What would you have had us do?" Marcel's voice matched the cool of the descending evening, tinged with its own darkness. "Should we have thrown Le Rocher here in its path instead?" Le Rocher, the boulder, the man of impressive girth who had spoken nary a word since leaving Le Cochon Gros, rumbled an approving sound.

"Better than to have done nothing." Dubois relaxed his stance and took on something more like petulance. "Better than standing around like a pile of useless bones staring at a wasted opportunity."

"Ah—" Marcel leapt away, positioning himself to address the entire party—"but there are no wasted opportunities if a lesson is learned. Our bones are useless, but our minds are alive. And what have we learned?"

"That Gerard is a liar." Dubois's response sent Le Rocher into action as he cuffed the teller of tales on the back of his head.

"No," Marcel soothed, "not a liar. He saw what he saw, and he came to tell. We made no error in watching the carriage drive through our town. Our error was to follow. To chase. There is a difference, is there not, between a hunt and a chase?" He took three steps to Laurette and touched his palm to her cheek. "What are we, *chérie*?"

"Lions, Marcel."

He kissed her sweetly, approving the response, then turned back to his men. "Émile Gagnon grazes his sheep not far from here. Sheep, as you know, do not think beyond the moment at hand. Sheep act on command. They startle and they move in one hapless accord, following and following and following some leader who doesn't know any more about their direction than does the poor one trapped in the middle of the herd. Sheep obey dogs. And dogs obey . . ." He paused, and Laurette knew he was thinking of *their* dogs. "Dogs obey commands too far distant for the human ear to detect."

The whistles, high-pitched with varied notes. The clicks. Cossette and Copine could hear them even when they had ranged nearly out of sight.

"We are not sheep. And we are not dogs. We are the lions, circling in wait. And I promise you this, my friend—" he clapped a hand to Dubois's chest—"the next time one of theirs escapes the flock and runs through our streets, we will strike."

Whatever animosity lived between the men evaporated as Dubois shook Marcel's hand with a bonding intensity.

"Now, go. Back to the village. If the men are still gathered, tell them what I have told you. Tell them we are prepared to rip the wool from the sheep of aristocracy."

Dubois seemed uncomfortable with his charge. "You are not coming?"

"I'll be along," Marcel said, turning to Laurette. "After I see *mademoiselle* safely home."

Laurette, so engaged in Marcel's speech, fought back her gasp of disappointment. She clutched his sleeve. "I want to stay with you."

"In time," he said—so softly that she knew she alone heard him. A command for her ears alone.

"Allons," Dubois said, urging the others with his bestowed authority. "And, Gerard, so help me, if it gets too dark, I'll light your hair as a torch."

They watched until the three silhouettes, each so distinctly different from the others, dissolved into the gathering darkness.

"This is where Gagnon brings his flock, *non*?"

Laurette pointed into the void. "Just over there. Renée took them out this morning." She felt the clench of Marcel's fist.

"If they harmed her in any way . . ."

"Why should they have?" Laurette moved herself to face him. "I'm sure it's as you said. The carriage was merely mired. Who knows that Gagnon didn't come to the rescue and send them on their way?"

"Refusing payment for his help, no doubt." Marcel's comment held no admiration for such supposed generosity. "Still, let me take you home. I have to know."

"Know what?"

"If she's unharmed."

"Why should she be harmed?"

"You didn't see how that driver . . . Dubois's boy was nearly run down."

"Renée is not a child to be run down."

"No. She is not."

Laurette felt him slipping away. His gaze fell somewhere in the engulfing grayness, no part of him touched her.

"Are you in love with her? With Renée?"

"Such a question," he said, fully seeing her again. "Are you sure you want an answer?"

"Oui."

"Then, yes, I do. I love her."

Laurette stepped back as if slapped. "But—but she is a *child.*"

"Moments ago she was not, by your own words."

"But she is younger than I am."

He shrugged. "Not so much." Then he laughed and wrapped her in a loose embrace, kissing her despite her feeble protest. "Do not be angry with me, *ma lionne.* I love her as I do my country. That is all."

"What does that mean?"

"She was abandoned by her mother in the same way our people have been abandoned by our leaders. Left to starve. Or beg."

"As was I."

"Your parents were taken from you, through acts of anger and justice. But hers? They were weak. She had you to fight for her. But now she needs something else."

"So you would fight for her?"

"I would die for her."

Laurette let the words sink in. How could the two of them be alone in spring moonlight speaking of nothing but Renée? She loomed everywhere—their words, his thoughts. An uninvited guest perched between them. Not big enough to overshadow, but small enough to nag. And now, if she didn't do something, Laurette would lose Marcel on his path to rescue Renée.

"And for me?"

"It is different." He placed his forehead against hers and blazed a trail down her neck with their entwined hands. "You are my moment. *This* moment. You are what is burning my blood right now. I can only promise that I do not love Renée half as much as I desire you."

Earlier in the evening, these words alone might have swept her feet from beneath her. After all, what had she become over the course of a day? A goddess. A lioness. The burning of his blood. And what had she been yesterday? Nothing. But half of her spirit remained moored to his declaration of love for her cousin. The world was ever changing, and Marcel a man incapable of a promise beyond a moment. Something told her that if he were given a choice tonight—if he were to see Renée—her moment would pass forever.

"Don't walk me home, Marcel."

"You cannot come back to the village with me tonight."

"I meant—can't we stay here? For just . . . for a little while?"

This time, Laurette did not wait for him to draw her close. He would not sweep her away. She touched his cheek and angled her face so that her lips could find their purchase. Pressing closer, she deepened the kiss until she was sure she alone consumed this thoughts as well as his breath. Marcel responded with enthusiasm, eventually surpassing her ardency and intent. Soon the heat on her skin matched what she felt when he held her next to the fire at the inn, bringing her straight back to that moment. His hands trespassed all boundaries. His lips muttered praise at every curve. Darkness fell and fell, until she didn't know if her eyes were open or closed. In time, she felt a breeze blow between them as he stepped away, but only long enough to lead her deeper into the grove. She gave herself over as the coolness of the evening air was replaced with the cool, damp feel of the ground beneath her.

His words stopped. All the promises of her beauty, her strength, her life—she fulfilled them as he wished. Moss entwined her hair. Grass stained her best chemise. She knew—had known, perhaps, since she took her first step into Le Cochon Gros—that the evening would end this way. And while a small voice urged her to stop, to guard her soul and body from this betrayal, a louder voice drowned out any warning. Her own, speaking, "Marcel," into the night sky.

His, answering, "Laurette . . . Laurette."

This exchange, this acknowledgment of one another to the night would serve as sacrament. These whispers, her vow.

L'épisode 6

Renée

MOUTON BLANC, CHEZ GAGNON

Rarely do I ever fret out loud about the scarcity of our meals, but when I do, Gagnon is quick to reassure with a Scripture about God's provision. This evening, his words prove true, because while Madame Gisela was traveling without so much as a change of stockings, she did have a hamper full of delicacies for a roadside dinner while the horses rested. There were pots of ground meat and two dozen rolls, fruit and cakes and jams and butter, as if they were planning to feed an army and not one stylish woman and her driver.

I was charged with bringing each item from the basket, and exercised my greatest self-control by not diving in or stuffing handfuls of grapes into my mouth.

"It seems so much," Madame Gisela says. "You must think I am quite the pig. But sometimes there are beggars, and it takes only a crust of bread to send them away."

My own hunger knots itself tighter, and I think that I shall refuse even a bite of all of this, lest she think me a beggar too, but Gagnon, opening a new bottle of wine, compliments her generosity. "You never know, *madame*, when such a morsel will bring the difference between life and death."

She has the good grace to look chagrined and holds out her glass for him to fill. "After today, I feel this drink will have the same effect."

Gagnon laughs. "I'm afraid, *madame*, that it will not rise to your standards."

Madame Gisela drinks and seems pleased. "This is the sort of wine I grew up with. It is the stuff of the court that leaves a bitter taste."

And so we dine, late into the evening, with candles lit all around. We learn that Madame Gisela is, indeed, a special friend of our queen's. One who wouldn't tell secrets, she assures, and so we ask for none, though I pepper her with questions about the fashions at court. Are the headdresses really three feet tall? Are some of the dresses really so heavy with silk and jewels that the women have to be helped from one seat to the next? Does the queen really wear a new pair of shoes each day so that her old ones might be discarded to the others who linger at Versailles? This, Madame Gisela deems too much of a secret to reveal, but uses the opportunity to reassure us of Her Majesty's generous spirit.

"What you see and what you hear from her enemies . . ." She looks away in tearful disgust. "Her Majesty hasn't a hint of cruelty or greed, let alone some of the more salacious accusations . . ."

Gagnon clears his throat and we fall into a silence that lasts until Monsieur Rascon, the driver, diverts us with a tale about the farmer he passed whose cow had thrust its head through the bottom of a feed bucket and was lifting the farmer clear off his feet as the man tried to free her. We laugh as he so brilliantly pantomimes the scene, and I wonder if Madame Gisela would ever have heard the story if she had not the opportunity to dine as a guest in the house of a man who insisted on equality at his table.

We have finished the first bottle of wine and are well into the second—a luxury, as Gagnon usually makes us mix it with water to last the week. My belly is full and my cheeks are warm from the firelight and candlelight and laughter. We are all in a state of mirth when the door opens and Laurette comes in from the night. Her face, too, is flushed, and her hair a wild, uncontained mass. I suppose I can attribute her appearance to a windblown walk from town, but something tells me she, too, has been enjoying a revelry of her own. As she comes closer into the light, I see that she is more disheveled than I first thought—her skirt damp, her sleeves stained, only her embroidered vest unscathed.

"Goodness!" I exclaim. "Did you take some kind of tumble on the road?"

Gagnon leaps to his feet. "Laurette! It's been dark for hours. Why hasn't that worthless Marcel escorted you home?" He is unsteady in both his steps and his words, taking both Laurette and myself by surprise when he punctuates his question with a hearty kiss to her cheek.

"He is staying at the inn," she says, abandoning her curiosity about our company to convey her displeasure at his behavior.

"So he is not to join us?" And now I know that it is all a ruse, even his intoxication, to gain assurance that our outspoken friend will not show up at the table. Marcel flares to anger at the mention of the queen. There could be no assurance that he would behave with civility in the presence of our guest.

"If only he'd known the more festive party was assembled under our very roof."

I jump up. "Let me fetch you a plate. There's plenty left."

"No, thank you." Laurette puts on an air, raising her voice to an unnatural pitch and looking down her nose at me. "This is nothing like the feast I had in town, and I couldn't swallow another bite."

I don't know why she's lying, as I couldn't imagine her letting pride get in the way of such delicacies.

"Join us for a glass of wine, then," Gagnon says. "We so rarely have guests; we should not be rude."

"Begging everyone's pardon," she says, with something like a curtsy, "I am tired from the walk and only popped my head in to wish you all a good evening."

More and more her behavior is puzzling, and I try to get her attention to send a private inquiry, but she avoids my eyes and takes her leave without suffering an introduction to our company. When she's gone, Madame Gisela asks, "Your sister?"

"My cousin. Laurette."

Gagnon appears to be at a loss to explain her behavior, but diverts attention by filling our glasses with the last of the bottle before declaring that he must be off to begin repairs to the broken wheel.

"Are you in any shape for such an undertaking?" Madame Gisela is flirtatious in her question.

"I've accomplished much more under far worse circumstances," Gagnon says with a convincing slur. "Nothing like a little hard labor to restore sobriety."

Monsieur Rancon goes off with Gagnon, his demeanor leading me to believe that he will be less than helpful in the process. Thus it is left to me to clear the dishes from the table and carefully store what is left over on the pantry shelf. As I cover each crock with a scrap of cloth and place each piece of fruit in a basket, I plan the following day's meal, knowing I'll have fresh eggs and milk for some kind of breakfast. Madame Gisela watches from a reclining position in the best chair, never offering to lift so much as a finger. I don't know whether to resent or admire her ability to be so resolutely unhelpful.

When I finish, she insists that I accompany her to her room. She is accustomed to having a maid help her prepare for bed, and under these circumstances I will have to do.

"We'll see how you are going to mend my dress," she says over her shoulder. "Unless you've forgotten."

Forgotten? I've thought of little else, and so I enter this forbidden room for only the second time in all my days here. The linens have been left folded at the foot of the bed. I spread them across the ticking, which has flattened over time, and listen to Madame Gisela tell me of the rooms at Versailles. The silks hanging from the walls, the bed that stands so tall the queen needs a stool to climb up on it, the carpets on the floors, and the halls that echo with conversation and frivolity at all hours of the day and night.

"Never a quiet moment," she says. The deep silence of the night descends upon us, but only for a moment. As if uncomfortable with the stillness, she speaks again. "This is his room, then? Your master's?"

I cringe at the word but reply, "Yes. That he shared with his wife. She died several years ago."

"And he has not remarried?"

"No."

"Nor ever had a woman here?"

"I wouldn't speak of such a thing if he had."

Madame Gisela laughs. "Not much of a gossip, are you? Then I don't know how you'd fit in at court."

"Well, as I'm not likely to be at court anytime soon, I don't imagine fitting in is a problem."

She laughs again, but when I turn, she is studying me carefully, chin propped in her hand. "Come. You're finished there. Help me with my gown."

I fight to hide my eagerness as I approach. She turns her back and presents me with a series of tiny glass buttons—two dozen, at least—fastened at the back, and stoops so that I can reach the top one. I'm struck by the coarseness of my fingers, the ragged cuticles around the nails scraping against the silk. Never have I touched anything this fine, this luxurious. My hands know only wool and canvas and any other material homespun on a loom. I fear I will leave a mark, that I will shred the fibers with my rough skin, but no. I slide each button free, and as I do, the gown loses its life. Its form. It is a single garment, and as I move to the front to hold it as Madame Gisela steps out, it collapses into nothing more than an armful of fabric. Beautiful fabric to be sure, but the power is gone.

Madame Gisela stands before me, clothed in a mass of petticoats stretched over the wire and leather contraption that gave the dress its form. I untie the top petticoat, and have to follow her instructions to unlatch the harness of the pannier and unlace the corset. I comment that she must feel like a prisoner in such constraints, and she laughs.

"Never let them tell you there's no price for beauty. It comes quite dear. Now, to mending my dress."

"I can't simply mend the tear," I say, running a finger along the torn silk. "I don't have the proper thread, and I think any such mending would look terribly patched. But I thought, something like a cutaway."

"What do you know about the cutaway?" Madame Gisela sounds more curious than accusatory.

The idea had been so clear in my head—perfectly so until I had the fabric in my hand, but I willed it back. "I could turn it under and bring the flounce up and around to frame it. That would hide the stitching, since my thread is so coarse."

"And then? Leave this gaping—I don't even know what to call it? To show my petticoat beneath? It is not one meant to be seen."

"I know." I don't want to mention that I've seen such in the unflattering cartoons.

"I don't have the proper underskirt."

"No . . ." I studied the plain white muslin of her petticoat. "But—I have an idea."

"I daresay you do." Her expression is almost one of pride, as if she played a role in my revelation.

I promise to return and make my way through the empty, dark house and out into the yard. A wide shaft of light spills from the open barn door, and I pause just outside to listen. Monsieur Rancon is nowhere to be seen.

From my vantage point, I can see Laurette, stripped to her chemise with a heavy shawl draped over her shoulders. She is sitting on the ladder's rung, hair spilled soft. "You'll be able to fix it, then?" she asks Gagnon. Her question is tinged with an urgency beyond curiosity.

"I hope to." His voice is terse. Without betraying my presence, I crane my neck to see him busying himself with his tools, never quite meeting her eye. "I had an uncle who was a wheelwright. Did some work with him when I was younger. Just need to replace a spoke, fit in a new piece, and true it. We'll have our friends on their way by dawn."

"And that's a good thing?"

He pauses in his work. "It's a very good thing, Laurette. For all our safety."

"You needn't worry," Laurette says. "Marcel stayed in town."

Gagnon glances up, something unidentifiable in his face. Less than anger, more than concern. "You shouldn't have gone there."

"I had to get away, after so many days cooped up with the rain . . ."

"Then go to the fields with Renée."

"I'm not like Renée."

Gagnon says nothing but returns to his work.

After a moment, Laurette rises and turns to climb the ladder. "Good night, then."

"He's a dangerous man," Gagnon says to her retreating figure, "and I hope I don't live to regret inviting him to my table."

I wait until Laurette has disappeared and a few breaths more, sensing that the moment newly past between the two was not meant for me to share. Then I open the door wider, allowing the creak of its hinges to announce my presence, and ask an obvious question, "Where is Monsieur Rancon?"

"He's chosen to sleep in the carriage," Gagnon says, and I can see that he is forcing some levity into his reply. "Protecting it with his life, though I don't know how much of a fight he'd put up if anyone made a claim to it."

I look at the unfamiliar tools. "Will you have it mended by morning?"

"I hope to, yes."

"Then I must hurry, too. It seems we both are charged with mending tonight."

I climb up to our loft, certain to find Laurette awake since it was only moments ago she left Gagnon, yet her form is perfectly still, as if in a deep slumber. This evening, it seems, is one for deception all around. She offers no reply to my whispered greeting, and I have no idea what I would say to her if she did. All my life, our last words of the day have been to each other. But tonight, this intrusion of strangers and old friends has wedged something between us.

I grope in the darkness and find my basket. I know what I have inside will be perfect, but I won't know until dawn if it will be enough.

⁂

The sun is coming up as I bite off the thread at the final stitch. I want to rise and work the crick out of my neck, but I've spent the night covered in heavy, fine silk, and I can't say when that will happen again. Only the sound of Madame Gisela calling me from the bedroom summons me to stand.

"Oui, madame," I answer her impatience. A glance out the window reveals Gagnon and Monsieur Rancon working to reattach the carriage wheel. Today, despite his inevitable protest, I'll make certain that he takes to his bed until dinnertime, at least. Laurette and I can see to all the chores.

"Renée!"

For the first time in my life I feel like a servant as I unfold myself from the chair and gather up the silk so that not a bit of it touches the floor. The dress is heavy, and I can't imagine the burden of carrying such weight every day.

"I don't suppose you've anything that can pass as a dressing gown?" Madame Gisela stands in the middle of the room wearing only her chemise. Her hair is plaited loosely over her shoulder, and in this state she looks completely at home in this simple peasant's room. "I'm not accustomed to going to breakfast dressed for the day."

"No, *madame*." I walk past her and spread the gown across the unmade bed. "But if you like, I can make something up and bring it in here to you? But I must tell you that the carriage appears to be repaired. I don't know how late of a start you will want to get this morning."

"What time is it now?"

"Nearly six o'clock, I think. Shall I go?"

Madame Gisela yawns, stretches, and heaves a sigh. "*Non.* You are right, I suppose. Now, show me what you've done."

My stomach flutters with nerves as I direct her attention to the alterations I made to the gown. "See here? I've taken the flounce, lifted it, and patched lace in the gap. It might not look special here, but I believe once you have it on, it will look like the hint of a cutaway with a lace petticoat beneath."

Madame Gisela bends forward and lifts the mended portion

close to her face, angling it to better catch the gray morning light.

"Where did you get this lace?"

"Forgive me, *madame*. I know I misspoke." My face burns with shame. "It's not lace, not in the truest sense. I don't have a fine-enough thread or shuttle. This is just a crochet stitch. But it's small and fine, and—"

She waves off my protest without a glance. "It's exquisite, Renée. As beautiful work as I've ever seen."

"Truly?" Now I'm doubly glad she's not looking at me, because I'm sure my joy must seem childish.

She stretches her arm, regards my work, then brings it close again. "Flawless. Do you know what kind of price you could fetch for such work?"

"It wouldn't matter if I sold it for half a sou or a thousand livres, my people here have no money to pay. I do little things for myself, or for Laurette. Or for what I can trade."

"A waste." Madame Gisela tosses the gown back on the bed as if it didn't hold more value than this entire estate. It is the second time someone has said such of me.

I work to revoke all of the freedom bestowed upon her last night, cinching her corset, buckling the cage, tying the petticoats, rolling the stockings, and knotting the garters. I brush her hair with my own brush and fashion it simply, dressing it with a length of my crochet. When all else is accomplished, I hold the dress for her to step into and patiently refasten each of the jeweled buttons in the back. Fully dressed, she turns, and I see my design. Before I can stop myself, I clap a hand over my mouth in delight.

"I don't suppose you have a full-length glass here?"

"*Non, madame.* But—can you see?"

She glances down, extends her leg and contorts her body. Then she emits her own satisfying giggle.

The effect of my work is that of an invisible hand lifting Madame Gisela's skirt. Flirtatiously, as I've seen some of the women do outside of Le Cochon Gros in Mouton Blanc. The kind of women Gagnon tells me not to look at, as he himself tears his eyes away. But this is no salacious invitation. There is no leg exposed, only lace—and thick, wool lace at that. Colored and textured, sturdier stuff than the skirt itself, but stitched to be light as air.

"Such a clever idea," Madame Gisela says. "How on earth does a shepherd girl have such a clever idea?"

I shake my head, feeling no insult at being called a shepherd girl. Her next words, however, stop my breath.

"You must come with me."

"Come with you?"

"*Exactement.* To Versailles. The queen will be mad for this. And I can only imagine what you might create given the resources—why, what stitching those little hands can do!"

I allow a single swirl of imagination before my better senses prevail. "I couldn't possibly. This—this is my home. I'm needed here."

"Nonsense. Your Monsieur Gagnon can manage quite well without you. The countryside must be teeming with orphans in need of a place to live."

I must have lost control of my mask of strength, because she breaks into a little frown and puts a maternal arm around my shoulder. "Oh, I see I've offended you. Forgive my brashness, but I know what it is to be what you are. I *was* what you are, though not orphaned to be sure. And not quite as poor, but only because the country was not quite as poor. But I was a simple country girl until I married a man who became a guest of the court. Believe me when I tell you that our Marie is a good and gentle woman who relishes any opportunity she can have to bestow generosity and reward. I would welcome you, Renée, as one of my own family. I will see to it you are introduced to the royal dressmakers. To Mademoiselle Bertin herself. Our 'Minister of Fashion.' What a relief your quick work will be."

By the time she comes to the end of her speech, it seems all decided, despite my not having said a single word of agreement or protest. She has relinquished her hold on me, and all her belongings are gathered and snapped inside her valise when a knock sounds on the other side of the door. I open it just an inch, as if to keep in the secret of Madame Gisela's proposal, and look up into Gagnon's tired eyes.

"Tell Madame that she should try to be en route within the hour. That will get her to Paris late tonight."

"Open the door, Renée," Madame Gisela says, and I obey. In a single breath she repeats all she has said to me within the past moments, framing her declaration as if I have already agreed to her terms. Midway, Gagnon looks at me, questioning.

"I have not said I would go," I tell him, denying the newly formed tug of desire.

"But do you want to?"

"Of course not!" I speak too quickly to be believed. "How could I leave you after all you have done for me?"

"Child—" he lays his hand to my cheek—"I did not take you in with any thought of holding you against your will."

"But I'm free to stay, aren't I?"

He draws me close and my arms wrap around his waist. I close my eyes and feel the roughness of his shirt, smell the night's labor. He plants a kiss on the top of my head and says, "It is the dream of all of us that France will be a place of freedom to make such choices. I would miss you, Renée. But I suppose like any father, I should have known that such a day might come."

Until this moment I've never thought of Gagnon as a father. He is not by nature affectionate or authoritative. I love him, and I obey him, but only as a natural response to his kindness and wisdom. It pains me to see how easily he can bear to let me leave, but his decisiveness fuels my own. Still, I need to hear it said plainly.

I look up. "Shall I go then, Gagnon? With her?"

"I will not decide for you, *ma fille*." He looks over my head toward Madame Gisela. "Our Laurette has prepared a breakfast for you and your driver, *madame*. Go, eat. Allow Renée some time to seek the counsel of our Lord."

"Very well," Madame Gisela says, though she doesn't sound at all pleased to have her personal wishes handed over to one more sovereign than the king. "But I—"

Whatever she had been about to say is silenced with a glance from Gagnon. She sweeps out of the room, obviously disappointed not to have received a comment on the flirtatious design of her garment. When we are alone, Gagnon goes to the tall dresser in the corner, opens the fourth drawer, and draws out a small book. He leads me to the bed and sits me down upon it, kneeling at my feet.

"This belonged to my wife. My Denise." It is a book of the Psalms, obviously loved and cherished and faithfully read by another life. A strip of faded blue silk marks a page, and Gagnon opens to it. "'In thee, O LORD, do I put my trust; let me never be ashamed: deliver me in thy righteousness. Bow down thine ear to me; deliver me speedily: be thou my strong rock.'" He presses the open book into my hand. "God is with you in whatever you choose. No matter where you are, you're never far from him."

"Tell me what to do, Gagnon."

He rises, shaking his head. "You're sixteen years old. This is not my decision to make. I obeyed God when he told me to feed you. To shelter you. And I'll obey him now as he tells me to hand you over to him. Read this prayer, let it be your own."

He turns back at the door. "Just know this—Madame Gisela will leave within the hour."

Within the hour. My time to decide is measured in minutes. Left alone with the open book, I read:

> *For thou art my rock and my fortress; therefore for thy name's sake lead me, and guide me. Pull me out of the net that they have laid privily for me: for thou art my strength.*

I pause and pray—have they laid a net for me, Lord? Am I being lured with promises of . . . what? Surely not wealth, as I will be a servant. Surely not a roof and bed, for I have those here. My mind reels with the praise of Madame Gisela. Have I laid my own net, to be ensnared by my own pride? I read the next verse:

> *Into thine hand I commit my spirit: thou hast redeemed me, O Lord God of truth.*

These are the same words of Christ upon his death, and a fear grips me. This place had been marked. Are these the words Denise heard before she died? Here, in this house. In this room. Could this be a place to cut life short? I know I am weak. I know how I suffer, and I wonder if what Madame Gisela offers is truly life. I close the book, keeping the scrap of silk safely nestled within. I've never made such a decision by myself before. I don't know that I've ever made *any* choices in my own destiny. Part of me wants Madame Gisela to stride in, take my hand, and drag me away, just as Laurette did when we could no longer care for ourselves. To my shame, the words of the psalm lose their power. Madame Gisela has no authority to take me, Gagnon has no authority to keep me, and God's will is frustratingly unclear. I hear Laurette's voice, pleasant in conversation with Madame Gisela. Last night was the first in memory that the two of us did not sleep and awake in each other's presence, and it feels already like the first chip of a chasm between us. Each of us holds a secret—I, Madame Gisela's proposal; and she . . . I don't even know how to name it, but there's something. We've never had secrets before, and I've less than an hour to divulge mine. I've always relied on her strength, but never took stock in her wisdom. This morning, I will need both, and I take a deep breath before calling her to me.

⚜

L'épisode 7

Laurette

MOUTON BLANC, CHEZ GAGNON

He was gone when she awoke, but the steady rhythm of Gagnon's labor had soothed her troubled conscience to sleep. She could only guess how much he suspected of what transpired the night before with Marcel—the memory of it sullied with the gray of morning. Hurriedly, Laurette dressed and went out into the yard, finding the carriage with a fully repaired wheel gleaming in the piercing light. Gagnon and the driver, the latter dressed in a sleep-rumpled livery, worked together to harness the horses.

"We're going to take it for a quick drive," Gagnon said, handing up the reins before climbing to sit beside the driver. "Can you prepare a meal for our guests before they leave?"

"Of course, Gagnon." She could only imagine what was left over to eat. After a brief stop at the well, where she splashed her face in the bracing, freshly drawn water, Laurette went inside, past the window seat with Renée's abandoned mending basket. She heard muffled voices from behind the bedroom door, girlish squeals that piqued her interest, but she'd been assigned a task. There were fresh eggs in the basket, half a loaf of bread to slice, a thumb's worth of butter, and, after nosing through the cloth-covered crocks, slices of ham and sausages. She took half a sausage for herself and ate it, cold, while she stirred the eggs and shreds of ham together to cook in the sizzle of the bit of butter. She added a pinch of salt and a bit of dried rosemary, thinking such might be welcome to the palate of a fine lady like Madame Gisela.

Her mind reeled, thinking about what Marcel would have to say about cooking for their guest. That is, if he came back to see her this morning. Two scenarios filled her with equal fear—what Marcel might do to bring shame to Gagnon, and what Gagnon might do to keep Marcel in his place.

When Gagnon returned and summoned Madame Gisela to breakfast, Laurette opted not to join her, politely thanking her for the portion she'd already eaten. Soon after, Gagnon went back outside. She'd just determined to follow him and warn him that Marcel and his friends knew about the carriage when Renée called to her from the bedroom.

"In a minute?" Laurette responded.

"Please." Renée's voice conveyed an unfamiliar urgency. Laurette thought back to the night before, her cousin's soft presence in the loft and her refusal to respond. Gagnon had no need of her warning. He knew—everything.

"Excuse me," she said, remembering her manners.

Their guest offered a smile that could only be described as cunning and said, "By all means, say your good-bye," before closing her teeth over the fork.

Laurette frowned, not knowing what the woman could possibly mean. Renée's distraught face only added to her confusion.

"Shut the door," she said, as if in possession of a great secret, "and come here."

Laurette crossed the room and sat next to her cousin on the bed, marveling at the normalcy of the act, when just yesterday the room was still a shrine to the dead. "What is it? You look like you've seen a ghost." More to the fact, she looked like one, her pale face nearly translucent, her eyes wide with blue shadows beneath.

"Yesterday . . . ," Renée said, and launched into a narrative much as Laurette suspected. That she had seen the carriage fall as she guarded the sheep, that she had fetched Gagnon to fix it. She spoke in reverent tones about Madame Gisela's torn skirt and her hours spent mending it. "And so she's asked me to go back with her."

Laurette, only half-listening to the details of the evening, shook herself at the last statement. "Go back with her? Back where?"

Renée shrugged. "I—I'm not even sure that I know. Only that Madame Gisela is a friend to the queen, and she thinks she will be impressed with my—what I can do. She says I could have work there. With *her*. As a seamstress."

"How—what did Gagnon say?"

Renée withered and looked at the small leather book clutched in her lap. "He said it was my decision to make. And to pray."

Laurette found the first of his responses surprising, the second less so. How could this not be his decision? Renée was . . . *his*. Wasn't she? Weren't they both? But then her own actions had forged a new allegiance for herself. Had Marcel asked, she would have returned with him to—to wherever he went when he wasn't here. And she wouldn't have asked Gagnon's permission or blessing, and she certainly would not have prayed. She'd held that very book in her own hands, even opening it to run her eyes across the words, but knew they would not give any answer she desired.

"What should I do, Laurette?"

"Why are you asking me? I don't even understand what—where you'd go. Would you ever be back?"

"Of course!" But then her determined smile collapsed. "I suppose. Oh, *Cousine*, what would you do?"

Renée was imploring, her small frame burdened with choice, leaving Laurette woefully unqualified to take it from her. But she could lighten the moment. She chuckled. "Leave this place and go live in a palace?"

Renée responded with a wan smile. "Think how much Marcel would hate the idea."

"Yes." Laurette sobered. "Think of it." And with that thought, a window to darkness opened. Perhaps if she were gone, Renée wouldn't haunt his thoughts. When Marcel saw her ambition, how quick she was to seize an opportunity to abandon the only home she'd ever known, would his love for her diminish? The moment the idea took life, she wished to squelch it, but it had inhaled the possibility, and she could hold it no longer. "It can't matter what he thinks, Renée. He's nothing to you."

"And what is he to you?" A question tinged not so much with suspicion as concern. "I know you were with him last night. I heard you and Gagnon talking."

"Never mind about that." She hoped to push the question away with her words. "It's nothing. He's nothing to either of us. But you, now—close your eyes." Renée obeyed, and Laurette was struck by the translucence of her cousin's skin, the pale lashes against her cheek. Had she always been so wraithlike? Her pale, thin lips began to move in silent prayer. "Listen to me," she said, not caring that she interrupted a sacred conversation. "When you think about what this woman said to you—what she offered—what do you see?"

Renée closed her eyes tighter, knitting her sparse brows together. Then, a transformation that reached Laurette's own heart.

"It's like a dream," she said, her voice almost sleepy and far-off. "Only, a dream I don't remember having." She opened her eyes. "Like a gift someone is giving to me, but not a gift I ever asked for, because I never knew it existed. Does that make sense?"

Laurette couldn't help thinking back to lying with Marcel. That, too, had been a dream, but one that had been burning within her since the first spark of imagination. If only the thought of it could bring the same kind of peace that seemed to consume Renée at this moment. How perfect it might be if he loved her.

"Of course, Renée." She swallowed the darkness, scooted closer, and took the girl in a careful embrace, relieved to escape from her large, searching eyes. "Of course you should go. It's a good dream, and if you wake up from it, put on your shoes and walk home."

Part II

Le Printemps et l'Été (Spring and Summer) 1788

Sous les étoiles et la lune et les nuages gris . . .

L'épisode 8

Laurette

MOUTON BLANC

Ten days after Renée shut herself behind the royal crest on the carriage door, Laurette awoke in the grip of a memory. A happy memory, in fact—one of the few she carried, and thus had been safely stored in the subconsciousness of sleep. She was no more than five years old, Renée a stumbling toddler haunting her every step. Their mothers were alive and robust, serving platters of food along a table that stretched from the house to the barn. The demons that would possess her father had yet to manifest, and the knife in his hand posed a threat only to the woolly coat of the sheep in his arms.

It's shearing day, and there's a race—a contest between the shearers to see who can clip the most wool in the time it takes for the children to run the perimeter of the pen. Laurette lags behind the rest, clinging to Renée's hand lest she be trampled in the mix. She passes Émile Gagnon, a gangly boy too old to run, too young to shear. He shouts something encouraging, but the words are lost in the fog of dreaming. Soon, everything else is lost, too. The sound of her father's laughter, the hope of seeing her mother, and the feel of Renée's tiny hand.

She woke up with her hand clenched in a fist, her lungs stinging with the effort of breathing—not from running, but from the strain of fighting the guilt that would greet her first waking thought, and every one throughout the day to come. She flung off her blanket and sat up, instinctively wary of the low, sloping roof, and brought her blanket up to bury her face. Where was Renée waking up? What kind of day awaited her?

Laurette's would be the same as ever, cooking and serving porridge to Gagnon, morning chores, and then another long, silent day as he prepared for the upcoming shearing. In his morning prayer, he would ask God to protect the unborn lambs, and in the evening after supper, she would drift off to sleep to the sound of his blades against the whetstone. During the hours in between, he would be gone, taking the sheep far off to graze sparingly. Hungry, tired sheep were much easier to handle in the shearing pen. They wouldn't be gassy or bloated, less likely to expel waste on the shearer.

"Weaker, too," he'd say. "Won't put up as much of a fight."

In the days of Laurette's dream, it seemed like half the town came to Gagnon's farm to help with the shearing. It was a time of joyous celebration. Her father would earn wages to last half the winter. Women planted their gardens and cooked up the last of the winter stores. The evenings were filled with music and dancing and wine—all in excess. Between the bleating and the challenges and the laughter, there was never a moment of silence. But as time passed, as Laurette grew, as the land rebelled with drought and the far-off government waxed with greed, all of life became subdued. The work that had once been a celebration became nothing more than a task to be completed.

"I'm going into town today," Gagnon said later that morning, spooning the last of his breakfast porridge. "See if I can scare up a couple of men to help."

Laurette took the empty bowl. "Why bother?" Never before had she spoken back to Gagnon about anything involving the work of the farm, and her impudence surprised them both. She cleared her throat and adjusted her tone to one more subservient. "I mean, there's so few this year. It seems to me you could get the shearing done yourself. If nothing else, there are laborers closer by—"

"Who have their own labor to do. And who will want wages I can't pay. In town I'll find men with idle hands and empty bellies. They'll work for what I can feed them. Even that wastrel Marcel—might do him good to work a few days and eat food earned from honest labor."

She'd seen nothing of Marcel since their night in the forest, and though it was never far from her thoughts, the mention of his name brought the memory out full force. Her face flushed and her words teetered with indecision. With encouragement, Gagnon might think her too eager; with protest, he might be suspicious. She opted for deflection.

"Renée might be gone, but you still have me. Surely these hands would be enough?"

She thrust them in his view, momentarily pleased that they were chapped and red, evidence of hard work. Still, he laughed.

"I've known you to be here at shearing time your whole life, Laurette. And yet I've never seen you touch a clipper. Seeing how well you can butcher a chicken, I think it's best for the sheep that we keep you away."

She indulged him with a smile before succumbing to a quiet thought. "This will be the first shearing without Renée."

He took her hand, squeezed it, and let go. "It will."

"Do you think—will she ever come back home?"

"Only God knows. He directs our steps. And, today, he's directing me to Mouton Blanc."

Laurette spent the day in fidgeting chores, scrubbing what needn't be scrubbed, sweeping what needn't be swept—nervous energy to keep her mind and body occupied so she wouldn't stew about an inevitable reunion with Marcel. She tried to imagine what she would say, alternating between an angry confrontation and a flirtatious invitation, both of which had the same text: *Where have you been?* The unspoken nature of the question was neither brash nor brave. It burrowed deep, hidden beneath layers of shame—both at the memory and the desire to be with him again.

With all of the house neat and tidy, she reached for the key to the master's room to find it missing from its place, the door unlocked. Cautiously, not knowing what to fear, she opened it and found the bed made up and smooth, a curtain fluttering in the breeze, Gagnon's shirt hanging from a hook on the wall. The curse lifted.

The sun was nearly set when she looked up into the horizon to see three silhouettes approaching. The unmistakable Gagnon, with his cropped hair and broad shoulders, Marcel with his mane of curls distinct in the red-gold light, and Le Rocher, twice as wide as the two put together.

"Now, that's one to feed." She slapped the newly milked goat on her flank before sending her back to the barn. Of all the men she'd seen gathered around Marcel at Le Cochon Gros, surely there were others in greater need of work and a meal. Le Rocher looked anything but hungry. She stood as they approached, smoothing her skirt and wishing she'd had time to wash her face and fix her hair. Soon she would know whether to greet Marcel as a new lover, or an old friend. The chaste kiss he offered upon walking into the yard resolved her question, and without doubt she knew why Marcel would choose Le Rocher to accompany him. He wouldn't speak about that night.

"Makes him a great keeper of secrets," Marcel said later, after dinner, when the four sat around the table with empty plates and an empty bottle.

"Do you not speak at all?" The wine had given boldness to Laurette's tongue, releasing it after a meal spent holding it.

Le Rocher raised his eyebrows and tapped a sausage-sized finger to his temple. His head might be shaved clean, but he had beard enough to compensate.

"His father—" Marcel turned to him. "Do you mind my telling? His father picked him up by the throat when he was a baby, trying to get him to stop crying. Crushed it. Never has been able to make a sound since, have you, *mon ami*?"

Le Rocher shook his head, then pounded a fist on the table hard enough to make the plates jump.

"Other ways to get a message across, right?" Marcel tipped his glass, emptying it again. "Room enough in this world for all."

Later, when the promise of a full day's work called for an early bed, Gagnon caught Laurette by her sleeve on her way out the door. "I don't want you sleeping in the loft tonight. Not while these men are here. I don't trust them."

"Marcel has slept here—"

"That's different. You had Renée with you. Those two will sleep in the barn; you'll come to my room." He looked away and took a breath. "What *was* my room. Now, it is yours, Laurette. For as long as you wish."

He gave her a candle and directed her in, where she found all of her belongings waiting. When had he done such a thing? He must have noticed, as she was busy preparing supper, how Marcel stood close behind her, whispering into the nape of her neck. But these had not been a lover's whispers. While she had braced herself for words of desire and longing, she instead was besieged by accusation.

"How could you let Renée go?"

"How could you conspire to send that poor lamb into the viper's pit?"

She could still feel the words hot against her skin, and Gagnon obviously mistook them for another kind of passion. Laurette's possessions were few enough to have been transported while she stirred the stew.

"*Merci*, Gagnon." She dipped her head in gratitude, took the candle, and closed the door.

⚜

The task of shearing Gagnon's flock took a scant five days, and might have taken less had any of the participants felt a rush to complete it. But the weather was pleasant, the company entertaining, and the sheep by and large compliant, as long as they were not subjected to the blades of Le Rocher, who proved to be terrified of hurting the animals, and thus clumsy with the shears. He and Laurette assumed the task of leading the sheep from the corral to the pen, handing them off to Marcel and Gagnon, who waged a friendly competition with each fleece. Once, when a feisty ewe fought every step of the way, dislodging Laurette's cap in the battle and bringing her hair cascading down, Gagnon made a joke that he might just shear her instead.

"That mane of yours might fetch a hefty price for a wig."

"Yes," Marcel said without humor, "and then the cocks at court can steal flour from the mouths of our children to powder it."

"No talk of that here," Gagnon said. "You'll stir yourself up, and the animals will sense your anger."

The ewe became compliant in his arms as he turned her and took the first clip up her exposed belly. Marcel started in on his own, and for the next several minutes the only sound was that of steel slicing wool in a regular rhythm. As if choreographed, the sheep were turned, wool cut up and under the hind legs, the front, around the head and face, and finally a cascade down the back while Gagnon whispered words of soothing praise. After, Laurette took the wool—all in one piece due to Gagnon's experience and skill—and laid it out on a table to pick through for clumps of twigs and dirt and other undesirable elements. It was taxing, disgusting work, especially in a certain area where she trimmed down around the sheep's tail, but her reward came from running her hands along the underside, soft and warm and soothing to work-worn skin.

"It seems strange," Laurette said, snipping with her smaller shears, "not to gather up the scraps for Renée."

"You should gather them anyway," Marcel said, standing and stretching. "She might be back."

"And if not," Gagnon said, "she left her carders. I'll teach you. Pity you haven't learned already."

"Maybe," Laurette said, "but I'll never be as good—"

"No talk of that here." Marcel made no attempt to hide his good-natured mockery of Gagnon. He captured the timbre of his voice and chastising tone. "The animals will sense your sadness. Now, Le Rocher, fetch me a sheep—a big, beautiful, plump one."

Laurette turned before Gagnon could see her blush and ran for the corral.

On the last day, they worked well into the evening, the final sheep a spirited male who required the attention of both men to safely take his wool. He scrambled out—nicked—with Gagnon at the chase to finish him off. That night they supped with nothing but bread, butter, and wine, Le Rocher nodding into his cup.

They gathered around a fire outside, craving the fresh spring air after a day spent in the flying dust of a shearing pen. The flames leapt lazily, occasionally emitting a spark that caught the attention of the dogs, who would snap up their heads as if to catch it.

"Shearing is a young man's job," Gagnon complained. He was stretched out flat on his back, and extended his arms and legs as though caught in a torture device.

"Easy, *mon vieux*," Marcel said, raising his glass. "You have a few good seasons left in you."

"We'll see what I don't have to sell. Or butcher. Next year it might be just me and that old one."

"And if you get rid of the ewes, he'll probably kill himself."

The two men laughed as easily as if there'd been no lady in their midst, as did Le Rocher, who only half heard the joke. Once his laughter—a strange, breathy sound—died, his cup fell from his hand, and the night noises were joined by his snores. Moments later, Gagnon's breath was equally deep and even, his body motionless save for the rising and falling of his chest. Silently, swiftly, Marcel rolled until he was at Laurette's side, up on one elbow, trapping her with his other arm, head nestled in her open chemise. It happened so quickly, so shocking—given the presence of the other two men—that she made no protest at first. Then, coming to her senses, she grabbed a handful of Marcel's curls and lifted his head.

"Have you lost your—"

But he kissed her into silence, drawing himself up and covering her so that she'd no idea if they had an audience or not on the other side of the fire.

"Take me to your bed," he whispered, so low that the words felt more like caresses in the night.

Laurette shook her head in protest. Not because of fear, or modesty, or any other quality that she should possess, but because the last time he kissed her he led her down a path of surrender and left her at the end with nothing but moss in her hair and stains on her skirt. Why should a night spent in a bed prove any more satisfying?

"Non," she said, only to be kissed again. She forced her head to turn away, but everything below it seemed poised to rebel. Summoning the strength of both body and spirit, she escaped from beneath him and scrambled to her feet. Cossette and Copine leapt to attention and flanked her as she walked into the house, stationing themselves at the door behind her.

"Laurette," Marcel called after in whisper.

She stopped at the doorway and turned to find he'd followed, only to be kept at bay by the protective dogs. With a soft sound, she rewarded their vigilance with a rub to their heads before sending them away to give Marcel clear passage inside. He wasted no time, taking her in a distanced embrace, ducking to meet her eyes.

"What have I done, *chérie*?"

"Ten days you were gone. Not a word. And since you've been here? You haven't—" tears stung her throat—"you haven't even *looked* at me."

"I'm looking at you now. I've been looking at you all these days."

"I mean, since . . ."

"Nor have you come to me, *lionne*. Because he keeps you here, doesn't he? Like a prisoner. Not like he did Renée, selling her off at the first opportunity."

"Why is it you can only think of Renée? When she is gone and I am here?" She buried her hands in his dark, thick curls and pulled him close, kissing him with a ferocity intended to command his thoughts.

He responded, returning her fervor, and when at last he did pull away, his voice was hoarse with impatience. "Answer me. Do you want me in your bed?"

Her bed. A gift from Gagnon. Her whole life a gift from Gagnon.

Marcel responded to her hesitation. "Of course you do. See how you have lured me here?"

"I don't know what I want."

"I think you do."

He bent to kiss her again when they were surrounded by soft light.

"Go to bed, Laurette."

The quiet authority of Gagnon's voice filled the room as much as did the candle in his hand. She jumped away as if burned by its flame.

"You've no authority over her, Gagnon," Marcel said, though he remained standing with Laurette between them.

"Perhaps not. But in my home I have authority over you. You're not invited to sleep inside. Leave my house now. Good night."

She waited for Marcel to fight for her, but no such argument ensued. Instead, he implored, "Laurette?" Nothing like the tone he'd used to convince her to call down the dogs.

"*Bonne nuit*, Marcel." Something inside her loathed the diminishing form of the man who had so recently commanded her body and spirit. She could not bring herself to watch him walk past her, past Gagnon, and out into the night.

At the sound of the latch, Gagnon's shadow covered the door and all the wall around it, stronger than any iron peg could hold. His face, gold in the light of the candle, cocked to the side, held an expression beyond reading. Curiosity? Enlightenment? Like he was encountering an entirely unknown creature—familiar, yet newly shed of a disguise. She knew her hair was a tumbled-down mess, but he'd seen her in such a state before—clothing askew, skin flushed, breath unsteady. She almost longed for shame, and might have taken it on if not for the fresh, small wound he delivered when he didn't fight for her, either.

"I won't warn you again," he said, salting it. "You have a place in my home for as long as you like, but he does not. Not in my home, not at my table, not again. He's a dangerous man in dangerous times. You have to trust me on this. Do you trust me?"

She thought about the sheep. Simple, stupid. "Yes. Of course I do. And, I suppose, after tonight it will be time for me to take my place back in the loft?"

"It is always your choice, Laurette, to come and go as you please." He took her hand and placed the candle within it before leaving her alone in its light.

⚜

L'épisode 9

•

Renée

VERSAILLES

For the first week, I know nothing other than the walls of Madame Gisela's apartments. She escorted me under cover of a massive velvet cloak and brought me immediately to a warm bath, where I was stripped down and scrubbed clean with sweet-scented soap. My hair was washed, too, then combed through with a foul-smelling oil, though I protested that I kept my scalp clean and had never been plagued with any vermin. My words fell on deaf ears, as the maid assigned to bathe me declared she would not take orders from a barn-dwelling peasant. For three days I was kept away from any open flame, lest my hair combust upon my head.

And I ate. And ate, and ate. Pastries and meat and fruit in all forms—fresh, jellied, baked into yet more cakes and pastries. Vegetables boiled and mashed into soups enriched with cream. Cups of hot liquid chocolate that made me feel as if I'd landed in a different, wonderful world. After the first three days, I was actually sickened by the spoils, my stomach not used to being full, my body unfamiliar with such richness. I moaned, doubled in pain, and took only broth for a day. It felt like a punishment, even though it was savory and delicious, and I learned to eat as Madame Gisela does, with dainty pinches, and enough left on the plate to feed the servants twice over.

I've been given a soft bed that I share with Madame Gisela's daughter, Amelie, the girl Madame Gisela claimed to be close to my age but is only eleven years old, the same age as the queen's daughter. They, too, I learn, are the closest of friends.

Through Amelie's eyes, I see a world I could never have constructed from my own imagination. She wears stockings and shoes every day, even though her feet never touch any surface that isn't polished like silk or carpeted with fine wool. When, to Madame Gisela's delight, we learn that Amelie and I have the same size feet, I am afforded the same privilege, though I am not excited about the prospect. I'm given new clothes, too. Simple dresses in the shepherdess design, once a favorite fashion of the queen. The first time I am brought this soft, flowing garment, belted to make my bust appear fuller than it is, I laugh.

"I could never graze the sheep in this. It wouldn't stand up to the wind and rocks."

"It's a fantasy," Madame Gisela says, pinning my hair in a simple design. "Nothing here is real."

I am real enough for Amelie, who resents my presence almost immediately, seeing me as a rival for her friendship with the princess, Marie-Thérèse, though I explain over and over that I've come to work, not to play, and that I'm too old to play, and that I wouldn't know *how* to play even if I were so inclined. To prove myself, I take to altering her clothes, making sleeves longer and shorter at my desire, transferring ribbons from one little gown to another. In a bold move, I cut panels from one discarded dress (tossed aside for a minor stain) and sew them onto another, creating a mix of patterns that Madame Gisela declares delightful.

"Like a little patchwork," she proclaims, as if patching one bit of clothing to another is a trick to be admired.

"There's a knack to it," I tell her, "to find fabrics that will work. If you're not careful, if the weaving doesn't match, the stitches will pull away when you wash the garment."

"We don't wash our garments often," Madame Gisela says in the indulgent tone she's adopted for me. "Something else you'll learn."

It is this particular endeavor that brings me my first introduction to the queen. "She has to come to you," Madame Gisela continued to reassure me during the first weeks of my stay. "Do you understand? One cannot—*I* cannot—simply walk up to her of a morning and say, "*Bonjour*, my queen, here is the delightful little seamstress I plucked from the countryside for you."

Each time I would reply that I had not come with any such desire. That I had no desire at all, only a bewildered sense of adventure and a heart of curiosity.

On an afternoon when Amelie is plagued with the sniffles of an early summer cold, I amuse her by taking the panels cut from the two dresses and fashioning the same dress for one of her favorite dolls. It is not a new thing for her to have matching gowns made for her playthings, but even my untrained eye can see the superiority of my creation. My hands thrill to work with the fine thread and bits of silk; my patterns match perfectly, down to the thin, painted veins of the tiniest vine. My eyes are sharp without need of a glass, my fingers nimble and without callus.

The day Amelie is permitted to play with the Princess Marie, a summons is sent to Madame Gisela's apartment within the hour.

"Do you see?" She shows me the very note, written in a hand less elegant than I would expect of a queen. "Never underestimate the power of innocence." Her eyes glitter, and I suspect she holds her tears back only out of fear that they might smudge the ink on the hastily written note.

"Why is it so important to you?" My question seems too bold for my station, but I've nothing to lose in asking. "That I meet the queen? It matters much more to you than it does to me."

Her smile is brave. "You can say that because you've never met her. You don't know what it's like to be her friend and then . . . not to be. We came here together, you know. All those years ago, I was one of her ladies-in-waiting. We learned this ridiculous language together and spun tales of fantasy. She was already married, of course, but still a young girl. Like me." She touched my cheek. "Like you. But I've fallen, you see."

"Fallen?"

"Out of favor. Out of fashion. She so desperately wants the love of her people. *These* people. I fear I'm too much a reminder of her past."

"But look where you live." The grandness of the rooms, I'm ashamed to say, has long since grown comfortable. "At her leisure, *non*? And you travel in her carriage; her servants serve you."

Madame Gisela makes a dismissive sound. "Anyone with a decent set of stockings can claim a spot in Versailles. And the carriage? They are always looking for us to take drives out into the country to measure the animosity of the peasants. Had I been viciously attacked rather than rescued by your handsome guardian, there might have been some rueful consequences for that little town. My dear husband, whom you've yet to meet, as he is far more interested in his mistress than his wife, is a member of Parlement, and almost as unpopular with the court as I am. It was his decision, you see, to send me on my little jaunt. You've no idea how happy I was to come back with such an unexpected treasure."

A treasure. How Laurette would tease if she heard me lauded in such a way.

"Come," Madame Gisela urges, pushing me toward the door. "Marie is fickle in her taste and temperament. We must take our audience before she forgets her summons."

Before coming to the palace at Versailles, my idea of heaven was Gagnon's fields in the lush green of spring, blue skies imparting a gentle breeze upon my face. Heaven smelled of life and earth, felt like a full stomach and a quiet mind. To be in heaven meant to be drowsy with purpose, rested from labor, a good day stretched equally before and behind each eternally living moment. But on this morning, my first visit to the queen, everything I thought I knew of beauty disappears like so much dust. Here, in her private quarters, everything is golden—all the colors of the course of the sun brought into one room to shine in simultaneous chorus. The sharpness of dawn reflected on the pillars, the richness of evening on sumptuous carpets. Having shouldered through so many crowds and conversations, without the chance to catch my bearings or my breath, I am immediately embraced by the tranquility of this room. Not silent, by any means. Amelie and another little girl pluck tunelessly at a harp standing in the corner, and the woman seated on the velvet sofa in the room's center speaks at a rate and volume more robust than necessary for the two women standing, listening, with their hands clasped and heads bowed.

Madame Gisela bows her head and elbows me to do the same. I obey, and hear the small sound of a clearing throat. Then, an explosion.

"Gi-Gi!" Forgetting all protocol, my startled head snaps up in time to see the woman leap from the couch, her dressing gown falling from her shoulders as she does, and fly across the room to take Madame Gisela in a warm embrace. Immediately the two are laughing and rattling off to each other in an unfamiliar tongue, which brings twin glares of disapproval from the two ladies who maintain their subservient pose.

It is not until this moment I realize I am in the presence of the queen, Marie Antoinette. She is tall and matronly, her figure on full display beneath the soft fabric of her gown. I've seen her only in portraits, and there are some features that have been truly represented on canvas—her forehead, for example, is high, her jaw thick, her nose long, but no painting can ever represent what it means to be alive in a single moment. No artist, for example, could ever capture the fact that she blinks with the rapidity of a hummingbird, or that she furrows her brow when she communicates in French, clearly searching for words and phrases after all her years as our sovereign. This I notice when she at last pulls herself an arm's length from her friend and asks, "How long has it been?"

"Too long," Madame Gisela says with a lightness only I can mistrust.

"Les affaires," the queen says, pronouncing the phrase with a hard *z* sound and an unusual syllabic emphasis. "But never mind all of that. Here you are now, and our girls . . ."

She gestures toward the young princess, Marie-Thérèse, who shares most of the features of her mother, including the soft curls of reddish brown, though the queen's bear the earliest flecks of gray. Or, perhaps, the remnants of powder.

"My Amelie has been longing to come play with the princess."

"And Marie-Thérèse the same. But who is this new little plaything?"

She refers to me, but when I start to speak, I remember my instruction to remain silent unless specifically addressed. Not knowing if I've been spoken to, I look to Madame Gisela for direction.

"This—perhaps you did not get my letter? This is the girl I discovered in that village up north." She uses her own language to attach an adjective to the word *village*, an unflattering one if her expression holds any clue.

The queen claps her hands. "Oh yes! The little seamstress. I saw what you did to my gown, naughty thing. Letting it get torn." This, said to Madame Gisela with all humor of friendship. To me, directly, she says, "And I saw your clever mending. Yes, I saw this days ago and was cross at first, but I was quite impressed with your work."

"*Merci, madame,*" I say, surprised to find my voice sounds much the same when speaking to a queen as it does when speaking to mere mortals.

"If you had seen her when she first arrived," Madame Gisela continues, "starving. Weak. I don't think I exaggerate when I say that I may have saved her life bringing her here. I believe she can serve you well. Or the princess, even."

"What a happy accident for both of you," the queen says. "And what a stroke of timing. Bertin is always in need of women who have quick brains and talented hands. Do you know I've lost three of my tirewomen in just this past month? Two dead. Nasty fevers. And one with a baby put there by one of my guards." She giggles, inviting us to join her, but I am in too much awe at her ability to so easily dismiss death. "So, too," she continues, "good timing when your husband is in such decline in the court's favor." Her smile has not wavered. "Do you think, *ma belle amie*, that I will put in a good word with my husband to save your place here?"

"I—I hadn't thought . . . ," Madame Gisela stammers.

"Viens!" The queen spares her friend and summons Amelie, who approaches reluctantly, pouting to have been pulled away from her play. She pulls the girl close and lifts the skirt to examine the stitching from the other side. "Perfect. So small and neat. This is your work, *non*? The panels?"

"Oui, madame." I've now spoken four words to a queen.

"And how did you choose the fabrics? To go together? Because it doesn't appear they would fit, but the effect is appealing."

"They are both inspired by the same palette, *madame*. If you'll see, the blue in the stripe? It is the same blue as the outer petals on the floral print. And so, they complement each other. Like siblings separated, if you will. One set of threads destined to strike out and be a stripe, the other to stay behind in the garden. And look how the prodigal is welcomed home."

It is something I would have said to Laurette, and something that would have earned me a cuff to my ears for such wasteful thought. The queen, however, is enchanted.

"I can only imagine Mademoiselle Bertin's reaction to such a tale. Thinking she is the only one with an artist's eye! Tell me, little one—though not so little, I can see. How old are you?"

"Almost seventeen." It is a deceitful approximation, but adding the phantom few months makes me feel much older.

"And your name?"

"Renée, *madame*. Renée Brodeur."

"Well, sixteen-year-old Renée, you have no parents?"

"Non, madame."

"And would you like to live here? At Versailles?" She adds the last question lest I think she means *here*—in her personal apartment.

"Madame Gisela is kind to have brought me here," I say. "I only follow as the Lord leads."

At my words, the queen makes the sign of the cross, her jewels clacking in the holy gesture. "As we women are fated to do, I suppose. Men, they can forge their own paths. We obey." She reaches out and grasps my hands, holding them tight at first, then loosening her grip and examining them on her open palms. "Exquisite, aren't they? Light as little birds."

"I said the same thing, *madame*," Madame Gisela says. The queen and I both turn, as if we'd forgotten her presence entirely. Indeed, little Amelie has gone back to play, and I just now notice her absence.

"Did you?" the queen says. "And is this the dress our little bird was wearing when she came to us?"

"You know well it is not," Madame Gisela says, and for a moment I worry at her boldness. "It is one of Amelie's, as she was so malnourished when she came, it fit perfectly. Her own clothes were—"

"Quite suitable, I imagine," the queen says, "for her station. Made of strong stuff, I suppose, and well stitched. Am I right?"

I nod. "Though I'm not so sure they were well suited for this place."

"And I'm not so sure that dress continues to fit 'perfectly.' Am I right, again?"

I'm torn, conscious of the fact that the band below my bust cuts into my flesh and that my shoulders strain at the sleeves. I must either contradict my queen or risk appearing ungrateful to my hostess. My mind works quickly. "I assume it is like all fashion: perfect in all ways, but not perfect for all time."

"Oh! My love, my love, my dear love." The queen grabs me and pulls me forward, planting a kiss on each of my cheeks, twice over. "The next time I am cross with Mademoiselle Bertin I will bring you to intervene on my behalf." She turns to Madame Gisela and releases a torrent of what sounds like praise in their mother tongue—praise that brings reassurance to Madame Gisela's expression.

"Do you have things with you?"

"Things, *madame*?"

"Just this." Madame Gisela speaks for me, producing the small cinched sack I brought from Gagnon's.

"What's all there?" The small question comes from behind me, and I realize it is the princess, speaking for the first time. She is years younger than I, but we stand nearly at eye level. I do not allow my voice to condescend.

"Not much." I open the bag and produce my few treasures,

beginning with the book of Psalms, its faded blue ribbon unmoved.

"You can read?" the queen asks admiringly.

"Yes," I say, though I'm ashamed to admit that I haven't opened the book once since my arrival. "This is wool that came from our sheep. I carded and dyed it myself, and I can spin it, too, to make a thread." I take out my favorite hook. "And with thread, and this hook, I can make—well, anything."

The princess's gray eyes grow wide, and she turns to her mother. "May I learn, *Maman*?"

"Of course, Madame Royale." The queen draws her close, and I have to look away. Rarely in my life have I ever seen affection between a mother and daughter. Even when my mother was alive, she was always tired, busy, aloof. The sight opens a wound too long ignored, and my throat burns with inexpressible pain. "Take her, now." This to the nearly forgotten ladies in the corner of the room. "Find her a spot in the clothiers' chambers. And you—" to me—"rummage through all you can find. Fabric, garments, thread, patches. Clothe yourself as you wish. I look forward to seeing what you create."

L'épisode 10

Laurette

MOUTON BLANC

The flock yielded only fifteen new lambs that spring, three of which were too weak even to nurse. Laurette did what she could, feeding them with cloth soaked in goat's milk, but in the end they were butchered to be served as Easter supper.

"It is a reminder," Gagnon said that night, "of God's provision for us. The death of his Son, the Lamb of God, sustains us for eternity."

"I don't see why we couldn't have one of the culls," Laurette said, trying not to think about the tiny creature sacrificed for her plate.

"You'll be thankful we didn't, come winter."

But with the warm days, and nights that allowed a window to be wedged open for a sleeping breeze, winter seemed a lifetime away—both the winter to come, and the one newly past. Already, Renée had become a fleeting thought, brought to Laurette's mind less frequently during the day, sometimes not at all, until it was time to take the light into her room. Dutifully, she said a nightly prayer, wishing her cousin shelter and warmth before sinking into her own cozy, comfortable bed. She had not, in fact, returned to her straw ticking in the loft, no matter her intentions to do so after the shearing. Nights loomed lonely with no one to talk to in those moments between wakefulness and sleeping, but there was a certain comfort to hearing Gagnon's healthy snores coming from the other side of the wall. He was always asleep long before she was, though he would not take himself to bed without knowing she was safely tucked away. Once, when she heard him speaking, she pressed her ear close to the wall, worried he might be trying to commune with the departed Denise. Instead, he was in prayer—fervent, vocal supplication for Renée's safety, and forgiveness for his part if she suffered in any way.

⚜

It was the third week in April, all the remaining lambs appearing ready to thrive, when Gagnon finished the last of his breakfast porridge and told Laurette to leave the dishes to soak.

"You're taking the sheep out today. Some of them, anyway. The old ones."

"Alone?"

He chuckled. "Of course not. I want them to return. But there are things to do here, and I cannot devote my time to shepherding, much as I enjoy the tranquility. It's time you learned."

Laurette took his bowl. "What's to learn? The dogs do all the work."

"*Exactement.* It's time you learned to call the dogs."

They headed out toward the forest road, leaving Copine at home to guard the ewes and lambs. Gagnon explained that Cossette would respond to her alert if needed.

"From so far?" Still, after all these years, she was amazed at the dogs' abilities.

"From so far, and more. I once took Copine into town with me, and her hackles raised right there, in the middle of the market, for no reason. I got home, and two wild dogs had come and killed three of my lambs. Do you remember that day?"

"Renée and I were inside, watching. We didn't know what to do." The memory of it still brought a rush of fear.

Gagnon stopped and took her chin in his hand. "There was nothing to have done without endangering yourselves. Always, you are more valuable to me."

They stood still while the sea of sheep ran past them, Cossette first behind, then circling, then behind again, keeping the animals at an easy trot, rounding up any inclined to stray.

"Would be easier with her partner here," Laurette observed as they walked again. "Not so much running."

"Yes. That is the charm of a dog, though. The ability to adapt without complaint."

Laurette recognized the teasing and jabbed him in the arm with her elbow. "I've not complained, have I?"

"Not so much. But then, you have not adapted."

"I miss her, you know. Do you think she misses us?"

"I don't know. We can see where she is missing. Like right now, can't you picture her? Beside you? On this very path? And up there—isn't that the rock where she liked to sit? But wherever she is, we've never been. She doesn't carry our shadows."

The sheep scattered themselves comfortably on a low knoll, Cossette walking a leisurely patrol among them.

"Now," Gagnon said, "we begin. A simple whistle. Let me hear you."

Resigned, Laurette puckered her lips and blew a single, soft note.

He laughed. "Now, you know better than that. Move your jaw, just so. Jut your bottom teeth to the front."

Laurette obeyed for his approval.

"Yes, good. Now, your tongue up to the roof of your mouth." He craned his neck and opened his mouth, displaying his instruction, then closed it again, offering an encouraging nod. She mimicked, and blew, producing no sound but the hiss of air.

"Hopeless," she said, working her mouth back into a lax, comfortable place.

"Nothing is ever hopeless." Gagnon continued as they walked, demonstrating the different calls, followed by a clacking noise in his jaw that brought the dog to a halt after each. This one would bring it herding to the left. This one to the right. This note was for Cossette, this for Copine. Stop—the clack. Go, come, hunt.

"Hunt?"

"You've seen it. Where they crouch and stalk, like wolves about to pounce. It startles the sheep into moving."

Then he sent Cossette through her drills, the dog running in joyful obedience, the sheep with their heads ever up, seeming equal parts terrified and confused.

"Poor things, let them eat," Laurette said. "How would you like to sit down to your supper only to be sent running around the table for no reason at all?"

Gagnon made a final call, and Cossette came running, her black, white, and brown coat laid flat with speed. She came to a halt at his feet, and he rewarded her with an affectionate rub between her ears.

"Try again?"

She did, with no better results. Only a weak, breathy note that exacted none of Cossette's attention. "My lips were not designed to whistle."

"Perhaps you should whistle for Marcel. He is a dog that would respond."

All their teasing was gone, along with any breath Laurette

might summon to reply. She covered her mouth, as if doing so would hide and trap its transgressions.

"Forgive me," Gagnon said immediately, seeming shocked by his own words. "I don't know what I was thinking saying such a thing. Oh, Laurette, Laurette . . ." He reached for her, but she pushed him away with a violence that earned a growl from Cossette.

"Who are you to say—?"

"I am nobody, Laurette. I don't know why . . . I did not mean to hurt you. Only that I have seen him, you know?"

She didn't know. She didn't want to, but her glare compelled him.

"In town. With women, Laurette. Other women. No better than a dog. So, that night, here—I don't want you to think that I'm keeping you from a man who loves you."

"No better than a dog."

"It was a stupid thing for me to say. Can we—a simple command. No whistling. Just tell her to go."

Like a storm's wind, he'd changed direction, and he assumed the ugliness of his words had blown away. She shook her head. "What?"

"Back to where we were, eh? Point down to where the herd is, and say 'Go!'" He mouthed the last word, though Cossette's ears perked up in anticipation of a command. "She has to learn to obey you."

"Why should she? If I am no better?"

His head drooped in frustration, his words measured. "I did not mean you. I said that *he*, Marcel—"

She couldn't listen anymore.

"I don't want to command the dogs, Gagnon. I don't want to graze the herd—that was Renée. Always Renée. And Renée is gone, because of me. I told her to 'Go!' and *poof*, she was gone. I can't fill her place, and I won't do her work. I will take care of you, tend to the house, and if that is not enough, then send me away, as you sent Marcel. Tell me. A single word, and I'll go."

Cossette let out a high-pitched whine, and Gagnon followed with three shrill notes that sent her to the farthest side of the herd. Laurette watched; it was easier than looking at the man standing in front of her. There was no sound other than the occasional bleat, and when the dog reached her destination, she sat. Even from this distance, Laurette could detect the smallest movement of the dog's head—the only movement of her stone-still body—at the merest step of a sheep.

"You see? How powerful you are, Gagnon. Send me away."

He matched her challenge. "And where would you go?"

He was right, of course. There'd been no grand lady to take her to Paris, and it seemed no room for her with Marcel, unless she were willing to bed down with the others. No better than a dog.

"It doesn't matter, does it? I could go, and then when you look at me, you wouldn't see her. Renée, or her shadow. Because I am the reason we have nothing but her shadow."

"I don't see Renée."

She looked up to find him watching, his eyes weighted with the effort of holding her gaze. "Tell me."

"Very well, then," he said. "Go, Laurette. Go home. Make my supper, and wait for me there."

The humorous glint in his eye cooled her temper. Rather than risk igniting it again, she obeyed quietly, turning and walking away at a pace too slow to be seen as retreat, but quick enough to dissuade her from looking back. A warm breeze blew against her face and she hummed a tune, hoping it would carry back to Gagnon, taking with it a message of reconciliation.

She stopped, though, when another sound caught her ear. The farm was still a blur in the distance when the distinctive bark of Copine carried from it. It was angry, meant to sound the alarm of an intruder, and Laurette spun in place, not sure whether to run back to fetch Gagnon or forward to confront the danger. It might be something as harmless as a hungry fox seizing the opportunity to kill a chicken, or one of the nomadic poor hoping to beg a meal. If it were a fox, she couldn't spare the time to fetch Gagnon; if a man, she couldn't risk facing him alone. She closed her eyes against the sun and clenched her fists at her side.

"Laurette!" She looked back to see Gagnon approaching at a quick pace.

"Do you hear the dog?"

He stopped, looking surprised. "*Non.* I just came to—" The look changed to one of concern. He touched her arm, urging her to follow, and continued on at a run. Laurette could not keep up, but she tried, knowing he was purposely creating a distance between them. Besides, he was not encumbered by skirts. She could ignore the burning in her lungs and the protest of her legs, push past the instinct to stop, lag back, and let Gagnon face the intruder alone.

She arrived seconds behind him, breathing sharp at a dead stop. Copine stood silent beside him, guarding not a fox, not a man—but definitely a thief. Two, in fact. Two boys, aged nine or ten she'd guess, but their thin frames made them seem younger, and their haunted, shadowed eyes were those of old men. The taller of the two held a chicken under his arm, its neck broken and body in the throes of listless twitching.

"What have we here?" Laurette fought to make her voice steady.

"Hungry children," Gagnon said, and both boys sagged in visible relief.

Laurette propped a hand on her hip and glared. "And we're just going to let them steal one of our chickens? She's one of our best layers."

"No," Gagnon said. "We are not going to let them take the chicken. Do you know what to do with a chicken, boys?"

They dropped their gazes and shook their heads, slowly, as the fowl came to a dead stillness.

"Then Mademoiselle Laurette will cook it for you. Would you like that?"

They nodded, but their grim expressions did not change. Laurette recognized their look of shame.

"Not for nothing," she said with mock sternness. "You killed it. You clean it. Chop off the head, scoop the innards. Pluck out every single feather. You want to eat? You have to work."

They seemed pleased, and the younger tugged at the other's arm, as if he'd need convincing

"Chopping block is over there." Gagnon pointed to a smooth stump with a small ax propped against it.

Later they feasted—the skin and meat flavored with herbs, the drippings mixed with cream and sopped up with hunks of dry bread. Between wolfing mouthfuls, the brothers—Philippe and Nicolas Choler—told their story. They'd traveled from a village not far away with their parents, who like so many others poured into the city of Paris in search of work.

"And could they not find it?" Gagnon asked, carefully picking at his small portion.

"Not enough," Philippe, the older brother, replied. "Not enough to feed all of us."

"And there was no place to live," Nicolas interjected. "Just rooms where we had to sleep on the floor."

"We woke up one day and they were gone." Philippe spoke with the emotionless tone of a man while Nicolas beside him studied his emptying plate. "Easier to feed two mouths rather than four, I reckon. I suppose he's taking care of our mother, and I'm taking care of him."

"I'm sorry we stole," Nicolas said, a child's quiver to his chin.

He was nine years old, Philippe eleven—much the same age as a hungry Laurette and Renée when they stormed hand in hand into Le Cochon Gros.

"You didn't steal," Laurette said. "You worked for your supper. And I for one am grateful. Now I have an excuse to raise up a younger bird to take her place."

"There's room for you here as long as you like," Gagnon said, and Laurette exhaled for what seemed like the first time since stumbling upon the boys. She knew it was only a matter of time before he would make such an offer. Calculating as he looked at them, she figured Philippe would be close to the same age as Gagnon's son would have been had he lived. Their presence at the table filled more than the void left by Renée. Their vitality brought back beating, lost hearts.

"Do you know anything about keeping sheep?" he pressed.

"Non, monsieur," Philippe said.

"We don't know anything about anything," Nicolas added before Philippe jabbed him.

"Are you smart?" Gagnon said, fighting a smile. "Do you have a teachable spirit? You must listen to everything I say, and do everything I tell you, and you'll have food and a bed for as long as you do."

"And your first order is to wash the dishes and the cooking pan," Laurette said, enjoying the spark of authority. "After that, take a wash for yourselves. There's a little creek just beyond the grove outside the fence."

"Oui, madame," the brothers responded in unison.

"Mademoiselle," she corrected. "And I am Laurette; this is Gagnon. We are too poor for such formality."

⚜

The last rain of the spring, the rain that kept them huddled under Gagnon's roof for three days, the rain that ruined the roads and upset the carriage and delayed the shearing, the rain that seemed to whisper a promise of God's provision and protection—it was the last they would see for the season. *Avril, Mai, Juin,* all passed with nothing but cloudless skies and relentless heat. On the occasions that Laurette journeyed to market in Mouton Blanc, she beheld the grim future. Crops, grown no higher than her knee, took on a deepening shade of brown with the passing days. What she carried spoke of no more prosperity. Wedges of cheese from their goats' milk had diminished in size and flavor. Eggs were too precious to leave their own baskets at home.

She began to slice the bread thinner, to take only half a slice for herself, to spoon porridge from the pot and claim to have eaten as she heaped the boys' bowls. She walked the half mile to the stream and back with water for her garden, keeping the bucket not quite full so as not to slosh a single precious drop on the way. The boys were trusted to take the sheep farther and farther afield, and she sometimes "forgot" to put two turnips in their sack lunch, or sent the crust of bread without butter to soften it.

But it was a welcome distraction, all of this planning and parceling, because it kept her mind free of its own singular pursuit. While carefully dusting the last of her flour into the mixing bowl for bread, she didn't think about Renée and the sumptuous feasts she might be enjoying. And she didn't think about Marcel, wondering if he had food for that day. In standing at the gate, watching for the boys' return with the flock, she wasn't searching for Marcel's familiar silhouette on the horizon. And at night, when each boy offered a sweet kiss to her cheek as they wished Mademoiselle Laurette good night, she could almost forget what it felt like to be kissed by Marcel.

Almost.

On a June evening Laurette sat in front of the empty hearth

with the boys' sweat-fragrant heads in her lap as they listened to Gagnon tell stories of his favorite hero—the mighty Odysseus. A single candle burned, casting a shadow on the wall which he transformed into the one-eyed giant who could scoop up a man and devour him in a single bite. The boys thrilled to the story as she and Renée once had, and cheered when Odysseus craftily used the sheep to escape the giant's cave. So caught up were they in the fantasy that they did not, at first, notice the two new faces at the open door. Gagnon had his back to them, but spun around at the smallest flick of Laurette's gaze.

"Vous-êtes?"

The boys knew who they were. Immediately, Philippe was on his feet crying, *"Papa! Maman!"* with Nicolas at his heels. The boys engulfed their parents in an embrace of such affection, Laurette turned away, both from the reunion of the family and the unmistakable longing in Gagnon's eyes.

"Come in, come in," he bade them, indicating Laurette's seat and sending her to bring stew and bread.

She pulled him aside and spoke low, hoping he would overlook the hint of resentment in her voice. "There's no fire to warm it up."

"Look at them," he whispered. "I believe they will suffer eating it cold."

He was right, of course. The couple—which was the man and which the woman determinable only by their clothing, as they were equally gaunt, and the mother's hair shorn within an inch of her scalp—took the bowls in shaking hands. They shunned the proffered spoons and gulped the tepid stew straight, mopping the sides of the bowl with the last of the bread.

"Would you like more?" young Nicolas asked, as if man of the house. "There's enough, isn't there, Mademoiselle Laurette?"

"Of course there is," Gagnon answered for her, because there wasn't enough, really.

Laurette scraped the pot and gave their guests all that was to be the next day's dinner, along with three cups of water and the last of the cheese.

"We went into town," Monsieur Choler said, "and someone told us our boys were here. That you'd taken them."

"Taken them *in*," Madame Choler clarified, only to be silenced by her husband's hand.

"Had them here slaving for you, is how I see it." He looked to his boys, squinting one eye as if bringing them into focus. "Tell me what this Monsieur Gagnon has had you doing of a day?"

Philippe and Nicolas spoke over each other in their excited rendition of a day's labor. Rising with the sun, calling to the dogs, chasing wayward lambs, games of pirate and soldier in the fields, Laurette's good food at night, Gagnon's stories, each a bed of his own in the loft. Monsieur Choler, however, grew only more bitter in his expression at the tales.

"And what's he paid you in wages?"

"Wages?" Philippe looked from his father to Gagnon and back. "What's wages?"

"Did you not hear?" Gagnon said, calm in the face of accusation. "I fed them. Sheltered them. Taught them a trade. Just look, you can see how healthy they are."

"I can see that they've been working for nearly three months and don't have a sou to show for it, that's what."

Laurette managed to catch a glimpse of the mother's eyes before she looked away in shame at her husband's rant.

"I figure two francs to be a fair price," Monsieur Choler continued, "each. Though I might be talked down a half for Nicolas, as he's younger."

Gagnon laughed and instructed the boys to wish their parents a good night and take themselves off to bed. The comfort and ease with which they obeyed brought a new pain to their mother's eyes, but having been silenced once, she did not speak again. Instead, she embraced them, kissing both and telling them how fine and handsome they'd grown before releasing them into the night.

"Now," Gagnon said after closing the door, "it appears you are attempting to sell your own children to me, and I've sent them away to spare your dignity."

Laurette poked her head from the kitchen. "Why, if anything *they* owe *us*. If we calculated the cost to feed them—"

"Non," Gagnon said, gently interrupting, "we do not calculate the cost of food when we offer someone a home." He turned back to Choler. "That is what we did, *monsieur*. The boys were given a home, as theirs abandoned them. And they are welcome to stay, as long as they like. But I'll pay them no wages, as I have none to pay. And I'll give you nothing for the privilege."

"Keep them." Madame Choler found her voice at last. "We cannot—we can barely feed ourselves. We've lost our farm, and there's no work."

"There's work plenty," Choler sneered. "Just not a man willing to pay for it."

"Not able," Gagnon corrected. "I can either pay the boys or feed them. I cannot do both. It seems to me at their age, food is more important."

"*Seems to me*, then, that boys that can work might fetch a price from someone more willing to pay. You're not the only man's kept his land, Monsieur Gagnon. If we can beg a bed off of you for the night, my family and I will be gone by morning."

Laurette stormed in, tasting bile at the back of her throat, sickened at Choler's suggestion.

"You *are* going to sell them?"

"Just a fair trade, is all. Until I get myself sorted out."

"Please," his wife begged, clutching at his rags, "let them

stay. Here. Do you see how they are cared for?" She turned to Gagnon. "You care for them, I can tell."

"They are good boys," Gagnon said, the compliment rife with reassurance. "You raised them well."

"Enough!" Choler rose, knocking his chair behind him. "They are mine, and I will do with them as I please." He stormed from the house and could be heard shouting the boys' names, calling them from their beds.

"Monsieur—" Madame Choler threw herself at Gagnon's feet, clasping his hand in hers—"I beg of you, keep my boys. My husband is right in one thing: we have been everywhere, looking for work and a home. We finally found a small room in Paris, but it is so dangerous there. Crowded, you know? Everybody looking for food, fighting for jobs. My husband worked one day laying bricks, and the man next to him was killed, only for the chance to take his place. We came to fetch our boys, but who knows if what we left will be waiting for us when we get back? Please, for the love of Christ—"

"Was this your plan all along?" Laurette asked, unmoved by the woman's display. "To extort money from whatever soul was kind enough to take your children in?"

"Laurette," Gagnon cautioned.

"Of course not," Madame Choler said. "Who could plan such a thing?"

"Go to my room, Laurette. In my dresser, in the top drawer, there are some coins." He looked into the mother's eyes. "I do not know how much, but what is there is yours to take. And to leave the boys with us."

"Oh, how God is merciful!" She peppered Gagnon's hands with kisses washed by tears. "I knew, when I saw the light from your window, and how the townspeople spoke so highly of you . . ."

Laurette turned and left, wondering if Marcel had been one

of the townspeople to speak so highly of Gagnon. She paused just for a moment, as the door to his room was still kept shut, if not locked, and wondered if his suspicions would be aroused at the fact that she'd taken no candle to guide her. But she knew this room as well as she knew any other in the house, and not even the darkest night could confuse her. She went straight to the bachelor, straight to the drawer, and found the pile of coins, knowing the amount fell short of the father's asking. How many days, her belly sharp with hunger, had she thought of these coins? Renée mended their dresses with patches, or tied rags around their shoes, or threw dried sheep dung on the fire—what tiny bits of comfort these coins might have provided. And now, she scooped them into a scrap of cloth, knotted it, and returned to find Madame Choler standing, drying her eyes with the fringes of a threadbare kerchief.

Laurette pressed the money into Gagnon's hand. "It will not be enough."

"No," he said. "It won't."

He strode from the house, Laurette and Madame Choler at his heels, to find Choler and the boys in the middle of the yard, protectively flanked by Cossette and Copine.

"Your father's summoned you to say good-bye," Gagnon said. "It's best you stay here with us for a while longer."

A hideous grin spread across Choler's face. He looked straight over his sons' heads at Gagnon. "Come to an agreement, have we?"

"Say good-bye to your mother," Gagnon directed, and as the boys were distracted by Madame Choler's embrace, Gagnon pulled Choler equally close.

"This," Gagnon said, depositing the money in Choler's vest pocket. "And your life."

"My life?"

"Step foot on my land again, whatever your intentions, I will see it as a threat to my boys, and I will kill you. Do you understand me? Our transaction is complete."

Choler understood, if the twisted expression of fear was any indication. Still, in the face of mortal danger, Madame Choler appeared grateful, mouthing *Merci* over her shoulder before shuffling away behind her husband.

It was the first time for Laurette to see him refuse a night's shelter to a stranger. Laurette ushered the boys to the loft and came out to find Gagnon standing in the yard watching the shuffling figures of the Cholers retreat into the night. She came alongside him and noticed another first—the loaded pistol taken from its place above the hearth resting in his hand.

L'épisode II

Renée

VERSAILLES

The workroom is a landscape of silk and wool and linen, great spools of each in every color beyond creation. There are patterns and florals and stripes, and a bin the size of a feeding trough filled with scraps. It is from this bin that I have pieced together my own clothing, creating a paneled skirt and vest made from the same materials that dressed the most important woman in our country. But I know better than to flaunt my theft. Everything Marie Antoinette wears has been designed by the famous Mademoiselle Bertin and meticulously recorded by the court's scribes; I fear I would be taken to task for the few inches of fabric featuring the sprigged pattern of peonies the queen wore to receive the archduke of Provence. So I strip the fabric to unrecognizable proportions and wear it with the reversed side out to further disguise its origin.

I carry all the tools of my trade with me. Three scissors—the largest sharp enough to cut through velvet without leaving a hint of thread; the smallest can reach between fabric and flesh to snip a wayward stitch. They are wrapped in silk and housed in a leather pouch I wear around my waist. Inspired by all the guards and soldiers milling about, I fancy these my weapons, though I pray I never need to use them. My sleeves are full, not only because the style is cooler in the heat of summer but because I've fashioned a special hem wherein I store spools of thread. On my wrist I wear a boar's hair cuff festooned with needles of various sizes. Other pockets have been stitched into my patchwork skirt, filled with measuring silks and sticks of chalk and thick paper packets speared with pins.

The result is something that makes me look somewhat like a gypsy, according to the women who share my duty.

"Ridiculous," Madame Gisela sneers the first time I don the garment after snipping the last thread. "You look like someone more suited to living in a tent and stealing horses than stitching garments for a queen."

Behind her criticism, though, lurks a grudging respect for my skill. I crafted the garment in only two days, working blindly without a pattern, sewing every stitch myself. She declares me to be a fine little seamstress. *Une couturière.* From that moment, I have no other identity at Versailles. When, in the chaotic hub of activity in the queen's dressing room, a call comes out *cherchez la couturière*, the call comes for me. My hands are small, my work is fast, and my stitches precise. I can finish a hem on a sleeve with the queen's arm inside of it, and not come close to nicking royal flesh. I can tack fallen lace on a gown's train while the gown itself is in motion, racing through the maze of halls on its way to a royal engagement. More than once I've been summoned midstep, on my way to another task, to mend the stocking of a notable man set to have his audience with the king, or to stitch in a kerchief for a woman whose dress exposes more bosom than her father will allow. I've had powdered wigs in my lap as I stitch ribbons and bows into them. I can thread a glass bead and anchor it to a bodice before it drops to the ground.

I do not know the idleness of a moment. When I am not engulfed in silk, I am running through the endless passages of Versailles on one errand or another. To the king's apartment to mend the tear in his favorite hunting jacket. To the chapel, where a clumsy altar boy singed the cloth on the table of the sacrament. It seems the tiniest mishap earns the cry of *"Cherchez la couturière!"* And I am sought out, found, and escorted.

And my reward? A coin, usually, or two—especially if I've mended the garment of a gentleman. Silver coins, too. The first I ever held came into my possession the day I reattached the sleeve of an archduke's shirt after he had some unfortunate encounter with one of my queen's ladies. I hadn't held out my hand. In fact, I'd barely been able to look him in the eye, only worked as quickly as I could to escape his hot breath and grumbled insults at the young woman who had put up such a fight against his advances. It was he who said, "Here, girl, and be off without a word," holding out the coin as if something distasteful. Part of me wanted to refuse taking silver from such a pig of a man, but something Gagnon used to say slipped into my mind. *"The wages of sin is death. Wages for the pure of heart are fairly gained."* I had committed no sin. I'd performed my task as I would whether or not I was complicit in some unrighteous deed. So I took the coin and slipped it into a long pocket I'd hidden in the panels of my skirt. The first time I touched silver, and the first time I sewed a secret. But far, far from the last.

I ask Madame Gisela why these people would bother with my work. Any man or woman who could drop a coin into my hand could surely purchase something new. Surely the woman whose sleeve I altered to hide a bloodstain of which she would not speak had a dozen other gowns in her own home.

Madame Gisela wrinkles her nose. "Squatters. They don't want to lose their spot."

Their spot, meaning their chance. The opportunity to hold the king's ear and unleash a complaint, or plead a case, or beg a favor. These people populate the halls of Versailles not as invited guests, but as citizens of France, members of the Second Estate—nobility, no matter how tenuous the claim. Madame Gisela clings to her apartment as a special friend of the queen, with no recourse should that friendship be severed. Some of these who wander claim temporary residence, too. Or invite themselves as guests, even spending nights sleeping on the floors in obscure hallways. They shuffle outside the dining halls, hoping to slip into a place at the table, or they buy provisions from the farmers who hawk their wares in the outer courts. One woman paid me to tack on a fresh panel to her bodice and refashion her sleeves so that she might don a wig and present herself as a noblewoman newly arrived, rather than the same who had been hiding behind her fan for a week.

So I keep their coins and I keep their secrets, and with my nose inches away from their outward show of wealth, I listen.

"They are pouring into Paris," one man sneers. He is stuffing his face with something roasted while I fashion a patch in the seat of his breeches. *"Looking for work. Unskilled and unwashed and passels of children clinging behind."* He doesn't see me as I work, and only tosses two coppers at my feet when I return his breeches.

I want to ask about Mouton Blanc. Has there been rain? Does a man named Émile Gagnon still have the largest herd of sheep, and do men still gather at Le Cochon Gros to drink wine and sing? But asking questions brings attention, and I'd rather remain invisible, lest somebody realize I'm nothing more than a peasant girl with a handy needle.

When I get up, the coins clink in my deep pocket, and I

wonder how many sheep Gagnon would have to shear to fetch such a price. Or would it be enough to pay the taxes on his land? Or to buy a new dress for Laurette? I have more money than I've ever known in my life, and no means to spend it. Though other servants complain of hunger, I can't quite remember what it feels like. Always there is a platter of this and baskets of that set up in the servants' dining hall. I have a small but proper bed in the corner of the sewing room, and nobody's come to collect any kind of price for it. When I am chastised for not wearing shoes, I make my own, woven of sturdy cloth and fashioned snugly to my foot with straps crisscrossed up to my knee. Already I am on the lookout for leather and full of ideas for shoes for the winter. But what is my cousin facing back home? Does Laurette have shoes? Will there be food on the table? I left before the shearing, so I have no idea what resources Gagnon will have to provide for the winter. I don't know what crop he will harvest in the fall. I don't know if he's seen a drop of rain this summer.

But I do. Deep down, I know the answers to all of these. Because I listen. The rich talk about the poor, the peasants, the lives and land ruined by the drought. Violence and uprisings and villages that have been emptied of their people because there will be no crops to harvest, and thus no food, and thus no reason to remain and wait to die.

And it is a shame I carry deep within me that I don't ever, ever want to go back.

⚜

"Can you help me?" I ask Madame Gisela one afternoon. It is the third of July, and unmercifully hot. I've sent her a note asking for an invitation to speak with her, in the way I have observed such things done at court. Neither of us are noble, and I am far below her class, but the very act of penning a message and imploring one of the pages to take it to her apartment made me feel every bit a lady. More exciting, she replied in kind, listing a day and time favorable to her schedule, as she put it.

"What more can I do for you, my dear?" she asks at the appointed time. She is sitting on the high-backed sofa—a bit shabby, I notice, having seen so many other fine furnishings in my travels throughout the palace. "Already you have achieved a status above anything I could have imagined. They talk about you as if you were a sprite."

"I have money." I whisper this, as if shame taints the sum.

She raises an eyebrow and dismisses her maid. "It is rude to speak of such things. And I couldn't possibly begin to think of a price suitable for my service to you."

I sit, heart in my throat, mortified at her misunderstanding. "Of course not, Madame Gisela. And I wouldn't think to insult you by having myself, a poor country shepherdess, thinking a great lady like yourself would even touch a coin from my hand. But I'm wondering if you could help me—somehow—to send some of it home. To Gagnon, and my cousin. To help them."

A look of disappointment tinged with embarrassment flits across her face, and I glance aside as she composes herself. "That seems an undertaking. I don't know that I'll be able to smuggle you away, given that you've made yourself so . . . useful."

"I don't wish to be smuggled away, Madame Gisela. Only this little bit—"

"How much?"

Hesitantly, I reach down deep and pull out my modest pile of wealth. It is not everything; some I've sewn into the hem of my skirt. But it is enough for her to raise *both* her eyebrows.

"People at court are more generous than I imagined," she says, calculating. "You must be a very silent little girl."

"I am."

"I could have it transferred into a note for safer passage

by post, but there's no telling if anyone in your little Moulin Blanc—"

"Mouton Blanc."

"—would have the means to cash its value. Better you should keep it here, *chérie*. I can find a safe spot where it won't be under the noses of that rabble of thieves you work with."

I'm taken aback, wondering if she would lump me in with such disdain. "I keep it all on my person. Unless I'm assaulted in my sleep, I think it will be safe."

She sniffs, unconvinced. "Suit yourself."

"Still," I say, hoping my professed need of her will restore me to her good graces, "will you help me to post a letter?"

"Do you need me to write it for you?"

"No, but thank you. Gagnon taught us well. Me, anyway. But I haven't any paper, or knowledge of where—"

"Come." She stands and motions for me to follow back into her bedroom. Even close to midday, it is dark, with curtains drawn to combat the merciless heat of summer. "I don't have a proper morning room in this place, so my dressing table often has to serve duty as a writing desk." She mentions this as if giving voice to a deep embarrassment, and I say nothing. She produces a short stack of stationery and a quill, and I give full attention to her instructions about the ink and the blotter, not wanting to waste a precious drop or page.

As she's leaving me to my privacy I ask, "Please, may I write two letters? Will you post them together to Mouton Blanc?"

"Avec plaisir." She gives the tight-lipped smile that I've come to know carries the foremost of her affection and leaves me to the dimness.

The first letter I write to Gagnon. That I am fine, that I am well and fed. That I spend my days—every day—doing what I love to do. That God's favor has shone upon me, and the gift he bestowed upon my hands has given me a life I could never have dreamed possible. That I miss him, and Laurette, and the dogs, and the sheep. But that I've found a place, and I pray for his prosperity back where I will always call "home." I sign it, *With love, Renée.*

The second letter, in which I will enclose the first, is composed of just a very few lines. To Marcel, in care of Le Cochon Gros. Simply a plea. To deliver my letter to Gagnon with a kiss to each cheek, and for my cousin, too. And then, as a secret between us two, if he can, to come to Versailles and ask for me, Renée, *la couturière.*

L'épisode 12

Laurette

MOUTON BLANC

As spring disintegrated into summer, bone-dry days stretched into dark nights offering no respite from the heat. Philippe and Nicolas escaped the stifling loft and took their mats to the thatched roof to sleep beneath the luxury of the night breeze. Tonight, they'd escaped entirely, having taken the flock to the farthest corner of Gagnon's land to graze. "As I did when I was a boy," Gagnon said. "As most shepherds do in the summer, I suppose." They'd be gone for the next two days at least, eating sparingly from the sack of food Laurette had packed for them and drinking from the stream that marked the property's border.

"Renée and I never did," she pointed out, surprised by her petulance. Gagnon's growing affection for the boys made her lately feel without an ally. They were eager to learn all he had to teach, from farmwork to Scriptures, leaving her with the frequent feeling of being just shy of inclusion. She cooked, she cleaned—much as she ever had—but she was not a wife, not a mother, yet earned no wage to buy loyalty. She had a room, a roof, a bed, and food if she prepared it.

Weeks before, she'd contracted a mild summer cold and taken to her bed, declaring herself too weak to go to the market in Mouton Blanc, too ill to spend time preparing whatever food lay about the cupboards. And what happened? Gagnon, Nicolas, and Philippe didn't eat, at least nothing beyond tearing off a hunk of bread and washing it down with well-drawn water. Not at proper mealtimes, either. Purely at the will and whim of their appetites. Worse, nothing beyond the same was offered to her. Oh, Gagnon offered to try his hand at a stew, but the thought of him battering around in the root cellar was enough to bring about Laurette's healing.

"Girls are different," he said. "They lack a certain sense of adventure."

Laurette wanted to reply that Renée had enough sense of adventure to ride off in the queen's carriage, but bit back the words. Enough that she had mentioned Renée's name; no need to summon her spirit. Laurette didn't want to spoil a rare evening that found the two of them alone, her place in the house restored.

"It's quiet without them," Laurette said, staying with the subject she knew he would welcome. They sat in the cottage's open doorway, the sweet smell of his pipe smoke drifting out and away, his frequent contribution to their dialogue. "Though it's nice to only make half the supper. I hope I sent them with enough. Still, like as not, they'll come back with the appetite of a bear." She knew she sounded like a nattering old woman, but knew a prolonged silence might send him packing off to bed. "You don't suppose we need to worry about wolves, do you? Those boys, out in the open field."

"Not with the dogs," Gagnon said, pipe clenched between his teeth.

"What about us? Left here alone without our ferocious guardians? What if a wolf comes here? Or worse?"

He took the pipe out of his mouth and looked over, matching her humor. "If a wolf comes, I'll shoot it. If a man? I'll have him ask you a question and watch him run to get away from the sound of your voice."

"I suppose I've no need to worry. You'll be asleep soon, and the sound of your snoring would scare away the fiercest creature."

They had perfected this banter, sharp salvos that protected from the tedious questions of the summer. Would they see rain? How long until all crops were lost? How would anyone survive the winter? Such questions invited only hopelessness. Better to light a spark, complaining about those things that brought true comfort. Laurette knew Gagnon was just as content to hear her speak as to sit in silence, and his snores were comforting on the other side of the wall. And now, in the summer, when they slept with windows and doors wide open, the sound snaked into her room as if no walls existed.

But the wolves? They existed, though not the carnivorous wild dogs of children's stories. Marcel said once the true wolves were the poor of France, driven from their farms as the crops in their fields grew brown and withered and died. They'd come to live in a world where a day's work wouldn't earn enough money for a single loaf of bread. Idleness and gnawing hunger drove men into fruitless actions, abandoning their families in the guise of searching for a better life, only to band with each other in aimless roaming.

While the boys' father had taken heed of Gagnon's warning, other haggard shells of men knew no better. More than once Laurette awoke to the sound of Cossette and Copine, furiously barking in the yard, keeping an animated stack of rags at bay. The dogs would not attack without Gagnon's command, but no man could know that. The first time Laurette saw them, swelled to nearly twice their size, teeth bared and ears laid low, she feared they'd turned rabid. But Gagnon, with a single word in a stern voice, brought them down, though their eyes remained on our unwanted guests.

Nobody was ever sent away without water and food—enough for that day and the next. But they could not stay the night, lest one night stretched into two, and they could not cloud the air with anger and accusation.

"No man can withhold the rain," he would say when a wanderer cursed our king. "Only the Creator commands creation, and God brings the heat of summer to us all."

Such was the path of Laurette's wandering thoughts, leaving her at a silent fork, where she could wonder if Marcel had become one of those ragged vagabonds, or speculate about Renée's fortunes. She let the silence linger for a bit more before asking, quite involuntarily, "Do you think . . ." Catching herself, she let the thought drift away with the pipe smoke.

"Do I think what?"

She dug in, pitching her voice so he would not think the question purely rhetorical. "Do you think Renée knows anything of our misery?"

"I didn't know we were miserable. Our well still has water. Our stream not yet depleted. Rain is not the only means of God's provision."

"But do you think—?"

"What would give you peace, Laurette? To imagine Renée suffering? To know that she did not escape your misery? Or to imagine her rejoicing in our plight while she lives the luxurious life of the elite? Which of these fantasies would you like me to confirm?"

Despite the sternness, she sensed no anger in his tone. It was Gagnon's way, to herd her thoughts the way the dogs directed the sheep, edged with fear, but no real threat.

"I've no fantasies about Renée. I barely think of her at all."

"Only every day?"

So he could read her thoughts as well as herd them. "No more than you, Gagnon."

⚜

The first of the lambs were old enough to be taken from their mothers. Gagnon had promised several in trade, along with the only two baby goats born that spring. The lambs were due to their neighbors in exchange for being lenient when their land was encroached upon for grazing, and the goats to merchants in town for an agreed-upon line of credit. The bit of money left from the sale of his wool was all but useless in Mouton Blanc. Piles of silver could not be consumed, but a goat meant milk and cheese for a merchant's family.

"You're coming with me," Gagnon announced.

Laurette hadn't been to the market in the center of Mouton Blanc since the opening days of summer, when there was still hope of rain, and while the place had been a shadow of its former self, there were still vendors with heaps of spring vegetables and skeins of brightly-dyed yarn from a long winter's spinning. So, too, had the open square been populated with wine-soaked visionaries gathered around a man elevated high on a crate in their midst calling for all men to act together in defiance of the aristocracy. That man had, of course, been Marcel, who feigned oblivion to her presence, acknowledging her only when Gagnon's hand gripped her elbow, tugging her away.

"Why me?" This would not be a simple walk into town. It meant the handcart, as the journey would be too arduous for the baby goats, and to leave them to themselves would mean a constant chase to return them to the path. Never mind that Gagnon would assuredly handle the cart, and she would only be responsible for carrying her part of the conversation. Much as she longed for even a glimpse of Marcel, she dreaded the idea that her glimpse would not be enough. Worse, that it would go unnoticed. "Take the boys. Let them wrestle to keep the kids in the wagon."

"I trust your charm to negotiate a better price."

They took the forest road, as the canopy of trees offered some respite from the heat. For long stretches, the only sound was the rumbling of the wheels and the occasional bleats of discontent from the passengers nestled in the hay. Laurette would bleat back, and then speak soft, reassuring words.

Gagnon teased. "You can speak to a goat but you can't whistle to a dog?"

"These poor babies miss their mother. I want to make them feel better for a little while if I can."

"Well, be sure to give them a nice kiss good-bye."

"I would have liked to have had a final kiss from my mother." She spoke more to the speckled sky beyond the treetops than to him, and he responded with silence.

In some ways, she supposed, she was no better than these little goats. At the moment, their world was this cart, rumbling along the road, the sides too high for them to see beyond. By sunset, they would have a new home, and would live out their days as God intended, and die at a butcher's hand. Powerless.

"No wonder they see us as animals." Her building sadness brought the words aloud.

They'd come to a narrow patch in the road, and Gagnon walked ahead of her. Without pausing, he glanced over his shoulder to ask, "Who sees us as animals?"

"The elite. The rich, the nobles."

He chuckled. "Those are Marcel's words coming out of your mouth."

"I'm capable of my own thoughts," she snapped. "The Church, too, I think. I've yet to meet a hungry priest."

"That's because you don't go to Mass. Our Father Pietro has no flesh to spare." He turned around again.

She ignored his remark. "Look how we live at the mercy of the earth, Gagnon. We eat what animals eat. We share our land and our home with them. We discard our children, let them be taken away without any kind of a fight. How the Cholers left their sons without question. How we traded Renée—"

"We did not *trade* Renée." By now the road was wide enough for Laurette to have come alongside him, but he still did not look at her.

"You're right. With a trade, you get something in return. We gave her away and have nothing."

Gagnon dropped the cart, sending the little goats tumbling into one another. "And just how would you have liked to be *compensated*, Laurette?"

"I just meant—no wonder they don't see our lives as having any value, because we don't value them ourselves."

"*They, they, they.*" He wrapped his hands around the cart handles, squared his shoulders, and lifted it again. "More of Marcel. Dividing the world into two parts. Us and them. Rich and poor."

She had to trot to keep his pace. "What else is there?"

"There are good rich men, and bad. There are good poor men, and bad. And even in those camps—the good and the bad—there are gradients." They'd come to the outlying streets of Mouton Blanc. One of the scattered shacks had been her home, but now was unrecognizable, deteriorated to weathered walls. A few men cast leering glances at Laurette, seeing a young woman in a tattered dress, no different from those eking out a living on the other side of the sagging doors.

Gagnon stopped again and stepped toward her protectively, taking her face into his hands and drawing close enough to block away the ugliness of their surroundings. "Some poor men murder their wives. Rich men do, too. Some poor men are kind, and I have to believe that there are kind men living in places of power. You must never, Laurette, find your esteem in the eyes of anyone other than our heavenly Father who loves you. The way men determine the value of others means nothing."

He drew her closer still, and placed a kiss on her brow, something he'd never done in all their years together. The touch of it was surprisingly cool, given the heat of the day, the weight of the air. The scruff of his whiskers stimulated her skin; the touch of his lips drew every thought from her head to that very spot, galvanizing them into one: *This is a kind man.*

The market square of Mouton Blanc looked to have suffered the same ravages as the surrounding farmland. The line of shops stood with open, empty doors, their signs bleached from months of unrelenting sun. A few carts dotted the empty space, each with half-empty baskets of wilted green things. The loaves in the baker's window were small, and marked with a price that made Laurette's blood run as hot as the near-noon sun above.

"What has happened?" She looked to Gagnon, sincerely expecting a response.

"Drought has happened," he said. "But our bones aren't dry yet. See? That woman, she has beets. When's the last time we had those at our table?" He slipped a coin in Laurette's hand. "Go, buy all she has. I'll make our other trades."

Laurette lifted her market basket from the cart and proceeded. The woman with the beets looked like one herself, round and red, with a few long, twisting whiskers growing from her chin. She sniffed at Laurette's coin, and offered only half her wares for the price.

"You're mad," Laurette said, more shocked than offended. "This is twice what they're worth."

"Won't buy me a week's worth of bread," the woman said. "And for all that I'm better off with my food than your silver."

"Robbery," Laurette muttered, pushing the woman's hand away and choosing the largest and darkest of the beets. They would make a fine addition to supper, boiled and mashed. The tops she would dice and fry up in salted butter—a treat the boys hadn't yet had at her table.

She'd brought with her two small rounds of soft cheese, and wandered the tattered remnants of the market deciding where to make her trade. Perhaps a crock of molasses. Or a cake of sweet-smelling soap from the man whose luxurious wares ensured his poverty. She strolled, barely moving forward, inclining her head and giving deep study to the sparse offerings. Marcel's words echoed in her head, and she tuned her ear for his voice. There was no crowd today, no stage, no audience. Across the way she saw Gagnon, rid of the goats, engaged in conversation with Monsieur Girard. Both men spoke with furrowed brows, hands cupped to disguise their words. Elianne, Girard's homely daughter, looked on with an expression of unabashed longing. If Gagnon turned his head, or stepped even an inch closer, he would find himself ensnared.

Intent on rescue, Laurette quickened her steps and sidled next to him, saying, "Don't the two of you look like quite the conspirators?"

"Some conversations call for softer voices," Gagnon said, and Elianne heaved a sigh behind him.

"Come!" Girard clapped him on the back. He was a good head taller than Gagnon, and the blow was hard enough for Laurette to wince against it. "A glass of wine before we start our journey home. My name is still good here, I think."

"Yes, let's." Elianne smiled, bringing no improvement to her face as sweat glistened between the range of blemishes on her brow.

"Perhaps one?" Gagnon looked to Laurette as if garnering permission.

"Of course." She remembered the darkness of Le Cochon Gros, the long tables and loud voices and the court Marcel held in the corner. Girard and Gagnon led the way, the first with his trunk of an arm settled across the other's shoulders. Laurette and Elianne followed, creating a hodgepodge of a procession. Soon enough, it was obvious Elianne was setting a slower pace, increasing the distance between the men and the girls.

"How is it between you two?" Elianne whispered.

"What do you mean?"

"Do you share his bed?"

Laurette felt a twinge of pity, tempered by amusement. "I share nothing."

The darkness inside Le Cochon Gros was at first both blinding and paralyzing. She stepped over the threshold, stumbling straight into the center of Gagnon's back, and stood stock-still as he held her steady. Soon enough, shadows emerged, becoming shapes of men and women in varying shades of gray. Here, as in the market outside, the atmosphere was subdued. No slamming of pewter cups on wooden tables, no shouted challenges to drink another and another. No impassioned gathering around a single voice. No Marcel.

It was Elianne's hand, thin and moist, that took hers and led her to a bench, and her sour breath in Laurette's ear asking—something. The question was lost in a rush of blood and thought. She broke away and tugged for Gagnon's attention.

"I have one more trade to make. The cheese. I thought I might get some molasses for the boys, they've worked so hard. I'll find you outside."

She couldn't miss the look of triumph on Elianne's face, but neither did she care. Outside, once again in the jarring light, she headed straight for the low, long building where she knew she would find Marcel, or nobody. Every spring she came here with Gagnon, their sheep pelts piled high and bound. Every spring she waited outside, as women were strictly forbidden to attend the weighing and the auction. But there'd be no weighing today; the auction house was merely another door for Laurette to open, step inside, and adjust to the darkness.

And to the dust. It floated, carrying a sheep's worth of wool dancing through the air, illuminated by the sunlight shining through the slats of careless construction. Great hooks hung from the rafters, five in all, each with a half-moon scale and a chain with a swaying platform beneath. Dubois hunkered over one of the platforms, adjusting an iron sphere, then stood to read the scale's bouncing needle.

Laurette made a small noise, and he turned.

"What do you want?" he said by way of greeting. Then he laughed, picked up the sphere, and moved to another scale. "As if I didn't know. Let me guess, that curly-headed bastard sired a bastard of his own."

Laurette felt a new band of sweat soak through her chemise, and her mouth filled with too much of a dusty protest to make a sound. Not that Dubois wanted to hear.

"I reckon it's been, what? Four, five months since we took our little jaunt out in search of the carriage? Made fools of all of us, he did. And then that runt of a cousin of yours disappears right along with it. You know, I knew her mother, like almost any other man in this godforsaken place. Good a chance as any that she's mine. But you? You've probably got a good idea who's the *papa* of your brat. Not that it'll do you any more good than if you didn't."

The chain creaked in protest as he dropped the sphere on the platform, causing the needle to spin so violently Laurette could hear it from behind its glass. She moved her basket to cover her belly, knowing it to be round, yes. But soft, and—to her relief—empty.

"I'm not . . ." She stopped, too ashamed to say the word.

"Well, that's a blessing anyway," Dubois said. He rubbed his hand over his graying whiskers, squinting at the needle, willing it to stop. "Because he's gone."

"Gone?"

The scale lost its appeal as he turned to her. "You didn't know?"

"I only know that I haven't seen him. Where did he go? I assume Paris, like everyone else."

Dubois shrugged, took a bit of chalk out of his pocket, and wrote something on the dark metal of the hook. "He got a letter. From her, you know?"

"Her?"

He picked up the sphere, went to the next scale, and repeated the process. The answer to Laurette's own question rang with the weight, her eyes locked on the needle, and her mind screamed in protest of learning what she already knew.

"The girl. That little cousin of yours. Did she not have a letter for you, too?" He laughed again, the sound of it mimicking the rhythm of the needle. "Yes, yes. He comes in one day with this paper. Finest paper any of us have ever seen. And he won't let us have a look, whether we could read or not, and just says he's been summoned to the palace. *'Summoned to the palace.'* Exactly what he says. And then he grabs that silent brute Le Rocher, and they're gone before supper."

Laurette said nothing, owed him no explanation, not that he would hear over the sound of his own rusty laughter. Mutely she turned, hearing him laugh even after the door closed behind her. She made her trades without haggling, the expression on her face clearly showing she would not be budged. The very thought of going back into Le Cochon Gros made her cheeks burn even hotter than the afternoon sun, and she lingered in the street, fingering a strand of ribbon on a rag man's cart until he finally took pity on her and said, "Go on and take it, now that your hands have dirtied it up." No softness in the kind gesture, but she thanked him sweetly, wrapped it into a coil, and willed Gagnon to find her.

⚜

They walked back with the Girards, at least to the point past the woods where their paths diverged.

"Are you sure you wouldn't like to come to our house for some supper?" Elianne asked. "There's plenty."

Laurette bit back the fact that they, too, had plenty, and allowed Gagnon to decline the invitation.

"The boys will be wanting supper, too. We'd best get back to them."

The foursome said their good-byes and went their separate ways. Once she was sure their friends were out of earshot, Laurette asked Gagnon if he realized Elianne Girard was in love with him.

"Nonsense," he replied. "Her father and mine were great friends."

"You haven't noticed the way she looks at you?"

"How does she look at me?"

"Like she's hungry."

"As we all are."

It was a cryptic reply, and one that would remain so, as nothing in his tone led her to believe he would expound on its meaning. She suspected he was holding back a comparison to her feelings for Marcel and wondered if he'd heard anything about Renée's letter from the men in Le Cochon Gros. He hadn't mentioned it, but neither had she, and it gave her an unsettled feeling to think they were walking side by side holding the same secret.

Gagnon was one who could carry on the rest of the journey in companionable silence, but her questions ground upon each other with every step. What did he know? What wasn't he telling her? And if he knew of Renée's letter, why would he withhold such a treasure? She had her reasons, wanting to protect his feelings. He might be hurt to know that, given the opportunity, Renée summoned Marcel instead of him. Perhaps he was offering her the same gift, guarding her heart from the man who would run off at the crook of her cousin's finger.

She should ask, flat out—*What did you hear of Marcel?* But she held off for a few more steps, crafting her question to allay any criticism, and said, "What news did you hear at Le Cochon Gros?"

"Nothing you would find interesting, I'm sure."

"More of what you and Monsieur Girard were discussing so secretively before you went inside?"

"I don't wish to spend the remainder of our walk in an argument."

Our walk. As if they were enjoying a summer stroll rather than trucking home a handcart with a pathetic bundle of beets and a small jar of molasses to speak for an entire day's trade. "I'll be good. Quiet and agreeable like Elianne."

To that, he had no comment. "There was an incident in Saint-Michel—you know the place?"

She did, a village not far—maybe a day's walk to the east. "What kind of incident?"

"The mayor's house was burned to the ground, as the mayor and his family slept inside. The whole family killed at the hands of the villagers because they thought he was hoarding their grain, driving up prices."

"Was he?"

Gagnon looked at her incredulously. "That is your question? If he were, does it justify the murder of his children? People are afraid, and that fear is turning into anger, and that anger is bringing them to unspeakable acts."

"Do you think anything like that could happen here?" She

thought back to the night before Renée left, the anger that fueled Marcel and his friends in their vengeful chase.

"I don't know. I hope not, as long as cooler heads can prevail. Now Saint-Michel is overrun by the king's soldiers; people have lost their homes to them. They've had to take food out of their children's mouths to feed healthy men. Those are the consequences of succumbing to anger, Laurette. And it only takes one hothead like Marcel to encourage such an action."

"Marcel isn't here."

"I know."

She feigned innocence. "Do you know where he is?"

He hesitated long enough for her to wonder if he was formulating the perfect phrasing for his answer. "In Paris, I suppose. Or Versailles. He'll never be able to plant his seeds of rebellion here. The good men of the village won't allow it."

"That's not why he left." Her intention to hide the secret folded in her desire to defend him. "He went to find Renée."

L'épisode 13

Renée

VERSAILLES

For the remainder of the summer, the queen has taken up residence at the Petit Trianon, though I've yet to understand anything *petit* about it, other than in comparison to the palace of Versailles with its labyrinth of hallways echoing with the voices of milling strangers. Only those especially invited by the queen are allowed to accompany her on this sojourn. For some reason I have been included in that number. It's particularly puzzling because in this place, the queen abandons much of her fashion, choosing to wear simple gowns—sometimes spending an entire day in a dressing shift.

"She's taken to you," Madame Gisela says with some consternation when I pose the question to her. "Marie has always been partial to pets. You are a pet to her, Renée. Stay loyal and close. Stay interesting, and you'll have a place always."

I'm not sure I appreciate being likened to a *pet*, but the sentiment about the queen is true. Her inner circle, those brought to this sanctuary of gardens and comfort, have been hand-chosen.

I have a proper room here, one that I share with three other girls, rather than a spot squeezed in between the dozens of other sewing women. And I've been given leave to pursue what I please. She is especially pleased with my execution of a quilted dressing gown—just warm enough for the earliest hours of the summer day, heavy enough to conceal the details of her figure as it is without structuring undergarments. The first I made with a layer of thin wool stitched between silk and cotton, with wide sleeves cut at the elbows. Now she wants more for her responsibilities at the palace. Ones that she can wear to receive guests in the morning before she's had time to fulfill her beauty regimen.

The sewing room at the Petit Trianon is nothing like that of Versailles. There are only two cutting tables and a single wall shelved with bolts of fabric. But it is mine, completely. The only other woman here in this capacity is a doddering old maid whose hands shake too violently for her to thread a needle or be trusted with scissors of any kind. At the palace, her duties are relegated to pressing down the seams of a completed garment. She is here only as a matter of protocol, because to have me here alone would elevate my status beyond what I've earned.

This, I suppose—this paring down of those who serve—is the queen's way of establishing normalcy in her life. The entire staff numbers fewer than fifty people, and though this château sits on the grounds of Versailles, there is a feeling of being a world away. The gardens here have been allowed to be overgrown and untamed, not groomed into submissive designs. The paths wander without intent. At Versailles, I imagine a bird flying over the gardens would look down and see something that looks like intricate green embroidery. Here at the Petit Trianon, I imagine a bird might think a bit of its own green forest has been uprooted and transplanted, exposed roots and all.

Whenever possible—and the queen is so generous with both the grounds and with time—I come out here. Once again free to wander without my shoes, I let my bare feet linger in the soft grass of the open spaces and tread the smooth stones of the paths. The treetops provide an escape from the sun, and on the rare occasion when a breeze presents itself, they rattle their waxy green leaves in tune. It's the closest I ever feel to being at home.

I hear that, in years past, the queen amused herself with life-size sculptures of livestock—living out her fantasies of being a poor farm girl. Perhaps that's another reason she's drawn to me. I'm the girl she never was. Now I feel like I could just emerge from the other side of the garden and find myself in the grazing field, with Gagnon's sheep in the distance and Laurette by my side. There are days when I'm tempted to try, when loneliness takes hold and I want to hear a familiar voice telling a common story.

But then I'll be summoned. *Couturière*, the queen is not happy with the cut of her gown. Can you fix it? *Couturière*, the princess wished to have a blue ribbon stitched to her skirt! Come, before she realizes it has been forgotten. *Couturière*, the queen's guest so admires your work she wishes to meet you and kiss your nimble fingers.

And I think, how have I come to be so fortunate? Why does God allow me to live and breathe each day doing only what I love, with such ample reward and blessings for the pleasure?

Here, those of us who work in service to the queen gather for a late supper every evening, when the lion's share of the work is done and she and her guests are engaged in their choice of frivolous pursuits. We'll have a hearty lamb stew, or a platter made of the cuts of meat not suitable for serving, with loaves of good dark bread and sweet water to drink. We take turns telling stories, though I am more content to listen to theirs rather than share my own. These people, after a lifetime in shadows, know secrets without bounds, and they spare no details. By mid-August I know the deviances of all the great men of France, the nobles and clergy alike, and the part of me that seeks to preserve my life compels me to stay for as long as I am welcome. When the day comes that I am not, I'll gladly take my needles and thread and return to Gagnon.

⚜

It is late in the evening, too hot to retire to my stuffy room, so I am biding time in the garden, lying flat on my back on a bench of stone and studying the stars when I hear someone calling me.

"*Couturière! Couturière*, are you out here?"

A part of me wants to roll off the bench and hide beneath it until the search is called off. A summons this late often means that I'm being called in for the queen's amusement. I've taught her little dogs to obey some of the whistled commands I used with Cossette and Copine, and while her little mops are far too spoiled and stupid to do any real work, they will sit and roll and dance on their hind legs according to my whistle. They will only obey me, and I don't feel amusing tonight. I am tired and have been drowning in the day's oppressive heat since rising early in the morning. But two things compel me to sit up and listen. First, this is not the shrill tone of one of the queen's ladies, too consumed with jealousy of my favor to ever speak with true kindness, let alone deference. This is a man's voice, and a familiar one at that—one of the queen's personal guards. Bertrand. Second, he isn't shouting for me, as is the usual case for my summons. He is whispering, more like an act of warning so as not to startle me upon turning a corner.

"I'm here," I say, sitting up and straightening my skirt, preparing for him to see me.

He walks through a canopy of vines allowed to grow pell-mell over a trellis, and my breath catches as it does every time I see him. His fair skin stretches like snowy plains along the contours of his smooth face, and his shoulders are half as wide as I am tall. Among those assigned to guard the queen, he is the most physically impressive and, surprisingly, the youngest. Unsavory rumors decree that he was chosen for those attributes, and that his duties extend far beyond merely keeping the queen safe as she sleeps in her bedchamber. But I know that not to be true, just as I know none of the rumors about our queen having unnatural appetites are true. And if Bertrand is aware of his role in such lies, he bears the weight in silence.

"There you are," he says. "I knew I would find you here."

I can't imagine that he even knows who I am. We've never spoken before, though I've spent my fair share of time glancing at him over my needlework as he stands guard at the entrance to the queen's apartments. I don't know the color of his eyes, as I've never seen him up close. Now it's too dark to make a determination, but the fairness of his skin leads me to believe that they are blue, and the moonlight reveals that his lashes are as pale as the hair on his head, giving him a ghostly appearance that I choose to explain the bubble of fear in the pit of my stomach.

"How did you know I was here?"

"I know everything about Her Majesty, and you belong to her."

I move to stand. "Has she called for me?"

"No. Something else. Come with me."

I follow without question. He walks, his massive back straight, shoulders squared. His coat flaps in time with his steps, to the point where it could be its own rolling drum. He's replaced his tricorn hat. Feeling like some escorted prisoner, I run to catch my steps with his.

"Is there trouble?"

He does not look down. "I can't say."

"What *can* you say?"

Apparently the answer to that question is *rien*. Nothing, for that is what I get in reply. He leads me to the very edge of the garden, then along its wall. When we finally stop, he reaches into a pocket within his coat and produces a key. We are at a cleverly concealed door, overrun with brambles.

"This," he says, holding the key, "was given to me in confidence, and with the assurance that I would return it within the hour. Now, you'll have to forgive me for accompanying you, but as I said, my duty is to Her Majesty and you are a part of Her Majesty; therefore, my duty is to you as well."

He places the key in the lock and, before opening the little rounded door, draws his sword. In a fluid motion, he opens the door, ducks through it saying, "Make way," and then calls to me.

Speechless, I obey. Already I can see that there is firelight on the other side, and when I walk through, I find a field of light produced by a semicircle of soldiers—some on horseback—holding torches aloft. In the center a man stands with all the defiance he ever displayed at our table back home.

"Do you know this man?"

"I do."

He's grown thinner since I last saw him, his face sharp, his hair long and wild about his face where it is not contained in the tie at the nape of his neck. His clothing is little more than rags draped on his frame, his shirt open nearly down to his navel, and I can see his breath beneath his ribs.

"Renée," he says, and without thinking, I run to him. My arms could wrap twice around his waist, and I don't think a bit about the fact that my face is pressed against the rough skin of his chest. He does not embrace me in return, and I soon realize it's because his hands are chained behind him.

"What have you done?"

"Apparently he was making quite a ruckus," Bertrand says, "storming around the grounds at the palace asking for you. And not so politely, I've been told." As he speaks, he walks closer, and I step away.

"Is that a crime?" Marcel asks, looking like a boy next to Bertrand.

"It is if the king's guard says it is. It is if he's been turned away, escorted from the property, and told that he's no right to speak to anyone in the queen's care."

"I'm just a seamstress," I say, my allegiance with Marcel. "I've no need for protection."

For the first time since emerging from the garden, Bertrand looks at me. "I'll beg your pardon, but that's not for you to decide." Then he regards Marcel. "You are not in prison right now only because of our curiosity. So say your piece. Or declare your love, or whatever it is you have decided is important enough to risk your freedom. Go on . . ." He makes a wide, open-armed gesture and backs away.

"May we speak in private?" Marcel asks, looking at Bertrand as if they were physical equals.

"No," Bertrand replies, with no further elaboration, but he does take an additional step away.

"Come now," Marcel says, and the chains in which he is bound clang with his truncated gestures. "If I were some kind of a spy, would I really have been shouting my intentions? I've known Renée since she was a child, and I'm merely here to determine her welfare on behalf of her former guardian."

"Gagnon." I grasp Marcel's shredded sleeve. "Is he well?"

"He is. He sends his love."

"And Laurette?"

"The same, *ma petite*."

"Did you give him—"

"Of course I'll give him your love when I go back home."

The way Marcel interrupts me, it's clear that he does not want me to mention my letter, or that he is here at my invitation. Whether my silence on that part is meant to protect me or him, I don't know, but I respond with an innocuous "Please do."

"Messieurs," Marcel says, now speaking to the soldiers surrounding him, "I beg of you. Look at the beauty of this girl. So far from home, she's been. And we've missed each other so. Can I not convince you to give us just a few moments? Over there—" he gestures with his head—"in the shadow by that wall. A few simple moments for a proper reunion?"

I blush at the implication, even more when Bertrand breaks his show of strength to send me a look of amusement. *"Mademoiselle?"*

"I'd—I'd like to hear about my family. In private, as we are not used to public scrutiny."

Bertrand directs his gaze to a soldier on horseback. "What say you, Lieutenant, sir?"

The lieutenant grunts permission.

"One more thing, if I may," Marcel says. "The chains? May I not be rid of them for the purposes of one chaste embrace?"

Rough laugher, and a comment from the back about some embracing not needing hands at all, which prompts Bertrand to raise his sword and call for order.

Marcel shrugs. "Come." His feet are bound, and his steps shuffle as we walk toward the wall, to a place of pure dark, hidden from the garden torches and outside the circle of the soldiers' light. Once we are cloaked in blackness, I embrace him again, wary that his bones might break. Months ago, at the idea of Marcel seeking me out, presenting himself to my arms, I would have allowed myself to drift into a sweet, peaceful death. All dreams fulfilled. Now, my heart quickens with fear.

"You received my letters?" I speak the question directly into the fabric of his shirt, my nose inches away from the stiffened stain under his arm. The odor is atrocious and I have to force myself not to wince.

"I did."

"Madame Gisela took them to the post for me. It's been so long, I wasn't sure . . ."

"Soundly delivered to Le Cochon Gros."

"And Gagnon and Laurette? They are pleased to know how well everything has turned out?"

"I had to come for myself to see. I wondered if perhaps your letter had not been written under some duress. Or a desire to hide your true status. But now I see—you are so important as to be escorted by mountains with every step."

It is a joke, and I laugh. "I believe he's more intended to be a wall between you and the queen."

"Ah yes. The queen." His voice takes on a familiar bitterness, one I well remember from our talks at Gagnon's table. But here, the edge is sharper, and I realize his words—along with his body—are a knife's hilt away from Her Majesty. One leap over the wall, a few quick steps . . . Now I know why the chains are kept in place. "How is it you have become so familiar with Our Majesty?"

I feel wary. "I'm not so familiar."

"Familiar enough to be here. Only her closest companions accompany her here. Everyone knows that."

"Let me make a new shirt for you." I tug at his rags playfully. "Look at you, so thin now. I can make it from scraps. A waistcoat, too, if you like. And breeches the same as theirs." I point to the soldiers behind us, and he makes a hissing sound.

"I want nothing that puts me in league with my oppressors. And I'd rather live out my days naked than clothe myself in the scraps of the nobles."

Self-consciously, I smooth my skirt, taking no comfort in the perfect exposed seams. "I've access to plain linen, too, if you'd rather."

"I'd rather not." He takes a step closer, and I find myself trapped between his body and the wall. Still, even at this proximity, the darkness reduces him to little more than a voice wafting on sour breath. "Why did you write to me?"

"I have some means to help Gagnon."

"Then why did you write to *me*?"

His question begs an answer beyond what I have to give—that I knew Marcel would come to me and that Gagnon would not. I tell him this, the simple truth, and he laughs.

"You thought I could not resist your charm?"

"I thought you could not resist an excuse to leave Mouton Blanc."

"And why did you tell me to keep my visit a secret?"

"In case—what if something were to go wrong? And you didn't find me? That would only heap more worries upon his head, don't you think?"

"You think he worries?"

"About me? I don't know. But, from the talk I've heard, about the crops, this dreadful summer."

"So, we come back to your letter. And why you summoned me here. What means do you have to help Gagnon? Do you have rainclouds stitched into your ridiculous dress?"

I smile at the insult because it feels good to be teased again. "I have money." My voice is so low, I barely hear myself.

"Comment?" He's not teasing anymore.

"Not much, I don't think. Truly, I don't *know* how much. Maybe nothing, maybe a fortune. People, at court, they pay me sometimes when I stitch for them, or when they want to know some secret I might have."

He leans in, so close now that I can feel his lips brush the lobe of my ear. "What secrets?"

I can't think. When I inhale, a strand of his dark curls brushes my mouth, and when I exhale, it stays and moves with my words. I feel the backs of my legs turn to icy fire, destroying the muscles that hold me upright. I've nothing to clutch but

Marcel, so I do. "Silly things, mostly. Ladies want to know what the queen will be wearing to a banquet or a ball, and I tell them. Once a man wanted to compliment the color of the queen's gown but didn't know the name of the color in French, so I told him." He's right up against me as I speak. I can feel his breathing against the length of my body. Relaxed, slow, calm, though how he could be under the circumstances I cannot understand. "I've little use for it, beyond the small coppers I keep for when I go to the markets. I have all I need. Will you take it to him for me?"

"In case you haven't noticed, I'm not in a position to act as your banker right now. Do you really think these barbarians will set me free and let me abscond with a bag of gold you fetch from the queen's chambers? Your big white mountain would come tumbling down on me like an avalanche."

"I have it here. In my pocket."

He stands straight, so suddenly that I'm knocked back a step. "Are you crazy?"

"I've not really a place to call my own. Don't worry, it's down deep, and I've fashioned a button to close it up. And I keep them all bundled—the coins—so they won't jingle when I walk. I already look enough like a gypsy, don't you think?"

I don't know if he's smiling back at me, but I hear the rattle of his chains. He's thinking. If we were back at Gagnon's, he'd be up from the table, pacing the room, previewing his words with his hands, gesturing as if to capture the very thoughts as they flew from his mind.

"Eh!" shouts one of the mounted guards. "*Les amoreaux!* We will not extend the entire night for your pleasure."

"Please, sir!" Marcel shouts over his shoulder. "You are a man of romance, I can tell! I beg your indulgence for just a little while longer. Think of your first love!"

Ribald laughter responds.

"Renée. Take hold of my shirt, and walk back, back, back, until you are touching the wall." He continues as I comply. "Your money is no good to anyone if we do not find a way to release me, but that will come later. There." We've come to the wall, and Marcel makes another in front of me, he is pressed so close. "Now, put the coins in my pocket. Not all, if you don't wish to. Keep what you want."

"No, I have it here, ready. I have since I sent the letter."

"Good, then. My breeches pocket, I think. So far I haven't seen these animals strip a man to that indignity."

"You're sure they are intact?"

I feel him grin. "It's where I stash all that I steal. Food, I mean. I carried a single apple for three days."

Marcel remains close, so close that some part of me touches some part of him with even the slightest of movement. I reach into the deep secret pocket of my skirt, find where I've sewn in a buttoned pouch, and pull from it the coins, wrapped tight in a square of muslin and knotted twice. The bundle is silent as a stone when I drop it into Marcel's pocket, and it is with great relief that it doesn't fall straight through to the ground.

"Good girl," Marcel says. "Your generosity will be your reward, but I wish I could convince you to come away with me. You've a crafty mind."

"We don't know that you're going anywhere yet, Marcel." A thought occurs to me, and I place a staying hand on his sleeve. "One more idea, a safeguard. Let me sew up your pocket, seal it halfway down, so even if you get—I don't know, tossed—it won't fall out."

"And how will you manage that?"

Reaching blindly into my belt, I pull out the threaded needle. "I keep this with me. Nothing makes a seamstress more nervous than having someone watch her thread a needle. Makes her go all blind and thumbsy." Then, working deftly with the skills memorized by my fingers, I set a series of swift stitches resulting in a pocket that, were anyone to thrust a hand inside, he would find to be empty.

Revolting sounds and lewd comments continued to flow from over Marcel's shoulder, making references I would not have understood just a few months ago. "What they must think of me," I say, wishing I could cover my ears to block them out.

"Your heart is pure, same as mine. Let their thoughts be their sin to carry and confess to the Lord at judgment."

"It's not often I hear you speak of our Lord, Marcel."

"And it's not often anybody will for much longer. Save to cry out for mercy."

When I'm finished, I snap off the thread, and Marcel bids me to rise up for a kiss—a chaste one to my cheek, and then I loop one arm through his confinement and walk him back into the soldier's light.

"Finished with her, are you?" the lieutenant says, but his laughter is cut short by Bertrand.

"Enough of that." Then, to Marcel, "You've said your good-byes. Now, go."

Marcel rattles his chains. "It doesn't appear I'm at liberty."

Bertrand addresses the assembled guard. For the first time, I allow myself to take a look at the lieutenant, the one who appears to be in command. His breeches are pristinely white, his coat a blue sea with islands of brass, and his head—bald as an egg—currently uncovered as his hat rests on the pommel of his horse's saddle. The lower half of his face is all a trim, white beard, every bit the shade of his breeches, his nose broad, and his lips entirely without humor. In every way he bests Bertrand—in age, authority, rank, and utter contempt for the prisoner at hand. And yet, when Bertrand says, "Release him," there is a subtle shift in the confidence of his seating.

"You've no authority, boy." The last word an insult to both their offices.

"I am second in command of the guardianship to the queen."

"And this nuisance of a man is a threat to the queen?"

"Is it now a crime to be a nuisance?" Marcel says, assuming thc air of a solicitor. "A crime to make inquiries on what is known to be property free and open to the citizens of France?"

"It is if I say it is." The lieutenant speaks directly to Marcel.

"And yet, Lieutenant," Bertrand says, taking slow, measured steps until he is standing a sword's length away from Marcel, "you chose to bring this nuisance to the queen's private retreat? By whose authority? Whose invitation?"

"Just wanted to shut him up is all."

"Then you should have slit his throat when you had the chance."

Bertrand touches the tip of his blade to Marcel's throat, and though Marcel is able to remain stoic at the steel, I leap forward and cry, "No! He is a dear friend of my family. He has brought me news, that is all."

"Well, that's not *all*," the lieutenant says. In an instant, Bertrand has resheathed his sword, and in a swift motion, hauls the man clean off his horse and throws him to the ground. The air is filled with the sound of half a dozen blades drawn, feet hitting the ground, and the rattle of a set of chains as Bertrand shoves Marcel to the side and places himself in front of me.

The lieutenant yells, "Stand!" even as he struggles to his feet, and his men reluctantly resheathe their weapons. Once up, he refuses to dust off his breeches, though somehow I know the stain of dirt infuriates him. He steps to Bertrand, his nose barely in line with the younger man's throat. "I suppose there's no need for the queen to get word of any of this unpleasant business."

"Take two of your men," Bertrand says, "and escort this person back to . . ."

"Saint-Canus," Marcel says, without affording me the slightest glance of warning.

"Saint-Canus," Bertrand says. "Wherever such a wretched hole of a place might be. Flank him, and send a message that his fate is that of anyone who takes it upon himself to disrupt the royal peace. Then he is to be left unharmed. Will you repeat my request to your men?"

He does so, using a more vulgar term to define their prisoner, and two of his soldiers remount while a third escorts Marcel to stand between them.

"Am I not to be allowed a horse?" Marcel asks over his shoulder.

"Did you ride a horse to Versailles?" the lieutenant responds.

"And these?" Marcel presents his chains.

"Leave them," Bertrand says. "Let someone in—what was it? Saint-Canus?—find a way to set you free."

Marcel shrugs. "*Eh, bien. Au revoir*, Renée. I will give your love to your cousin."

"And Gagnon!" We are at quite a distance from each other by now, and I'm forced to peek around Bertrand to say anything at all.

The only sound is that of hooves and shackles, and we all stand in silence, looking in the direction of their disappearing light. A full three minutes, I'd say—maybe more—the remaining soldiers staring at the darkness, the lieutenant staring at his soldiers, Bertrand staring at the lieutenant, and my vision consumed by the ground beneath me. Why did Marcel lie about our town? In all my days I've never heard of a place called Saint-Canus, though there are villages enough dotting the countryside surrounding Paris. Perhaps he wanted to protect the people of Mouton Blanc from seeing him in chains. Or worse. I prayed I'd given no reaction to make them doubt his word.

When the night fully engulfs the prisoner and his escort, the lieutenant turns around and somehow makes himself taller with an imperceptible rise of his feet. "What is your name, boy?"

"Bertrand Thiron, second in command of the queen's personal guard."

"Any experience as a soldier?"

"It's not been my pleasure, sir." It's a thing to behold how Marcel's absence brings these two men to a gentleman's level of conversation, yet somehow Bertrand holds command. Without an exchange of salute or acknowledgment of any kind, the lieutenant and his soldiers mount their horses and ride off at a quick pace in the direction opposite of the previous dispatch. They take the light with them, leaving Bertrand and me without even a sliver of moonlight. Only stars, and they are not bright enough for us to make each other out clearly, and for that I am grateful.

"I'll escort you back to your quarters," he says with the formality of a total stranger, which, until this evening, he has been.

"I can find my way."

"Your quarters are my quarters, *mademoiselle*. I'm just on the other side of the door."

As we walk, he obviously alters his stride to meet mine. I don't know if I should thank him, or apologize, or if I'm allowed to speak to him at all, now that our official business has concluded. If I have learned nothing else in my time here, it is to remain silent until spoken to. Soon enough, Bertrand complies, eerily matching my thoughts.

"How did you come to be acquainted with such a liar?"

"What makes you think he is a liar?"

"The name of the town is Saint-Cannat. So either your friend does not know the name of his own hometown, or he is lying."

I say nothing, as neither choice would allay suspicion.

"And I am inclined to believe he is lying, because you are from Mouton Blanc."

"How do you know?"

"I heard you mention it once or twice. You were telling the princess all about the white sheep on the green hillside. It sounds like a beautiful place."

"It is." Then I remember. "Rather, it was, when I left. I pray it is still."

"Your family is still there?"

"They are."

"And your friend?"

I smile—to myself, as Bertrand hasn't looked at me once during all of our conversation. "As long as I've known Marcel Moreau, he's never had a home. He drifts, you know? Nights here and there."

"So his next night will be in an imaginary town?"

"Not so surprising if you know him." I look up, keeping my step and holding my gaze until he is prompted to look down at me. "Why didn't you say something before you sent him away?"

"Because I don't care where he goes. Or if he goes anywhere beyond the first bend in the road. As long as he doesn't come back here."

Part III

L'Automne (Autumn) 1788—
Nouvel An et le Printemps
(the New Year and Spring) 1789

Accordez-moi le sommeil de
rêves tranquilles. . . .

⚜

L'épisode 14

Laurette

MOUTON BLANC

Gagnon kept the underbellies of the sheep sheared clean throughout the summer that they might cool themselves on the ground when they lay down for the night. The boys had to take them beyond the stretches of his land, to that of neighbors who had no livestock left to graze. Days stretched endlessly under bone-dry skies and unrelenting heat. More than once, Laurette thought of the last day she spent with Renée, out in the field, staring into the sky, creating stories with the clouds. What clouds had she seen these past months? Nothing but wisps in the morning, gone long before the last spoonful of porridge was swallowed.

And autumn brought no hope.

Gagnon's meager harvest was brought in with less than a week's labor and hardly worth the effort of driving in to the mill. The fate of all of France's fields could be no better. Laurette pulled from her garden, already rationing its yield in hoping to make it last through half the winter. Grain was siphoned from the sheep and given to the goats so they would stay healthy, giving good milk even in the leanest months.

For the first time since developing the curves of a woman's figure, Laurette had evidence of a skeleton beneath her flesh. Even her arms lost their plumpness, and her body felt like a bundling of sticks within the volume of her dress. She felt the sharpness of her clavicle, and the pain with even the slightest collision of her bones if she knocked into a doorway or brushed a hip against the table. And the thirst. With well water drawn and drizzled along the rows of her garden, down the furrows of what was left of the wheat, the crock was filled twice a day when the boys were home with the sheep, only once when they were out to pasture, their skins full to bursting with the rest. Her throat dry, Laurette spoke little, as did they all, so the days lived and died not only with heat, but with arid silence as well.

It was mid-October when Laurette finally emerged from the house in the predawn light to meet a corner of chill in the air. Nothing near the crispness of autumn that usually came with the death of a healthy summer, but a hint, at least, of a respite to come. She crossed the hard-packed yard, sensing damp coolness there, too. Her steps quickened to the well, and she coaxed a tune out of her morning-dry throat as she began pumping the water. Soon, another sound came out of the lingering night shadows. A hiss—no, a *psst*. And her name, spoken like a long-held secret.

"Laurette."

She paused, looking over her shoulder toward the barn, up at the loft's window, though she knew the boys were afield.

"Laurette."

And he emerged, as she knew he would, looking every bit the man she remembered in his gait and bearing, but hardly recognizable in his appearance. His chest stretched full and healthy beneath his open shirt, and she assumed his legs hidden beneath long, loose trousers boasted strength as well. Only his hair gave a moment's doubt to his identity. Gone were the long, curling black locks that had been so prevalent in her dreams she'd awoken with contorted fingers. In their place, a tight black cap, much like the wool of the sheep in summer. The look aged him, and a certain fear stirred within her—a fear she liked to think she would have heeded that night when he urged her down in a bed of moss. But then her heart began to race, two beats to each of his steps, reminding her that her fear was useless to prompt resistance.

"Just like old days," he said, close enough to pick up the battered cup from the wood block next to the pump and hold it out for a drink. "Slipping in for a night in Gagnon's barn. Only this time with no pretty girls in the loft to tempt me."

Not imagining any right to refuse, Laurette filled the cup and watched him drink it down in three swallows, with a waste of it dribbling down his unshaven face.

"You should go," she said, even as she filled the cup again. "As far as I know, you are still not in his good graces, and I'm not exaggerating when I say we've nothing to offer you."

He finished, wiped his mouth with the back of his sleeve, and cocked an eyebrow. "*We*? Sounds very domestic. I see the boys he took sleep in the loft. Does that mean you have taken residence in the house? In his bed?"

Were it not for the cool of the morning she might not have felt her cheeks flush at the suggestion, but she owed him nothing. And besides, there were more pressing matters.

"You heard from Renée." It was a statement, not a question. A challenge for the truth.

He gave half a blink in surprise. "I did. She wrote to me."

"But not to us? To Gagnon?"

"She sends her love."

Laurette exhaled a breath she didn't know she'd been holding. "So you saw her? In Paris?"

"Not Paris."

"Where?"

"You're not likely to find her. It was not easy for me to do so, and I'm a man of resources."

Laurette snorted. "What resources? Those fools from Le Cochon Gros who hang on your words? That bald, silent stone that follows you?"

"I've made new friends since leaving this place. Friends that your man would be interested to meet."

"He's not my man. And he doesn't know about Renée. That she wrote to you or that you went to her. Monsieur Dubois told me, but I kept it from Gagnon. So please—"

"It's all right." Marcel reached for her, touching her shoulder, frowning at the thinness he found within. "I've many secrets to keep. What's one more? But do you think the man would welcome me to his table one more time? For whatever you can spare. I haven't eaten in two days."

She wasn't sure she believed him. She'd seen plenty of starving men; none of them looked like Marcel. "I'll see what I can send on with you."

"I want to see him."

"Marcel—"

"Then see me." Gagnon's voiced carried from the doorway. How long had he been standing there? What had he heard? Had she noticed, she would have stemmed the conversation, but Marcel's mischievous grin gave no such assurance. Gagnon stepped out now, arms wide. "See me, drink my water, and leave. I've rarely turned any scoundrel away from my home, but you may need to be an exception."

"Mon ami," Marcel crooned, "you will still hold a grudge over such a small thing? You have never been tempted by a

pretty girl in the moonlight? Come now—" he flicked his gaze between Laurette and Gagnon—"you surely have."

"And there, *mon ami*, is why you will never be welcome in my home. Have you had your fill to drink? Then go."

"I have news of Renée."

Gagnon raised a brow in surprise. "What news?"

Now it was Marcel's turn to hold his arms wide. "What breakfast?"

Laurette thinned the morning porridge with water and goat's milk, stretching two servings to three, and turned the bread into lacy slices. At the table, she dutifully made the sign of the cross with Gagnon, but locked open eyes with Marcel throughout the prayer for God's blessing on the meal, on the day, on the boys, and on France.

"You still pray?" Marcel asked before digging his spoon into his food in a way that testified to his hunger.

"What is a man without prayer?" Gagnon replied. "Or a nation without men who will turn to God on her behalf?"

"I don't see that it's doing much good."

"Then perhaps more men should pray." Gagnon pushed his bowl across the table toward Marcel and tore off a corner of his bread. "Tell us about Renée."

"She wrote to me some time ago." Marcel barely looked up from his food. "To let me—us—know that she was alive and well, but I did not want to share this news with you until I had a chance to see for myself. And so . . ." He spoke of his journey first to Paris, where he and Le Rocher prowled the streets, haunting pubs and shops.

"Why didn't you go straight to her?" Laurette asked. "From her letter, didn't you know where to find her?"

"Yes, but not *how* to find her. Before this, like you, I've never been more than a half day's journey away from Mouton Blanc. Never to a city, and never to a palace. So I wanted to know—what does one do?" And it was during that time that he met like-minded men—and women, too, he made clear to Laurette—willing to share with him openly their frustrations and their hunger for justice. To see the wealth of the nobles transformed into bread for the people. "You would like these men, Gagnon. Men of great thoughts, yes, but soon of action."

Gagnon waved off the idea saying simply, "Renée."

"I went then to Versailles, as she indicated. It is a place for the public, you know? So I went wherever a man like me could go. Into the great hall, just looking and looking for her. You can't imagine the beauty of this place. Gold in the walls, men and women of fortune milling around, jewels around their necks the size of duck eggs. I just started asking, 'Have you seen *la couturière*?' That is what they call her there. And at first, I got only puzzled looks. Or I was knocked off my feet, kicked like a dog. But as I am a citizen, I have a right to a certain space of marble tile. And then one day I asked a woman, and she looked thoughtful. Like she was thinking, trying to know, and then—as polite as you can imagine—she says, '*Non.* I have not seen her in some time.' That's when I knew, my first confirmation, that she existed in this place."

Laurette listened, mesmerized, unable to imagine the sights Marcel described.

"So," he continued, "I become a little more aggressive with my questions. *Bolder* might be a better word. And I learn she is not at the central palace of Versailles, but at the queen's retreat, a place called the Petit Trianon. A place with no access for the poor. I will spare you the more lurid details, but say only that I was put under arrest and chained, held at the point of a sword of the king's guard."

Laurette was now at the edge of her seat, porridge cold and forgotten. She, like Gagnon, edged her bowl across the table, as if in payment for the end of the tale. "But you saw her?"

Marcel smiled indulgently. "Yes. She was escorted to me in the shadow of a mountain."

"And she looked—" Gagnon had to pause to gather strength to his voice—"she looked well?"

"Plump as a Christmas goose, and dressed in the scraps of the queen. Still, no taller than this—" he held his hand to his shoulder, level with the back of the chair—"but with life in her eyes and flesh on her bones. Not like the rest of us."

"Merci à Dieu," Gagnon said, though not as a passing statement. His eyes were closed as he voiced a prayer of gratitude for her safety and provision. Laurette kept her eyes resolutely open and watched Marcel lick cold porridge off the back of his spoon.

"They keep her like a pet, you know," he said, once Gagnon's prayer ended. "Did you not hear? She is plumped up, ripe for slaughter, dressed in rags. Silk rags, but rags nonetheless."

"Are you saying she wished to leave?" Gagnon asked, his concern tinged with hope.

"I'm saying they've cleansed her of any thought that she might."

"But she is not ill-treated," Laurette clarified. "What did she say? How long was your visit?"

Marcel made a bitter sound. "Not long, as—you'll remember—I was in chains at the time. She sends her love, and with Gagnon's permission, I'm to give you a kiss, Laurette. From her. And then I was escorted away, my chains removed after a promise given to never return."

"It seems to be a promise that follows you," Gagnon said.

"And see? Already I've broken it once."

Silence followed as he mopped the sides of all three of his bowls with his single slice of bread—a silence during which he said nothing about the soldiers freeing him from his chains in the middle of a deserted road, with no village of any name in sight. Nothing about Le Rocher and his men, emerging from the surrounding trees, having followed his every move, prepared with their own knives and bludgeons to ensure his freedom. And nothing about the coins, once sewn tightly into his pocket, long since unbundled and traded for what he could buy. Food, clothing, loyalty.

Gagnon broke the silence. "That is it?"

Marcel nodded, his mouth too full of bread to speak.

"Then we have concluded our business. I wanted news; you wanted breakfast. You're better fed than any of us, so you'll be on your way."

"Can you really not go back?" Laurette asked. "Would they recognize you?"

"I would not go back alone, and I would not go back for Renée. I need to find like-minded brothers and go back as a force. Not every poor man can be absorbed the way Renée was absorbed. No, we remain slaves to the land—*their* land that they tax and take. And what do we do? Nothing. Nothing but starve in payment for our labor."

"As long as I've known you," Gagnon said, "I've not known you to do any kind of labor."

Marcel was undeterred. "My labor is for you. To be a voice for you, if you won't join me with your own. There are pockets of men in Paris, men of action. Actions for your benefit."

"I need no action from you. I need nothing beyond my God, my land, and my home."

"Well, *mon vieux*. It will not surprise you to hear that I have a favor to ask."

"Nothing you do or say would ever surprise me, my friend." His smile almost implied a begrudging affection.

"I need a home for the winter. For myself and my friends."

"There's no room for you here."

"That, I understand. You know I've no roof, nor do the men

who travel with me. But I thought we might be given shelter in the weighing shed. Dubois has no use for it until spring. There is more than enough room for us to bed down."

"Eh bien?" He looked confused. "Go. What have I to say in it?"

"I need you to negotiate on my behalf with Dubois. He respects you more than he respects me."

Gagnon laughed. "Why should I do such a thing for you?"

"Because I can do something for you in return. I may not be a man of means, but I am a man of resources. What do you need?"

Laurette wished she could jump up and speak for Gagnon. What would she say? What wouldn't she say? Food, flour, meat, shoes, firewood—an endless list. But Gagnon did not consult her. He did not even look at her. Instead, he cast his eyes across the room to the empty hearth, as if an answer might appear in place of the winter's flames.

"Food," he said finally, to her short-lived relief. "Food for my sheep. For the winter, I'll need grain." He calculated. "Twenty bags of it."

Before she could stop herself, Laurette gasped. Not so much shocked at Gagnon's choice but the gall of the amount.

Marcel, however, took the pronouncement in stride, as if Gagnon were asking him to gather so many sacks of pinecones. "I can do that."

"Before winter?"

"*Tout à fait.* In fact, for an invitation to winter in your cozy loft, I will bring you twenty-five."

Gagnon looked intrigued, amused in a way Laurette had never seen. "Be here before the first snow with thirty, and you can have a bed inside."

"Done." The men stood and shook hands. Shortly after, Gagnon bid him *adieu* and walked him out the front door, across the yard, and from what Laurette could tell, up to the hill crest, as she stood at the door and watched until both were out of sight. When Gagnon returned, alone, she made herself busy, raking the soil to prepare her fall garden.

"Intriguing about Renée, *non*?" Had she not spoken, he might have strode right past her without a word.

"Yes." He stopped but seemed uneasy, shifting his weight from foot to foot. "And a relief to know she is safely delivered." Without warning, he took the rake from her and reached it to the farther corners of the garden, obviously attempting to escape conversation through labor, but she would have none of it.

"Thirty bags, Gagnon? How is any man going to find thirty bags of grain this winter? Grain for *sheep*?"

"He won't."

"Then why—?"

"Because even a scoundrel like Marcel Moreau will know better than to ask for shelter without them."

"But suppose . . ." She knew a side of Marcel that Gagnon didn't. "Suppose he does?"

"Then I give him a bed." He plunged the rake into the packed soil and pulled it through, creating a soft, tilled layer.

"But—where?" When she was really wondering, *Whose?*

"That, *ma fille*, is a question for the winter."

⚜

L'épisode 15

Renée

VERSAILLES

There is a hall in the palace composed entirely of reflections. A wall of mirrors faces a wall of windows, with glass-baubled chandeliers suspended from the ceiling. The archways are gold, as are the statues, and to run through it means racing past your own reflection a hundred times over. Of course, rarely do I have a chance to run through this particular corridor, as during the day it is almost always packed with dignitaries and those with a desire to rise in rank and reputation with the court. Thus, the floor is dull and scuffed, and it is here that I keep my eyes trained whenever I am on an errand in the middle of the day.

But when it is deserted, like it is this morning, I allow myself a sprint, at least partway, until some servant of the household spots me and raises a threatening eyebrow. Then I walk slowly, with careful, silent steps, and breathe in the grandeur of this place. Everywhere is beauty—beauty that gets lost behind the vulgarities of ambition. There was a wedding not long after my arrival here. I stood at the back of this hall, flattened against my own reflection, and watched a fat, blotchy-faced man take a girl less than half his age in marriage. She looked like a frightened rabbit with her paw trapped in the snare of his hand, and he like a drunken squire ready to sit down to dinner. Nobody in the room wished them well. The men made crude jokes about the night to come, and the women, snide comments about the groom's health, longevity, and fortune.

This morning a new element lends itself to glisten in the hall. Outside, the courtyard is covered in fresh, unbroken snow. When the sun hits it full strength, the glitter will be blinding, but now it is a matte, perfect white, just emerging from the gray of dawn. I remember the magic of fields of snow in moonlight, the dogs romping through, sending up crystal clouds, new flakes dark against the sky. Once Gagnon's cottage was buried halfway up the door, and Laurette and I had to climb out of our loft window, walk across the drift, and holler down the chimney. Here, even the snow falls by design. A perfect cushion on the garden benches. A frosted layer on the disciplined greenery. Pathways shoveled and salted to make safe the king's steps.

This speaks to the very heart of my errand.

I was awoken this morning with a nudge to my shoulder and a voice close to my ear whispering, *"Couturière. Couturière. Lève-toi."* I opened my eyes to find Bertrand mere inches away, close enough that I could see the fine white whiskers growing along the strong line of his jaw. Later, as I walk through the Hall of Mirrors, I look out upon the snow and think of them, how soft they might feel beneath my palm, and I regret not claiming the confusion of sleep to touch him.

Instead, from the darkness I grappled to find his name and muttered it questioningly, with only my voice as proof that I was not in a dream.

"I've been sent to dispatch you to the king's apartment, with a message from Her Majesty."

Immediately I was fully awake. "Is everything all right? The children?" For this past week, since the eve of Christmas, after so many late nights and rich treats, Marie-Thérèse, Louis-Joseph, and Louis-Charles have been sleeping with their mother in her enormous bed. As a favorite of the princess, I've been allowed to stay near, helping her with the gifts she planned to present to her parents in the New Year—a quilted case for her father to store his spectacles, and a silk pillow for her mother, specially constructed that she might lie down upon it without destroying her coiffure. I've taken to sleeping on one of the sofas in the queen's antechamber, one of the lesser-used against the wall. It is more restful than my narrow cot in the crowded room of tirewomen, and the room is kept warm enough that I need only a single blanket. Never in my life had I slept a winter's night without waking to the sight of my own breath, and this morning I awoke to the sight of Bertrand, second of the queen's guard, with a message for the king.

And he was smiling.

"They are fine. Still sleeping. She wants to take the children for a sleigh ride this morning, and the dauphin left his warmest boots in the king's apartment. Would you fetch them?"

"Why would she send me?"

At this, he looked chagrined. "Actually, she sent *me*. But with so many guests in the palace, I don't want to leave my post for something so trivial."

"And my life can be spared?"

"It gave me a reason to go to you. To be the first person you see in this New Year. Why would I not take that opportunity?"

I'm never sure how I should take his words. True, we have become friends since that night of Marcel's visit. I know that he is twenty-five; he knows that I am seventeen. We are both children who lost our mothers far too young, though his father is still alive and well and employed in the king's stables. He makes jokes about my size, pretending not to see me when I am near, and urging me to stay away from all the rat traps hidden throughout the palace. And when I tease him about his massiveness, he tells me he is descended from the hordes of Vikings that stormed through France, leaving destruction and bastards in their wake. When I tell him that Marcel called him my "mountain," though, there is no laughter, and I take care not to mention him again.

The Hall of Mirrors is not the shortest route to the king's apartment; that would be the secret door in the queen's chamber, but I love having this hall to my own devices. I pause every step or so and take the time to examine myself in the mirror. *What does Bertrand see?* And then, I run—a sprint that brings me to race against myself as my reflection flashes and disappears and flashes again. For those tiny bits of time I'm not alone here, not the only shepherd girl, the only daughter of questionable parentage, the only girl dressed like a quilted gypsy.

The attendant at the king's apartment looks at me as if I'm little more than a bundle of scraps when I arrive, breathless, at the door.

"I've a message from Her Majesty the queen for His Highness."

The soft folds beneath his eyes are shaded gray, and the two armed guards on either side look like their first order of duty will be to prop the man up, as he appears on the verge of collapse. The hour is not unduly early, so I can only surmise that he, too, participated in the festivities of the New Year well into the night, and the strong odor of old wine wafting from his breath confirms my theory.

"Leave it with me," he says, soft hand exposed, "and go."

"It's not written, sir. I'm to fetch something for Her Majesty. The dauphin's boots? His fur-lined, as the family would like to go on a sleigh ride this morning. Doesn't that sound like a fine idea to celebrate the New Year? But it's so cold, you see . . ."

I know that if I prattle on long enough, he will wave me through, and I am not mistaken.

This is not the first time I've been to the king's rooms. He is not a man overly concerned about his clothing, but those who surround him have sharper eyes, and I've been summoned to tack and mend lest he go out looking like a sovereign in a pauper's coat. My first visit was startling, as his favored decor consists of hunting trophies staring with dead glass eyes. The chambers are every bit as masculine as my queen's are feminine. To think that the most important marriage in France exists in two entirely separate homes. I asked Madame Gisela once how they managed to have children at all, having become quite comfortable in discussing such matters.

"That was the question on everyone's lips for years," she said, tapping her chin in a way I'd come to recognize as a signal that she was choosing not to say all that was on her mind.

I am brought through to his office—a room that was once a bath and has been haphazardly redecorated for its new purpose. Meaning a desk and table and chairs have been brought in, but the paintings of water nymphs and aqua-themed frescoes remain. The clash invites the king to be perpetually conducting business underwater. And not for the first time, when I find myself face-to-face with the king, I have to remind myself that I am, in fact, in the presence of royalty. For he is an unassuming man. Not terribly tall, somewhat fat, nearsighted, and with hair that must have been thinning since he was quite a young man. Not bald, but sparse. To see him now, in sleep-rumpled clothing and without a wig, is what I imagine it must be like to see a turtle without a shell. He is all soft.

A host of men, all dressed for the formality of the day, surround him, and I'm forced to stand outside their circle saying, *"Pardon, messieurs? Pardon?"* before one of them finally acknowledges me with an impatient hiss. I repeat my mission three times, twice interrupted by a declaration that His Majesty has greater needs to attend to, until finally it is the king himself who quiets his advisers and draws me to his side and says, "Speak, girl."

"Her Majesty wishes to take the children on a sleigh ride, and *le monsieur—le dauphin*—requires his fur-lined boots. She believes they may be in your apartment, perhaps in your sleeping chamber, as he came here for a lie-down after playing outside the other day." It is the longest single sentence I have ever said to him, and he rewards me with attention.

"I am quite occupied here, you see." He gestures behind him. "But you are most welcome to go through that door and look for yourself. I daresay you'll be more efficient at finding the things than I."

"Oui, monsieur," I say, offering a curtsy and a smile. Refusing to acknowledge the grunts of the men around me, I enter into what appears to be the king's bedchamber. His bed is smaller than the queen's by half, heaped with furs and blankets but only a few flat pillows. Our queen is known to lounge abed for more than half the day if she has no official duties, even receiving visitors and entertaining guests (only women, of course, despite what I've heard in scandalous rumors) when she feels too ill or too listless to leave it, but this is clearly a place for a man to sleep. The bed is both unmade and undisturbed. Just rumpled, like the king himself.

I've left the door open behind me, so I can hear every word spoken in my absence.

"Your Majesty, we must insist—"

"Is it too much to ask for even a modicum of respectable behavior?"

"And how, pray tell—" this the voice of Louis—"is an afternoon sleigh riding with her children in any way disrespectful?"

"Now, in these troubled times—and they are troubled,

Monseigneur—it is more important than ever that our queen appear devoted to *this* country. Our traditions. With all due respect to her native Austria, we do not engage in sleigh rides in France. Not on the grounds of the palace."

I remain frozen in place, allowing my eyes to roam the room. It will be a challenge to locate a small boy's pair of boots, and the king's greatest secret might be his slovenly habits. Clothing is draped over furniture, books and papers are scattered throughout, as are knives and pouches and stockings and shoes. Obviously none of the men berating the queen are charged with tidying up.

"I will not forbid my wife to spend an afternoon with her children," Louis says, and I find myself smiling with pride for him, and soon after shocked at his adviser's tone.

"It is your sovereign duty to protect her—as her husband and her king—from those who would wish her harm. You know the public sentiment. How much worse would it be if she were to begin this New Year by reminding us all, once again, of her foreign roots? Better she should be aligned with our traditions."

"Our traditions are dying." This, spoken softly, is a voice different from the one so vehemently opposed to the queen. A beat of silence follows his solemn pronouncement. Uncomfortable in the heaviness of the moment, I move around the room, happily spying one little boot peeking from underneath the bed. I fish the other out of the darkness. Hoping to distract from more berating, I rush out, holding the boots aloft, as if the fur that lines them is my trophy.

"Success!" But the ring of faces is stern, wigs in authority, mouths set in disagreement.

"Hold, girl," says the king, and he riffles through his untidy desk, finally producing a clean scrap of paper. He dips his quill and begins to write—short, choppy strokes. The only sound is that of the nib on paper, but I can well guess the flow of thoughts onto the page. He rolls the blotter and folds the sheet carelessly, forgoing the seal, as I'm sure he thinks I cannot read. He hands the paper to the spokesman for the gathering, who makes no bones about unfolding the page and reading the note within. He grunts in assent and hands it to me.

"Take this to Her Majesty. And be quick about it."

"Oui, monsieur." But I offer no curtsy, or even the slightest dip of my head. For all I know this man is no better born than I. He notes my disrespect with a narrowed eye, and I think he might be on the verge of warning me to say nothing to the queen about what I've heard, but then I realize: he wants her to know. He would say it to her face if given an audience to do so. I could tell from his tone that he is one who revels in the gossip, who gets some satisfaction from the slander.

The Hall of Mirrors has come to life in the interim, the business of the palace fully commenced. The holiday has brought anybody of birth or means to Versailles. Red-faced squires and pale, water-eyed dukes. Children, too. Some clinging to their mother's skirts, fearful of the endless reflections of strangers, and others boldly behaving as I do in private—running up and down the length of the glass, intermittent shouts as they race past themselves. My stomach churns at the idea of delivering this note to the queen. How could her behavior be any more appalling than what I see here? Who among these people has a right to pass judgment on what might bring her joy?

I make my steps heavy, plodding through the grandeur, my eyes fixed on the tiles beneath. Black, white. Black, white. I'm clutching the dauphin's boots close, willing my nose not to wrinkle at the smell of damp-dried fur and little boys' feet. He may be a future king, but his boots are of no finer quality or craftsmanship than those Gagnon made for me every winter from the pelts of the goats he'd been forced to butcher. Though, unlike these, mine were always lined with wool, giving the warmth of an extra sock stitched within. Last winter, I'd stitched them myself.

The children are awake when I return to the queen's apartments, and two of them are nesting in her bed. The dauphin, Louis-Joseph, is gone, no doubt to be examined by a physician before any outing for the day. Louis-Charles is quietly setting up an intricate battle at the foot, having molded the silk covers into hills and trenches. Marie-Thérèse lies curled at her mother's side, speaking softly of a dream, oblivious to the fact that her mother is only half-listening, if the expression on the queen's face is any indication. She stares as if the gilded walls of the chamber have disappeared, leaving vast plains of someplace both fearful and wonderful before her. Protocol demands that I not speak until she speaks to me, and though I'm standing squarely in her vacant gaze, she is gently startled when she finally sees me.

"You have found them? The boots. Children are so careless with their things."

"*Oui, madame.* I have also this, from His Majesty." None of her ladies are in the room, so I'm compelled to give her the note myself. She does not dismiss me, so I'm forced to watch while she opens it, adjusts the paper to her weak vision, and takes in the brief message. Her countenance loses all traces of contentment. Not all at once, but with the registering of each word, and her entire body ripples in a sigh of disappointment. She transforms before me, aging into a woman with thinning hair and shadowed eyes. Nothing about this woman would invite salacious ridicule. She is not an enemy of France, but a woman trapped within its dictates. Her daughter senses the change.

"*Maman?*"

"We are not to have a sleigh ride today, *chérie.*" She crumples the paper in one hand and pulls Marie-Thérèse close with the other. "*Papa le Roi* says we mustn't."

"Why?" The princess whines and pouts. Though in face and feature she looks like a replica of her mother, here the difference shows clear. Perhaps, as I imagine, the queen was petulant on her arrival as a child bride deposited in an unfamiliar country, but now a hardened woman lurks beneath the soft flesh clearly displayed within the billows of her nightdress.

Though I doubt Louis said as much in his quick missive, she says, "He thinks it is too Austrian. And that we won't appear to be loyal to France if we do." Her tone is flippant, but I hear a wistfulness in her voice. She notices me again. "You grew up in this country, did you not, *couturière*? Out and away from here. Did you never go for a sleigh ride on such a fine winter's day as this?"

"Non, Madame la Reine." I don't know if her look of surprise came from my response or the fact that I took no time to consider or remember.

"*Jamais?* Never? But certainly such an activity is no great luxury. We—that is, my former country—cannot be the only people to engage."

"Most of the people—all of the people—that I know are poor, *madame*. If a farmer must choose to have wheels or runners, he must choose that which will be used more often. When the snow is too deep to drive a cart, we stay home. And to drive a horse through snow at any speed is impractical. Grain is expensive, and often our animals are quite weak during the winter. Perhaps the king—" I stop myself not only because I fear I am overstepping the boundaries of my response, but also because, were I to be completely correct, the objection came not from the king, but his advisers. The note, though written in the hand of her husband, was not, as I'd witnessed, a message from his heart.

"Go on," she prompts, allowing me to change course.

"Perhaps the objection is not so much about France, but

about the poor. This has been a particularly harsh winter. You have said it is no great luxury. But to people like us, it is unimaginable. Maybe he wants to spare the feelings of those who could never afford such an indulgence."

"But do people—your people—really watch us so closely? Why do you care?"

"We don't watch you," I say, picking my words like slivers in a finger. "We can't *see* you. But we hear. And we can only hear what we're told, and sometimes, *madame*, we aren't told the whole truth. If we only hear from your enemies, we think you are our enemy."

"Enemy!" Louis Charles shouts, furiously pitting his soldiers against each other.

"Maman?" Marie-Thérèse sounds frightened. "What does that mean?"

The queen strokes her daughter's hair and makes a soft shushing sound. Even without words, it sounds nothing like French. She bends, kisses her daughter, and looks at me. "Is that what you think?"

"No, *madame. Pardon*, of course not. I only wish that everyone could see you as you are now."

"But then I would not be queen. I would be like any other woman worried about feeding her horse throughout the winter."

"Even worse. You have to worry about feeding an entire country."

Her head drops with the weight of the idea.

"I think, perhaps," I continue, "it is just as well. The dauphin's boots were not properly dried. Or—and I do not intend to insult a craftsman—constructed. Were he to wear them out today, he might fall ill. Give me some time to stitch in a better lining, and in the afternoon, when the sun is out and it's a bit warmer, you could all go for a New Year's walk together. That's what we liked to do when I was a child."

She laughs. "You are still very much a child."

I smile a consent. "We would find an unbroken field. Gagnon would instruct us to walk in it and make our mark. Make designs with our steps."

Marie-Thérèse perked up. "What design would you make?"

I turn my full attention to her. "I would build." And as I speak, the memory is so clear I can feel my hands burning with the cold of the snow. "I would build a gown. Pile the snow into a skirt." I mime the actions as I speak. "Form a waist, a bust. I would spend hours sprinkling it with evergreen needles and branches. Oh, if you could see."

Marie-Thérèse is entranced, and I feel somewhat guilty at how quickly the idea of the sleigh ride has been abandoned.

"We will walk," the queen says. "We will make our mark." She sends the children away to wash up and dress and take breakfast. I assume I am dismissed too, but the queen stops me. "I have a gift for you, *couturière*."

"A gift, *madame*?"

"For the New Year." She climbs out of bed and crosses the room to an ornate chest of drawers, lacquered white with a floral print accented with gold leaf. She opens one of the small drawers on the top row, rummages for just a moment, and comes away. "I'm sorry to say I do not remember who gave this to me initially. I get so many things, you know. Too many. For a year I honestly had no idea of its purpose, and now that I know, I have no use for it."

I smile, wondering if she has any idea of the ungracious connotation of her words, but at the same time I bubble with the anticipation of receiving a gift from the queen. When she places it in my hand, I am in awe of what she's given me. It fits as if by design, gold filigree warm against my palm.

"A knotting shuttle," I say, to make sure the queen knows I understand its function as well as its beauty. "It's exquisite."

"You know what this is?"

"*Oui.* I have a friend, back home," I say, speaking of Elianne Girard. "She had one—not nearly as beautiful as this. Bone, I think. It was one of the few things I truly envied. She didn't know how to use it at first, either." Too late, I realize this might be insulting, to equate the queen of France with an unknown farm girl back home, but she laughs.

"Perhaps, then, people are not so different after all. And you? Do you know what to do with this thing?"

This thing. Worth more than anything I've ever known in my lifetime. "Not now, but I can learn. I'm sure one of the women here can teach me. Or, I'm clever. I'll teach myself." I finally tear my eyes away from this treasure. "Thank you, *madame.* Your Highness, thank you so much. I—I didn't think to get a gift for you. I had no idea . . ."

To my utter surprise, she reaches and tucks her hand under my chin. "You gave me a great kindness this morning, my girl. Insight—something I know how to use. Never underestimate the value of loyalty."

L'épisode 16

Laurette

MOUTON BLANC

On Christmas Day Monsieur Girard had sent word to every family within an hour's walk to come to his home the following week for a New Year's dinner. Each was to bring two loaves of bread, one other offering, their own plates and cups and spoons, and a contribution of firewood. They arrived to find a rough-constructed table stretched from one end of the great room to the other.

Laurette had been in the Girards' home dozens of times, and while it was larger than Gagnon's, she would never have considered it grand until this day. The walls seemed to stretch to accommodate the party—fourteen in all: Monsieur and Madame Girard, Elianne, Gagnon with Laurette and the boys, the aged Monsieur and Madame Tournac, and the Norrin family. The three Norrin children tumbled into the Girards' house looking like nothing more than bundles of listless rags. Round, hollow eyes stared out above layers of mufflers, and even when they'd been freed from their winter wear, they did little more than cling to their mother, leaving great trails of snot on her skirt. Soon, though, the fire warmed them, and Philippe and Nicolas had them entranced, taking turns in a peg-board game.

"They are good big brothers, *non*?" Gagnon held the youngest Norrin while its mother unpacked their offering to the meal. Laurette looked on, able to decipher neither the nature of the Norrins' food nor the gender of the child in Gagnon's arms. The food was a greasy gray mass half-filling a wooden bowl. "Gravy," Madame Norrin explained, "though it turned mostly solid on the walk." Laurette's stomach, empty as it was, lurched at the thought of it.

Then, to her surprise, it lurched again in a completely different way at the sight of Gagnon and the child. It couldn't have been more than two years old, with soft brown wisps jutting from beneath a knit cap. Tiny hands protruded from a shirt that must have been handed down from an older sibling, because the sleeves were rolled and rolled to cut the length in half. The child had gone to Gagnon's arms as naturally as if it belonged in such a place, much to the relief of its mother and indifference of its father. Gagnon cupped his hand against the knit cap and pulled the child close to whisper something Laurette desperately wished to hear.

The child whispered back.

"Jeannette!" He pronounced the name victoriously and commenced a stroll around the room, singing:

"Ne pleure pas, Jeannette,
Tra-la-la-la-la-la-la-la-la-la-la
Ne pleure pas, Jeannette,
Nous te marierons, nous te marierons."

It was an ancient song of tragic love, but Gagnon simply sang the first verse over and over, promising to find a man to marry the weeping Jeannette. He bounced her in his arms with every *tra-la-la* until her solemn expression was transformed and her sweet voice chimed in.

"He was meant to be a father." This, spoken straight to Laurette's ear by Elianne Girard. If a woman's gaze could bring a man's child to her belly, Gagnon would be a father by nightfall.

"He is as good as a father to Philippe and Nicolas," Laurette said.

"And to you, *non*? Orphan child taken in?"

"And to me." Though she had always thought of Gagnon as a peer, if an older one. And in this moment especially, she didn't see Gagnon in any fatherly light. He'd let his beard grow during the winter, a soft covering of dark copper that masked the gauntness of his face. Little Jeannette reached up a hand to touch it, and Laurette's fingertips twitched in jealousy. When he broke off his song to growl like a bear and nibble her tiny fingers, she squealed in delight.

Laurette brought her own to her lips. They were red and chapped, nails bitten down to the quick. One finger, the third on her right hand, sat at a strange angle, never having healed properly after her hand had been caught under the hoof of a startled goat. She had the hands of an old woman at nineteen.

"He needs a wife, *mon amie*." Elianne stood beside her, speaking out of the corner of her mouth. "And if it's not you or me, then that little brat will grow up and snatch him away."

Laurette forced a laugh and jabbed her elbow. "I believe he'd wait that long before taking either of us."

The meal was plentiful enough to have been served on a mountain by the Savior himself—or so claimed Girard. But he spoke something near the truth. Plates were passed more than once, and even when the guests sat back declaring they couldn't hold another bite, some dishes in the center still held traces of food. Two loaves of bread remained intact, and even Madame

Norrin's gravy found a home mixed with another sauce and poured onto plates to be mopped up with crusts.

"There is no better way," Girard said, "to usher in a New Year than to do so with a full stomach."

Voices rose in agreement.

"And with prayer," Gagnon said when silence settled again. He stood and crossed himself. "In the name of the Father and the Son and the Holy Ghost . . . ," and he entered into a prayer of thanksgiving for the bounty of their feast and the health of those gathered, though the Norrins' middle child burst forth in a rattling cough. He prayed good health and fortune to our king and our queen and their children and our land. And he asked that God would remember all of them in the year to come. The year of our Lord, 1789. That the decade would end in peace and prosperity for all.

All gathered said amen and opened their eyes to find Gagnon waiting with a wide grin.

"Good food," he said, "full stomachs, and prayer. And?" He looked to old Monsieur Tournac.

The old man sported his own sparse-toothed grin. "Wine!" he declared, bringing out—with the help of Monsieur Norrin—a good-sized jug from beneath the table.

"À la bonne année!" the party shouted, one echoing to the other as cups were filled and clattered together. Nicolas, Philippe, and even the older Norrin children were given a celebratory amount, and in the spirit of the holiday, Laurette touched her cup to Elianne's.

The evening was spent in conversation, stories about the days when Mouton Blanc was a thriving town, when *le roi* was still a harmless boy married to a strange foreign girl, and when—while none of them lived in excess—there was never a New Year's Day spent wondering if there would be food enough until spring. Laurette sat back, her dwindling cup of wine providing a slow, steady stream of warmth, listening. She had no stories to contribute. These days were before her time. Before Gagnon's, too, as his contributions were through the eyes of a bright-futured boy.

What she lacked in story she made up for in song. During the lulls between tales, someone would hum a tune, and she bravely ventured in, ever confident of her voice. They sang carols that dated back to Charlemagne, ballads that told stories of young lovers destined to be apart. To her surprise, old Tournac led them in a bawdy tune that made Madame Tournac swat at his arm repeatedly, though she blushed and joined in on the rollicking chorus.

Darkness fell, taking the great room with it. Philippe and Nicolas sat in the middle of the floor, their backs propped up against each other, heads nodding in sleep. The Norrin children had been assigned to laps—Madame Norrin and Elianne with the older two, little Jeannette coiled upon the enthralled Madame Tournac. Her curly head nestled in the old woman's shoulder; no doubt both were grateful for the extra warmth. Lit only by the dying fire, as no one wanted to dislodge themselves to light a candle, the party turned to shadows. Girard poked halfheartedly at the fire, sending a few sparks. "Say, Gagnon," he said, tossing on a final log, "what do you know of that girl Renée?"

"That she is well," Gagnon said in a way that prompted no further question. He and Laurette sat next to each other on one of the dining benches, close enough that, on several occasions throughout the evening, their shoulders touched, or their arms, even their hands in gesture. He pressed against her now, purposefully, lest she try to add to his statement. Under any other circumstances, his prompting would suffice, but she was warm with wine and fire and song, and she leaned forward to escape.

"Well she may be, but she'd be a fine sight happier here. At home. It is enough."

"Home," they echoed, and a silence descended, deeper than any other of the evening.

"One more song," Gagnon said, "before we head out to *our* home."

"Surely not," Elianne said with a force strong enough to disturb the child in her lap. "*Papa*, we can't let them go. It's late. It's dark."

"It's a clear night," Gagnon said. "And we've Cossette with us. She could lead us home blindfolded."

"Do you mean if she were blindfolded?" Nicolas piped up. "Or if we were?"

Gagnon laughed. "Both."

"Are you sure?" Girard asked. "There's room enough on the floor. Or we'll all be warm packed together in the beds."

"I am sure." To punctuate, he stood and stretched, emitting an enormous yawn that caused all in the room to follow suit. Even the sleeping Jeannette.

Elianne did her best to appear enticing, drawing the drowsy child on her lap closer. "You said one more song."

"On second thought, maybe it's best not to disturb the little one," Gagnon said, touching his hand to her cheek. "Besides, I should save my voice to sing us home, right, boys?" Philippe and Nicolas groaned good-naturedly as he reached down to haul them to their feet.

"Take your bread with you," Madame Girard said with a lazy wave of her hand. "We've not touched it."

"It will only freeze on the walk. Come, Laurette. Help me get our things."

After a flurry of lamplight and well wishes and worry, they were wrapped toe-to-nose in coats and scarves, three socks within each boot, and caps pulled low over their brows. Gagnon was correct about the night being clear. The moon shone bright on the snow; the stars glittered like sunlight on a stream. Girard sent them home with a lamp, which Nicolas carried out in front, Philippe close at hand. The path they'd cut on the way to Girard's was still fresh, as there'd been no snowfall that day, and only occasionally did one of the boys drop off into a fresh drift.

"That's why you're in front!" Gagnon shouted, though the night and the snow muffled his voice. "You find all the traps!"

Not even halfway home, Laurette felt the cold seeping through all the layers of clothing, and as she had no more layers of flesh, the chill settled into her very bones. "Why did we have to leave?" She hated the complaining tone in her voice but felt powerless to corral it. "We could have spent the night. I'd welcome a warm floor right now."

"There wouldn't have been enough food in the morning if we'd stayed. Think of it: four more mouths to feed."

"I told Madame Girard to make *pain perdu*. It would have fed the crowd."

"Mmmm . . . will you make that for our breakfast?"

"With what? You gave away all of our bread."

"Then will you make more bread?"

She murmured something like an agreement, not wanting to invite more cold air with speech. Feeling cold was becoming something from the distant past; her body had gone beyond to a place of near numbness. Her feet were a memory, her legs a dissolving dream. Her thoughts a swirling mass—*bread*? Bread. Making bread . . .

Gagnon nudged her shoulder. "We're halfway, Laurette. Will you make it?"

Yes. What choice did she have?

"Tell you what—I'll sing. And by the time I get to the end of the song, we should be at the crest of the valley. *D'accord?*" Then, never one to wait for permission, he began: "'*Ne pleure pas, Jeannette—*'"

"Why are all the songs about Jeannette?"

"Are they? I haven't noticed. But if it makes you happy, I will change the lyrics just for you. *'Ne pleure pas, Laurette . . .'*" He sang the entire story of the tragic Jeannette—Laurette—and her love for the imprisoned Pierre, with whom she would rather die than marry a nobleman of her father's choosing. The ballad was eight verses long, with the lyrical *tra-la-la-la-la-la-la* intercepting each, and ended on the darkly comic note of the tragic Jeannette hanging with her beloved. It took some forced stretching of the notes in the chorus, but true to his prediction, they were at the crest of the valley when the last note wafted to the stars.

"Tell me, Laurette," he said, taking her arm to steady her down the slope. The boys and Cossette had gone ahead, half-running, half-rolling. "Would you make the same choice as the girl in the song? Would you marry a prisoner over a prince? Would you rather marry one of our weak, lifeless royals, or die for your lover?"

His tone was jovial, meant to keep her awake and engaged for the final steps, but her brain was too clouded for the question. Why would she die? And who was her lover? A pauper? A prisoner? A prince? She was nobody, had nobody. She muttered a response, and at Gagnon's prompting, repeated it. "I'll never marry."

"Oh." He made a sound of sympathetic disapproval. "And why would you say that, my Laurette?"

"Because I'll never leave you, Gagnon. And you'll never marry me."

She felt her lips move against the muffler, unsure if she had spoken the words loud enough for him to hear. He said nothing in response but brought his arm around her for an embrace strong enough to bring her home. There, a small fire burned, making the inside of the house only marginally warmer than outside. Its surly attendant added a log when they came in.

"You're home."

"We are," Gagnon answered, escorting Laurette closer.

"I still don't understand why I could not have accompanied you instead of wasting here, bringing in the New Year alone."

"The party was for friends and family only, Marcel. I count you as neither."

"Nobody asked about me?"

"Non."

"And you've brought me nothing home to eat?"

"Should I take food from the mouths of children to feed you, grown man? Bad enough you take from my table each day."

The argument thrummed in Laurette's ears like a pulse. It sparked daily, almost, brought on by too many hours in too close quarters without enough work to fill the day or food to fill the plates.

"I met our bargain," Marcel said, as was his reliable defense.

"With grain stolen from poor farmers just like me, no doubt."

"You've no problem feeding it to them. I don't see your sheep starving. Unlike me—"

"Stop!" Laurette wished for a moment for the muffled sound of a snowy night.

"Boys," Gagnon said, turning his attention to Philippe and Nicolas. "Take your stone and off to bed."

The boys knew better than to put up a fuss. Philippe took the metal tongs from their place on the hearth and picked up the large, smooth stone that had spent the evening in the direct heat of the fire. He carried it carefully to the bedroom he shared with his brother and Marcel, the three of them coming to nightly agreements as to who would get a spot on the bed and who would be stretched on the floor. Tonight, after a long, late walk, there would be no question.

Next, to Laurette, "Go into our room. Take off your boots and socks. I want to see your feet."

Thankful to miss the last remnant of the argument, Laurette—like the boys—obeyed. She took no candle, not trusting her fingers to grip one properly, but relied on her memory to guide her to the bed. She peeled off her gloves, letting them fall to the floor in a careless manner she would never permit under any other circumstances. Her hands were sore but apparently free of frost. All of the layers of clothing, scarves, shawl, and coat made it difficult for her to bend to reach her shoes. After a few grunting tries, she sat up, frustrated, and waited.

"It's getting colder every minute," Gagnon said when he arrived, carrying a lamp in one hand and a warming brick gripped by the tongs in the other. "I'll build a fire in here tonight."

A rare luxury. "What about the b-b-b-boys?" As she thawed, her teeth chattered.

"Them, too. Have no fear. Marcel will no doubt build a small inferno. Now, let me see." He lifted the bottom corner of the blanket and ran the brick beneath it before kneeling at Laurette's feet, gently removing her boots and one sock after another until he held her bare skin in his hands. He touched them gently, careful not to rub the flesh, and declared them beautiful and fine.

"My f-f-f-feet are not b-b-b-beautiful."

"On a night like this, any foot that is not frozen is beautiful." He wrapped them loosely in soft wool and instructed her to get beneath the covers while the stone was still warm. This she did, his back turned to her as he built a small fire in the stove. Somehow she knew she would be asleep before its warmth took hold, but felt comfort knowing it would blaze away while she dreamed. Slowly, still somewhat hampered by numbness in her fingers, she stripped to her chemise, moving carefully so as not to dislodge the soft wrapping on her feet. She climbed into the bed—*her* side—and pulled the covers up to her chin.

It was, by now, routine, the same as that first night when Gagnon had explained, calming her fears.

"You'll be warmest in here. With me. And safe."

"Safe from what?"

"Safe from him."

And then, like that first night, when she assured him she was *settled*, he opened the door and whistled, calling in Cossette, who jumped up and laid herself along the length of her. Laurette sneaked a hand out from under the cover and ran it through the thick, reassuring fur. Long after the fire died, the dog would keep her warm.

Then, too, like that first night, like every night, she listened to Gagnon undress, don his sleeping shirt, and kneel at the bedside to pray, imagining the sharpness of the cold floor against his bare knees. When he at last climbed into bed, he, too, reached a hand to Cossette's fur, this time—for the first time—finding Laurette's there. He held it, briefly. Too briefly.

L'épisode 17

Renée

VERSAILLES

I've taken myself to the farthest corner of the sewing room and have been hunched over here for the better part of two days. Tomorrow will be the fourth birthday of the youngest prince, and I have been charged with making the suits for both of the royal sons. Doing so for Louis-Charles is nothing taxing—thus I've been given full charge. Breeches and a waistcoat in a pale-blue velvet, befitting the colors of the Bourbons. I crafted a narrow collar, as he still tends to be messy when he eats, and I want no stains to mar his princely appearance. The sash, however, is a deep, dark indigo—wide enough to cover the lion's share of his breast to catch and hide any bits of chocolate or sauce that might dribble from his fingers. I've stitched a ribbon of interlocking dolphins—his favorite—up the calves of his stockings and instructed the shoemaker to add matching brass buckles.

The dauphin, however, is more of a challenge, and while I might be insulted at the simple task of stitching the younger brother's suit, I'm honored to have been given the responsibility for the elder's.

I'd always noticed something ungainly about Louis-Joseph's gait, but when he is not in the protective care of a governess, he is at his father's side or tucked up against his mother. He's never taken any particular interest in me, and truthfully neither have I in him. Where Marie-Thérèse seeks me out to help her create fashions for her dolls (or, more lately, for herself), and little Louis-Charles has the kind of bubbling, trusting spirit that makes him instantly friends with anyone who crosses his path, the dauphin is more guarded. He chases after nothing, tumbles nowhere, and talks in a hesitant, whining whisper that I can easily ignore.

"He has trouble with his spine, you see," the queen said when she drew me into her apartments the day they began planning his brother's birthday festivities. A low-faced Louis-Joseph stood beside her, and a dour governess behind him looking like she would need no prompting to leap over him and break me to pieces should I make any move or noise of harm. "Go ahead, Louis," the queen prompted. "Show her."

Keeping his eyes downcast, the boy slowly removed his voluminous shirt and revealed a monstrosity beneath. A corset, more like a cage, not like those we women wear to force our bodies to conform to fashion, but unyielding ribs of iron meant to discipline the boy's spine. It wrapped him from just below his arms to just below his hips, and when he finally lifted his face to look at me, his eyes spilled over with shame.

"Well, look at that!" I forced a bit of cheer into my voice. "It's like you have your own suit of iron. *Un véritable chevalier.*"

"I'm not a knight," he said, eyes downcast again. "I'm to be king."

"But of course," I soothed. "All the more reason to keep you safe and protected."

"I hate it," he said, and I could see why. Each rod was separated by a strip of thick canvas, all of it unyielding. Even with the light wool shirt he wore underneath, the contraption had to be a constant source of irritation. Immediately, I repented of all my thoughts that labeled him as sullen and lazy. The poor boy's burden was kept a secret from the court, and certainly from the people.

Now that I know, I've been employed to keep it too.

That very afternoon I made him a shirt of fine linen with a layer of soft wool batting, quilted with stitches running counter to the rods of the corset. The next morning, the queen summoned me to tell me how pleased Louis-Joseph had been, how very comfortable and bearable the shirt made the corset, and I had to bite my tongue to keep from asking why no one had ever thought to do such a simple thing before.

My challenge, then, was to find a way to hide his contraption from the prying eyes at court. Until now he's been wearing wide-cut jackets, but his little brother was graduating to that same style of clothing, and the time had come for a more sophisticated cut to the dauphin's *habillement.* I took his measurements and drafted a pattern that would narrow at the waist and have a flared hem to cover the bottom edge of the corset, the structure of the jacket giving the impression that it fits closer to his body than it actually does. As for the shirt underneath, I stitched a generous row of ruffles to serve not only as a two-tiered collar in front, but as a cascade that falls to his shoulder blades to hide the top.

The collar will serve another purpose, too. While the boy's irregular steps could point to an infirmity that might follow him into old age, other aspects of his health do not. I've heard in whispers that the king's oldest living son is not a healthy child. That he was taken away from the palace for a time to live in the château at Boulogne, where the king considered the very air healthier than he would breathe at Versailles. Since the turning of the New Year, though, there has been no sign he will outgrow this disease and live to be a man. Days spent abed, with fits of coughing rumored to be so severe, it is like his very life spews out upon the sheets. Even with my limited interaction with him, I can see how pale he's become, the faint blue shadows under his eyes in sharp contrast to the porcelain translucence of his skin. And so, the collar is designed to be a refuge should he take ill at his brother's celebration, to cover and catch his spasms. The material is a rich, absorbent wool, dyed by my own hand to the darkest shade of blue, lest—as has happened—he emits a stream of blood with his attack.

I sew secrets in every stitch, for it is important now more than ever for the family to maintain an aura of strength as the head of this unsettled country. For it, too, is sick. Weakened by drought, crippled by winter. As often as the dauphin takes to his bed, the villages around Paris rise up in protest. More than ever as I linger at the edges of the court, I hear stories of the frightened bourgeoisie, recounting tales of tax collectors being tarred, sheriffs forced at knifepoint to release prisoners of debt. They say there's nothing to eat, nothing to sell, nothing to trade. The worst they've seen in more than a decade, when peasants revolted at the scarcity of flour. I remember Gagnon telling me about those days.

"*La guerre.* War, with wheat as the weapon."

I keep my ears sharp for any mention of Mouton Blanc. By and large, our town seems to have escaped such violence, mostly due to men like Gagnon, and his father before him, and Monsieur Girard, and others who keep level heads and faithful hearts. But . . .

I lift my head from stitching the heavy hem that will keep Louis-Joseph's ruffled collar weighted in place. A year. An entire year has passed since I climbed into that carriage with Madame

Gisela. More than seven months since I gave Marcel my fortune. I've not heard a word back from him, and it's only during times like this, when I am engaged in mundane stitchery, that my mind wanders back to that night. Except, of course, when I think of Bertrand.

At the thought, I experience a rare slip of the needle and, pricking my finger, test the collar's ability to disguise the sight of blood. I smile as I bring it to my lips.

There is a knot of pain between my shoulder blades, and my fingers are cramped into place when I put the final stitch into the dauphin's suit. It is well into the evening, I can guess. The sky on the other side of the high row of narrow windows is still gray, but the room has been abandoned by my fellow tirewomen. They no doubt have gone to the servants' hall for supper, but the thought of elbowing my way to a place at the long, crowded, noisy table steals any appetite.

Instead, I make my way into the kitchen—the one dedicated to the feeding of the staff—and look for Agnès. She is a sturdy woman who could be aged anywhere from forty to sixty. I have never seen her without a cloud of urgency about her, one arm stirring, another reaching, her feet ready to take her from one table to the next to inspect the work of the undercooks.

"Supper's not for an hour," she says without losing count of her whips in the white stuff frothing around her spoon. "Not my fault that you haven't eaten yet today. Now, off."

"Could I eat if I fend for myself?"

"No dishes," Agnès says, pacing her words with her whips. "And take it out of here. I've got enough bodies to trip over."

"*Merci*, Agnès," I say and begin spying around the crowded countertops. I walk away with a jar half-filled with milk, two small brown rolls, and a square of cloth with a last bit of soft cheese inside. Already I know the cheese will be good, but nothing as rich and satisfying as Laurette's. Not for the first time I wonder what it would have been like if I'd asked her to come with me. She could have worked here in the kitchen, and the two of us could have found a bunk together, just like at home. But then a spirit of selfishness kicks in, for I don't know that I want to share all that I have. Versailles itself is an enormous house, but we all live very small lives here. Just as Laurette didn't want to share Marcel, I don't want to share my queen. Or her children. Or Bertrand. I wouldn't worry about sharing wealth because I have none of that. And I hardly know a day of leisure. Still, I am *somebody* here. I am *la couturière*. I am known and recognized, and now I've been entrusted with a royal secret, which I hold close to my heart.

All too happy to leave the kitchen, I take my food out to the gardens. There are still dozens of people—noble, no doubt, in their finery—strolling the wide pathway, but they give me no mind. I'm a fixture, the odd girl in the patched skirt. *La couturière*, though in these days I find my services less and less in demand. The grand balls and lavish suppers have all but ceased, with the exception of the youngest prince's birthday tomorrow. They say it is unseemly to put on such displays of wealth when so many are hungry, and lately when the king and queen present themselves to the public, they are met with boos and jeers and all manner of missiles. Unmentionable stains on the queen's gowns.

This evening, the visitors at Versailles, those who bother to notice me at all, perceive me in the same vein as the queen's dogs. Small, interesting, harmless. A few even take a moment to nod and say *"Bonsoir"* as I pass, and I pause in my steps to curtsy.

As the night grows darker, the orange light from the torches takes hold, and I quicken my steps to get a glimpse of my favorite fountain before full darkness descends. I've often thought that if I ever had the chance to welcome Gagnon here as a visitor, I would walk him straight through the palace without stopping and bring him here, to Apollo's fountain. It is a work of art that stole my breath the first time I saw it, exploring one evening weeks after my arrival. It still catches me unaware with its grandeur—the sight of the four horses bursting from the water, the god Apollo with the reins gripped in one hand, ready to drive his fiery chariot across the sky. Gagnon would tell the story of Apollo defeating the python. Before, when he told tales of Poseidon, his son Triton, and the conch he blew to command the sea, I could not bring my mind to create a picture, never having seen a sea, or a conch, or a merman. Here, the myth comes to life, and I think it is such a waste on the nobles who get to drink in its beauty every day, ignorant of the stories.

I settle myself on the narrow wall and whisper a blessing over my food.

A familiar voice says, "I knew I'd find you here," just as he did the evening of our first encounter. Bertrand's red coat is open to reveal his white shirt—open too. He's removed his hat and sword, both clutched loosely in his hand. "Have you ever seen it at dawn? When the sun hits, you'd think he really was a god, taking all the light and reflecting it back to us."

"I haven't, but I will now, someday. How is it you've escaped your duty?"

"It's my time to rest, but I knew I would not rest until I saw you. It's been days."

"Has it?" I pat the wall for him to sit next to me. "I hadn't noticed."

"I noticed for both of us."

And he kisses me. Not for the first time, either. Spring has blossomed with our kisses. Whenever we find ourselves with a moment, and a shadow, and a willingness to deny the danger of our action. The first was on a winter's night, after months of casting gazes aside and avoiding the smallest greetings when we passed. I'd come across him en route to his barracks, and I threw myself in his path, desperate to explain my transaction with Marcel.

"I gave him money, that's all. To take home to my cousin. I stitched it into his pocket. He is nothing. He means nothing . . ." My protests floated out on the cloud of my breath, and Bertrand interceded, passing his lips straight through and pressing them to mine.

Now his kiss is more gentle, but no less fervent, and I forget about my hunger and my aches as my body becomes full and fluid—a warm bath flowing beneath my skin, matched to the lapping of the water in the pool behind me. I feel him pull away, and open my eyes to see him looking at me with such earnestness, I can only respond with nervous laughter.

"What's so funny?" he asks.

"What's so serious?" I expect him to laugh with me, but his countenance sets. And now I'm growing fearful. "Bertrand?"

For the first time since I've known him he seems uneasy, and he shifts away, turning so I see his profile as he folds his hands loosely between his knees and gazes down upon them. For a moment I think he might be in prayer, though one with his eyes open, searching for God's answer in the tiles of the walkway. But when he speaks, he speaks to me. "I think we should go."

"Go? *Go* where?" My heart races because I know. I've known since our first kiss—maybe since the first time we saw each other—that this moment would come. There had been times, when we found true seclusion and freedom from duties, that I thought I could not kiss him enough, could not hold him close enough, could never get my fill of his touch and his words. And I knew, from the ragged nature of his breath and the violence with which he tore himself away, that he felt the same. Always, one of us would whisper, *"We should stop. We'll be seen."* The idea of interruption preserved my chastity more than any thought of sin. But now, with a cool head, I could rely upon my virtue. "Bertrand, I—I can't."

He looks at me quizzically, and as understanding dawns, flourishes a grin of pure delight then buries it in a kiss. When he pulls away, he is still smiling, but his eyes look beyond. "Not that you aren't tempting, but I mean *leave* this place. The palace. Versailles."

The shock of his suggestion quells my embarrassment. "Leave? But you guard the queen. You protect the mother of our nation. You can't just *leave*."

"I'm not a slave, Renée. Nor are you. None of us are."

"There's a wide berth between compulsion and loyalty."

"And what if loyalty takes me away from the queen?" He turns his head to look straight at me.

"How could it?"

"What if I'm dispatched to go to put out all these rebellious fires springing up?"

"The king wouldn't do that. You're too valuable here."

"Apparently I'm valuable anywhere. And if the king wants a show of military strength to intimidate the rebels, who's to say I wouldn't be first chosen to mount up and ride into some village to frighten some poor, starving farmer?"

"Have you been given any such order?"

"Non." He looks away again. "But I don't know what I would do if I were. I suppose in some ways I'm not entirely sure where my loyalty lies."

"With Her Majesty, of course." My answer is quick and sharp, as if I have some right to speak his response. Such boldness on my part should surprise him, as I'm sure few people ever speak to him this way, but he only regards me with his same measured, calm expression. When he speaks, it is with a tone of reassurance, as if I'm some kind of child with a fear of the dark unknown.

"With Her Majesty, of course. But as for the rest . . . I would give my life for the queen herself. But I don't want to take a life for the country."

I think about that moment, Bertrand's sword touched to Marcel's throat. Knowing Bertrand as I do now, I realize he would never have harmed Marcel. The lieutenant had been in far greater danger. I know, too, that Bertrand has been trained to kill. Would be expected to kill. I've never thought about whether or not he desired to kill—even an enemy. And who was the enemy of the king? Not another king. Not another country, but his own people. Farmers, craftsmen, peasants. The poor.

"Has it come to that?"

"It will, Renée. The people are hungry, and when there is no food, they'll be fueled by vengeance."

I put my hand on his arm. "All the more reason for you to stay. Here. It is no secret how much they hate her."

"Any man with a sword can take my place."

"It would take three."

Now he laughs, a low chuckle. "Think about your family, back in that little town you came from. What if royal troops showed up to keep order? Wouldn't you want someone like me there? One of you, on *your* side? Protecting *your* people?"

"My people are here now, Bertrand."

"But if I left—"

"You are not my only—I have Her Majesty. And the children."

"You're not a governess, Renée."

"I know—"

"You are a seamstress." He couldn't have been more clear in his intent to diminish my role.

"But today . . ." And I told him of the dauphin's suit, how I was asked especially to design and construct it. How the queen trusts no one but me with accessorizing her gowns, that I alone know how to strike the perfect balance to make her appear equally royal and modest and approachable. How Marie-Thérèse pouted because she was to have no new dress for her brother's party, as the queen declared she had two that had never been worn to a public appearance, and I appeased her by making her a skirt just like mine.

"Like yours?" Bertrand asks with the air of a man who doesn't tease me about my dress on a regular basis.

"Just like," I say, standing and offering a twirl. "The queen declared her daughter a Hapsburg gypsy and threatened to have her portrait painted in it just to infuriate her father."

"It's not often one sees a princess dressed in rags."

I hold my finger up to correct him. "*Royal* rags. Scraps from the finest gowns. But it made her happy."

He cups his hand to the back of my head and pulls me close. He murmurs, "You're a seamstress," against my lips and pulls away. He must think his kiss will take the edge off the insult. "There's a dozen or more women just like you who can take your place."

"There's not," I say, so offended by his declaration that I ignore the implication of it. Why would my place be vacant? "I'm a favorite of Her Majesty. Of the children."

"Ah yes." He is fully detached from me now. "A favorite. That's not a permanent position, you know. What was the name of that woman? Who enticed you to follow her here?"

"Madame Gisela." I already know his point. She was a favorite too. She brought me here as a token to secure her place. And then, suddenly, she was gone. Perhaps not suddenly at all, because by the time I myself marked her absence, weeks had gone by since I'd seen her. "What are you asking of me, Bertrand?"

"Nothing now. But soon." He gathers my hands in his and pulls us close to each other. He is sitting on the low wall, and I am standing, and my lips touch straight to his temple. "I've never known what it is to be my own man. To live on my own land."

"The king owns all the land." Such was the conversation during nearly every meal at Gagnon's table.

"Not forever. Not for long, from the talks."

The talks. Like those behind Girard's door.

"Would you even know what to *do* with land?"

He gives a sheepish grin and looks behind him. "I know a lot about horses."

"We'll be too poor to have horses."

Now the grin grows triumphant. "*We?* So you will go with me."

I take my hands away and study the pattern of my skirt. What most want to dismiss as poor gypsy patchwork, I see as hours of intricacy. Unlike my first foray, when I'd only had a single night to stitch, this creation was an homage to Mouton Blanc. Taken at a distance, one can clearly see the color gradation, from the blue sky falling right below my hips to the grazing green along the hem. White stitching swirls like wisps of cirrus clouds. (Gagnon taught me the different names.) Along the green, knots of wool, my sheep. Looking at my skirt I see two loves—my home in Mouton Blanc and my home here, for only here could I have the freedom and the means and the approval to while away time and fabric on such a frivolous garment.

"Are you asking me to leave tomorrow, Bertrand?"

"I'm asking you now."

"But to leave? When?"

He shrugs. "I don't know. But soon enough. When we can."

"Don't ask me again until you are ready to go. In the moment. Don't give me time to think and worry and plan. If I had known all my growing-up years that I would someday get into a carriage and assume life in a palace, I wouldn't have enjoyed a single day of the pastures and the sunlight. I would have known I was poor and been unsatisfied with all I had."

"I don't understand."

I touch his face, soft with whiskers. "All my life I've been content. Even when I had nothing, when I had only my cousin—both of us children—I was content. *She* knew I needed better. More. If you wait for me to decide it's time to leave, I never will. Because I'm content now. Don't make me long for something I do not have. For something I might never have."

He turns and kisses my palm. "You will have me, Renée, my love. For I do love you."

I want to retort that love is no more permanent than being a favorite. I think I might have loved Marcel once. For all I know Bertrand has been true to me since that winter's night, and I—of course—to him. But a declaration of love? I'll keep that tucked and stitched to my heart.

"Take your time," I say. "Make your plans and watch for your opportunity. And then, when our leaving will be a 'tomorrow,' come to me. Find me, and I will kiss the children good-bye a final time and follow you."

L'épisode 18

Laurette

MOUTON BLANC

That winter, more of the flock had been sacrificed for meat than any year in Laurette's memory. The grim expression on Gagnon's face every time he selected the weakest and touched his blade to its neck filled her with shame for her hunger. Not even the perpetually hungry boys could take joy in those feasts. They ate the roasted meat with reverence, spooning the stew with appetites fueled by desperation and regret. The pelts from those that would not live to the shearing were washed, though it was a sacrifice of firewood, and Laurette spent endless dark winter days carding them into fine, wispy strands.

Carding had always been Renée's job. Long winter nights meant tufts of soft, rolled wool piling up in the tall sack propped beside the chair. Laurette was clumsy with the carders at first, having only the vaguest memory of the process.

"Like this," Gagnon said on her first attempt, after she'd been able to produce nothing more than a gray mass more tangled than when she started. "It's important to keep them to the proper hand. Right in the right, left in the left." He turned the carders over and showed where, years before, he had burned the letters *D* and *G* into the wood. "See? This one? With the curves in the letter G? Like the curves of your fingers." He touched them, the fingers broken by the goat so long ago. "This handle in this hand. This other in the other. And you mustn't drag. If you can hear the nails scrape against each other, you're dragging too hard. *Attends?*"

Marcel spoke from his chair, closest to the fire. "Who knew you'd be so well suited for women's work, Gagnon?"

"It's a far sight better than being suited for no work at all, *mon ami.*"

That touch to her hands was the first since the New Year's night, and one of the few that transpired between them over the course of the rest of the winter. Their words were few, too, since it was almost always too cold to talk. The sharpness of the air pierced the throat.

Gagnon led in prayer every morning, evening, and meal—no matter if the meal were nothing more than warm broth and a single slice of bread. He quizzed the boys in the catechism, and Laurette listened to the answers, learning some for the first time. Marcel listened, too, though often not with quiet reverence.

"How did God form his people through Moses?" Gagnon asked. It was a bitter-cold afternoon. The small fire struggled to provide both light and heat, leaving all in the room huddled within a mass of gray. Except Gagnon, who sat closest to it, catechism tilted to the light.

Philippe and Nicolas responded in unison, "By setting them free from their captivity in Egypt."

"Exactly correct."

"And so," Marcel piped in, uninvited, "who is to get credit? The man, Moses, who risks his life and takes his staff in hand to defeat Pharaoh? Or God, who was content to watch from heaven throughout their enslavement?"

"God worked *through* Moses," Nicolas said, his response as sincere as he presumed the question to be.

"Yes," Marcel said, "but without Moses, there would be no action, and there'd have been no freedom. In times of great peril, my boys, God is useless."

A silence without fathom followed, broken only by the sound of tiny shards of ice hitting the windows. The boys were struck dumb at such blasphemy spoken aloud, Laurette in shock at Marcel's arrogance, and Gagnon clearly fighting the urge to strike the man dead on God's behalf. The hand not holding the catechism flexed in and out of a fist, and Laurette felt her own chest rising and falling to match the control of his breathing.

"You will not speak such of God in this house." Gagnon kept his eyes trained on the fire, not trusting himself to look at Marcel.

"We're bringing in a new age of freedom, *mon vieux*. A man can say—"

"Not in my house, see? I am sovereign in my home. A fifth generation within these very walls. It is *my* France within these walls. *My* God who protects us and gives us our bread every day." By now he was out of his chair, brandishing the catechism just short of Marcel's nose. "You may choose not to acknowledge him as you wish, but I will not allow you to speak aloud against him, do you understand? It is the least you can do, as you eat *his* bread, and you are warmed by *his* fire, and you are protected by *his* walls, *his* roof."

The boys had scuttled across the floor to cower at Laurette's side, neither of them ever having seen such a display of temper. She had, but in the past his anger had been sheathed in a frighteningly calm demeanor. The display before her seemed to be that of a man on the brink of explosion.

"Comprenez-vous?" This question he addressed to all, sweeping the catechism in a wide arc, lest the boys or Laurette be

tempted to complaint by Marcel's boldness. All but he answered vocally *oui*, and Gagnon continued the lesson. Laurette returned to her carding, and Marcel returned to reading one of the dozen pamphlets he'd peruse until it grew too dark to read.

When that darkness came, Laurette set a pot of goat's milk to warm over the fire, which later she would pour over cubes of dark, stale bread. This was their supper nearly every night, and all took themselves to bed before the sensation of fullness—no matter how incomplete—wore off. The boys went to Laurette not only to give her a kiss good night, but to receive a swipe of lavender oil behind each ear, a precious substance to speed sleep. Then, with a hot stone from the hearth and one of the faithful dogs, they made their way to bed, with instructions to get straight under the covers and say their prayers from within. Sent off next, Laurette, at some point Marcel, and last, Gagnon, who often waited until he was sure she was asleep, though most nights he was wrong.

Nights like this night.

With the tension of the outburst still thick in the air, Laurette had taken herself off quicker than usual, bidding a hasty good night the moment Gagnon deposited her heated stone in the burlap sack she took to bed. Her feet warmed by the stone, her body warmed by the dog, she listened to the muted conversation coming from the great room. One low voice rumbled after the other, rancor diminished, their tones distinguishable even if their words were not.

When at last Gagnon came into the room, moving with expert silence in the dark, she made no pretense of sleeping.

"What did you say to him?"

"I said a lot of things." His weight disturbed the mattress, causing Cossette to let out a canine grumble.

"He's just passionate, you know."

"Oh, I'm well aware of his passions."

They rarely talked while sharing the bed, and never once about Marcel. "There's nothing like that between us, you know. Maybe once, a long time ago, but not now. I don't want him, Gagnon." She'd pulled the blanket up to her nose and felt the steam of her words.

"It's a good thing. Because one of these mornings, we will wake up and there will be birdsong in the air. And on that morning he leaves."

⚜

As in all things, Gagnon's words proved true. The first song of the lark still pierced the blinding shafts of sunrise when Marcel, pack thrown over his shoulder, disappeared on the horizon. The last weeks of winter had been unbearable—oppressive cold, cavernous hunger, and a physical closeness for which God had designed sheep, not human beings. Laurette had found herself spending hours in bed—sometimes close to entire days—for the sole purpose of solitude. And warmth. And a burning hope that she might dream of food and be a little satisfied in sleep. But she arose the morning Marcel left, giving him half a loaf of bread and a wedge of cheese for his breakfast while Gagnon and the boys attended to the morning chores. The house itself exhaled in his absence.

Spring came with the promise of eight new lambs, five goats, and sweet new grass sprung up in the absence of winter's snow. Somehow, as only boys can do in times of hunger, both Nicolas and Philippe managed to grow a full three inches over the winter, making even Nicolas tall enough to handily wrangle a sheep when the time came for shearing. The flock had thinned so, there'd be no need to hire even a single set of hands to help, which was fortunate because Gagnon had neither the funds to pay them nor the food to feed them.

Every day during that week in April, Laurette listened to

Gagnon giving special instruction to Philippe: how to hold the ewe, to direct the blades, to speak calmly and maintain control while she completed her task of cleaning the wool, trimming out clumps of dirt and other, smellier masses. She tried to pass this task on to Nicolas, but Gagnon laughingly refused.

"He's better suited to walking the animals into the barn."

"And what does that say of me?" Laurette asked, indignant. "That I'm better suited for snipping around the bottom half of a sheep?"

"Look at him." Gagnon pointed with his shears at the mud-speckled boy whose hair grew out as sharp as his bones. "Would you trust him to clean anything?"

They laughed, and another chip of winter fell away.

On the day he decided to take his wool into Mouton Blanc, Gagnon left before dawn to go to Girard's to borrow a cart and horse while Laurette made other preparations for the day's trade. Flour, of course—though she dreaded what price they'd pay for it. If rumors and all that Marcel railed about proved to be true, that expense alone could take half of Gagnon's pay. And seeds for her garden, a little sugar if there was any to be had. She'd also have to get word out that they needed to buy or trade for chickens, as their brood had been all but decimated over the winter. There'd be no luxury of clothing or shoes, though she'd see if she could find leather scraps to mend the ones they had. All of this she recorded in her mind, envisioning the market, seeing the booths and storefronts, planning the route she'd take while Gagnon shouted with the others in the weighing house, fighting for his price.

She'd just given the boys their orders for the day—to air out the tickings from their loft beds and check every fence post in the sheep corral—when the Girards' cart came into view with two distinct silhouettes on the seat. Gagnon, of course, she recognized, even at a distance with the sun behind obscuring all features. The other she knew only to be a woman, thin and hunched. Elianne.

"I have my own trading to do," Elianne said as soon as Gagnon brought the wagon to a stop. "So *Papa* suggested I go with you."

"Did he?" Laurette lifted her hand as a pretense of shielding her eyes but sent Gagnon a hidden look of amusement. "Well, isn't your father exceedingly logical?"

"You can tell her what we need and stay here if you like," Gagnon said. "I know there's much to do."

"Nonsense. I'll be ready to go as soon as you and the boys load the wagon."

Without extending any invitation to Elianne, Laurette took herself inside and went straight to the room she'd reclaimed the morning of the first birdsong. She ripped off the rag tied around her head and ran her fingers through her hair before plaiting it into a single, loose braid. The skirt she wore was the only one that fit around her emaciated frame, but she did have one chemise cleaner than what she currently wore, and the green vest stitched with peacock feathers, though it, too, looked depleted. In the kitchen, she added another few slices of bread to the sack dinner she'd prepared and congratulated herself on her generosity of spirit. There was no way to stretch the cheese.

They rode with sparse conversation, Elianne in the middle, talking about little more than the relief of the spring and the hope of a better summer. Whenever possible, Laurette offered something tart, at which Gagnon would laugh and Elianne would appear confused.

At the first sight of Mouton Blanc, however, all three fell into a sober silence. It was one thing to see the dilapidated shacks on the outskirts of town looking all the worse for weathering the winter, but the market center itself looked to have fared no better. Every building appeared a lifeless gray, half the windows boarded up. The few people in the streets wandered with no outward show of purpose. The open market had completely disappeared. Not a single farmer with a single seed. Laurette thought of her garden, the patch of land that was meant to feed them for the summer and the months to follow.

"Where is everyone?" she asked, more to herself than Gagnon, but he answered anyway.

"Home. Hungry."

The only sign of normal life came at the weighing house, where a few familiar faces gathered at the door.

"Thank God the king still needs wool," Gagnon said, "because there's nobody left here to buy it."

Tradition held that no women—not even widows—were allowed into the weighing house, but Laurette had crossed that threshold before and had no qualms about doing so again. The world had changed since the first time Gagnon had left her and Renée as young girls sitting in the back of the wagon, legs dangling, with a sweet bun to eat while they waited. On this day she left Elianne to her own devices and walked beside him until Dubois met them at the door.

"N'entrez pas." His looming frame blocked her entrance. "It is men's business that we do in here."

Indeed she could hear the business roaring inside, men's voices raised, numbers shouted among a host of vulgarities and insults.

"Go," Gagnon said, seeming surprised that she'd accompanied him in the first place.

"Go? Where? There's nothing—"

"Wait outside with Elianne."

Laurette obeyed, but without any pretense of grace. She huffed past the stranded, bewildered Elianne and straight to the baker's, recognizable only by the faded signboard hanging above the door. There were no loaves in the window and no enticingly yeasty scent wafting through the open door. The shelves along the back wall were bare and the establishment empty until Madame Ledard came out of the back room, where the ever-burning brick ovens used to make this place a warm haven in winter.

"We've got nothing," she said, wiping her hands on her apron, though there was clearly no flour to dust away. "The man has journeyed three days out looking for flour, and God help us what the price will be when he finds it. Go home."

She turned to leave, but Laurette called out, "Wait. You're sure you have nothing? Not even a single sweet bun? That maybe you set aside for yourself but you'd take a trade for?"

Madame Ledard propped her hands on her ample hips. "What have you got to trade?"

Laurette felt the burn of tears at the back of her throat and forced a weak smile. "Nothing, just like you. But Gagnon's selling his wool as we speak, and—it's just, it was a hard winter. And I can't remember the last time I had anything sweet."

To her surprise, Madame Ledard disappeared and came back with a single, small sweet roll and placed it directly in Laurette's hand. "Do you remember, when you girls were so little, and your *maman* gone, how I fed you?"

Laurette nodded, tears still at bay but gathered in her eyes. Any day she and Renée came to the baker's, there was always a baguette left from the day before. Or a few rolls with scorched bottoms that no one would buy. Or a tart with its top shell smashed and its filling seeping out into the cloth.

"That's the worst part about these days, you know?" Madame Ledard went back behind her counter, as if a line of customers stood at the door. "So hard, even to do the smallest Christian duty. It's bad enough to have nothing to sell, but worse to have so little to give."

"Thank you," Laurette said, pressing her thumb into the brown, crusty top to find it pleasingly soft underneath.

Madame Ledard held up a hand. "It feels good to give something."

Laurette heard the door scrape open behind her, and from the enraptured expression on Madame Ledard's face, knew immediately who'd entered the store.

"Any left for me, *Tante* Belle?"

"Just one," she said before scuttling back, leaving Laurette alone with Marcel, seeing him for the first time since he'd disappeared with the birdsong.

Although only weeks had passed, his hair had grown, or perhaps it only appeared so as dark curls fell beneath a red knit cap, along the corner of one eye and nearly touching his cheek. He remained thin, but the pallor of winter was now a healthier gold, and his eyes were bright. Health—that's what she saw. A man of health and vitality, as rare to see in these early days of spring as in the days of snow.

Madame Ledard presented him a pastry identical to the one Laurette held. "I gave the other to this young lady."

"I can think of no one more deserving. This is the true bread of life, but no sweeter than the hands that made it."

Madame Ledard giggled and blushed like she was still the young girl who first came to this shop to work beside the owner's son. She made a shooing motion with her apron. "Get on, both of you. Go outside and take in this beautiful day. Find some hope to bring back to the rest of us."

Marcel thanked her again and opened the door, ushering Laurette out before following. It was he who fell into step with her, though she couldn't say that she would not have followed him. Their silence fell easier than it should, and when Marcel did speak, it was with a deceptively familiar ease, as if nothing but camaraderie had ever passed between them.

"Your man is fetching a good price for his wool."

"He's not my man."

"Not anymore?"

"He's never been my man."

Marcel looked at her, his brow disappearing beneath the cap. "Never?"

"Never."

He made a noncommittal noise. "At any rate, he's brought in the finest quality of anybody today—of any I've seen yet. Healthy wool. Healthy sheep."

It was obvious he expected some kind of acknowledgment for the feed he provided over the winter, but Laurette would give him none. That was business best left between the two men; she'd brokered nothing.

"Come have a drink with me, Laurette. I have an open bottle waiting for me at the pub."

"I don't think so," she said. "Gagnon will be waiting. . . ."

"He'll be haggling with Dubois for an hour at least to get even half of what is owed him. Come. One drink, two. Get yourself cheered up for the long ride home."

"And what makes you think it will be a long ride?"

"Because no wagon rides smoothly with three wheels."

Laurette dipped her head to hide her smile. When they turned the corner, she spied Elianne on the opposite side of the nearly deserted market, speaking with an older woman—Madame Tournac, as revealed when the woman turned her head to give a peek within her bonnet. She, too, bore the toll of winter, appearing to be able to stand only through her grip on Elianne's arm. Laurette knew she belonged with them—another woman withered by winter. She should be the third in their conversation, worrying about their gardens and the summer and the rattling cough that seemed to have taken root in their lungs.

Or she could go with Marcel. What would it be like to sit in an upholstered chair next to a fire burning with somebody else's fuel? To sip wine and bring some life back to her blood—pink to her cheeks, light to her eyes.

She never spoke consent; neither did she offer further protest. Instead, she pinched a bite off the pastry and let the sweetness melt on her tongue. A side glance showed that he did the same. And with that shared experience, they walked across the threshold into the semidarkness of Le Cochon Gros.

As before, Marcel was greeted with a general chorus of raised voices and cups. *"Mes frères!"* He acknowledged them with a tipping of his cap, bringing to Laurette's attention how many of them wore the same. Like a poor man's uniform, for Marcel was the only man not dressed in near rags.

He took her to his table, where, as promised, a dark bottle sat upright. A boy no older than Nicolas scurried over with a second glass, wiping it with a nearly clean cloth en route. Marcel motioned for her to sit and was about to do the same when the room fell into utter silence, prompting a curse as he looked behind her to the open door.

Two men walked in. Rather, one man, and a relative giant who had to wait for his companion to enter first, as the breadth of his shoulders would not allow them to walk in side by side. Both were bareheaded, and the taller of the two had a shock of hair as blond as sweet new straw. They were given no greeting and offered none in return. While the smaller took a table, the giant went to the bar and ordered a bottle of wine, his sheer size guaranteeing the keeper's service.

"Who are those men?" Laurette asked, instinctively whispering.

"None of ours." Marcel pulled his hat low, then took the bread from Laurette's hand and dropped it in his shirt pocket along with his own. He grabbed the wine bottle by its neck, the two glasses with his fingers, and said, "Follow me," heading directly for the stairs at the back.

"Where?"

"To my room."

"I don't think—"

He looped an arm around her shoulders and spoke directly into her ear. "Come. If you kick up a fuss, I'll be a dead man in the morning."

She allowed herself to be escorted without further questions up the dark, narrow steps with Marcel close at her back, then through the door indicated with a whisper and a prodding of the wine bottle.

"I shouldn't be here," Laurette said as she heard a latch slide behind her.

"Well, you are. And you'll stay. For a while at least. Two glasses of wine, yes? And the delightful pastry from Madame Ledard. And then, free as a bird. Free from me, anyway. He'll no doubt lock you right back into your cage."

She heard the wine pour into the glass; then he took her hand and wrapped her fingers around it.

"To Gagnon," he said, touching his glass to hers. "Drink. Drink up, and you'll get your bread."

Laurette obeyed, not for the bread, but for the taste of the wine, instantly feeling her nerves settle—a warmth that sparked at the top of her head and spilled until an ensuing dizziness brought her feet to the edge of the narrow bed. Sitting upon it, she found it to be nothing more than an unyielding plank and thin mattress, apparently the source of the sour smell that permeated the room.

"Why do you hate him?" she asked, taking the bread from his hand. "He's been good to you."

"Why do you love him? He's done nothing for you."

She swallowed, thankful for the time to gather a reply. "I don't love him."

"You shared his bed all winter."

"Only so we—*he*—could give one to you."

"Glad I could be of service."

The room, lit only by a window thick with beveled glass, was the color of dark ash, and—Laurette expected—just as filthy. It contained nothing but the narrow bed and a rickety table where Marcel set the wine bottle before settling beside her.

"How long after I left did you leave his bed? Or have you?"

"Of course I have."

"Why, *of course*?"

"I told you. It was only so you could have a place for the winter. He is a generous man even to his enemy."

"And what makes me his enemy?" He refilled his glass. "Because I desire you? Or because you desire me?"

The wine rushed around his declaration. But then, perhaps the wine inspired it. "Neither."

"*Exactement.* I am his enemy because I desire equality with him. Equality for all of the brotherhood of France, so that nobody can look to their *land* or their *generations* for superiority. What are you to him, Laurette?" He took her glass, refilled it, and passed it back. "I'll tell you what you are. *Rien.* Nothing. You are nothing. Not his wife, not his daughter. Not his lover. He pays you no wage, so you are not a servant. You are owed no inheritance, and he is too pious to make you his whore." Laurette gasped at the idea, and he laughed. "Why the shock? At least a whore knows her place. Where is your place?"

She steeled herself. "With Gagnon."

"Beside him? Or beneath him?"

No amount of steel could withstand such an insult. She threw her glass to the ground, mindless of its shattering, and moved to slap his face, but he tossed his own empty glass onto the mattress and caught her arms, drawing her close. "I know you remember that night, Laurette. You *gave* yourself to me."

"And you tossed me straight aside." A year of shame roiled up from where she'd kept it tamped down.

"Because of *him*. That night after the shearing, he treated me like I was some kind of animal. Threatened my life if I came near you. He's locked you up, Laurette. And he uses his piety as a key."

"He saved my life. Took me in."

"Like those boys," he said with derision. "A cozy little family, aren't you? I saw it this winter. *Maman, Papa. Les deux fils.* Two sons for which you get all the drudgery of being a mother with none of the comforts of being a wife. You should know such comforts."

Laurette fought his kiss at first, tried to pull herself away, but he held her in place, and his lips tasted so sweet—like unfinished wine. Slowly, he loosened his grip, testing her to see if she'd flee. She didn't. She leaned in, taking his face in her hands, bringing her fingers through his thick curls, knocking the red cap to the ground.

"Laurette, Laurette . . ." He trailed her name with kisses, across her cheek and down her neck, pulling her closer, his body pushing hers until she felt the mattress against her back.

"Non." She pushed against him and felt him smile.

"I'm sorry. Of course, not here." He moved away, his only touch a soft holding of her hands. "Come with me, Laurette."

She should have repeated *non* but instead asked, "Where?"

"To Paris."

"Paris. As what, Marcel? Your wife? Your sister? Your lover?" The ugliness of his tirade took hold. "Your whore?"

"As my equal. As a part of something."

"Gagnon would never let me go."

"You don't have to ask him. He doesn't own you. Besides, I know exactly what he would say." He straightened his back, appearing taller, and transformed his stature to broaden his shoulders. *"Go or stay as you wish, Laurette. It is yours to decide."*

It was a flattering impersonation, carrying Gagnon's warmth

and compassion, followed quickly by the real voice, stripped of all that, accompanying a pounding on the door.

"Laurette! *Ouvrez la porte!* Marcel!"

Marcel leapt from the bed. "Ah, Laurette. Look, your knight has come to your rescue." He slid the latch before Gagnon's fist could land on the door one more time. It came perilously close to landing on his face.

Gagnon shouldered through the door. "Come. We're going home."

"It's not . . . I mean, nothing—" Laurette stood, took a step, and immediately sat back down, wincing in pain. She lifted her foot and spied a shard of glass embedded in the arch. She pulled it out. "Stupid glass."

Gagnon stepped forward. "Let me see."

"I'm fine."

"She's fine," Marcel added, taking half a step to stand in front of her, then moving aside at Gagnon's approach. He scooped her off the bed like she weighed nothing and spun to fit her through the door. Somehow he maneuvered her down the narrow staircase, where they were met with applause from the patrons downstairs. To a man, they held their cups up in salute, shouting mocking, debauched cheers to a young lady's virtue. Even the two strangers joined in, amused at the local display.

Marcel went no farther than the bottom step. "You've no quarrel here."

"I've a quarrel where I find it." He kept her aloft, skirt gracing the tabletops as he carried her outside.

"Gagnon," she said, eyes burning with the sunlight.

"Not a word," he said, not stopping until he brought her to the water pump in the middle of the square. There he deposited her unceremoniously on the ground, took a cloth from his pocket, and held it under the spigot while he worked up a stream of water. Kneeling in front of her, he wiped the bottom of her foot clean and transformed the cloth into a bandage, wrapping it around twice before tucking the loose ends. "Can you stand?"

She held her hand up and he gripped it, lifting her.

"Can you walk?"

She rolled her foot to the side and found she could take a few steps with relatively little pain, but took his arm for the limp back to the wagon, where Elianne sat waiting, hands primly folded in her lap.

"Did she send you to my rescue?"

"She did."

They said nothing else for the rest of the walk to the wagon, nothing as Gagnon lifted her up beside Elianne, and nothing as they drove away. Elianne attempted conversation about the warmth of the day, the growing lateness of the hour, and ultimately convinced Gagnon to stop outside a grove to eat the dinner Laurette packed the morning that now seemed to have happened a lifetime ago.

"I was worried about you," Elianne said finally, picking the softer bread from its hardened crust. "*Papa* says those men, in the red caps? They're dangerous. Plotters against the king."

Laurette left her bread untouched after the first disappointing taste. "Perhaps our king is a tyrant."

"Do you see?" Elianne had never before sounded triumphant. "How he's turned her head?"

"He's turned nothing." She looked over to meet Gagnon's eyes and clutched his arm before he could look away. Her skin crawled with shame as she offered a silent plea for forgiveness. Yes, she'd been a fool to be caught up in such a moment of spring madness. But that's all it was. A moment. Madness. A sip of wine falling into a stomach too long empty. A soft touch after a winter of crowded solitude. A desire to be something other than a withered, old, forgotten woman. But she couldn't say any of those things, not with Elianne's beaked nose so close to their conversation. She could only repeat, "He's turned nothing," and pray for an opportunity to plead her case later.

Gagnon stood. "Finish up so we can be back by dark."

For this leg of the journey, Elianne would not be silent. After trying and failing to convince Gagnon to favor them with a song ("I've not forgotten your voice since the New Year"), she spoke of their new litter of pups, offering his pick to train up as herd dogs. She took it upon herself to examine the bandage on Laurette's foot and, seeing the blood soaked through, tore a new one from her underskirt.

"It's my natural tendency to care for people," she said, "which is why I was so concerned when I saw you going into the tavern with that rebel. It's no place for a sweet girl, and Lord knows he's no fellow to go with. Just shows it's never too late for you to need the attention of a mother."

Laurette could not hold her tongue. "A mother?"

"Everybody regards you as *his* daughter, of course." She inclined her head toward Gagnon. "But a girl needs a mothering influence. I'd be lost without mine."

"Was it your mother's suggestion that you accompany Gagnon and me today? Because I'm sure it wasn't his."

Elianne's sallow face fell, and she looked out over the steadily passing landscape. Gagnon nudged Laurette's arm. "Enough."

⚜

The gait of the horse lulled her. She closed her eyes, remembering Marcel's arms wrapped around her, only to be jolted awake to find herself in Gagnon's. His body against her back, her head drooped onto his shoulder. Her foot throbbing in pain. They were riding Girard's horse because of her foot. It was too late, too dark, and too far to walk—three reasons enough to have accepted the family's invitation to take supper and spend the night, but Gagnon had refused. The boys were at home alone, after all. And Elianne showed no enthusiasm in the invitation.

"Can I ask you a question, Gagnon?"

"I don't know. That would entail talking to me, something you haven't done much of since I pulled you away from Marcel."

She ignored him. "What am I to you?"

"Is that your question? Or his?"

"Mine."

"You are . . ." There was a series of hoof-falls before he continued. "You are my Laurette."

"What does that mean?"

She felt him shrug. "It means what it means."

"Does it mean that you love me?"

He transferred the reins to one hand and brought the other to her face, his touch warm against her cool cheek. Turning her head and leaning his body, their faces were closer to each other than Laurette could remember. So close that she could see nothing else. Not the stars, not the sky, and least of all, the image of Marcel.

"Do you need me to tell you, Laurette? Do you not know?" Then he took his touch away, settled back, and the heavens came into view again.

The silence that accompanied this ride was nothing like the silence in the wagon with Elianne. This was comfortable, familiar, like a night by the fire transported to a worn path under a blanket of moonlight. Rather than speak, Gagnon began to sing—a soft song about a young woman whose lover sailed away, a favorite of theirs, though the boys declared it too sentimental. She felt the song rumble through her, experiencing it in a way she never had before. Always, by the comfort of the fire, having never seen the ocean, Laurette would try to picture a ship, a shore. The endless stretch of sea, the horizon into which her lover disappeared. Now the vastness of the night stood in place of the sea, and though Gagnon was close enough to share the beating of his heart, he felt a world away.

An ache formed within her. What if he disappeared? What if *she* disappeared? Like Renée. No need for a ship or an ocean. Just two turns of a carriage wheel. Marcel was a force in and out of her life; Gagnon, her only constant. A part of her, like this moment, positioned as her spine, keeping her upright and steady as the world moved beneath.

She woke up when it stopped, and in one fluid motion, Gagnon dismounted the horse, bringing her with him, cradled close to his chest. He carried her through the empty house and deposited her on her bed, whispering good night. She heard him leave, knowing he was heading to the barn to put up the horse and check on the boys. But he'd be back. Not to her room—never to her room. Never to her bed.

Yet he loved her. He'd said as much, and it was more assurance than Marcel had ever given. Even more, he cared for her—fed her, sheltered her, spoke to her first and last each day. Solicitous of her comfort without overt emotional indulgence. Gagnon would never permit her to wallow in pity, but he allowed her intermittent moments of joy. There wasn't a morsel of her mind or soul or spirit that didn't belong completely to Gagnon, but that wasn't enough to assure her place, because her body remained under Marcel's power. Nothing else explained her reaction to his invitation, his kiss. How was it he could be away for months at a time, never darkening her thoughts, yet a stolen moment in his presence destroyed her defenses?

She'd given herself to Marcel once, and he'd given nothing back, least of all a place beside him. Until this day, she'd never considered her place beside Gagnon to be precarious, to be so easily dislodged. And yet, outside of Gagnon's view, she'd fallen right in step with Marcel, on the sidewalk, up the stairs, to his kiss. If only Gagnon fully possessed her . . .

Up, she was surprised at the pain in her foot and found a position that allowed her to take the few steps over to the table, where a basin of cool water waited for her to clean her face, a coarse brush to drag through her hair. She unfastened and dropped her skirt, her shirtwaist, and the corset beneath. Dropped her chemise and stood naked in the cool breeze coming through the open window. The house had been left as such to take on the spring air, bringing new life to the room so long choked by cold and smoke. Her room smelled of fresh earth and green grass, the slightest sting on its edges raising her skin to gooseflesh.

In a few brief, breathless steps, before she had the chance to lose her courage, Laurette limped from her room and slipped into Gagnon's, straight to the bed that had been hers throughout the winter, sliding between the familiar blanket and mattress. Once in, her pulse took on the rhythm of the horse's steps, bringing to mind the memory of his arms. *"You are my Laurette."* Here, he would finally see her unrealized value. He would know her as a woman—not a girl, not a foundling. There would be a final purpose to his rescue. Slowly the chills she suffered warmed until she felt nothing but unreserved peace.

Until he walked in the door.

Because of the darkness, he did not at first see her and had no idea of her presence until he sat on the edge of the bed. Then, at her slightest shift and whisper of his name, he leapt to his feet.

"What are you doing here?"

"I want to be yours, Gagnon. Like you said I was."

"Not like this."

He hadn't paused, not even a breath to think before speaking his rejection. The words stung as if he'd delivered them as a physical blow. The nerves that had settled into peace sparked again as anger. She sat up and knew his eyes had adjusted to the moonlight, because he turned his head as the blanket fell away.

"You didn't mind keeping me here while Marcel was in the house."

"To keep you warm, and to keep you safe. From him." He gave a bitter laugh. "But I see that did no good, as I pulled you from his bed this afternoon. Why, after that, would you think you'd be welcome in mine?"

Refusing shame, she extricated herself from beneath the blanket and came to stand before him. Her hair tumbled to the middle of her back, providing the only cover to her smooth skin.

"You've wanted me before, Gagnon. Émile. You must have."

Though they stood completely apart, she felt the turning of his head, the resistance and tension of the movement. Sensed the constriction in his chest. She took his hand and brought it to her lips, knowing every bit of labor behind each tiny scar and callus.

"Laurette." His voice held a warning for them both. But she knew if he would only touch her—once—whatever they lacked would be complete. How well she knew a single touch to conquer all good intentions. She moved his hand to lay it flat against her flesh, and he moved forward, briefly brushing against her as he reached for the quilt and draped it softly over her shoulders.

"This is what *he* wanted from you, Laurette. But it's not right in the eyes of God, nor in mine."

Now, despite her attempt at courage, humiliation flourished. Fully covered and untouched, she felt more disgraced than she did the night she brushed the green moss from her skirt.

"I'm sorry." She fought back tears. "I thought—"

"Don't be sorry." He placed a soft kiss to the top of her head. A father's kiss. "And know that my feelings for you have not changed. You are to me now what you were this morning. My sweet Laurette. *Ma famille.* But this cannot happen again. Do you understand?"

He spoke as if she'd committed a minor infraction of childhood disobedience. The same as he would if she left the gate to the sheep pen open or spilled a pitcher of milk with a careless gesture. She nodded and shouldered past him, forcing herself to walk straight despite the pain. In her room, she folded his blanket and set it at the foot of her bed before dropping her nightdress over her shoulders. Only when she was tucked away where she belonged did she allow the tears to flow unbidden.

Why had she followed Marcel? Tonight's actions were no less impetuous, as they flowed from the same source—a yearning for something other than the drudgery of each day. A means to infuse herself with a strength not drawn from her own dwindling resources. Her body, a wasteland of skin and bones, her teeth aching, her flesh dry and scabbed over from the sparks that landed when she sat too close to the fire. She was twenty years old now, with full memories of her mother being twenty years old. Poor and wretched, yes, but *alive* with a life she had chosen for herself. A life with a man whose passions ran so hot he'd killed her in their wake. A child of her own who clung to her long after life ebbed away.

Who would cling to her in death? If the harmless shard of glass that embedded itself in her foot had instead slashed her wrist, her throat, who would care? *Ma famille,* Gagnon had said, but her only true family had abandoned her without even so much as a word in her absence. She cried, not knowing for sure if her tears were born of shame or pity or a loneliness she would not have recognized before today.

"He's a fool."

Had she not buried her mouth into her quilt to mask her sobs, she might have screamed loud enough to scare the goats. Instead, the initial shock so constricted her throat that she could do little more than will herself not to explode with the impact. Marcel unfolded himself from the darkest shadow.

"What—what are you doing here?" Her words choked with the same staccato as those emitted in a nightmare.

"I followed. And I waited."

"How long have you been here?" The walls, she knew, were solid—enough to hold the house for five generations, enough to conceal their whispers.

"Since before you arrived."

"So, you saw—"

"Everything. Hence, the fool. If you ever were to give yourself to me so completely . . ."

"I did, once."

"And this should prove that you were meant for so much more. Get dressed, Laurette." He crossed to the open window, hoisted himself easily up and through it, and spoke to her from the other side, elbows propped on the sill. "Find your shoes and meet me at the barn."

"The barn?" Already she found her legs dangling over the side of the bed in anticipation of following through on his command.

"You won't alert the dogs. Or the boys."

She couldn't stop the fact that her tears were now more closely associated with the nervous laughter rumbling out of her. "Alert them to what?"

"To the fact that you are taking Girard's horse. Rather, *we* are taking Girard's horse."

"Oh, really?" She played along, waiting for her mind to catch up with her heart and her words. "Taking it where?" But she knew.

"To where you belong, *ma lionne*. With me. In Paris."

Part IV

L'Été et l'Automne
(Summer and Autumn) 1789

Et au lever du soleil à l'est . . .

L'épisode 19

Renée

VERSAILLES

I've made Louis-Joseph a battlefield for his tin soldiers—a green quilted cloth the size of my arms squared, with odd-shaped bits of batting to simulate hills and valleys for strategic positioning. I pack it along with the soldiers in the long wooden box that serves as transport, knowing somewhere in the back of my mind that I will not see him—or the soldiers—again in my lifetime.

In the months since his little brother's birthday, the dauphin has been in a steady decline, so weak he can scarcely hold up his beautiful head without the propping of a pillow. He hasn't walked in weeks, getting from one end of the palace to the next by means of a wheeled chair, pushed by a brave nurse who fights tears behind his back. He speaks little and eats less, and continues to be haunted by a racking cough through which he regularly blood-soils his linens and nightshirts. These are burned immediately, lest lingering evidence of the king's weak line become more fodder for gossip. Any child can grow to be a ruler who cannot walk, but none live with the exhalation of royal blood. So rather than embellishing gowns or cutting coats from the finest velvet, I spend my time stitching new shirts for the king's heir, as he requires several every day.

Tonight, traveling in the darkness to avoid the angry throngs that gather at the palace gate and roads beyond, the royal family will go to Château de Meudon. It is thought to be a better environment for Louis-Joseph: fresher air, fewer people.

And I am left behind.

Versailles takes on a strange personality with the absence of the royal family. In many ways, business conducts itself as usual. There are meetings in the Bull's Eye Antechamber, nobles strolling the gardens, shouted political discourse and whispered schemes. But this time it is different. It is heavy and dark. Everybody knows the dauphin is dying. Everybody knows that France herself is in no better state. Our people are weak, our land near death, and our king and queen are sovereign only in title, for they are powerless to heal either one.

For the first time, I find my hands truly idle. On other occasions when the queen was away, noble guests tried to employ my services, but these days, any garish display of excess is dangerous. Men and women have had their wigs ripped off in the streets, the rebellious crowd screaming for the flour that gives them such a pristine, noble appearance. Ornate gowns have been ruined by unmentionable projectiles, jewels ripped from throats, silk shoes ruined by the continuous filth running in the streets.

So I look for ways to keep busy. Without any instruction from Mademoiselle Bertin, I go into the royal gown room and examine each dress, mending seams and repairing hems. Then, knowing the queen is unlikely to wear any of these in public for some time, and guessing that her tastes might be significantly subdued if she does, I divest them of even the smallest bauble of shiny pressed glass, replacing the embellishments with decorative stitching. I take a few of her older gowns, cut them down for Marie-Thérèse, and save the scraps to make a colorful new skirt for myself.

This flurry of menial activity serves many purposes. Gagnon always said that busy hands are soothing to the soul, and all those hours when my vision is trained on a single inch of silk and the bright thread stitching through it, I'm not thinking about the young boy who was never really a child or wondering if he has breathed his last. I'm also creating a reason to be here, at Versailles, and not declared useless and tossed out of the gates. And—most important with each passing day—the work gives me time to think about Bertrand. Late at night, my hands engaged with my knotting shuttle, making a trim for the queen's favorite shawl, I lose my thoughts in the mindless repetition of the pattern. I hear his voice and remember the feel of his lips on mine. The thread runs through my fingers and I recall the texture of his hair. My thread is the color of his eyes—cerulean blue. And every now and then, when all is dead silent around me, I can hear the wool against the gold, and it sounds like his voice when he says my name. I create knot after knot and imagine each to be a day we will spend together. By the time I reach the end of a row, we measure our togetherness in years.

Or we will, when he returns.

True to his prediction, he has been gone since mid-April, traveling through villages on orders to listen, report, arrest. He was to blend in, like a spy, which made me laugh.

"Never have I seen a man like you in my village. It would take three of them tied together to fill your uniform."

He was sent away the same day the queen left for Meudon, for it was assumed she would be safe there, locked away with Louis-Joseph, spared from public appearance, surrounded by people who were, perhaps, not quite so hungry and desperate as those outside the gates of Versailles.

And far, far away from Paris.

⚜

News comes of the dauphin's death in the first week of June with a page marching through the halls, his solemn pronouncement accompanied by a sonorous bell. I am in the queen's apartment, the outer chamber, on a settee tucked into a corner where, if I curl myself tight enough and remain still, I can pass an afternoon or more without detection. This announcement brings me to the floor, to my knees, crossing myself in prayer and beseeching God to welcome Louis-Joseph's spirit into heaven.

"And he was a good boy, Father," I pray aloud, heedless that doing so betrays my presence.

Weeping can be heard throughout the palace, most stirringly from the children's apartments, where the governesses who have been left behind make no attempt to hide their mourning. They, like I, stagger into the great hall, all of us looking lost and stunned—though why should we be? Whispers have always predicted Louis-Joseph's death. Since not long after his birth, I've been told. And nobody who spent more than an hour's time with him should be shocked at his passing.

Then I think, if this had been a poor boy, some wretched gutter foundling or a farmer's son, the child would have been given nothing more than a click of the tongue and a muttered, "Poor dear—better he be in his heavenly Father's arms." But as sumptuous as all good Christians know heaven to be, who could look at the luxuries of Versailles and think any child *better off*? How unfathomable to think about the abundance of food, the ready warmth and comfort, the physicians no more than a summons away. The medicine and money that separate the rich from the poor surely should separate the living from the dead, yet with all that, a royal status could not extend a single hour.

The next morning, we—yes, all the servants in the household—go to the chapel for an early Mass. The priest who says the prayers for our deceased prince wears three rings set with massive stones and speaks not a single word about the boy. He intones the prayers with a formality better suited for the crowning of a king rather than the death of a child. Perhaps our status precludes us from true familiarity and warmth, but that does nothing to squelch the tears of those of us who loved the boy.

In light of the dauphin's death, all of the royal guards have been summoned back to Versailles—not to mourn with us but to protect the family from the type of monster who might take advantage of its weakened state. Every other passing moment I chastise myself for my excitement. My heart is still heavy for my queen, but my steps are quick and I have to mask the smile that tugs at my cheeks at the thought of seeing Bertrand again. I give Mademoiselle Bertin any excuse to vacate my post at the sewing table—a pressing headache in need of a breath of fresh air, a favorite measuring tape left in my sewing basket in another room. At every opportunity, I roam the halls and grounds, my eyes alert for the man who stands head and shoulders above all the others.

Finally, on a ridiculous errand to inquire about the color of the horses' plumes in the funeral procession, I find him at the stables. It is my first time to see him in civilian clothing—dark-brown breeches, a blue linen shirt, and a vest made of what I can see from a distance is soft leather. I see him before he sees me, giving me the chance to study him, visualizing the gentleman farmer of his fantasies. How strong he looks! And prosperous, though I suspect the clothing is in good condition due to its lack of wear.

I've never seen Gagnon in anything quite so fine; still, I can picture Bertrand at our table, dunking a hunk of bread in his soup, laughing at something bawdy Laurette might say. In fact, he's laughing now at the groom's joke—something about me, given the man's gesture, but the moment Bertrand sees me, his laughter dies.

"Renée!" With an abandon never permitted in uniform, he runs to me and swoops me up. High enough that I am soon looking down at him. So strange not to see the sky behind his head. Dizzying, because he is spinning me around and around before bringing me in close enough for a kiss that makes up for all the time we spent apart. "You'll never guess where I've been," he says, setting me down at last.

"Where?"

"Your village. Mouton Blanc."

We are walking now, aimlessly, in the general direction of his barracks. I'm clutching his forearm to my side and tug it down to bring his gaze. "Did you! How was it? Were you there at the shearing time? That's always the most exciting . . ." But as I speak, I cannot miss the falling of his countenance, and I know that my own little village has not escaped the plague of poverty.

"It was months ago, and from what I heard, early in the shearing season. So perhaps things are better now."

He is lying to me, and I love him for his dishonesty, this man born to protect.

"But is it . . . safe?" By which I mean, have my gentle friends and neighbors succumbed to the fever of rebellion?

"I saw your friend," he says. "As charming as I remember. We were in a tavern—"

"Le Cochon Gros!"

"Just so, a colorful place. And he was there, talking to a young lady. He saw me, I think, and recognized me, and took the girl upstairs."

I laugh. "That sounds like Marcel, from what I remember. A pretty girl?"

Bertrand shrugs. "I only think of you, my love. In any case, they aren't upstairs for a quarter of an hour before a man comes storming in, goes straight up the stairs, and comes down with her in his arms. Carrying her, like this." To demonstrate—or with demonstration as an excuse—he swoops me up again, this time with one arm around my waist and another propped beneath my knees, and I feel like I'm flying.

"So, a hero?"

"Her father, I assume."

"Not her husband?"

He sets me down. "A husband would have killed your friend, I think."

An amusing story, to be sure, but it doesn't obscure the fact that he hasn't answered my question. My town. My people. Are they in danger of the king's discipline? Are they in danger of destroying themselves?

"So did you speak with him?" I ask. "Marcel. Did he remember you? Did he ask about me?"

Bertrand shakes his head. "You'll see the men now, wearing their red caps. That is their uniform for the rebellion, I think. Your Marcel wears such a cap, as did many of the men in the tavern. Nobody would speak to me. I waited for him to come back downstairs, waited as long as the proprietor would allow. He would not permit me to go upstairs—wouldn't even let me rent a room. And in the morning, they were gone."

"They?"

"Every man in the tavern who wore the red cap. Disappeared."

Before I can ask more, I hear the sound of the page's bell and my sobriquet, *"Couturière!"* between the rings.

I clutch Bertrand's hand. "I have to go and finish Marie-Thérèse's mourning dress. So sad, isn't it? To dress a child in black."

"Renée—" He captures my hand as if he hasn't heard me. "I'm relieved of duty for the next two days. Until the family returns. Meet me tonight, will you?"

"I don't know. I have to finish—"

"After, you can work through the night if you like. Can you finish the dress in two days?"

"Of course."

"Then you'll have no further duties tying you here?"

I don't answer. The ringing of the bell is closer, louder. The voice of the page irritated, because we can see each other now. I know this one; he'll ring the bell until he's close enough to nip my ear with the clapper.

"I have to go." I step back, our arms stretch, our fingertips cling.

"Tonight?" he calls out, even as my back is to him.

I turn my head. "Nine o'clock! Apollo's fountain!"

⚜

I find him waiting for me with a good bottle of peasant's wine—hearty and red—which he pours into a single cup to pass back and forth between us. I have leftovers from the servants' supper, a dish of a meaty pie with vegetables and gravy. This, too, we share with the passing of a single spoon.

"Let's always be just like this," he says, filling the cup. "After we are married. Let's have just one cup and one plate and one spoon."

"You sound as if you've made some sort of formal declaration for my hand. You've never even asked me to marry you."

He smiles and hands me the drink. "Will you?"

"Yes." And like that, it is settled. I've no one to grant permission or blessing, and I know it's what he wants to hear—a simple answer to a simple question. He leans forward and kisses me, then trades me the cup of wine for the dish of pie and wolfs more than half in three bites. I drink and watch, unable to imagine the two of us anyplace but here. In what way could I ever have a house to keep? What kind of room would he not fill? I'm still not accustomed to the sight of him out of uniform. And what would I wear if divested of my status here? How could I be *la couturière* without a queen to serve?

But all are questions for another night, until he offers up an answer.

"You'll have to leave this place someday, you know. It's not our home. It's where we work. Nobody dies here."

"I know." I glance over at the stone porpoise leaping from the fountain's ocean. "Do you know why I like this place? Not the palace, but here? This fountain? Because it is so fantastical. It's everything my life could never be before. A god, chasing gods. The stories that Gagnon would tell in the evenings—all of the stories of the ancient Greeks. The first time I saw this, I saw Apollo, ready to race the sun across the sky. And the most breathtaking of stories became real. I could swim out and touch him."

"It's not real, Renée. It's made from the same stuff as the sewers that run under the city."

"Every day I'm surrounded by beautiful things, Bertrand. My hands are buried in silk. Sometimes the very creations of my mind are worn by our queen. I don't want to leave that. Not yet. Someday I might rise to the level of Mademoiselle Bertin herself. She listens to me sometimes. My ideas."

"So this is another reason? Before, you did not want to leave the queen herself. Now her gowns are holding your affections?"

"You are as loyal to her as I."

"To the queen, yes, as is my duty. To the monarchy—" he lowers his voice to a whisper—*"non."*

I feel the flush rise to my cheeks. "Then you are—one of them?" I don't even have the word for what I mean.

The shake of his head is barely perceptible. "No, but I won't fight them, either. They have cause, Renée, for their anger. I've seen life on both sides—"

"As have I, don't forget. I wasn't raised here. It's been little more than a year—"

"And I don't think you'd be alive if you weren't. I've seen the desperation. The hunger. I won't take up arms against men who want only to feed their families."

"Have you been asked to?"

"Not yet. But there are orders being issued, dispatching more troops to Paris. My prayer—if I stay—"

"Please stay. Right at the queen's door. You don't know how much peace you give her."

He stands up and paces ten steps away from me, then ten steps back, his body a soldier's in common clothing. More than once he begins to speak, then sucks in a breath, reverses direction, and paces again. I take a bracing sip of wine, preparing to respond to the lambasting to come, but when he speaks, his voice is gentle. Frustrated, but soft.

"What if I forced you to choose?"

"Choose?"

"A life lived with me, or a life lived for her?"

He is standing close enough to see, but too far to touch, which is just as well, because he is beautiful tonight. Torchlight illuminates him without shadow, making his hair and skin a color that could never exist at any other time. Apollo at dawn. His rough linen shirt is open at the neck, exposing a smooth, muscled chest that I have touched before—I can still feel it soft and warm beneath my palm, his heart strong enough to answer my pulse. If I could touch him, he'd have the answer. If I could simply reach out my hand, I'd clutch his sleeve, pull him to me, and give him his answer with my lips, my breath. All of me. Instead, I am frozen, and in the infinitesimal time it takes for me to will myself to stand and go to him, he lifts his hands in surrender.

"Bertrand, please—"

"Tomorrow, when Her Majesty arrives home, I'll be there in full dress. Sword at the ready to protect her. But not for her sake, Renée. For yours." He walks closer, and even as I ready myself for his embrace, he stops and lowers himself to my eye level but makes no move to touch me. "I don't think you understand how reviled she is. How much they hate her. And I admit I don't understand your affection, but I promise you this: I will protect her because you love her. I'll defy any order that will take me away from her side, because I love you. Do you understand?"

I can only nod, my heart too full for words.

He reaches now and takes the wine from me. Stands and lifts the cup to the stars. "To our queen. Long may she live."

L'épisode 20

Laurette

PARIS

It was a hunger like she'd never known. Always before, with Gagnon, there was a crust of bread left in the corner of the wooden box. Or an egg beneath a chicken, or an animal to fall under the butchering knife. Being summer, there might be green tops of vegetables to pull from the earth, or a fish to catch itself on the line, or a rabbit to fall in a trap. But in this hot, crowded box of a room, there was nothing. No bread, no wine, and—though the day had long ago turned dark—no Marcel.

Laurette paced the few steps it took to cross from the bed to the window and back again. The tiny lodgings she and Marcel managed to acquire in the crowded house on the boulevard de la Madeleine were smaller than any of the accommodations at Le Cochon Gros, smaller than her room at Gagnon's, smaller than the loft above the barn where she slept her childhood away in safety and comfort. The mattress was flat, with only the moldy odor as proof that it contained straw within, and the blanket spread across it upon their arrival was sour and stiff. It crumbled the moment Laurette lifted it; the one she procured from a back-alley shop was only marginally better, though in fact the nights were too warm, the walls too close, the air too stifling to sleep with anything other than a sleeveless linen sheath for modesty's sake. Marcel, not even that. Beside the bed stood one uneven table. In the corner, one unstable chair. The saving grace of the room was the single, enormous window, stretching from just above Laurette's knee to near the top of the ceiling. Light. Air. When she left the window and the narrow door open, a breeze flowed through that made the confined space nearly tolerable. Being on the third floor, Laurette could spend a day on the unstable chair, careful not to let the unpredictable wobble toss her over the jamb, and watch the teeming streets below.

Now she searched for Marcel.

There was a time when she could discern his silhouette from a distance farther than her voice would carry. Here, in this place, her shout would be swallowed. There hadn't been a moment's silence since they arrived two months ago. Always the sounds of revelry and anger clashed upon each other, fueled by hunger and wine. This night was no different.

She spared the candle and let the room be lit by the torches in the street below, having no need to see anything more clearly. She could not read any of the pamphlets stacked untidily beneath the table, had nothing to stitch, nothing to do. Nowhere to go.

"My own little Bastille," she joked once when he came home one night at an hour close to morning.

"Not so," he said, stripping off his sour clothes and tugging at her own. "Those poor souls are all alone. You are not alone." He trailed kisses down her neck, then came up to her lips, tasting of salt. "And they spend their days and nights in chains. You are free to go at any time. Do you want to go?"

Sometimes, she thought, but said, *"Non."* Gagnon, too, always told her she was free to leave, and she'd ended up here. Where else was there to go?

She looked down into the street, the hour early enough for the crowds to move in solid masses. A gaggle of women shrieked over each other, locked in battle for a greenish piece of meat one held loftily over their heads. Others walked singly in the street, shouting for their husbands.

"Jacques Demeure!"

"Jacques Fontaine!"

"Jacques Montrose!"

So that was how a true Parisienne brought her husband home at night. Not by hiding within a window, wishing him across the threshold. Those were the true *lionnes*, patrolling the jungle for their mates. But Laurette was no more a Parisienne than she was a wife. Her feet would never grow accustomed to the feel of hot bricks and sharp stones; her lungs would never be satisfied breathing the air exhaled by a thousand strangers. And yet, her body would respond to Marcel's touch, her heart would cling to his words, even when the words denied over and over that they would ever be truly married.

"There's no God to please, and only a corrupt government to sanction," he'd say whenever she broached the subject. "I promise myself to you, for all the days that we are together. And I ask nothing more of you."

She could shout out the window, "Jacques Moreau!" and scan to see which of the dozens of red caps tilted to look her way, but it was still too early for him to be out among them. No, somewhere—and he was always careful to be vague in direction and detail—he gathered with others around a table much as he had in Le Cochon Gros. Only here, she suspected, he did not lead the conversation. He listened, just as she did on the rare occasion when she accompanied him to the dark taverns and rented rooms. He spoke little in the company of others, but repeated it all when she became the sole audience.

"The monarchy must be brought to their knees. To their death, even better. The citizens of France have no hope to seize a destiny so long as their futures are clutched in the greedy hands of the king."

The speech never changed, but the anger increased. Murderous intent framed every word, and Laurette made every effort to distance herself from that strain of Marcel's passion. Let him have his weapons, his blades and bullets and endless tirades. She didn't steal Girard's horse and ride with bandits to Paris with the intent to rebel against anybody but Gagnon. Whatever the squalor, whatever the acts of petty crime she witnessed and aided—all was worth it to keep her from facing Gagnon in the clear light of morning.

A familiar gait turned the corner, and Marcel looked up to find her in the window. Unbidden, her heart raced in the exact way it had since she was a young, young girl—her very existence rewarded by his smile. He held up a small canvas sack and yelled, "Supper!" above the street's din, then motioned for her to come down and join him.

Laurette shook her head. He no doubt wanted to go to some public house, entreat a fellow to trade a cup of wine for a portion of whatever food was contained in the sack, and ignore her for the rest of the evening. Instead, she leaned over and out as far as she dared. "*Non!* Come up. I have a surprise."

From here she could tell his dark brows danced up. "What surprise?"

She laughed. "I'm not going to shout our business from the window. Come, bring me supper!"

He disappeared into the building, and she knew to the second how long it would take for him to arrive at the door. Enough time to smooth her skirt and give a quick twist to the hair that escaped her cap. She met him at the threshold, greeting him with a kiss that carried him across and to the bed, supper momentarily forgotten.

"I know better than to believe you're not hungry," he said, pulling away. "And as it took some doing to bring this delicacy home, I propose we enjoy it first, and each other after."

Everything about him was humor and desire, and in that moment, there was nothing unpleasant about their life together. He loved her, surely. He'd said so often enough, dismissing the attentions of countless other women, claiming that no love but hers could sustain him.

She sat up beside him and gave her senses over to the enticing smell coming from the sack. "What is it you've brought?"

"Goose. Netted on the grounds of a bishop. *L'évêque pompeux.*" The descriptive nickname was delivered with puffed cheeks and a general air of portliness. "You should have seen. We were chasing the geese; he was chasing us. Never fear, my darling, that hunger will make you weak. Jacques and I were barely out of breath when that pious sack of fat gave out. 'Hold! Hold!' He couldn't even stand straight at the end. Luckily, his birds are equally obese. We took three—fat, juicy things. Been roasting all day."

"You just—are you saying you stole them?"

"I'm saying we fed fifty hungry people, at least. I was lucky to bring this much home." He reached into the sack and pulled out a white cloth stained with grease. What had been a savory, pleasant odor a moment ago now overpowered the tiny room, growing stronger in its heat.

"I'm sorry," she said. "I'm not used to—"

"Taking what you want? What you deserve? The days are over when the poor of France will sit in idleness, waiting for our king to throw us the crust from his table. And this—this man of *God*? Every morning I've watched him step over starving, wasting women and children on his way to his *church*. If he can ignore the teachings of Christ, so can I. So can we all. The country will be in a far better place if we live by the statutes of hungry men."

He unfolded the cloth, revealing several slabs of dark, greasy meat within. Picking one up, he gobbled it with the enthusiasm of a hungry stray dog. Goose fat shone on his lips, his chin, and he gave her a first taste with a kiss. "And, for you," he said, dangling a bite in front of her. "Before I get too greedy."

She bit. It was her first taste of meat in weeks. Already the texture was unfamiliar, the taste unwelcome. It was neither hot nor cold, and she forced both the smile and each laborious chew before struggling to swallow.

"It's rich," she said in an effort to explain her lack of enthusiasm. "I'm not used to such a delicacy."

"Well, get used to it, my love. We are going to turn the world upside down. The rich will be in rags, and the poor will be in the palace."

She thought about summer evenings sitting on the bench outside with her back against the cool stone wall of the cottage, watching the boys and the dogs chase each other in circles. "I don't want to be in a palace." A bit of goose remained lodged between her teeth.

"Then wherever you like, my love." He took another bite of meat and licked his fingers. "You said you had a surprise for me?"

She picked up a small piece, willing herself to ignore the feel of it against her skin, and nibbled. "It doesn't seem like so much now."

"Tell me."

"Well—" she fought past the smoky taste of the goose—"the other day I went out walking, and I was wearing the vest Renée made for me. You know the one—green? With the stitching? I was passing by a little chapel. I can't think of the street name, but just that way." She pointed in a vague direction. An observer might think she used vagueness to cover an untruth, but there had been a walk. There had been a church, and there had been the conversation that followed. "A woman—not noble I don't think, but with some measure of wealth—actually called out to me and complimented the vest. Called it exquisite."

Her story ended at that point, and the raucous laughter from the street underscored the silence between them.

"Et?" He leaned closer. "And? What then?"

"I told her *merci*. And that one of the seamstresses for the queen herself fashioned it for me years ago."

Marcel's face froze in a strained smile. "You told her that?"

"I did," she said, confused by his reaction.

"Why would you say such a thing?"

"I—I don't know." The last taste of meat gummed at the back of her throat.

"Do you know her sympathies? If she's one of us or one of them?"

"*Us? Them?* What do I know of us or them? I know she was a lady, and ladies find such details interesting. But I think—I didn't realize how I must have appeared to her." The embarrassment of the rest of the encounter took hold, and even in the street-lit dimness of the room, Laurette could not find enough darkness to hide. She turned her back to Marcel and touched her head against the bedpost.

Never had she been prone to vanity, but always she understood her ability to draw attention. Before that wretched summer, when her figure was full to bursting, she recognized the looks she received from both men and women. Lust, envy. Even Gagnon was not immune—*sometimes*. And Marcel certainly made his desires known since that very first night at the forest's edge. She'd been buxom and round, always with a ready laugh. Even without a glass she knew her complexion to be healthy and pink, her hair too thick and unruly to confine itself to any cap or braid or kerchief. And always, always, she'd been clean. Scrubbed. Fresh.

But that afternoon. How many days since she'd felt even a splash of water on her face? Because the fountain was far, and the women gathered at it spiteful and terrorizing. Days since she'd combed her hair. Her chemise stiff with sweat. Skirt frayed above her blackened feet. Yet, for some reason, on that day, with Marcel gone since the sunrise, she chose to don her green stitched vest and venture out alone. Her steps brought her to the church, to the woman.

"May I add, the stitching on this vest was done by my young cousin, who is now seamstress to the queen herself."

And how the woman had laughed. Head reared back, every healthy tooth exposed, great, shrieking laughter. How she'd pointed at Laurette, repeating the ridiculous phrase to all who passed, bringing the laughter into a chorus. Laurette stood, feeling each peal like a blow, ever more aware of her disheveled appearance, the layer of grime on her skin, the stench she must carry. From the corner of her eye she'd seen a brown-frocked priest in the doorway of the chapel. Out of the same corner, she saw him disappear.

"When was this?" Marcel mercifully allowed her to leave the rest of the story untold.

"A few days ago. It's not important. I guess my surprise was that I thought I might sell the vest. If it can catch the eye of such a woman—a *different* such woman might pay something for it."

"Never." He came behind her and pulled her close against him. "It means too much to you."

"Not so much." She'd come home and buried it, forever tainted, under the mattress.

His breath blew warm at the back of her neck, where he planted a kiss so small she might have missed it if not for the undercurrent of revulsion running under her skin. Not for him, but for herself, for she was no cleaner now than she had been that afternoon. Nothing had changed, or was very like to soon. In fact, given the true nature of her abandoned surprise, it would get much, much worse.

She felt him rummage around the forgotten meal, felt him take a new bite, heard the slurp of it. Next, his arm snaked around, a half-eaten strip of goose dangled in front of her. He nudged, and she opened her mouth, allowed him to feed it to her. Closed her lips over the tips of his fingers, tasting the grit of Paris along with the now-cold grease. She couldn't swallow, and when she did, it wouldn't stay. None of it.

Tearing herself from his embrace, Laurette leapt from the bed and staggered to the bucket in the hall, retching all the more when confronted with its contents. She heaved every bit of the ill-gotten prize from the bishop's yard, keeping balance with one hand on the wall, unwilling to drop to her knees.

She would tell Marcel, again, that it was the richness. So unaccustomed was she to fine things. She would not tell him the truth, at least not what she suspected the truth to be. Not tonight. Not with the shadow of shame still so dark upon her.

L'épisode 21

Renée

VERSAILLES

There is a painting in the Salon de Mars of the queen and her children—Marie-Thérèse at her side, infant Louis-Charles in her arms. The young dauphin, probably four or five years old, points to an empty cradle. I'm told the cradle in the painting wasn't always empty. It once held baby Sophie, just as the queen once held her infant daughter in her arms for a fleeting time. When the infant died, she was removed from the canvas just as she was removed from the world. Erased with a painter's brush, erased from conversation, living only in brief moments of lingering sadness in her mother's eyes.

Days after the dauphin's remains are laid to rest in the family crypt, she is told to appear publicly as a queen dedicated to the life of her country rather than the death of her son. She walks the halls, shadows of sleeplessness undisguised by powder, head held high, for if she allowed it to droop—even a bit—she would collapse beneath the weight of the invisible crown.

"I don't mind so much, wearing black," she tells me. She's

been home for three days and is preparing to go to the chapel for a special, private novena for her son. "Black and yellow are my family's colors. I wasn't allowed to wear a single stitch of either when I first arrived. They said, 'Not until you've done your duty to this family.' But I was sneaky. A feather here, a ribbon there. I think you would have been very handy to have had around back then, my dear."

She is not often free with terms of affection, and only because I am kneeling behind her, adjusting the train of her gown, do I allow my smile to linger.

She spends her days listening to those who, through persistence or subterfuge, have found a pathway to her ear. I watch from the side, small and unnoticed, continuously working on one small task or another. Since the revelation of her family's colors, I busy my hands with the knotting shuttle, working with yellow wool I've dyed myself, making trimming that will be appreciated by my queen and unnoticed by anybody else. Her parasol, for instance. Or the silk toes of her shoes.

One after another, women come in to have an audience with the queen. Each a copy of the last. They are skeletal in physique. Torn skirts reveal legs without an ounce of flesh. Their breasts are pendulous and empty, even those who come with equally emaciated children on their hips. "We are starving," they say. Not merely hungry, but dying. "You are a mother. Imagine what it is like to watch your child die."

And I drop a stitch. Do they not know? Can they be so ignorant?

But my queen is gracious. She learns she cannot give them enough money to buy bread, for there's little bread to be bought. So she sends them away with sacks of flour, barrels of vegetables, and bids them to return for more.

Men come sometimes, too, clutching hats no more than rags in their hands. They will not look their queen in the eyes the way the women will. They carry their poverty with shame, not challenge. They ask for work—fair labor for wages. Her Majesty will say, "Of course, of course," and tell them to go speak to one minister or another. They bow and thank her in a way the women never do, yet they never take her offering. They speak to no ministers. Who are they to wander the grounds, hoping to find the right overstuffed officer and submit their services?

True to his word, Bertrand is a constant at her side. On these occasions, when she is face-to-face with her country, he stands with his hand on the hilt of his sword, eyes in constant motion, watching to see if the pitiful soul in the center of the room is merely a distraction for an attack to come from the side.

"You frighten them," Her Majesty said once. "You look ready to attack."

"Not attack, Your Highness," Bertrand replied with all respect. "Defend."

She laid her royal touch to his arm. "Do not take a life on my behalf. It is hardly worth the effort."

Since then, to please her, he stands attentive, but with his arms at his sides. The queen says nothing, but later that evening, when she is well abed and I about to be the same, I lift the same hand that felt so at home on his sword and kiss it.

⚜

It is a hot afternoon, the air motionless and thick, and I'm listless. The queen, rightly gauging the mood of the people, has declared a halt to the design and construction of any new gown until warranted by some royal invitation or event. I've altered, mended, and otherwise stitched every garment in the gown room—both at the request of Mademoiselle Bertin and to appease my own need to stay busy.

My idle hands are a source of trepidation, for I cannot help but remember the warnings Bertrand gave about the queen's fickle nature, her tendency to toss aside those no longer useful or entertaining. I know Madame Gisela brought me here as an oddity. A scrawny poor girl with an exploitable skill. Like a pet monkey with a needle or a small dog capable of creating a perfectly balanced peplum. But I'm of little use now, and I notice with each passing day there are fewer and fewer of us numbered among those in service to the royal family. The long tables at which we take our meals are sparsely populated, and our food declines in both quality and quantity accordingly. Once, at our midday dinner, there was simply nothing. We—chambermaids, footmen, dressers, pages, porters—went into the kitchen and procured bread, cheese, fruit. After, the sentiment for many was that they could very well starve in their own homes without wiping the royal behind to do so, and a mass exodus occurred that evening.

Our queen has announced that she will not appear today, which has led to a loud grumbling among those who came with a hope to see her. Never mind that she has left word that all who come are to be fed—not only on these premises, but given food to take home to their families. Still, they raise blackened fists into the air and curse her generous heart.

"Thinking she'll buy our love with the scraps from her table."

Bertrand is right: I've never known this level of hunger or despair. Some of the men and women lingering in the courtyard might be mistaken for corpses abandoned there, if not for the curses they manage to utter at the nobles who pass by. They do not beg, though. No man sits with his cap upturned; no woman asks aloud for food. It seems they subsist on anger and pride.

Midstep, I feel a small tug on my skirt and look down into the wide brown eyes of a child. His hair is a tangled mass of golden curls, his face pinched but beautiful. He gives me a shy smile, revealing tiny teeth with spaces wide between them.

"C'est belle," he says, tracing a tiny finger—no wider than

new-spun wool—along my patchwork patterns. I can see why he would find it so beautiful. What he wears is little more than a rag draped over his shoulder. A shirt, really, tattered and torn at the hem so as to clearly reveal his gender. The woman who might be his mother is nearby, listless in watching the child.

"Merci beaucoup." I reach for his curls, which are soft, despite the rest of his dirty appearance. "Your hair is pretty, too."

The woman comes closer and draws him to her own threadbare skirt. "Do you think Her Majesty would want him?"

"Want him?" The question is so shocking I can only repeat it.

"I know he wouldn't be one of them, but she just lost her boy. Minc's about the same age. She could have him, might bring her some comfort. And I can't—"

"Madame!" I look to the boy, who is too entranced by the pattern of my skirt to give any comment, if he could even understand. "You mustn't . . ."

But already she is walking away. I pick the boy up; though his mother says he is the same age as Louis-Joseph, who was seven years old, this child weighs nothing, even less than Louis-Charles, who is only four. I walk swiftly to catch up with her, not wanting to frighten the boy by running, and I clutch at her shirt the same as he'd clutched at my skirt, though the gentleness in my touch is for fear that the garment will dissolve in my grasp.

"Wait," I say, holding both the mother and the child. "Wait here, and I'll bring you something to eat. Have you eaten yet today?"

Her eyes answer. They are utterly without color, the bones in her face sharp beneath her skin.

"And while you wait . . ." I dig into my pocket and produce a length of yarn, its ends tied in a knot. I look to the mother. "You know how to play cat's cradle, *non*? You played when you were a little girl?"

Something sparks, and she nods, lips a silent seal.

I loop the yarn in a simple pattern and hold it out to her. She hooks her fingers, so crusted with dirt I can hear them scrape against the wool, and takes it from me in a new configuration. The boy looks on, fascinated.

"You know," I say, "I was playing cat's cradle with this very string with the young dauphin just this morning. Stay here, teach your son, and I'll be back. Will you wait for me?"

Stunned, and maybe confused, she nods again, then sits down right in the middle of the bustling courtyard, bids her son sit in front of her, and begins the game.

Now I run.

In the children's apartment, their table is set for lunch. Rather, they've finished, based on the dirty dishes scattered about, and nobody's bothered to clear up. Today, this works in my favor. I dig through the sideboard and find a cloth, fold it into a smaller square, and fill its center with all I find on the table. Bread, fruit, cheese, pastries. I tie the corners together in a bundle and am about to rush back to the courtyard when another thought occurs.

A wreath hangs on the door to Louis-Joseph's room, and I allow only a single breath of hesitation before opening it and stepping into the gray light from curtains drawn against the sun. I'll need more light to complete my errand. I step to the drapes, but before I can pull them open, a voice bids me, "Stop."

Familiar as it is, I jump at the sound and spin to see her curled upon his bed.

"Forgive me, Your Majesty." I forget altogether to curtsy, but it is only the two of us here in the shadows.

"They won't let me speak of him. We royals, we are not to associate ourselves with death, you know. This idea of immortality, one king's life passing into his heir. One breath to the next. We are not to allow the shadow to linger. We are not to—what is the word?"

"Faire le deuil," I say. To mourn.

"That is it. They've taken everything from me. Everything. And all I've tried to do is be a good wife. And a good mother. And a good queen—but how? When God himself is against me? Starving my people. Stealing my children. No wonder they hate me."

She is dressed, still, in her nightclothes. Her hair, loose and long, spreads against the silk pillow. I set the bundle of food down on the floor, walk over, and kneel at the bedside, her face inches away. I tell her about the woman in the courtyard, her hunger and weakness, and her boy.

"He is beautiful, *madame*. Golden hair and big brown eyes. And the mother, she asked me if . . . if you would want to take him. She knows you lost your son, and she is willing to give her son to you."

"All the better for her boy," the queen says. "Not out of affection for me."

"There has to be some affection, wouldn't you say? Some trust? If she is willing to give up her child? Anyway, I'm here to fetch some food for them, and I thought—if you wouldn't mind—the boy is practically naked. I thought, if there were some clothes. Something he could wear."

I realize I am in the midst of confessing to the theft of the dead dauphin's clothing, but she doesn't seem to mind. Instead, she sits up and says, "Bring them to me."

"Here?"

"No, to my chambers. Take what you want from here and bring them to me."

She leaves, and with renewed purpose I rifle through all the clothing that will never be worn again. His formal ceremonial clothing has already been either stored or destroyed. Here I find all that has been forgotten—plain wool breeches, shirts of dark linen to hide stains of play and illness. Much of it seems never to have been worn. I finally settle on a simple complete suit, including a little coat. I can tell it is too large for the boy right now, but it should fit for a year or more, and well I remember wearing the same clothing through several ages.

I'm relieved to find the woman and child exactly where I left them, though my cat's cradle ring is now dangling from the boy's mouth. Quickly I explain that the queen will have an audience in her private chamber, and that they are to follow me. Inexplicably, this announcement sparks nothing in the woman's eyes, and I wonder if she fully understands what I propose. Still, she follows without question, leaving me to manage carrying both bundles—the clothing and the food—while also keeping the boy safe beside me.

When we arrive at the queen's chambers, Bertrand stands guard, eyeing me with more suspicion than he affords my ragged companion.

"What's happening, Renée? First *she* sneaks away, and now . . ." He shifts his gaze to the woman next to me.

"The queen has asked for her," I say. "May we pass? I can explain everything later."

He steps aside, and I'm puffed with pride, knowing the man charged with our queen's safety will bend to me.

She waits in her antechamber, poised on her settee as though she were receiving a peer. She's donned a simple day dress and has her hair tucked up in a cap, looking, I'm sure, nothing like this woman believed a queen to be. The little boy is drawn to her immediately, responding to her beckoning gesture, but the woman holds back, eyes fixed on the ornate carpet.

All aspects of protocol and manners are set aside for the moment. I make no introduction, as the woman remains stone silent when I ask her name, and the queen abandons all formality.

"I lost two sons," she says, skipping all the niceties of polite conversation. "The first to death. The second to the state. Because they do that, you know. Take him away. Give him a title and a purpose other than playing at his mother's feet. So, my good woman, cherish what you have here. He is a beautiful boy. Pray that he has a long life. That he will grow up to have an honest trade. What is his name?"

"It can be what you want it to be, *madame*."

For a moment, it seems the queen might, in fact, take the boy. She touches his dirty face and studies it, as if gauging how it will appear in portraiture. The artists could simply touch their brushes to Louis-Joseph's eyes, shading them to this dark chestnut brown, adding hints of burnished gold to his hair. This boy who could, like a weed, thrive on nothing—imagine the strength he could bring to the throne. Why had no one thought of this before? It is clear that she wants to embrace him, to take him in her arms and draw him into her lap, and I know if she does, he'll never leave the palace again. With visible restraint, she takes her hand away and withdraws into the public persona befitting her station.

"Take him home, *madame*. I will not take a child from his mother. But come back—send him back when he is of age, and I will see—"

"He won't live that long, *madame*." She is desperately brave, for even she must know better than to interrupt the queen.

"I'll see to it that you have food. See? The girl there already—"

"Food today is not food tomorrow."

"If you are alive tomorrow, come tomorrow. If the next day, come again."

"Oui, madame," she says obediently. She takes both bundles from me, her face unchanged from the moment I first saw her in the courtyard. The boy has remained silent throughout this exchange, the soggy string clutched in his fist.

I'm told to escort her out to the courtyard, and I do not

meet Bertrand's glance as we leave. The walk from the queen's chambers is just as silent as the walk to them, though my steps are heavier, bereft of hope. Somehow I know this woman will feed her son but not herself. I know, too, that she will not return when the food is gone. In a few days' time, all will be as it was before the boy ever reached out to my skirt. For her, at least. I, on the other hand, am forever changed. My love for my queen has been magnified tenfold, as has my frustration with her people. Bertrand may guard her person, but as long as I am able, I will guard her heart.

L'épisode 22

Laurette

PARIS

Laurette awoke to pounding on the door. She'd come back to bed after spending the dark hours of the morning standing in line for bread, only to be turned away like the twenty women in front of her when the supply was depleted. Marcel was leaving when she walked through the door, vowing to return with something before the end of the day.

"Ouvrez! Ouvrez!"

She knew the knocking was a leftover politeness from better days. The door had only a flimsy twig of a latch, and they had no right at all to lock it. Marcel had handed Monsieur Jaunir, the yellow-toothed, pock-faced landlord, a small stack of coins the day he walked Laurette over the threshold. She'd not witnessed another such transaction since.

"He's one of us," Marcel soothed whenever she voiced her trepidation. "A brother won't throw another into the street."

But the fist slamming into the door seemed quite capable of doing just that.

"Ouvrez! Ouvrez la porte!"

Laurette sat, knees pulled up to her chin, hoping to be still and small enough to disappear in the dimness. Marcel would be unperturbed by the situation, using his tongue as currency to secure another month. Or week, or day. She knew better than to plan for any longer range. Not for her life, or for the life growing within. Two months along, she figured. More experienced with the birthing of lambs than babies, her crude calculations predicted a child born midwinter.

A child still unknown to its father.

The pounding increased in volume and ferocity as the shabby wood bowed with the impact. She couldn't cower forever, and Jaunir showed no signs of going away, so with little choice she unfolded from the bed shouting, *"Arrêtez! Arrêtez!"* between blows. She pushed the latch to the side and opened the door, stepping away lest Jaunir's fist make a final statement.

Instead, the man himself stormed in. "Where is your man?" He looked around the space as if it afforded a place to hide, then to her when it was clear she was alone. The leer on his face suppressed any notion she had of telling the truth—that she had no idea where Marcel was, nor of when he would return.

"He's due back any moment. Five minutes," she said. "Just going to fetch some breakfast from a friend."

"That's a lie." He kept his feet planted but loomed closer with each word. He must have been substantially fat before the famine, because his jowls sagged like empty water skins on each side of his face, turning each pockmarked dint into a tiny pocket. "He left hours ago, caught up with that rabble—"

"Then why are you looking for him here?" Her head swam with hunger and fear, but she forced her body to steady itself under his threatening posture.

Jaunir smiled, grunted something that must have been

intended for a laugh, and held out a grubby hand. "Your rent, *mademoiselle*. Now."

"Marcel has all of our money."

"Does he? Then he must have some empty pockets now, am I right?"

"He'll be back this afternoon, I'm sure of it. Or better—" she took a step to the side—"I can go find him. Stop him before he spends it all elsewhere. Give you what we can."

Jaunir mirrored her step. "What you can give me is all that I'm owed."

"I can't." She held his gaze. "Not right now."

"You underestimate yourself." His meaning could not have been more clear as the empty hand, once reaching for rent, filled itself with flesh barely concealed by her nightdress. Revulsion roiled within her, and she looked away, hoping to prevail upon some hidden good nature. Instead he released her, turned, closed the door, and slid the latch back into place.

A fear like none she'd ever known quickened, entwining itself with her weakness, threatening to take her legs away. "*S'il-vous plaît,* Monsieur Jaunir," she said, forcing a tone of calm respect, as if entering any civilized transaction. "My husband—"

"Will be pleased that his woman has taken down what he owes by half." He bent to bury his hot breath in the hollow of her shoulder, his hands immediately gripping the tender flesh of her thigh.

"*Monsieur,*" she pleaded, abandoning all pretense of strength, "*s'il-vous plaît*, Monsieur Jaunir." But the weakness in her voice seemed only to fuel his intentions. Laurette looked to the window as her only escape, the inevitable injury or death in her fall a welcome alternative to the fate that awaited in this room. Finding some reserve, she pushed against him. "*Non!*"

"Slut!" He moved his grip up to her arms. "This is my room, isn't it? My bed. You are here at my pleasure, and now you are here *for* my pleasure. Fight me, and I'll take it all as what you owe and throw you out after."

Laurette felt the edge of the bed up against the backs of her legs. She fought her own paralysis as violently as she did his ardent pursuit, flailing and twisting, anything to keep her body in motion, his target deflected. Screaming would do no good—hadn't she herself heard cries from women at all hours of the day and night? *"Desperate men take desperate action,"* Marcel had said by way of explanation. *"We've been taught to victimize our own."* No one would come to her rescue. Only she could defend her honor and her body, though neither seemed deserving. Then a source of strength, as small as the second heart beating within her, grew to life. Resisting and evading his manipulations, she found a pocket of space and an unguarded moment to buck against him, bringing her knee up for a sharp, satisfying collision. Cursing, he fell away, giving her time to leap up and stand above his writhing figure.

"I'll not let you have me nor harm my child." *Child.* It was her first time to say the word aloud. Jaunir's face registered a passing disgust, but even he seemed unwilling to rape a pregnant woman.

"Get out," he said, his voice no more than a wheeze at first. "I mean it. For good." He made his way to the door with an ungainly step. Opening it, he turned. "I'll be back within the hour. If you're still here, I won't be so forgiving."

"I—I have to wait for my . . . for Marcel."

Jaunir spat at her feet. "Then you'd better hope he returns before I do. And that he finds a way to take care of his family. From the looks of it, you and that bastard both will be dead before the week's end. Just as well you'll be out of my hands."

When he was gone, Laurette felt her body turn to sand and fell heavily to the floor, her head pressed against the sour mattress. Her ears rang with her silenced scream, and she pounded her fist against the floor, welcoming the pain. Only after, her emotion spent, did she hear the sound coming from the street. Great shouts growing louder in a unified refrain. Summoning strength, she crawled to the window, peeking just above the sill to see a wave of humanity moving in a single direction.

"À la Bastille! À la Bastille!"

Surely Marcel must be among them. With a remaining tremor in her hands, Laurette dropped her linen shirt over her head and tied her skirt around her waist. A single bag of rough canvas would have to hold all their belongings, of which there were few: her hairbrush, a stub of a candle, their one cup. Marcel had a leather portfolio of his amassed papers—pamphlets, newspaper clippings, meaningless scribbles on cheap, thick paper in what she recognized as his hand. In an action heretofore forbidden, she untied the string holding the papers secure and laid it open wide. The stack within was untidy, and as she gathered the loose papers scattered beyond it, she took them up, laying them one atop the other. The back of her mind remained conscious of Jaunir's threatened imminent return, but the luxury of this rebellious moment stilled time.

Briefly, she hearkened back to the days when she would clean Gagnon's closed room, shut away by his grief. And then, for just a moment, the oppressive heat in the room gave way to a single, sharp, cold breath piercing the center of her lungs, and she remembered long, cold winter nights, Gagnon's warmth close by.

She ran her hands along the pages, amazed that mere printing on paper could bring her to this place. That it would move Marcel to such anger and passion, enough to capture her in its wake. Still—she knew nothing. None of it, the speeches, the songs. Hunger she understood. Nakedness and fear and poverty. But this? She held up a picture of a woman draped in a sash of three broad stripes, *tricolore*, and remembered the afternoon of celebration on the square, filthy hands grasping for swatches of red, blue, and white wool with the same eagerness as if such flags could be fed to their children.

Papers arranged, she closed the cover of the portfolio, only to have another small note fall from it. This was not like the others. Even with her roughened touch she knew the paper to be of fine quality. It was folded—and had been over and over, given the softness of the creases when she opened it. A useless gesture normally, as she had never mastered reading beyond a smattering of letters, but this she recognized.

"Renée?" She spoke aloud, as if her cousin could answer back in the printed words. She traced her finger along the name. The message, benign as it was, remained elusive. She saw only that her own name appeared nowhere, yet Marcel, for all this time, had been carrying this precious memento. What else was he hiding? "And why did you keep this?"

All this time, they'd made no attempt to find Renée. "We are in Paris, my love," Marcel said every time she asked if they might not venture out that day. "She is not here. And if she were, how would we ever stumble across her?"

"Is Versailles so far away?" Her ignorance, genuine.

"In distance, not so much. But in ideology—far enough that we wouldn't be welcome."

She'd persisted, waiting for sweet moments between them to see if he wouldn't take her to the palace, just for a glimpse. A peek at the opulence, a chance of catching her cousin's eye. But as time passed, as Marcel became consumed with his secretive late-night gatherings, as the soot of the city ingrained itself into her pores, the thought of reunion with her pretty little cousin dropped away like any other abandoned task. Consumed with the fear for the child growing within her and the man growing away, she'd given Renée little thought in weeks.

And now, nothing more than a name scrolled before her, she roared back to life.

Carefully she folded the note, imagining the truth it carried—that he loved Renée still. Pushing away the feeling that the words were intimate scribblings for his eyes alone, she stuffed the note in her skirt pocket and shoved the portfolio into the sack, no longer caring if the papers within were unduly distressed. She snaked her hand under the mattress to retrieve the green vest. This was not a day to wear such a fine garment, not with the lingering residue of Jaunir's touch. But, perhaps, someday . . .

Someday what? A reunion of cousins? An opportunity to present herself a lady? An event worth celebrating? Would she wear it as a bride?

Instead she ripped a strip of twine from the mattress seam and used it to tie the bag. The next tenant could wear the vest in good health.

A final glimpse around the room revealed nothing else to take. All erased, save for the bag she carried on her hip and what she and Marcel had created within her. She walked into the dark hall and down the narrow, waste-strewn steps, emerging under the white-hot summer sun. Immediately she lifted her hand to shield her eyes, but it was not the light that burned. The air smelled of smoke from unnatural fires, peppered with explosions. The shouts she heard from the window amplified a thousand times once she was down among them. She could feel the pounding of the footsteps in the street but could not bring her own to join them.

"What is happening? Somebody! What—?" But no one would respond. Men and women rushed by as if she were a phantom in the street, their eyes wild with unfulfilled violence. Laurette pressed herself against the wall, determined to wait until Marcel came back. Otherwise, how would they ever find each other? Then Jaunir's voice sounded over the surrounding chaos, his threats renewed. The memory of his breath on her flesh cut through the heat; his words and her muffled screams loomed beyond the noise of the crowd.

"I told you! Slut—if I saw you!"

She didn't wait to hear another word. Clutching her bundle, she took a single step into the street, and like a twig dropped into a running stream, was overtaken, swept along, propelled, her feet barely touching the ground. The crowd babbled nonsensically around her:

"La Bastille! It is ours!"

"Liberté!"

"Destruction stone by stone!"

She continued, stumbling, afraid to fall, knowing death by a thousand footfalls would follow.

Onward, and the shouts lost all vocabulary. A series of twists and turns through narrow ways and they burst through to a familiar image—la Bastille, the great, round stone structure. The prison. She'd walked here with Marcel often enough, heard him speak with disgust about the men hidden here. Locked away. Enemies of the state, held without trial. Voices for equality silenced by stone walls. "It will be their seat of murder," he'd said.

At once, the forward momentum stopped, and Laurette found herself trapped within walls of foul-smelling flesh. Using her bundle as a shield, she pummeled her way through, working toward a place where a low wall bordered the path to the prison. She scrambled up on it and stood, waist high above the crowd, her stomach lurching at the sight. Men—women, too, but most were men—with crude weapons raised high above their heads. Guns, yes, but swords and axes and clubs rushing across the footbridge, disappearing through the door. Soldiers wearing *tricolore* sashes over dirty uniforms mingled with men wearing the same over their rags. They fired shots over the bridge and ran with bayonets poised to plunge into the hearts of still more soldiers on the other side. A burst of cannon fire, and those charging in were scattered, limbs torn.

This was not a thousand men. Nor a hundred. What she saw was a single body, driven by a single purpose, shouting with a single voice. Covered in soot and blood, their features disappeared. What vanity it would be to search for Marcel—to pass her eyes from face to face in hopes of landing on his familiar visage. But she knew he was here. Everything he ever said, his dreams and ambitions, led to this moment. *"What use are words without action?"*

Finally he had his bloodshed. All of his words sprang to violent life.

Surely he was over the bridge. Surely he was through the door, never wanting to be the one left back. Left out. And what would he be at the end of this day? Would he return to their room on the boulevard de la Madeleine? Would he walk up the stairs, expecting to find her there? Would he be covered with the blood of the battle raging before her, empty-handed and expecting her to listen to the details of the day? Had they not the misfortune of eviction, she would have sat perched on the end of the bed, listening to the heroic tale as he paced the room, proudly displaying his marks of war. Maybe a bullet wound in his shoulder. Or a cut to his beautiful face—something that would leave a scar and inspire a story.

But she didn't want to hear this story. She didn't want to watch it. As often as Marcel tried to explain, she couldn't understand how rebellion would lead to food. How revolution would bring rain, how a new regime would end famine. These people, she knew, were hungry. Like her. Before her eyes, another fell in expedited death, a wound opening in his throat to issue blood.

"Liberté!"

"La mort à la Bastille!"

"La mort!"

The tone changed to one of celebration in a single, sustained note. She rose up on her toes, held one arm out for balance, and brought the other to shield her eyes and increase her focus on the scene ahead. A man, his clothing tattered and stained, held a pike before him. At the top of the pike, a severed head, mouth gaping, gore trailing in the open air.

"Mon Dieu." She clapped her hand over her mouth to stop the bile rising from her empty belly. No, not empty. Full—with a life too precious to look on such a thing.

Not wanting to be swallowed by the now-hysterical sea, Laurette walked the length of the wall, her back to the scene, retracing the route that led to a road that—if followed long enough—would take her to one of the city gates of Paris. The same that brought her in would take her out, and away. By the time the wall came to an end, so did the throng. She leapt down and found a much easier time working her way up the stream. Occasionally someone asked, "Did you see? The governor, I heard, lost his head in the battle." This, taken for a joke, produced laughter from great, empty maws.

Laurette, though, said nothing. She kept her head down, her bundle close beside her, trying to retrace the steps that brought her into this city. She'd been riding a stolen horse, Marcel walking beside. Others, too, La Roche with his silent girth, and nameless companions who came and went according to the supply of stolen food. Those days held the promise of spring, of love. Who knew but the girl of that day wouldn't have been in the middle of this fight? Other women were, wielding weapons alongside their men. Had Marcel told her that day to rise up, to charge forward and butcher an enemy, she might have obeyed without question. But today she was hungry, and hot, and lonely, and frightened.

Jaunir predicted she and the baby would be dead within a week, and nothing before had ever seemed so true. But they wouldn't die in Paris, not in the shadow of the death she witnessed today.

Here, the road became wide and smooth. Abandoned, with the people engaged in, or hiding from, the great rebellion. As she walked, she became aware of short, shuffling steps coming up from behind. She did not turn, would not stop. The steps grew closer until, from the side of her eye, she caught sight of a flash of gold—soft golden curls, and then a pair of deep-brown eyes looking up from behind them.

"Allô?" Smoke and heat gripped her voice.

"Allô," he said, keeping pace.

He was dressed, inexplicably, in clothing better suited to a prince. Clean tan breeches, white shirt—understandably not as clean—and a rich blue velvet vest. He wore shoes without stockings and had the bulk of his golden curls tied in a ribbon. In short, he was a beautiful boy, and had she not felt the soft touch of his hand taking hers, she might have thought him altogether a mirage.

"Where is your *maman*?"

"With God in heaven." A statement of practical truth.

"And your *papa*?"

He pointed vaguely behind them. "He lost me."

"Why are you following me?"

He thought for a moment and said, "Because you look like you're going away. And I want to go away."

No response could be more satisfactory. She squeezed his hand and led him.

L'épisode 23

Renée

VERSAILLES

"Everybody's leaving," Marie-Thérèse says. I am brushing her hair, careful not to let the bristles near her neck, as the red marks will last for days. She is not exaggerating. In these last weeks she has said good-bye to her aunt, uncle, cousins, and her beloved governess, Madame de Tourzel. Though without official permission, I've ingratiated myself into that abandoned post, as Madame Royale and I have always enjoyed each other's company. I cannot offer the same in the ways of courtly instruction or education, but there is no mood for such.

Since the death of Louis-Joseph, she and Louis-Charles have taken to sleeping in their mother's chambers, and the queen watches from her sofa—the very one on which she reclined the first day I entered this room. She has diminished to an almost unrecognizable degree, her hair faded with powder, her skin the same color—a wash of near-white, the same as the nightdress that encompasses her wasted frame.

She is drained in the same way her power has been drained,

as her husband the king and the very idea of royalty and the rule of monarchy crumble like the stones ripped from the Bastille at the hands of bloodthirsty rebels. The day after the fall of the Bastille, Louis was paraded in front of the rebels and forced to listen to chants of *"Vive la Révolution"*—this from the same mouths that once called for the long life of the king, believing him to be some sort of god, that the issue of an heir embodied immortality.

The people are their own god now. Their desires, law. The intangible supremacy of royalty now displaced by an elected National Assembly. Young, healthy Louis-Charles will not be the heir to King Louis's reign. That honor will go to the collective thoughts penned as *la Déclaration des droits de l'homme*. The Declaration of the Rights of Man. The philosophy declares first and foremost that all men are equal. Born equal and entitled to equal treatment. That prosperity will not hinge on birth or station. And that all men must live for the greater good of all other men.

When I hear these words, it's as if I'm hearing memories of Gagnon. This was true Christianity, that men love one another. And if they could not love one another in Christ, they could be compelled to do so through law. He always said that, in the eyes of God, he and the king were brothers. Now, with *la Déclaration*, France herself made it so.

People of the ruling class have always lived within arm's reach of the poor, with nothing more than an agreed-upon sense of superiority to insulate them from the physical touch of the masses. As the summer progresses, that barrier recedes, and the nobles who once lounged within the finery of Versailles scatter like a flock of geese at the sound of a gunshot.

"Well, they won't make me leave, I can tell you." The queen speaks as if making a proclamation to those who might influence such a decision. Instead, it is only her children, two remaining ladies, and I who attend. "They forced me to learn their stupid language, to hold my head high while they spread lies and vulgarities about me, to erase every memory of my childhood. They mock my family and my country now; after I have given *everything* to be their queen, they spit on it. *Vive la Révolution.*" She spat, muttering something in her native tongue. "I will not wear the *tricolore*. Do you understand, *couturière*? Never."

I am wrapping a delicate sausage curl around my fingers, gently brushing it into smooth perfection, but her tone calls me to look up. She is flushed, her chest and cheeks the same shade as one of the three detested colors.

"Not in a rosette, not ribbon-trimmed, not in a hat, not a silk shoe buckle, not in jewels, or buttons, or any conceivable *accessoire*."

"Oui, madame."

"They'll try, you know. They'll try to use Bertin as their puppet. All those cowardly bureaucrats who wet themselves at the voice of the rabble will climb into her ear and whisper that I must appear to be sympathetic. Minister of Fashion, they call her. Always, always it is that the people grumble and my wardrobe pays the price. Not again. If she asks you to stitch me up in the garb of the rebellion, refuse."

"Bien sûr, madame." Though I hope to never have such a confrontation.

The family is called in to breakfast, and I am left to my own devices for a short while, which has become the time I spend with Bertrand. Since that awful day in July, when we all learned of the people's capacity for violence, his duties have narrowed to the strict guard of the queen. Day and night he is at her side or in front of whatever door she is closed up behind. He is at attention while she sleeps, half a step behind her when she walks, keeping her always within his field of vision. From the day King Louis came back from his humiliating display, he—and all—have been urging her to take residence elsewhere. To take the children to Meudon, where the people of *la république* have no expectation of access. The palace at Versailles has always been open to all—not just the halls and galleries, but even the most intimate of spaces. More than once we have found people in all states of uncleanliness wandering through the royal family's private chambers. "They used to be in awe," Bertrand told me, "but now, nothing but contempt."

But Meudon holds too many sad memories, and whether because of pride or foolhardy stubbornness, our queen refuses to leave this place, her home. Thus Bertrand's duties have taken on a far greater sense of urgency. These hours of breakfast and dressing and consulting the agenda for the day mark the entirety of his freedom. Generously, he allows one half hour for me.

As usual, we walk out into the gardens. At the first opportunity of fresh air, he stops and fills his lungs, and I cannot help but think of the life he longs for. I have procured a bit of bread and fruit for our breakfast. We don't venture far, as I do not want to waste a moment of his precious time walking to an ideal spot. But there is a bench, the shade of a tree, and a sense of isolation.

When he comes to sit beside me, I tell him of the queen's tricolor decree. He laughs at my imitation, for I have perfected her tone and accent, delivered with the utmost respect and affection.

"It is a dangerous thing she's asking you to do, Renée."

"How so, dangerous? She has always had her own mind for such things."

"And it has won her no favors. The people—*our people*, Renée—we cannot underestimate the anger. The power. You know they dismantled the Bastille with their bare hands. This is not a gathering of disgruntled citizens anymore. This is an army. A war."

"I know."

"Do you? Does *she*? Does she really think she can dismiss it all by refusing to acknowledge the colors of their flag?"

"She is our queen, Bertrand. Still."

"A queen whose own army is divided. Every day, more soldiers have deserted. I'll be fighting against my own brothers in arms. And they'll have no hesitation in killing me." He takes my face in his hand. "They'll have no hesitation in killing *anyone*. You have to leave, Renée."

"And go . . . where?"

"Home. To your little sheep village." He smiles, knowing how much I hate it when he refers to Mouton Blanc as such. "Far away from this place, and farther away from Paris. We've talked about it before, I know. But so much has changed."

"Not so much. My heart is here, Bertrand. *You* are here. And—"

"But for how long?"

His eyes, blue as the sky on that last day I ever took the sheep to pasture, hold me, aloft as a cloud, suspended in their gaze. In them I see hurt and hope and an unhappiness so deep I cannot fathom the source.

"God alone knows the answer, Bertrand. He brought me here, to you. Do you not understand the *miracle* of circumstance?"

He pulls me forward and kisses me sweetly, then pulls away. "I do. And I see circumstances in my favor now. Before—I might have had the stigma of a traitor for leaving my duty."

"And what has changed?"

He bucks at my challenge. "What has changed is the magnification. If, tomorrow, they found my post abandoned, my uniform laid neatly on my bed, nobody would follow. Nobody would hunt me down, throw me in prison as a deserter, because now there is another side. Another *France*."

"Your duty is to your king."

"My duty now is to my country. To help her survive. And trust me when I tell you the monarchy will not survive. I don't mean their lives in the flesh; I mean the *idea*. The system. In the New World—"

"The New World is not our world."

"Renée, *chérie*—" he grips my shoulder—"this is not your world. You and I—we are tools, don't you see? I am a musket. You are a needle."

I think about the feel of the brush against my palm as I arrange Madame Royale's hair. Louis-Joseph's quilted battlefield. Louis-Charles's chubby hand tracing the pattern of my skirt. And Her Majesty, pointing her hand, devoid of jewels, charging me directly to protect her beloved image. "I'm more than a needle."

"You're not. Not to them. But to me, Renée . . . You are the only reason I'm here at all—to see you every day. But already, look how things have changed."

"Yes, Bertrand. They have changed." I cannot help feeling a little insulted, as he is speaking to me more as if to a child than the woman he has pledged to love. "You will see, though, that they will get better."

He smirks, and for the first time, I feel true anger toward him. "And how do you know this, my little *couturière*?"

"I am not a silly, stupid girl, you know. *La Déclaration.* That will change everything."

"*La Déclaration.* Do you think the men who paraded the head of the governor of the Bastille will care about a piece of paper signed by the king? Already he has no power. He just doesn't know it yet."

"Every year," I say, now speaking to *him* as to a child, "after the shearing, when the men would bring their wool to be measured and sold, always—no matter how fine the quality or how high the price—there was anger, resentment because the king's portion was so outrageous. *La Déclaration* gives them the rights to their property. To whatever is grown and harvested on that property. Do you see? To our land, our crops, our—our women. Our people. Isn't that what they want?"

"*They?* Has your loyalty so changed?"

"Has yours?"

I wonder if he can read the answer in my face as clearly as I can read his.

"*La Déclaration* has come too late," he says. "It is nothing more than an empty gesture from a frightened sovereign. These people—*they* don't want rights. They want blood. The king's, yours, mine. Any who oppose."

"But you don't oppose, really."

"I oppose their methods, but not their ideals. Oh, Renée—" He pulls me close again. It's like falling into strength. "King Louis is bringing in more soldiers, recruits from all over the country to shore up his army here. I won't be missed. Let's leave now, this morning. I have a little money. I've rights to my horse. We could ride out today and be married in Mouton Blanc on Sunday."

Because I am folded into him, I cannot see the grounds, the statues, the palace. I can see only our little town square, the market, the vast expanse of green pasture dotted with sheep, striped with dark earthen paths. The gurgle of the fountains holds none of the music of the stream. And to see them again—Gagnon, Laurette. To know whether they've changed as much as I have, or would they be as the day I left? Healthy and content. But the longing, real as it is, finds no purchase. I back out of his embrace.

"I cannot promise today."

"Renée . . ." There is unmistakable warning in his voice. I'm breaking the promise I made to him months ago, that the next time he asked me to leave, giving me a day's notice, I'd go.

Willingly. Unquestioningly. I told him, *"Don't give me time to plan. Tell me 'tomorrow' and I'll go."* And here he is, fulfilling my wishes, following my directives, and I am faithless in my response.

"The queen—hear me—she comes out of mourning next week. Give me time to help. To prepare her wardrobe as she sees fit. She trusts me, Bertrand, and she has so few people to trust."

"You would choose her over me?"

"Only if you force me to." My response is too quick, too sharp, and I wish immediately to take it back. I should have soothed, *"Non, non, mon amour. I choose you, now and forever."* But my heart speaks too quickly sometimes, and in this moment, with sickening clarity, I see where my heart has found its home. I don't deserve to be a part of his dream because I don't share it. At least not today.

His sigh comes from deep within his cavernous chest. An exhalation composed of every intimate part of him. "Don't you trust me, Renée?"

"With my life. With—" I dare not say *my queen*—"with the lives of those I love."

"I will not fight for them. Do you understand?" It is the second time today I am asked if I understand, though the queen's question seems more rhetorical in hindsight. "I will not take up arms against my brothers. Not in open battle, not in the streets."

"What if you had been there? At the Bastille?"

"I like to think I would have walked away. But I know I would not take aim at a hungry man fighting to feed his family."

"So you're leaving?"

An eternity of heartbeats sound before he answers. "Not without you. At least not now. But soon. I will remain at the queen's door as long as that door is at Versailles. But I will not follow. You may, if you choose. If you are allowed. But not me.

God brought us here to meet. But I believe our journey ends here too. Fair enough?"

I nod and say, "Fair enough," without voicing what I know to be true. That Her Majesty will never leave Versailles. She'll not be taken out like those others, hidden in their coaches, afraid for their lives—or at least afraid to lose the luxuries that define those lives. She'll not give in to the demands of those fueled by *la Déclaration*. I cannot imagine the circumstances that would pry her from her place.

L'épisode 24

Laurette

EN ROUTE

Laurette called him Joseph, named for the dead little prince she'd been told not to mourn. "It's the mercy of the revolution," Marcel had said as the bells tolled their somber proclamation. "One less tyrant in the world." She called him Joseph, too, because he never gave her any other name. When asked, he said nothing, remaining tight-lipped with eyes downcast.

"What did *Maman* call you?" He shook his head. "What did *Papa* call you?" At this, he looked confused.

She tried a game, listing every name she could think of: "Georges? Pierre? Alphonse? Robert?" But no response. He claimed a gypsy at the palace gave him his clothes, and that a grand ghost lady wept when she saw him. He told a single, fantastical story about a room where he came to life a thousand times and walls painted with gold. "Maybe you are an angel after all," she whispered into his curls one afternoon as he slept, head nestled in her lap. "Sent to guide me home."

That first day, they'd walked until the walls of Paris were

just beginning to fade in both distance and light. A small grove of trees hid them from the road, and a trickle of a stream gave much-needed refreshment. Laurette dipped the cup and gave it first to Joseph, repeating until he could drink no more. Before quenching her thirst, she took a great mouthful of water, swished and gargled, then spat it into the earth, expelling the smoke and grit of the city.

"I've nothing to feed you," she told him. "Nothing to cook, so we won't have a fire. Come close to me if you get cold." She didn't need to tell him, though, as he folded himself beside her, head propped on her bosom, and fell asleep before her next breath.

When Laurette awoke, she could think of nothing but the need for food. By her estimation, this day dawned as her third without eating, and God alone knew how many for the boy. She dared not ask. The stream from which they drank their breakfast was too small to provide even hope for fish, and the road too well traveled to think wildlife nearby. Besides, she had nothing to snare or skin or cook with, and the fuzz of hunger allowed only enough strength to walk. By some silent agreement, neither she nor Joseph talked about food—not in memory or speculation or complaint. It was an unknown substance, a secret packed down until hunger was nothing more than a constant, consuming ache.

When she and Marcel had traveled this road the first time, in the opposite direction, they had done so with the illicit excitement of thieves. Upon approaching a fellow band of travelers, Marcel would boldly ask to join in their fireside supper, offering to read from one of his salacious pamphlets in exchange for a meal. "Enough to share," he'd say with a protective arm around her. And, more often than not, the band would comply. They shared a brotherhood of discontentment and conspiracy, and Laurette would fall asleep listening to the rumbling talk of rebellion.

What they could not beg or borrow, they stole. An expert, Laurette crept through barns and coops, fishing warm eggs from beneath roosting hens or giving a cow a predawn milking. She stopped short of stealing livestock, justifying that everything she took would be replaced for the owner in time. Marcel's fawning approval when she rejoined him with her spoils was nearly as rewarding as the food itself. "I've always said you were my lioness. They hunt, you know. Work much harder than the lion." She basked in his glowing remarks, the chuckling assent of whoever joined their camp.

Leaving the city proved to be a different experience. Hourly, it seemed, a thundering coach drove up from behind them, horses at a pace suited for running to—or from—a battle.

On foot, weakened, with one child within and another at her hand, their journey would last three more days.

"Tell me again where we're going," Joseph asked.

"The house where I grew up," she said, fighting the lump of emotion rising in her throat. "The man's name is Gagnon, and there are two other boys—Philippe and Nicolas, older than you. And there are sheep, and goats, and two dogs named Cossette and Copine. And they can do wonderful tricks if you whistle just right. . . ."

She talked as the landscape became familiar. Up this path, and they would arrive at Girard's farm. This other, to the pastureland and through the woods into Mouton Blanc. Over this crest and—

Gagnon.

He didn't see her at first. Or, at least, he didn't recognize her. It might have been only a matter of months since they'd seen one another, but she knew how much she'd changed. She felt the itch of her scalp from her lank, sweat-stiffened hair, the looseness of her teeth, the sharpness of her frame.

He, however, had not altered, save for the fact that his hair was in dire need of a trim, as it poked out straight from his head like straw, and he must not have taken a razor since she left, as the beard usually grown in winter darkened his cheek. In this, though, she took great comfort. Those were her responsibilities, after all, to catch him on a summer night saying, "It's shearing time for you, *mon vieux*," and she would work soap into a lather and hum softly while gliding the blade along the planes of his cheek, his neck.

He stopped, and she watched him see her. Recognize her. Know. He ran his hand through his beard, across the top of his head—both hands—then started walking again. Slowly, purposefully.

"Laurette." He was so close now, she could clearly hear his voice, even though he choked on the word. "Laurette," he said again, this time as if claiming a promise. "Laurette." Pure joy as he stood before her, reaching and bringing her close. She stepped into his embrace, all—even Joseph—dropped and forgotten at her feet. He bent his knees, gazed upon her face, and kissed it. Her brow, her cheeks, her lips. He cupped his hand behind her head and drew her in.

So much—so much she had to tell him. To explain, to beg, but in that moment she took comfort in the vibration of his chest beneath her cheek as he spoke for them both.

"*Merci à Dieu.* Thanks be to God. You are home."

⚜

The first night of her return, Laurette went to the stream and bathed, an hour or more, letting the water wash over her, not wanting to emerge until the filth of the city had been taken at least a mile away. She ran her fingers through her hair, feeling it become loose and compliant, scrubbed her scalp and skin with crude soap, but felt clean just the same. After, she sat on the bank exposed, knowing Gagnon would keep the boys away—himself, too, as he'd loudly announced his presence when he deposited a blanket and a clean dress, walking backward as he approached. She sat on the blanket and let the sun dry her skin, ran the brush through her hair in thin sections, until it was all soft waves. Pressing her hand to her stomach, she prayed to God for the babe's safe deliverance from this weak, shriveled body.

She had a vague recollection of the blanket being tucked around her nakedness and being lifted in strong arms, carried, and deposited in a familiar bed. Not her own, but his—Gagnon's—that she had shared throughout the winter. When she awoke, light was streaming through, and Joseph, scrubbed to something pink, was tucked up beside her.

For days she did nothing but sleep and eat, the room passing from light to dark to light again. Lulled by the conversation on the other side of the door—Gagnon's low rumble, Joseph's inquisitive tone, the older boys' alternating teasing and authority—she cared not what thoughts were waking and which were dreams. All were safety and comfort. All were home.

Her strength returned with every cup of broth, poached egg, bit of bread soaked in warm goat's milk, weak tea.

"You've learned to cook while I was away," she said, propping herself up to eat a stew of clear, flavorful broth and soft vegetables.

"I could cook before you came to me the first time. Don't you remember? You were a hungry little thing then, too."

"Not so little anymore."

"No," he said, eyes averted. "Not anymore."

The first day that Joseph was allowed to accompany the older boys to graze the sheep, Laurette rose, dressed, and stepped out into the midmorning, breathing deep the abundance of air.

"It's not like this in Paris." She held her arms out wide. "Always there is another person, just here, at your fingertips.

And the streets are narrow, and they stink. Oh, Gagnon, you can't imagine the smell."

His response was little more than a grunt and a nod. "Can't say that it will be much more pleasant here today. Mucking the pen."

Laurette smiled. "Sheep dung is sweet perfume next to the stink of Paris."

And for weeks, that was all she uttered about her time away. In obvious obedience, Philippe and Nicolas asked no questions, and all were consumed with answering Joseph's endless inquiries. Laurette commended them on the garden, which yielded a generous amount of late-summer vegetables, and the small grain field looked to be equally promising, much more so than the previous year.

There was one part of her story, however, that could remain unspoken no longer. By early September the fluttering in her stomach, like a bird drying its feathers, was a regular occurrence, and she marveled that she could be standing at the table, ladling soup into bowls, and have it go unnoticed. Of course, she was the only woman in attendance, and even though the mound of flesh was still relatively modest beneath her voluminous skirt, it was only a matter of time before even young Joseph would take notice.

One evening when a brief, light shower left the kindling laid for the outside fire unusable, Laurette went inside and came back with a bundle of paper. "Here, use this," she said as Gagnon continued valiantly to strike his flint.

"What is this?" She'd rolled the paper into a thin white twig.

"Pamphlets."

Gagnon chuckled and renewed his efforts, soon building a modest flame. He and Laurette sat, arms close to touching, and called to the boys to finish their chores and come join them.

This had always been Laurette's favorite time, the end of the day with the sky stretched violet above. Especially now, with the first cool crisp of autumn. The boys came quickly, Joseph claiming the space beside her.

"Shall I tell a story, then?" Gagnon asked, unnecessarily, as he told one nearly every evening. He whistled for Cossette and Copine to join them, each dog settling herself against one of the older boys, leaving only himself alone, detached.

Laurette gently laid a hand on his thigh, as if to capture his attention, saying, "Tell a fable." When he did not flinch, she let her touch remain.

"Let me see . . . Once there was a dog." Cossette and Copine's ears perked, causing them all to laugh. "The dog had found for himself a tasty bone. One with all kinds of scraps of meat stuck to it. And he was taking it far into the forest, because he wanted some peace and quiet away from all the noise and work on the farm to enjoy it." He shifted his weight—infinitesimally, but enough for Laurette to take her hand away.

"As he was crossing the bridge into the forest, he looked down—and what do you think he saw in the water?"

"Fish?" Joseph guessed.

"No," Gagnon said, with a softness that stirred Laurette's heart as much as the spinning life within her. "Not fish; the water was too deep. And still. What he saw was another dog."

"His reflection," Philippe said.

"Yes," Gagnon affirmed. "And what do you think that other dog had in his mouth?"

"A bone!" Nicolas jumped in before his brother could.

"Yes, a bone. Now, this dog was a very selfish dog. *Well,* he thinks to himself, *why should I not have that dog's bone also?* So he bends low to bark at that dog, opens his mouth, and what do you think happens? The bone, it falls out of his mouth. *Le floc!* Splash! Into the water. He has nothing."

"Poor dog," Joseph said through a yawn.

"There is never a loss if there's a lesson learned," Gagnon said. "Now, off—all you boys."

They obeyed, all three to the loft above the barn, Joseph feeling like such a big boy to join them. When they were out of sight and the lamplight snuffed in the window, Laurette ventured a whisper.

"I was worried for a time, Gagnon, that I would be like that dog. Losing everything."

"Because you wanted something more?"

"All I ever wanted was to belong somewhere. With someone."

"You've always had as much with me. This was your home."

"And you told me, over and over, that I could leave. That I could go—anytime I wished." She'd been staring into the flames, and she turned to find him doing the same.

"So you left."

"So I left."

"And you've come back, just like before. Hungry, clutching an even hungrier one by the hand." He looked at her, a smile tugging on his lips. "So it is just like before? I take you in for a time, until you want . . ."

"I won't want to leave again."

"Where is Marcel?"

It was the first his name had been spoken since her return. "I don't know."

"Will he be coming for you?"

"I don't know."

"Do you still love him?"

"He's . . . he's not what I thought. I believed he loved me from the night—that night before Renée went away. But I don't know if he ever did. And he changed so much. When we got to Paris, it was like something took him over. This lust for blood, these *people*." She went on about the long stretches of his absence, his crimes—

"He stole Girard's horse."

She looked away in shame. "I know. I know he did."

"Girard named too high a price for it. I'm indebted to him."

"What price?"

He smiled, calculating. "He wanted me to marry his daughter."

There was no time to stifle her laughter, the expression on his face giving no encouragement to suppress it. "And what did you say?"

"I was tempted, for a time. Because we—the boys and I—missed having a woman in the house. Then I realized I didn't miss having a woman; I missed *you*. It wouldn't be fair to Elianne. Now, you have not answered my question. Do you love Marcel?"

"I'm going to have his child." That would have to suffice as an answer, because it was the only truth she could offer. Gagnon did not move, not a single muscle of his face or body. Not for a full minute as the flames danced beside them, casting shadows and filling the silence with hisses and pops. Laurette looked down into her lap, not embarrassed, but unsure. Then his hand crept into her field of vision, taking hers, and his other touched her face—warm from the fire—and forced her to look into his eyes.

"Has he married you?"

Tears pricked her eyes. "You must know he hasn't."

Illogically, he grinned. "Then, my sweet Laurette, I shall." He brought her close and kissed her brow. "If you'll have me. This will be your home, and I'll give the child my name."

It was a declaration, not a proposal, leaving Laurette to wonder if she owed any kind of response at all. The idea of marrying Gagnon seemed too natural to question, like something that had happened years ago, only to be newly discovered. She waited for him to tell her that she was free to refuse, free to take herself and Marcel's child to find whatever fate awaited. Free to return to him, if she liked. Surely it couldn't be this easy, to simply say yes and have—finally—a life and future assured.

"But should Marcel come for me . . ."

His grip tightened, thumb beneath her chin, holding her in place. "You won't be free to leave. He won't be able to take you. Is that what you want?"

She thought back to the night she left, when she'd offered herself to him—unmistakable in her intent. The motives behind this offer, however, were hidden, and an unwelcome shadow of doubt emerged. Was she a prize in some unknown competition? Was her child simply another foundling to be taken in? Would marriage somehow ease his conscience for having so easily lost her to the ills of the city and the dangers of the rebellion? For all she knew, Gagnon would take her as a wife for no other reason than to fend off future threats from Elianne Girard. Looking into his eyes, though, the motive didn't matter. Even in the firelight, she recognized their hue—gray and green together. The colors of promised rain and new life. He might never love her with the all-consuming desire that sated her hunger all those breadless days with Marcel. But neither, still, would he let her go hungry. Nor the baby within her, nor Joseph, whom he'd welcomed and fed without question. For them, as much as for her own life, she would accept.

"When, do you think?" She touched her hand to her stomach. "I don't expect the baby until—"

"Tomorrow."

"So soon?" She suspected he worried she might have a change of heart, and could think of no words to assure him otherwise.

"To wait much longer, I'm afraid, will set tongues to wagging more than they already will. Would you be content with just a small ceremony? The two of us, the boys, and whoever happens to be in the church to act as witnesses?"

She felt a rush of relief at the thought. "Of course. That will be perfect."

His look turned serious. "There's one other thing. Father Pietro will expect us to give Confession."

"I won't."

"You must, to take Communion. I've allowed you to—"

"Allowed?"

He changed course. "I've said little about your reluctance to attend Mass—all these years that you've been living under my roof. But this is different. Matrimony is a sacrament. If we are to be married in the eyes of the Church—"

"I don't care about the eyes of the Church."

"The eyes of God, then."

"I won't go behind that curtain and tell him everything I've . . ." The fire had burned down to embers and the night taken on a true chill. She longed for a shawl to wrap around her not for its warmth, but for its comfort. Something to hide behind, because the thought of all those words, her deeds spoken into the darkness, terrified her like a living nightmare.

"The Holy Scriptures tell us—"

"Please—" Her instinct was to tell him to *stop*, knowing she had no argument against God's Word, but then a fluttering within her, the fluttering of the child—*Marcel's* child—reminded her of Marcel's growing antipathy toward not only the institution of the Church in all its abuse of power, but also all of Christianity. He'd said precisely that the Church had no power to sanctify a marriage. Here, she seemed to be speaking his argument with her lips. "Please—" she softened her tone—"what does Scripture say?"

"That if we confess our sins, he—Christ Jesus—is faithful and just to forgive us our sins, and to cleanse us from all unrighteousness. *All* unrighteousness, Laurette."

She thought about the deliciousness of the bath she took

upon her return, washing the grit of Paris from her body. Sleeping beneath the sunshine, completely alone. *Alone.* "It hardly seems fair, Gagnon, when you have nothing to confess."

"I was cruel to you, Laurette." By now, with the fire nothing more than veins of orange in a dark pit and the sky moonless above, his face was obscured as if behind a confessional curtain. Here, though, the air was not warm and close, but wide and sweet, so that his words carried beyond her ears and clear to heaven, though she knew he'd whispered them to God in the darkness. "You came to me and I rejected you, even though I'd had thoughts . . . thoughts I could have made pure if I'd asked you to be my wife before . . ."

"Before I left?"

"Before Renée left." This, perhaps, God did not hear, as it nearly disappeared behind the hiss of an ember.

"What can I confess?" She felt tears, cold against her cheek. "What do you not know? What does God not know? Doesn't he see everything?"

"Confession is not for God's benefit. Or for mine. It's for you, Laurette. Speaking it brings your soul to the surface. Otherwise, sometimes, I think, our silence keeps the truth hidden from ourselves."

Since before Renée. She could tell by the direction of his voice that he was looking away.

"What shall I confess to, then? To being foolish? To being jealous of Renée and giving myself to Marcel the first time so that I could pull his love away from her? Foolish for wanting him and wanting him, even when he cast me aside? When I think about what I've done—how I must appear to you . . ." She saw herself, full-figured, eyes bright with wine, sitting in Marcel's lap at Le Cochon Gros, pinned beneath him beside the fire after the shearing, exchanging glances throughout the winter, walking along beside him in the spring. "I'm so sorry,

Gagnon, that I didn't listen to you when you warned me. And I'm sorry most of all that I ever thought you would—that you could see me the way he saw me. That you would want me the way he—"

"Enough with that." The weight of his hand on her shoulder brought the same comfort as a heating stone at her feet. Still, she took it and pressed her face against it, not caring about the tears that were now flowing freely.

"I'm sorry that I didn't trust you to take care of me. And I'm sorry I helped steal Monsieur Girard's horse. And I hate every minute I spent in Paris—every minute with . . . *him*. I've never felt so filthy and used and alone. Only—" she clasped his hand in both of hers and held it to her body—"I can't be sorry about the baby. I hate what I did—how I lived—with Marcel. But I cannot hate this child."

"Nor do I." Gagnon stood, bringing her with him, and drew her into his arms. He held her long enough for her to repeat the litany of her confession—every word spoken into the fold of his shirt. He said nothing in response. No words of comfort, no assurances that it was *fine*. All *forgiven*. He didn't try to hush her or draw out any more than she was willing to say. He asked no questions, showed no frustration at her repetition. He remained steadfast as ever until she sobbed herself into silence, midsentence. She turned her face to lay her cheek against his now-damp shirt and felt the cooling breeze against her skin, thinking, *I'll never have to say these words again.* She'd poured her sin and sorrow and felt—empty. Not depleted, but like a jug emptied of its soured remains and ready to be filled with something new. Her body carried Marcel's child, but her heart knew only Gagnon.

"Will you ask Christ to forgive you?"

"I want you to forgive me."

He stepped away, and she missed him immediately. "You

were restored to me the minute I saw you on the path. But to be restored to Christ, you must come to him."

Though the night itself was dark, she closed her eyes, not only to shut herself away but because she knew she was supposed to. "Holy Father—" She opened her eyes. "Will you hold my hands, Gagnon? Hold me steady? I feel dizzy." It was not a complete lie. Her head pounded from its onslaught of tears, and the darkness felt disorienting. Once in his grip, she closed her eyes again, but no more words would come. She pleaded, "Tell me what to say."

"Will you speak my words from your heart?"

"I will."

"Say, 'Father of mercy, I have spoken my sins. And I am cleansed with the blood of Jesus on the cross.'"

Laurette spoke them faithfully, perfectly, each phrase with a ring of truth as sure as her confession.

⚜

The market square in Mouton Blanc breathed the same resurrective air Laurette herself felt. It was nothing like the thriving days of her youth, when merchants shouted over one another in an effort to take coin or goods in trade, but there were signs of life: a hastily erected pen of late-born lambs, a few wagons with baskets brimming with summer vegetables. A middle-aged woman walked up and down with a tray of soft, downy chicks strapped to her chest. *"Chick-chick-chick! Three-a-copper!"*

Laurette tugged at Gagnon's sleeve. "Can we get some? Maybe six?"

"Of course," he said, tucking her arm in his. "What kind of a groom would I be if I didn't buy my bride a gift on her wedding day?"

It was then that the boys learned the true purpose of their journey—they'd been promised only an afternoon in town.

All three whooped in delight, though Joseph seemed short of understanding.

L'église du Mouton Perdu, the Church of the Lost Sheep, was a small structure, with a single, arched door that opened to an empty, dark vestibule. While many members of France's First Estate—the clergy—benefited financially from their strong ties to the ruling class, the priest serving here, Father Pietro de Salinas, was a poor Spanish transplant willing to pastor those in an equally poor French village. A dozen solid, backless benches—worn soft through the centuries—lined a narrow aisle; beveled glass in the windows bathed the chapel in gray. Three women knelt in prayer at the altar; three candle flames danced surrounding the empty alms box.

Aside from the triptych altarpiece depicting the Annunciation, Crucifixion, and Ascension, the only artwork in the chapel was a large painting on the wall opposite the window of Saint Germaine, saint and shepherdess. She was the patron saint of lost sheep and children, being an unwanted and unloved child forced to live with the animals she tended. Every spring, on her saint's day, the villagers at Mouton Blanc celebrated her legend, choosing one little girl to play the part reenacting her miracle. With one arm tucked up to resemble Germaine's deformity, the girl ran through the market, chased by the woman chosen to play her wicked stepmother. The stepmother would scream at the girl, accusing her of stealing bread from the kitchen, but when the girl opened her apron to confess the sin, a hundred flowers wafted to the ground. Laurette had never been chosen to play Germaine, but Renée had, and she'd practiced for weeks unfurling her apron to make the blossoms fly.

Father Pietro entered from behind a heavy drape, looking pleased to see so many souls within his little house of worship, and even more so when Gagnon informed him of the reason for their visit.

"So rare to hear good news these days," he said, clasping the thin hands that protruded like twigs from the voluminous sleeves of his black robe. "How soon until the happy occasion?"

"Today," Gagnon replied, his own hands clasped in pleading. "Now."

Father Pietro's dark brows rose high. "Is there a reason for such a hurry?"

Gagnon leaned closer and whispered, "The oldest reason known to Christendom."

Understanding dawned, and the priest stepped back. "Shall we, then, have Confession before the ceremony?"

"And have our marriage serve as penance?" Gagnon's words were tinged with humor. "Our sins are well known to our Savior, and covered by his blood, Father. We have confessed to him and to each other."

Laurette's heart swelled with gratitude for his intervention, but Father Pietro would not be so easily denied.

"You know well you cannot take Communion without Confession, and I will not join you as man and wife without knowing you come together fully restored to righteousness."

Behind them, the boys—all three—shifted nervously, but Laurette stood resolute. Who could know Gagnon and assume him to be anything other than righteous? One truth would clear him of the sin Father Pietro assumed. He need only say that the child she carried wasn't his, that he was offering to share his life as a gift. Instead, he placed a protective arm around her.

"We wish to be married, Father. To make a permanent home for these boys and the child to come. We will choose a marriage in the eyes of God over one in the eyes of the Church and save ourselves the fee." He punctuated his statement with a wink to Laurette—they were her words, after all—and a thin silver coin held eye level to the Father.

Without delay, and to the bemusement of the women at

prayer, Father Pietro pulled Philippe to serve as altar boy, holding a small plate of the host and later, a pewter chalice of sacramental wine, both of which he administered with Latin prayers and undue haste. Laurette took the bread to her tongue and sipped the wine for the first time since her first Communion. When, with practical efficiency, Gagnon and Laurette were declared man and wife in the name of the Father and the Son and the Holy Spirit, they exchanged a chaste kiss, after which Gagnon finally pressed the coin into Father Pietro's palm.

"I will see you at the baptism," the priest said. "If not before."

The atmosphere in the market square had erupted into something like a celebration by the time the newly married couple and their gathering of lost sons emerged from the church. Shopkeepers congregated in the street, and a steady stream of shouts poured through the open doors of Le Cochon Gros.

Though the scene before her was on a completely different scale, Laurette's mind went back to that terrible final day in Paris—the shouting and the macabre celebration. Even without the brandishing of crude weapons or the presence of the king's army, the revelry carried a hint of the same dark tone. Instinctively, she reached for Joseph and brought the two of them under Gagnon's protective arm.

"What do you think it is?" she asked, her fears in no way allayed by the lack of violence.

"Come." Gagnon ushered them into the street. Once they came to the door of Le Cochon Gros, he handed the care of Joseph to the older boys and took Laurette's hand. They walked in and were met immediately with a wall of noise. A cask of wine sat on the bar, and upon arrival, both Laurette and Gagnon were handed a cup and ordered by Saumon to fill and drink to their satisfaction. No less confused, they complied, Laurette surprised to find it tasted no sweeter than what she took from the chalice Father Pietro pressed to her lips.

"Gagnon!" The crowd shouted his name in chorus, and from among them, Dubois emerged, his face flush, his shirt stained. *"C'est une célébration, mon ami!"*

"How did you know?" Gagnon asked. "We've only just—"

"How did we know?" He bent first to Laurette, his face inches from hers, then stood tall again. "How did we know! All of France knows! And soon, all of the world!"

Another shout, and with it Laurette understood clearly that nobody here was celebrating the marriage of Émile Gagnon and the orphan Laurette.

"Vive la France! Vive la République!"

"No," she whispered, the wine turning sour. "No, no more." She found herself alone, Gagnon swept into the crowd of men, more shouts, more nonsensical talk. The room grew dark and insufferably hot. She dropped her cup, caring not that the wine spilled to the floor, on her bare feet. How could it be, after feeling blissfully complete only moments ago, that she could once again be left alone while men shouted praise to *la République*?

She groped her way through the crowd and was almost to the door when strong arms came around her, spun her, lifted her, and brought her down for her second kiss of the day.

"It has happened." Strange how she could so clearly hear Gagnon's whisper above the crowd.

"What has happened?"

"*La Déclaration.* Our rights, as men. As citizens. As equals. Laurette, do you know what this means?"

"War?" A supposition based on all she knew of Marcel and the scenes like this she'd so often witnessed.

"*Non, ma Laurette.* It is all we wanted, all we've asked for. *La Déclaration* will bring us peace."

L'épisode 25

Renée

VERSAILLES

The draftiness of the house never works in concert with nature. When it is hot, the rooms are stuffy, and more than once a day I have to run outside to feel a breeze. When it is cold, the drafts make it impossible to get warm. Rain is different. If it persists, then a certain dankness makes itself known, as men and women bring it inside, their skirts damp and coats dripping. A sudden downpour, however, can be a surprise. The sound is hidden in the height and thickness of the ceiling, and many of the inner rooms have no windows.

Today, the rain is torrential, a steady stream from the sky, and it has brought the rabble of Paris into the halls of the palace. They've come for a royal audience and are at first disappointed. The king has been out hunting, and Her Majesty at the Petit Trianon, where she escapes more and more frequently without her usual assortment of companions. In earlier times, under ordinary circumstances, a disgruntled crowd would raise no alarm. After all, people came day and night to wander the halls, rarely with any expectation of being seen or heard. But these are not ordinary times, and this is not an ordinary crowd. On this day, Versailles is overrun with women. Poor, rain-soaked women driven by hunger and unsatisfied by platitudes.

The queen is sent for and returns, entering through a little-used door that allows her to bypass the Salle des États, where the women have gathered on the promise of an hour of the king's ear. Armed guards flank her on all sides, Bertrand at the rear, capitalizing on his height to scan for threats. I know better than to distract him when he is thus engaged, and nothing in the queen's demeanor makes me feel like I am invited to keep the family company. She is obviously angry, and by the words she spouts between the perfect cadence of their footsteps, it is clear her anger is directed at her guards.

"You stupid, stupid—" and then a word from her mother tongue that is clearly not a salute to their strength and loyalty. "Behaving as you did at that, that . . . farce. When will you learn these people are animals? *Sauvages. Bêtes.* They have no more sense of diplomacy than a rutting stag in spring, and nothing near the grandeur. Or usefulness."

She is speaking of a banquet a few evenings ago, held in honor of new recruits brought in to replace the king's depleted army. It was, at first, to be an affair for the soldiers alone, free of any royal presence so that the men could conduct themselves in a manner suited to their station: raucous, with bouts of challenge and good-natured violence. Since the death of Louis-Joseph and the fury of the rebellion, the king and queen have by and large abandoned any show of royal excess. On this night, however, they were compelled to make an appearance, to show acceptance of and appreciation for the men newly dedicated to the healthy defense of France. And so, the little royal family complied, dressed in simple yet elegant clothing, down to the velvet breeches of Louis-Charles in his first official outing as dauphin.

All had gone well, according to Bertrand's whispered account in the wee hours of the morning when the queen was abed and his duty relieved. His words were saturated with wine, his face flush, his uniform disheveled—but he seemed, for the first since I've known him, completely at ease.

"Until—" and here he took on the manner of a boy facing chastisement—"the wine was flowing a little too freely, and . . . some—not me—got careless. And started shouting for death to the rebels and throwing those tricolor ribbons on the ground. Stomping them, calling for blood. Just what soldiers do. Bloviate, you know? Empty words. When we are alone."

But someone saw, and someone told, and the next day the newspapers of Paris were filled with the gross exaggeration of the king and queen calling for the death of the rebellion—of the rebels themselves. Never mind that they were long abed before the first cockade hit the floor.

The queen still intersperses insults between the steps of her escort, and I catch Bertrand's eye long enough to send up a sympathetic smile and a quickly blown kiss. He would never return the gesture under circumstances such as these, but I am rewarded with a brief twinkle of a blue eye that only I could ever notice.

The evening is falling, and the women refuse to leave. Refuse, as if one ever has a right to stake a claim in another's home. The king has been summoned from his hunting and will face them alone, which, given our queen's current humor, is a better choice than relying on her sisterhood to soothe them.

Their shrieks and shouts echo, as I imagine the banshees from Gagnon's late winter–night tales. While other souls in the palace make their way to their own chambers and business, I have no business to attend to and no chamber worth retiring to at this hour of the evening. Following the noise, I come to the Salle des États, which looks like a demented market square in the wake of a hurricane. The women, dressed in their aprons and caps, stand facing their king, who paces the length of a raised platform at the front of the room.

"All that is in the royal storehouses is for you to take!" His voice, weak and tremulous, hits a pitch not much different than that of the enemies gathered before him. "Flour enough to make all the bread you need to feed yourselves and your children."

"He thinks we want bread!"

"What use is bread without blood!"

While the shouted threats are frightening, my heart grows cold at the mutterings that never reach the king.

"Rip her head off, I will. Take her jewels right off the bloody stump."

"Fancy her, mourning the death of one son when I've buried three just this summer. Seems the score should be evened up."

"Limb from limb, I say. Send half of her back to that cursed place."

All of this while the king shouts concessions over their heads. Sugar, he says. And hunting on the royal grounds, if they have the guns and ammunition to shoot clean. They laugh at this, claiming no need for guns when they have clubs and claws, brandishing all manner of knives and hatchets for good measure.

Suddenly, every word, every threat, every warning Bertrand has ever spoken comes to life. He saw this. He knew this night would happen, that the hatred of the people would leave the streets of Paris and make its home here.

I've been winding my way through the crowd and am about to make haste for the queen's chambers to warn her of this imminent threat when something catches my eye. At first, I can't place the memory, only that I have seen something familiar. Something—then it is gone. From my sight, not my mind, and I stop in place and turn full circles, trying to find it again.

Not a face, though every woman here bears a countenance so streaked with mud as to hide any familiar feature, but a—

There, with her back turned. It is darkened from the rain, and I need to work my way to see the front again, but I'm certain it's her.

"Laurette!"

The din is such that my shouts dissolve, but I persist, garnering a little more attention each time until she is within arm's reach, and I touch the familiar green material of the vest, knowing when she turns around I will see my peacock-feather stitching. "Laurette?"

She turns, and for a moment I convince myself that this is her, *ma cousine*, my Laurette. But then, the face beneath the grime twists into a sneer, and she shoves me away.

I clutch at the vest. "Where did you get this?"

"What do you care?"

"I made it. For somebody. Not for you."

She pushes me away again, harder, and I lose my grip. "It's mine."

"It can't be."

"Are you saying I stole this?" She cackles, catching the attention of the women around her. "Do you believe this? Here I am, wearing clothing I found in my *own* home. And she's calling me a thief!"

"I'm not—"

"Who is she to call me a thief?" By now she's not merely shouting rhetorical questions to the crowd. I'm surrounded by a dozen or more women who look just like her, only dressed in rags—the kind of rags that might have inspired pity at one time and would do so again if I didn't feel their gaze like so many tiny daggers.

"Have you seen her before?"

"Do you know her?"

"Is she one of us?"

"She's one of *them*."

And I'm encircled, trapped. "*Pardonnez.* I'm nobody. Just a servant here. A seamstress, and I made that for my cousin. Back home, and I don't know how it would be *here*. She would never—"

"Not good enough to be *here*." She turns my words into a mocking insult and grabs my wrist, holding it out for display to her audience. "Because hands that stitch for Her Majesty could surely not stitch for the likes of me, eh?"

"Please." I dare not try to take my hand away, lest she imagine further insult. "I just need to know what happened to the girl I made this for. How did you come to have it?"

She measures me, releases me, and lets fly a stream of spit at my feet. "I took up a room with a certain kind and generous friend, and found this stuffed under the mattress. It's mine, *juste et honnête*. And just because you work for *her* doesn't mean you have the authority to take it away."

A woman behind me scoffs. "If we had our way, the queen herself wouldn't have the power to take it."

Yet another, "If I had my way, she would not have *hands* to take it. Chop 'em off I would, and take the jewels with me. Now *that's* something to steal."

They laugh again, sounding like a flock of grackles before a storm. So entertained by their imagined violence are they, I am able to slip away. I don't know how to make sense of what I've seen. Laurette in Paris? Now gone from Paris? Without once trying to find me? For surely, if Marcel made it back to Mouton Blanc with my messages, she would know where to find me. How to find me. And did she come alone? With Marcel? With Gagnon? I know many of the people here are from the countryside, transplanted to the city looking for a means to survive. But Laurette? What would take her away from home?

By now evening has fallen and the king makes his final proclamation: that they all must go. All but one.

"Being but one man, I cannot negotiate with a hundred voices. Choose one of you to speak with me, and the rest—go back to your homes, assured that I will do all in my power to meet your needs."

They respond to his pronouncement with jeers, several in the crowd wondering if he is a man at all. Contrarily, given all their bravado, few seem willing to take on the honor. In a final sorting, one steel-eyed woman steps forward, and the rest disperse as the king's guards herd them like sheep into the main hall and toward the courtyard. Then out to the front steps.

I follow, hoping against hope that perhaps—somewhere—Laurette is here. If nothing else, I want one more conversation with the woman in the vest. If I can get her alone, away from the need to posture in front of her friends, perhaps she could tell me where . . .

But she's gone. I've lost track of her in the wave of women.

Late into the night, an uneasy peace falls on the palace. I've taken myself to the sewing room but cannot bear the oppressive solitude. Feeling restless and useless, I follow the muffled voices to the door leading to the queen's apartments and open it just wide enough to make the conversation clear, even if the speakers remain out of sight. There are half a dozen at least, their backs to me so I see nothing but suits and wigs and bits and pieces of Her Majesty, divided like a triptych behind them.

"All the grain stores in the city?" she says. "He'll open all of them?"

"So he said, *madame*." The dog in Her Majesty's lap emits a low growl when she is proffered a sheet of paper. "Which the woman demanded in writing."

"*Pfft.* Demanded. I'll bet my crown the slut can't read her own name."

"That may be, *madame*." Now I recognize the voice—the same adviser who denied the queen an afternoon sledding with her son on his last New Year. "But His Majesty bids you sign it as well. A gesture of good faith."

"Good faith." There is a rustling as she takes the paper, then the angry scratching of a quill. "Faith in what, tell?"

He seems to know better than to answer, only hands the document to a page and dispatches him to the king, who awaits in his office. "And now," he says, with a far less submissive air, "let me ask you again to consider moving yourself and the children into the king's quarters. It would be safer for everybody and less of a strain on your guard staff if you consolidated the family for the night."

The detail who escorted the queen to her room stand at attention in a semicircle around her, two men facing each door. Bertrand faces the one I'm peering through, and I learn that I am not as invisible as I would like. He's looking directly at me, all hint of humor gone. I should close the door, but instead I open it a pinch wider.

"I'll not have fishwives and banshees dictate my habits," the queen says disdainfully. "The children are asleep—and a time we had of it getting them so. They're frightened enough without being dragged out of one bed for another. My mind is clear on this. Now go."

I know she's rankled him, but he speaks no more, and soon the queen is left to relative solitude—just her and twelve brave, beating hearts encased in the men who guard her.

The hours tick by, and nothing seems more unlikely than sleep. The queen is abed with her children, Bertrand and his men at attention, and I tucked away on a sofa. I've closed my eyes off and on, attempting rest. In between the bouts of darkness I see Bertrand watching, and we make silent promises to each other.

This will be our last night.

Come dawn, come tomorrow, we leave.

And dawn is fast approaching.

⚜

At first I think the sound is nothing more than an echo of all the grumbling we heard throughout the night, but something is different. It's sharper, familiar. Close.

I sit up on the sofa and listen.

The voice—the woman wearing Laurette's vest. Her screeching tone is unmistakable. The last I heard it, she was laughing, though she's not laughing now. The hairs on my arms rise up at the sound, because I remember, too, *why* she was laughing. The macabre jokes. The threats. The bloody fantasies of—

"Mon Dieu!"

Bertrand and his men are already at full alert, and I follow him and six others he's ordered into the queen's bedchamber, where a lantern burns low. She sits straight up in her bed, blanket clutched to her breast, children beside her.

"Madame," says Bertrand, "you must—"

"I hear them," she says, her voice eerily calm.

"Madame," I say, "there's no time! Quickly, to the king's chamber!" Without waiting for any kind of permission, I shake Louis-Charles awake. Marie-Thérèse is already clutching her mother's sleeve.

"They'll find me," the queen says. "They'll follow me straight there and kill him—"

"Nobody's killing anybody," Bertrand says. He picks Louis-Charles up and hands him to one of the soldiers before parting the panel that hides the door to the hidden passage straight to the king's chamber. "Go, and be quick! Run." They leave, two running ahead of the queen and Marie-Thérèse, three behind, one carrying the sleepy boy. I'm left standing, closing the panel, aligning it with the others to hide its existence.

"What are you doing, Renée? Follow them!"

"I'm not leaving you. Nobody wants—"

An explosion of violence on the other side of the door calls to him. In a single voice the guards shout, *"Halt! In the name of the king!"*

To which the women chorus, *"After tonight there'll be no king. Nor queen neither, once we've had our way!"*

"Stay here," Bertrand commands me. "Do you understand?"

Obedience is my reply. I'm frozen—not in fear, but in contemplation. Calculation. By sheer volume, I know that the women outnumber the remaining guards, and their intent is clear. They want the queen. Her flesh, her blood, her life. If they know she isn't here . . .

In the time it takes me to cross the room, I say two prayers. First, that God will protect my queen, and second, that Bertrand will forgive my actions.

The sight that greets me when I burst into the antechamber is nothing I could have imagined. The women who surrounded me in the Salle des États have multiplied threefold, as has their anger. They are armed, too. With knives, sticks, and pistols, though their weapons hold far less threat than their clawed, grasping hands. In front, the one with the green vest—I've ceased thinking of it as Laurette's. There's no time for that now, and I tuck the question of my cousin away, forcing myself to forget in the moment.

But she has not forgotten.

"Her!" The woman points to me, wielding a baton of rusted iron. "Still fancy me a thief? All of this, and I'm taking only what's due to me. Just the flesh from her foreign bones to pay for what I've lost!"

She charges, and Bertrand aims his pistol, shouting, "Halt!"

But she will not be stopped. None of them will. Like a gathering storm of rags and anger and iron, they rain—relentless. The men, disbelieving that the fairer sex could ever be moved to any act of true violence continue to brandish their swords in a threatening posture, repeating, *"Halt! Halt!"* As if mere words could stand as a bulwark of defense.

I, however, see the truth. The women carry weapons in their hands, but they carry hunger in their bellies, dead children in their hearts, broken men in their arms. They suffer all that my queen has suffered, and while she hides behind a wall of soldiers, they have only hopelessness as refuge. They will run the men over on their way to her chambers. They will tear the panels from the walls in search of a hidden door. They will find it, they will follow, and unless every man in the regiment is armed and waiting in the king's apartment, they won't stop until the last bit of royal flesh dangles from their rusted blades.

Desperate for Bertrand to follow my thoughts, I shout, "Stop them! At all cost!"

The explosion from his pistol coincides with my command, and before I fall silent, the intricate stitching of peacock feathers is wasted, shot through, singed with fire, and fallen to the floor.

A new howl rises up, an unholy sound of fresh despair.

Bertrand turns his head to me and says, "Save yourself!" It is a split second, but enough time for a murder of soot-faced women to descend upon him, weapons abandoned.

I can think only to distract them, so I slither through, successfully maneuvering around their focused anger, and come out the other side at the door that leads to the main hall. A dozen soldiers approach, and I run to meet them halfway. "Make haste to the king. She is there, with the children."

From behind me I hear sounds of battle, as much as any fought on soil. My only desire is to run from it, to follow the guards and see my queen safe in Poseidon's shadow. Better yet, to flee to Apollo's statue and wait for Bertrand to come find me in the approaching dawn. I've yet to fulfill my vow to be there at that hour, to see the myth fulfilled of a god racing through the heavens with the promise of a new day.

A brace of women, bloodied yet carrying renewed fervor rush past, shouting, *"Au Roi! Au Roi!"* They have obviously discovered the empty bedchamber, but not the passage, as they pour forth spewing new threats and sporting fresh wounds. The soldiers follow, looking for all the world like they are returning from the field. Four of them, uniforms askew, hats abandoned, weapons drawn—they run in pursuit. The fifth, a stone-faced man named Alsace du Vin known for his easy charm and ruthless wit, emerges and stops short in front of me.

I look behind him. "Where is Bertrand?"

He lays a hand on my arm. "Go to him. I'll send someone."

His words stain as much as his touch, which leaves a red print when he withdraws his hand.

No.

My shoes, soft leather laced up my calves, feel like lead, sinking with every step. The first time I walked into this room, I'd been awed by the ornate decorations, the silk, the gold, the opulence of life. There'd been the humming chatter of conversation. Laughter, stories. A truly welcoming heart.

Now.

The acrid scent of gunfire lingers, and the silence.

Near silence.

The sound of labored breath permeates, and I see him, my mountain, flat upon the floor. The intricate pattern of the carpet obscured by blood.

I rush to his side, kneel at his head. His face is a new shade of pale, his lips utterly without color as I press mine to them. When I rise, his eyes are open, blonde lashes half-mast.

"Is the queen safe?" His lips do not move.

"She is, my love."

"You have to leave now. Will you promise me? I couldn't . . ."

Blood is pooling behind his head, trickling out of his ear, staining my skirt.

"They would have killed her, Bertrand. You saved her. You got her away. You protected her."

"I wasn't trying to protect her. I'm sorry, but I wasn't. I was trying to protect you, Renée."

My name is the last he speaks before his countenance turns to peace. His gaze flutters wide, and I know he is picturing the cottage on a farm, riding the horse hc earned the rights to. For him, it is a clear day—evening, the sky violet and orange. For me, the storm outside rages on, loud enough that I can hear thunder over the shouts of murder in the palace and the echoing footsteps of its citizens. His eyes, though, are clear blue, full of wonder, even as the rest of his body goes perfectly still beneath my palm. I bring my hand to my lips, pressing his final heartbeat against my kiss.

I feel like I could stay there forever, even if it meant the rest of my life surrounded by death. My love, just beyond my touch, a stranger in my cousin's clothing, and I to blame. I've made promises to both Laurette and Bertrand, promises to return home, but how?

I touch my fingertips to Bertrand's lids and close his eyes, leaving a crimson stain on the pale flesh. His brow is cool to my final kiss. Then, as much as I hate that first, final separation, I force myself to stand. I'll speak no words to his departed spirit, knowing I'll be overflowing with speech when we are united again.

"Mademoiselle."

The thought that I am the only living soul in the room causes me to yelp at the intrusion, and I turn to see a familiar figure. Not in face or being, but dress. Patched breeches, stained shirt, bare feet, red cap.

"You startled me," I say, feeling instantly guilty for the

healthy pounding of my heart. "There's no one here. Only me, and I'm nobody."

"Oh," he says, a wicked grin spreading across his grime-smeared face. "You're not nobody. You're a combatant. An enemy of *la République*. And you are coming with me."

⚜

I face this new day with my hands bound behind me, coarse rope chafing my skin. They've not bothered to check my pockets, so they don't know I have scissors within reach to cut through, and a solid gold knotting shuttle to reconfigure the strands into something beautiful. But then, I'm not inclined to do either. Numbly, I follow my instructions, up the steps into the grain wagon, where I'm loaded in alongside valets and cooks and chambermaids and soldiers.

Soldiers.

Five prisoners away, I lock eyes with Alsace du Vin, who breaks his gaze to look at his handprint in Bertrand's blood on my sleeve. Silently he questions, and I answer with a shake of my head.

We are leaving Versailles in the direction of Paris, traveling behind the royal carriage, where, according to the conversation around me, the king, the queen, and their children are safely aboard. They are prisoners now, just like the rest of us, and I can only pray that they have been spared some of our indignities.

Let her hands be free, Lord, that she might hold her children.

I pray, too, that the carriage blinds are drawn to block out the sight that we must endure. On either side of the road, in a line that appears to stretch the entirety of the dozen miles to Paris, mobs of rebels jeer at each turning of the wheels. My mind journeys back to that afternoon with Madame Gisela, the rich upholstery of the carriage my first taste of luxury. And the hours before, when the kindness of Gagnon protected her.

Now face after face twists in anger; tattered bodies dance, their weapons raised in victory. Another and another and another—red caps and gaping mouths. Some women hold thin children to their breasts while others hoist them on their fathers' shoulders to get a better view. They meld into a single visage, like a walk down the hall of mirrors, the same face reflected over and over again.

Until . . .

My mind is dull with hunger and fatigue and loss, but in an instant life shoots through me. Tattered clothing, yes. Victorious in rebellion? Yes. And the red cap—only in this is he changed. The black curls fringed beneath it are achingly familiar.

I worm my way through my fellow prisoners, ignoring their protest, and press my body against the side of the wagon. Its wall rises to the middle of my chest. I lean over and shout.

"Marcel!"

He doesn't hear me, see me. We're passing, and I turn my head to look back and shout his name again, adding, "Laurette! Laurette!" in case she is nearby. We roll on and on. He grows smaller with each turn of the wheel, becomes just another indistinguishable silhouette. Still I shout his name. My cousin's name. Somewhere within the wagon, new commands are issued, calling for *"Silence!"*

But I will not be silent.

"Marcel! Laurette!"

Until I feel the blow of something hard and sharp at the back of my head, and everything goes black.

Part V

L'Automne (Autumn) 1789—
l'Été (Summer) 1791

Réveillez-moi pour voir un jour glorieux. . . .

⚜

L'épisode 26

Renée

À LA COURT

I lose track of the days and know only that when I am brought up from the prison where I've been held—shackled—in a cavernous room with countless other women, it is a bitter-cold wind that blows against my face. Still, the air, choked as it is with chimney smoke, is welcome, and I gulp in as much as I dare.

There are five of us taken out. We shuffle in step, prodded by guards who make crude comments with each touch of the stick. I am the smallest, and probably the youngest, though the conditions of the prison have turned us all to crones. I am thinner now than I ever was in even the leanest times in Mouton Blanc. I can feel the dryness of my skin, unwashed since my arrival—water is far too precious to waste on something so frivolous. My lips are cracked with the cold; they split and bleed if I open my mouth too wide to speak or eat. There's little chance to do either.

For those sharing the same plight, we women do a poor

job commiserating with or comforting each other. When it was learned I was a resident at the Palace of Versailles—albeit a servant—hatred rained down on me from all sides. Noblewomen of the Second Estate, resentful of our equality as prisoners, blamed me for being one of the class responsible for our misery. Those like me, poor and without any crime to claim, mistook my silence for aloof disdain. They teased me unmercifully for the colorfulness of my dress, calling me the queen's gypsy along with far more degrading names. Sensing my clothing was made from the scraps of the queen's, in one accord they ensured that I was fed nothing but scraps from their own bowls when the guards came with buckets of pale, tepid soup.

I would have wrapped myself in pity and prayed for deliverance if not for the two images that came to haunt me every time I closed my eyes. First, I saw the woman; no, not the woman—the vest. The green velvet vest I stitched with golden thread as a birthday gift to my cousin on our last New Year's together. I saw it—see it, still—with a black, smoking hole in its center. I do not see the face of the woman. I cannot, much as I try. The only face I see is Bertrand's. I see his blue eyes staring up into mine, the color draining. I press my hand to my heart and I feel his at its last. And I hear his voice, *"for you"*.

He is dead because of me.

Laurette was here because of me.

While I may not be guilty of the crime they accuse, I'm no innocent in circumstance.

"I need a priest," I said to those who guard us when I could catch one's attention. "I need to make Confession."

But they laughed and told me to bide my time, that I could make Confession to the council of the brotherhood that will judge me, as there is no God in heaven to forgive what I've done.

Today is my day to confess.

We are taken into the court chambers, where the gallery is full of men and women jeering at our appearance. Their voices blend into a wall of noise, sparing me from the vocabulary of their taunts. At some point, someone must have said something amusing, because the resounding laughter bursts forth as its own unique sound. Once we are sitting on the bench at the front of the gallery, our shackles are removed, and a man wearing a soiled shirt and red cap walks the length of us, pistol drawn, promising to mete out justice here should we move or speak without being called.

At the front of the chamber, a bailiff pounds a gavel for order, and the noise of the crowd dies down to a murmur as three men take their places behind the table on the raised platform. They look like no other judges I have ever imagined. No powdered wigs, no black robes. These are rough men, well dressed but looking ill at ease in their attire.

"Citizens! Citizens!" The bailiff calls for silence. "The court of the citizens of *la République française* is in session today to hear accusations against her enemies!"

The crowd roars in excitement, and it takes a good bit of pounding to get them quiet again. The first of us accused is a middle-aged woman, Madame la Fontaine, who wears the same dress she did when she first arrived at our prison two weeks ago. It is torn at the sleeve from the struggle at the time of her arrest. I offered to repair it for her, but she refused, saying she would proudly display her fight against this mad band of hooligans bent on ruining her country.

She is led to the front of the room, to a platform just below and to the left of where the judges sit. On her own power, she steps up and turns to face the audience. A small iron gate closes in front of her, and though it is no taller than her waist, it reminds us that this woman is a prisoner. Anyone who testifies against her will do so from behind a podium directly in front of the judges, as will anyone here to speak on her behalf. Today, there is no one.

Madame la Fontaine is charged with being an enemy of the republic, and before the bailiff can go into any further detail, she collapses into tears, begging forgiveness for her misguided thoughts, promising to renounce her finances and position in honor of the new order of the world. With a strike of the gavel, she is forgiven and handed a prison sentence to last only as long as it takes for her property to be satisfactorily disbursed.

The entire ordeal lasts less than five minutes.

She is led away, much to the delight of the gallery. The gavel sounds again, and my name is called. "Renée *la couturière*! Accused of inciting violence against the people, and the murder of citizen Anne de la Rue."

I shake as I stand, feeling the jeers of the people wrap around me. My desire is to remain immobile, but someone removes my shackles, and I am shoved forcefully up to the platform and shut behind the little gate. Locked in. When, finally, the room is silent—though even the silence is thick with hate—my crime is read for all:

"On October the sixth, when the citizens of France were engaged in the lawful detention and arrest of our heretofore king and his wife, our former queen, you, Renée *la couturière*, in employ at the palace at Versailles, did make violent efforts to thwart them in their mission, and those efforts resulted in the murder of Anne de la Rue, a good citizen of Paris who gave her life for the freedom of its citizens. How do you answer these charges?"

I think back to that night, remembering it as clearly as any of my life. Their faces twisted in hate, weapons raised, intent on tearing the flesh from their queen, bringing death to her home. And I can see the woman—Anne—as vicious as any other of them. And my voice. *"Stop them! At any cost!"* Not caring in the moment if that meant taking their lives. *Her* life. In truth, not caring now.

"I have no answer, *messieurs*."

My response does not please my accusers. No amount of shouting down would quell their protest, the pounding of the gavel no more effective than the tapping of a finger in a moment of frustrated thought. Not until one rises among them, standing from his seat and making his way through the thunderous sea of protest, does a wave of calm ripple through.

Marcel, red cap in his hand, hair bound at the nape with a length of blue ribbon, shirt miraculously white—he rises as the tricolored embodiment of their cause. "I have something to say about these charges."

One of the three judges, the one sitting in the center seat, pounds a small round stone on the table. "Are you a witness to her crime?"

"I am a witness to her life." By now he's come to the railing that separates the gallery from the court stage, and he steps right over it. "I have known *mademoiselle* since she was a child. Since we both were children. She is incapable of the violence of which she is accused."

The crowd takes in a single breath, mine joining in the shock of his appearance and statement.

The judge smiles a smile that bodes no good for me. "Citizen—"

"Moreau."

"Citizen Moreau, we are not here to judge the idyll of the accused's childhood. We are here about the events that took the life of citizen Anne de la Rue."

Without any ruse of asking permission, Marcel approaches, bypassing the witness podium to lean against the prisoners' gate. His handsome face is inches from mine, infused with an air of experience and power that has chased away the listless rogue. He knows something—something about Laurette. He conveys as much with his eyes, his gaze reaching out to build a sort of trust between us. I feel that my life is in his hands, as much as it had ever been in Bertrand's.

"Did you kill her, Renée?"

Truth—real truth, not truth driven by my conscience—comes forth. "I did not." His eyes prompt for one more word. "I did not, *citizen*."

"Did you instruct the soldiers to kill her?"

"I begged the soldiers to stop her."

"To save the queen?"

I know better than to answer this, and he rewards my silence by not pressing the question.

"Did you ever think, Renée, when you were a poor shepherdess living off the charity of your community, sleeping in the loft of a barn, that you would one day be a resident of the grandest palace in all of France—" he adopts a wide gesture—"in all of *Europe*, put in the position, little thing that you are, to defend a woman who has more than enough resources to defend herself?"

"I never imagined anything," I say, unwilling to denigrate my queen.

"Would it surprise you to know that Anne de la Rue, the woman so tragically murdered that night, lived a life very similar to your own? To what most of us have experienced? That she was poor too. Came to the city with no thought of such a vile confrontation. Wanted only to find work and food for herself."

Marcel steps away from me and paces the length of the judges' table. "You see, I knew Anne de la Rue." He pauses. "Intimately. I loved her very much."

The crowd is enthralled, but I am not fooled. Forcing my mind to return to those frightful moments, I see the woman—Anne—with greasy, lank tendrils creeping from beneath her cap, her uneven figure and fish-eyed expression.

Even without the grime of poverty and unnatural fury, she would not be a woman suited to Marcel's taste. I have no doubt that somehow he and Laurette became lovers, and he is the common person who brought my handiwork to rest on this woman's frame. He may have used Anne's body, but he did not love her—a truth on which I would stake my life.

"Isn't it safe to say, citizens," he continues, weaving this tragic tale like a timeless ballad, "that many of us have been moved to actions that could never have been ascribed to us when we were children? What part of our childhood trained us to take up arms against the injustice that bound us in poverty and fight for rights we never knew existed? When we were mere boys stacking blocks, did we ever think we would tear down a mighty stone structure with those same hands? If I, the lover of the murdered woman, can ask for mercy, surely you can find it within you to grant it? Anne herself, a citizen more devoted to the cause than we will ever know, would have wanted as much."

He holds them—every eye and heart and soul and mind in the gallery, on the bench—in shackles, and charged with dispensing justice. His words have commanded more silence than any stone or gavel ever could. I grip the railing, hating him. Hating every serpentine word that has ever dropped from his tongue, but knowing he is saving my life. Blood for blood is what these people understand. He has given them something else. Innocence for innocence.

"You were in service to the former queen, Marie Antoinette?"

It is a heartbeat or so before I realize the judge at the center of the table is addressing me.

"Oui, monsieur."

"In what capacity?"

"Seamstress, sir."

He frowns. "Not a highly important position?"

"Non, monsieur."

"And yet you were in her chamber that night?"

"Oui, monsieur."

"To warn her?"

"I thought, *monsieur*, if they—the family, the queen and her children—escaped . . . if they got away, there would be no cause for anyone to be hurt. That those who wished her harm would simply . . . go away."

"And now, in your current circumstances, do you remain loyal to our former sovereign?"

"I am alone, *monsieur*. My loyalty is to Christ, into whose hands I commit my life."

A whisper ripples through the crowd.

"Well," says the citizens' judge, "Christ has delivered you to me. And I remand you back to prison." He punctuates his pronouncement with a rapping of the stone.

"Citizen, please!" Marcel moves from the witness stand to place himself directly in front of the bench. The bailiff moves to restrain him, but a single glance from the judge allows him to remain free. "She is but a child. New to the city, unaware of the distasteful cruelty of her former mistress. We cannot fall into the same patterns of injustice that enslaved us for so long."

The impact of his words registers on the judge's face as he holds the stone aloft. He looks to Marcel, to me, and confers quietly with the men on either side.

"Very well," he says with an air of final authority and turns to me. "We will allow you to live out your life in loyalty to the woman who is responsible for your circumstances." Then, to the guards who brought me here, "Remand her to custody at Tuileries."

I don't know what this means, but a sense of calm enfolds me even as I submit myself to once again be bound.

"S'il vous plaît, messieurs." Marcel has sidled between me and the men who escorted me here. "A prisoner bound for a palace

surely need not be shackled like a common criminal. I will escort her myself." His hand closes around the crook of my arm.

"I don't reckon that'll happen," the guard says with a knowing smile. "Bit too familiar with the testimony for my blood." He leans in close, almost nose to nose. "I don't trust you. She'll ride back in the cart she come in."

I've remained silent, eyes downcast throughout the exchange, and submit my hands to the ropes. Once bound, I'm taken back to the crowded bench, where one by one my fellow prisoners hear their verdicts.

Guilty of treason. Death.

Guilty of treason. Death.

A movement catches the corner of my eye, and soon I feel Marcel's breath on the back of my neck.

"Don't turn," he says. If I did, even a fraction, his lips would grace my cheek. "It is a good thing, going to Tuileries. They don't want royal blood on their hands. Do you hear me? They say they do, but they don't. The king is stripped of power; it is enough. I've saved your life."

"Laurette?" My single word holds a life of questions.

"She is safe, as far as I know. Home, from what I have heard. Gone since the day of *la Bastille*."

He has no reason to lie, so I allow his words to be truth. It is a small hope, but as two more are pronounced dead, it is enough. Until the day comes that I, too, can return to Mouton Blanc, his words will keep her alive in my mind, in my heart. I will see her, will walk with her in the fields, will talk with her late into the night. All this time past will be but a moment. Soon and soon, our feet will share a path.

L'épisode 27

Laurette

HOME

A month after the wedding, as news of the nuptials trickled among the people of Mouton Blanc, Monsieur Girard hosted a celebration at his home, complete with a roasted hog, a cask of wine, and a dense, sweet cake. There were twenty people or more in attendance—some Laurette knew, others barely familiar faces drawn by their own hunger as much as a desire to celebrate.

Elianne, never one to exude an air of charm or joy, looked especially pinched and sallow, moving Laurette to pity.

"I'm sorry," Laurette said, finding a moment to catch her alone. *Catch* being the most appropriate word, as she'd chased her back into the kitchen. "I know you had your sights set on him—"

"My father had his sights set. I knew better. Gagnon's always had a heart for taking in strays. Like you and—" she looked down meaningfully at the now-unmistakable mound under Laurette's skirt—"whatever bastard you're carrying there. How could I compete?"

Laurette drew back, feeling Elianne's truth over every inch of her, clear to the fingertips that itched to slap her face.

Others, though, no less aware of her condition as evidenced by their own whispers and glances, were kind enough to keep their silence. Gagnon, long known for his generosity, was remembered in kind, and the new family was showered with the best gifts their neighbors could afford. Bottles of wine, a sack of flour, a crock of butter. Skeins of yarn, a pitcher with a beautifully painted pastoral scene that Laurette declared she'd be too frightened to use. To the boys' delight, they received five jars of preserves and a basket of pears, which meant special treats after supper for weeks to come. Finally, the grandest gift of all: the young milk cow given by Monsieur and Madame Tournac, born to them last spring.

"We won't be able to feed her through the winter," Madame Tournac explained. "We pray you'll be a blessing to each other."

Father Pietro attended and prayed a special blessing. "We are all adopted into the Holy Father's family. His sons and daughters through the miracle of mercy." He brought with him the registry book for l'église du Mouton Perdu, and with all eyes watching, recorded not only the marriage of Émile Gagnon and Laurette Janvier, but listed below the names of Philippe, Nicolas, and Joseph. For safe measure, he baptized each, pouring water over their heads from a pewter chalice. "That they may all be reunited as a family in heaven."

The walk home was slow going, as the young heifer seemed in no hurry. The boys took turns leading her; those not in charge of the rope carried the bundles of pork and food gifts. Laurette and Gagnon lingered behind, close to Cossette, who circled them constantly, redirecting any step that veered from the invisible path.

"We'll see our first frost tonight," Gagnon said, seeming unconcerned about their leisurely pace.

"How can you be sure?"

"I'm sure because I wish it to be."

His voice had dropped to something low and secretive, and somehow brought her to blush. "And why do you wish it to be?"

"Because it means winter is coming." He took her hand and brought it to his lips, keeping their coordinated stride. "And that means, Laurette, my love . . ."

They stopped, allowing the boys' lamplight to move ahead. The world grew dark around them, and she felt the promised chill.

"What does it mean, Gagnon?"

But she knew. When she first returned, she and the shy, frightened Joseph slept in Gagnon's bed, though it wasn't long before the boy begged to join his brothers—*mes frères*, he said—in the loft. And then, long after, even after their wedding, now a month past, she remained. Alone. That first night, exhausted from the walk from town and the excitement of *la Déclaration*, Laurette had collapsed upon it within minutes of walking through the door, mindless of any wedding-night expectations. And after, each evening, the two danced around the question, ending with a chaste kiss and Gagnon's own declaration that she looked tired and needed her rest, and he would stay up with his pipe for a while.

Though there had been moments. Touches, glances. Once, when Joseph fell asleep at her feet, Laurette said, "Perhaps I'll just stay in this chair all night. I hate to disturb him."

Gagnon scooped him up, saying, "I'll take him to my bed tonight," leaving no doubt where he planned to take himself. But then, while being lifted, the child cried out for his *maman*, and Gagnon laid him in Laurette's arms, all other plans abandoned.

Now, with the question left unanswered between them, she felt him lean forward, his touch to her face and his kiss.

It was by no means their first. Here, too, with this bit of

uncharted affection they'd been testing one another. Pecks to her cheek as she scrubbed dishes, a kiss to his brow as he read through his printed copy of *la Déclaration*. Every night before retiring to their separate rooms, every morning meeting between them. But tonight, he held her, his mouth upon hers, a bit of warmth in the chilly air as he moved upon her, coaxing.

It was the first time, after so much time, after that first night with Marcel on a bed of moss under a canopy of moonlight, after all the nights and days in the tiny, hot box of a Paris room, after accepting the new life growing within her—this was the moment she felt truly a woman. Desired, protected. Gagnon's kiss held a promise that he, too, had stumbled upon the same realization. Stumbled, righted himself, and was now proceeding with sure footing.

He released her slowly, her mind echoing all the times he told her she was free to go, free to leave his home and pursue what life she would. Now, no force could make her more of a prisoner than this kiss.

"I think you are wrong," she said when the cool of the evening once again touched her lips. "It is far too early and too warm for the first frost." She smiled at his look of quizzical disappointment. "But I need no such reason to share your bed. Tonight, and forever, Gagnon—"

"Émile," he prompted.

"Émile. I am your wife, am I not?"

"You are. In the eyes of God and our friends. And our sons. And this one you carry."

"Venez!" the boys called from their paces ahead.

"Allons-y," he whispered. "Let's catch up and put them to bed."

⚜

The baby was born just past dawn in the bitter-cold first days of February. There'd been no time to call a woman to come help with the birthing, as the pains started well after dark, and a swirling snow portended a dangerous journey to the Girards'.

"All will be well, my love," Gagnon reassured. By now Laurette was well versed in the nuances of his heart. His words were meant to reassure her while constructing a wall between this night and the night all those years ago when death took his first wife and his son away. He built the fire high in the front room and brought her in beside it, the flames seeming to wave in rhythm with her pains. Through the hours, the only sounds were her labored breaths and his whispered assurances that she was strong, she was loved, that the baby girl would be a blessing to the home.

"You're still so sure it's a girl?" Laurette asked when a pain cleared itself away to make room for words.

"I am." He mopped her brow with a cool cloth.

"How can you be?"

"Because it is what I want. It's what I see in my heart."

She didn't question further.

It seemed right, somehow, that he alone would bring this child into the world. She'd known, all those years ago as an abandoned, hungry girl, that this man would restore her life. Gagnon took her hand, led her around the room in the times between birthing pains. He told stories when she asked, remained quiet when she demanded, and laid his hands upon her when she cried out in fear.

"She is making her way, my love," he pledged. "We will see her before the dawn."

"I don't want the boys to come in and be frightened."

He grinned. "I put the dogs in their room at the door."

Gagnon was almost perfect in his predictions. The morning sun was glinting off the new day's snow when Laurette delivered a new life into his hands. The soft mewling was lost at first, masked by Laurette's own heaving sobs of relief, but the cries grew strong and robust once she took the squirming bundle, wrapped in dark, soft wool, into her arms.

"Hold her close," Gagnon said. "Touch her face, her cheek."

Her.

Laurette did as he said, grazing a knuckle along the soft, pink flesh, and felt a surge of life when the babe turned her face, the cries softening once again. "She's beautiful."

"As is her mother."

Gagnon guided her through the final stages, but Laurette paid little attention. She knew nothing but the depth of the tiny girl's brown eyes, felt nothing but the weight upon her breast. She held her nose to the cap of dark curls and breathed in the essence of her daughter.

"I've never felt so important in all my life," she said. Already the pain was dissolving into a distant memory. As if it happened to some other woman in some other place, far from this cozy, familiar room.

He laughed. "It is something, isn't it? To know that you will love this child from the moment of its first breath."

She knew that he, too, was far away. With some other woman, in this same house, yet not this place. All these years, and he still loved the tiny boy. Loved the woman, too. Laurette would always share her affections, and the boys—all three—would in some way be shadows of the life his firstborn would never know. This little one, however, knit them together. Born of Laurette's flesh, born to Gagnon through mercy. From her womb to his arms, without the time for a breath to pass between them.

At some point before the final, crucial hour, he had built a fire in the little bedroom stove and assured her that the room was warm, the bed soft, and she and the little one had earned a day of rest. He helped her from the chair and held her arm as she took her first steps as a mother, the baby cradled against her. The day loomed full of promise, but the bed yawned an invitation. Gratefully, she sank within it, propped her head against the pillows, and felt a tugging within her breast as her girl's soft face rooted against it. An unknown instinct took hold, and she moved the fabric of her nightdress aside, inviting the first droplets of milk to draw the babe's mouth closer until they were perfectly seamed together.

All of this under Gagnon's protective gaze, free of any hint of embarrassment or shame.

"What shall we call her?" he asked, sitting gingerly on the edge of the ticking.

"Aimée, because she is loved." Then, another thought, another ghost. "Aimée-Renée."

⚜

L'épisode 28

Renée

TUILERIES

If not for the armed guards at the door, we might not know we are prisoners. It's easy to pretend they are here for our protection. Daily, hordes of rebels pass by, shouting praise for the revolution and calling for our blood. I would like to think that, should such a breach occur again, an event like the one that brought murderous rebels into the chambers of the queen, those men posted at our doors and gates would leap into action and dispatch the would-be assassins.

But then, these men face in, not out. They interrogate every visitor who crosses the threshold, inspect every package—even the most mundane grocery delivery. They wear the uniform of the revolution: long breeches and the tricolor cockade, and they look at us all not with fear or respect, but disdain. None would sacrifice his life to save any of the erstwhile palace's royal guests. Their loyalty lies beyond the paint-chipped walls of this dwelling, silently echoing the jeers of the rebels.

Though certainly a royal residence, Tuileries is nothing like

Versailles, and even I—a peasant shepherdess—can ascertain the difference. There are ghosts of the tile factory it once was hidden in the architecture, especially in the hall where the household servants are kept. Entire wings are blocked from use, deemed dangerous because of their leaking roofs and aggressive mold. The king holds court—to the extent he is allowed—and has his private apartments on the first floor, Her Majesty on the second. And those who reside with them have taken apartments throughout. I think back to Madame Gisela, and wonder what she would think of the turn of events. Vindicated? Remorseful? Would she consider it still an honor to be part of the inner circle of the queen's companions if being such put her life and freedom at risk? Or is she like the others, willing to trade her jewels and gold and weapons for emigration documents—scraps of paper giving her permission to get in a carriage like the one that brought me here and drive it to the coast, board a ship, and join the English bourgeoisie?

I'm told that this place was once a favorite of Her Majesty's. From the days before, when Paris welcomed their young, fashionable queen, ushering her from one festivity to the next while the stodgy Louis drank his warm chocolate at home. Those were the days that the rumors worked in her favor—stories of illicit lovers in any one of the dozens of the palace's apartments. But since the turning of that tide, when her husband and children begged royal dedication and the grandeur of Versailles, Tuileries has fallen into the disrepair of disuse.

Again, all of this is whispered to me by the staff transplanted from Versailles, serving at the leisure of the Assembly. I am not numbered among them. They can pass in and out, going to the market and to coffee shops and to the celebrations in the street whenever there's word of another member of the Second Estate pulled out of his carriage and dragged into prison. They flaunt their freedom, singing the songs of the revolution as they perform the household tasks. I, on the other hand, am a prisoner. A rare common girl living under the punishment of power. And, though she offered me no welcome upon my arrival, displayed no acknowledgment of my presence for the first month of my residence, and has yet to show any gratitude for the actions that most certainly saved her life the night the women of Paris stormed her chamber, I place myself as often as possible in the queen's presence. It is enough that Marie-Thérèse flew into my arms at the first moment away from her mother's watchful gaze, and Louis-Charles entrusted me with his favorite wooden toy soldier to protect me like Monsieur Bertrand. By and by, I am allowed more time with the children, as the queen cannot find a nanny who does not look at them with sidelong, treasonous eyes.

For her part, the queen—or now simply Madame, since referring to her by a royal title is grounds for accusations of treason—refuses to act like a prisoner. She and Louis make daily excursions—he to the countryside, under guard, to hunt; she to pay social calls on those unwilling to visit her in the dank, crumbling parlor of her cramped apartment. As they are not allowed to have a chapel at Tuileries, the family goes to Mass every Sunday, and when I am once again enfolded to her favor, Madame allows me to accompany them. These are some of my very few opportunities to walk out on the streets.

And what frightening times! We are flanked by a contingent of the former king's guard, those yet to desert in search of the blood-glory of the rebels, and they alone stand between us and the violence of the crowd. Their bodies bear the brunt of stones and bricks, their blue coats stained with spit. They are not permitted to carry weapons, or the route to Tuileries might be scattered with the heads of the poor. But they retaliate with their shoulders, their elbows, their feet.

I can imagine Bertrand here, a full head and shoulders

above everything. My mountain, Marcel called him. A fortress. A bulwark. Yet, in the end, as vulnerable as the walls of the mighty Bastille, which had been torn down by the hands of peasants. These days, remnants of its stone walls are rounded and smoothed and worn as baubles in place of pearls.

On Tuesday afternoons, a routine since the first bitter-cold days in December, Madame assembles a guard and takes an afternoon to visit one of the neighborhoods struck by poverty. She brings baskets of food from our own kitchen and stacks of warm clothing and blankets. It is because of this, I think, that I have been admitted into her good graces, for I am capable of knitting five pairs of stockings a day, now that I have no other royal duties to attend to. I also have the trust of Mademoiselle, and have made her my apprentice. She is getting quite good—precise and detailed, though not nearly as fast. We make caps, too, and warm wool sleeping sacks for the smallest of children. All in black or brown, never the colors of the revolution. If we are given skeins of red or blue wool, I am charged to dye them black, and I live with the telltale sign of the deception beneath the nail beds of my fingers.

I am not permitted to accompany Madame on these excursions, but Mademoiselle is, and we spend long, cold afternoons next to the small fire in the parlor knitting in preparation for the next one.

"They are so nice to her, you'd never know," she says, brow furrowed in concentration. In moments like this it is painfully clear that she will never be the beauty that her mother was in youth. Mademoiselle looks too much like her father from the nose up, and like her mother's worst features from the lips down. Her skin is perpetually blotchy in the cold, her teeth crowded, her eyes small and close and pale. Her lips are pink, but not in an inviting way, and even when chapped with cold, manage to make moist popping syllables when she speaks.

"These women, who sit around her and *ooh* and *ahh* over her dress, and say '*Merci*, our angel of mercy.' And the next time they are there with more children, more mouths to feed. And Mother, how she loves them. Takes them into her arms, settles them on her lap, and says, 'If you were mine, you'd never know a hungry day.'"

She pauses, lobs a mild curse at a dropped stitch, rips out a row, and begins again. "I'm always wondering, *Are these the same women that ran through our house that night?* And I think, if they knew truly the kindness and generosity of her heart . . ."

"I've often thought the same," I say. I'm using the shuttle Madame gave me to create tiny yellow flowers from thread pulled from draperies I found stored in the attic. I attach one to each of our stockings, a hidden signature of the former queen. "Perhaps if she'd had more opportunities, before . . ."

Mademoiselle wrinkles her nose. "It wouldn't matter. These are selfish, stupid people. They take her gifts and then curse her on the street."

"Do you ever—does she ever worry for her safety?"

She shrugs. "I don't think she cares anymore, one way or another. If they don't want her as queen, she's happy enough not to be queen."

"And you?" It is a bold question, far above my station, but present circumstances have erased a multitude of formalities.

"You know I can never be. Our laws won't let a girl—"

"But it seems those laws are changing. Or, perhaps, you'll be married to a prince? Like your mother."

She knits for what seems like ages, her nailbitten fingers snagging at the wool, before responding, and when she does, her voice is a whisper so low the sounds of the needles overpower it. "I don't want any of this. Not to be married, not to rule. I don't want to be what they hate."

⚜

Summer arrives without any of its usual welcome respite from the cold of winter. The garden space at Tuileries is overgrown and untended, without even a hint of the majesty of that at Versailles. I know Madame longs for an escape to the Petit Trianon and complains more loudly of her confinement with each passing day.

"They trust me enough to allow me into the streets to feed their poor," she complains. "But a single step beyond the city gate makes me a fugitive."

She's grown fatter during our time here, and every dress that she was able to summon after her arrest strains at the seams in a manner no corset can relieve. I've taken to sneaking them away at night and altering them as I can—adding panels of material cut from the skirt to the bodice, cutting more generous sleeves in the name of *la mode*. It is becoming the style to wear plain white dresses fashioned from cotton or muslin, with indistinguishable waistlines and an absence of any kind of structure. When I mention once, quietly, that she consider such a gown to make her appear more approachable to those she has alienated, she lets forth with a laugh so bitter I taste the black gall behind it.

"I was reviled for wearing such a thing years ago," she said. "Didn't look regal enough. Said I looked like some poor shepherd girl. And now—"

"The people, Madame. They are impossible to please."

"Do you know, when I first came here—" her face goes dreamy with nostalgia—"when I was just a girl—fourteen years old, imagine, to marry Louis. I rode out from my home, and a carriage met me midway. A point, they said, in the direct center between my old home and my new. I stepped out of my carriage and there, in the middle of the road, they made me strip naked. A girl, fourteen. Bare to all. I had to leave everything. Down to my stockings and pants. And they dressed me in their clothes. Their colors, their fashion. And I've been a slave to them ever since."

The two extremes of her reign interplay as she speaks. Her voice is that of the petulant girl, wronged and embarrassed and angry, the sharp whine incongruous with the soft folds of her face. Her eyes spark with memory, then cool to steel as they take in the cold shabbiness of the room. I have no words to soothe or encourage; even if I did, she is too far away to hear them. She is back at that same crossroads between her beloved homeland and this dreadful one, stripped of both the girl she was and the woman they forced her to become.

"It is time for me to go home."

⚜

In early June, when she summons me and asks me to bring my measuring tape especially, my mind spins with possibility. Madame Bertin has vanished along with anybody who might be sympathetic to the royal plight, and wouldn't be allowed to design a new gown if she were discovered living comfortably down the street. It's been so long since I've crafted anything new—nothing, really, since the mourning gown after Louis-Joseph's death. I raid the children's room for some drawing paper and charcoal, and stand outside her open parlor door at our appointed time. There's no one here to announce me or to keep me from barging in. I clear my throat once, recalling the importance of never addressing our queen until being first addressed. It seems to me by the subtle shift in her posture, an infinitesimal rigidity, that she is aware of my presence but is choosing to ignore me. A remnant of the status from her former life. Part of me senses that, were I to say, *"You called for me, Your Majesty?"* I would face chastisement for forgetting my place. And so I wait, and wait, until finally Marie-Thérèse and Louis-Charles come careening around the corner.

These two, she cannot ignore, and they run to her with a joy-filled familiarity, eager to show off the day's treasure: for Marie-Thérèse, a new volume of poetry; for Louis-Charles, a new set of dominoes. Madame fawns over each and then happens to look over their shoulders to see me patiently waiting.

"Maintenant, mes enfants," she says with a final kiss to each face, "off with you while I have a chat with *la couturière*. You can show me more after supper."

They immediately depart, and for the first time I notice the absence of a once-familiar sound—that of shoes clattering and echoing in the halls. Not because the halls of Tuileries don't echo—the floors and walls are largely stone and bare—but because the children's feet, too, are bare. As bare as mine ever were in summer. Suddenly my soft leather slippers feel uncomfortable and confining, and I envy that measure of freedom.

We exchange no pleasantries once we are alone. In fact, she treated me with more warmth and familiarity on the day we first met than she does in this moment. She does, however, summon me close until I am standing right next to the small sofa on which she sits. Then, to my utter amazement, she pats the cushion next to her.

I am sitting beside the queen. She may be merely Madame to the bloodied rebels of Paris, but in my heart she has suffered no change of station.

"I need you to do something for me," she says. As she speaks, her eyes dart between my face and her open door, and her voice is far softer than necessary.

"Of course, Madame. I am always at your service."

She responds with a thin, strained smile. "You know, so much of my wardrobe has fallen into such disrepair, I need some new things. More appropriate, I think, for my current activities."

"Activities, Madame?"

"Something that would make me less . . . *reconnaissable*. Now, people see me on the street and they say, 'There she is! The queen!' They can spot me from a mile away. They recognize my gowns. I need something . . ."

"Plain?"

"Bourgeois."

I let the word sink. "Of course, Madame." Already I am thinking of the endless sea of fabric in the garment room at Versailles. Here, I will have to crawl through unused wings looking for something suitable, for I doubt I will be able to visit any of the shops in the city.

I voice this concern, but she waves me off. "You're a resourceful little thing. Always have been. If the people—*those* people—learn that I am indulging in a new gown, no matter how *modeste* . . ."

"I understand." I put the bit of charcoal to the page and begin a sketch, thinking of the garments worn by the ladies who still come to call. I almost suggest borrowing something from one of them, simply altering it to fit Madame's distinctive figure, but something tells me she would have none of that.

"And for Marie-Thérèse as well."

I don't look up. "In the same vein?"

"Oui."

I feel a smile tugging. "If I may be so bold as to say so, Madame, I think it is a good thing when Marie-Thérèse accompanies you on your visits. It's important for children—for poor children—to see such kindness. And I think it's good for her to see such poverty."

Madame doesn't respond, and it's like a thin window of ice has grown between us.

I continue to sketch until her hand stills mine. "This—this won't be like the others. Remember when all of the court would be waiting to see what beautiful creation I would wear into the ballroom? All the silk. The candlelight, the music. The gold." I glance up to see her gazing at the ceiling, where a water stain is creeping from the corner. "And the wigs! Oh, such towering, ridiculous things." Her laugh is a private affair I am not invited to join. "And now I ask for nothing but a plain brown dress. Something that will make me look like the wife of a prosperous shopkeeper."

This last word is delivered with a laugh too. Yet another from which I am excluded.

"I could never please them," she says. "Any of them. Louis, such a boy when we married, had no idea what to do with a woman." She leans forward. "Never learned, either. But always, I looked too Austrian, my French was inadequate, I looked too much like a little girl, then too much like a whore, then too much like a peasant. If I wore a new gown I was wasteful; if I wore one a third time I was disgraceful. If I danced too much, I was no more than a country trollop, but if I didn't dance, I was a stodgy, humorless Hapsburg. I wish I'd never come."

"Madame!" Impulsively I touch her sleeve. "You cannot mean that."

Rather than pull away, she covers my hand with hers. It is warm and dry and heavy, and as she leans close, I permit myself to stare into her features with a forthrightness I've never been allowed. There is no beauty in her at this moment. Not a trace. She might as well be the ghost of a tile cutter from the first generation of this crumbling palace.

"I would rather be dead," she says, chopping her words with the accent of her native tongue. "A spinster at my mother's side, my children nothing more than dreams that never lived, than to give myself over to the bloody hands of those animals outside."

And that's when I know, without any lingering doubt, that she has no intention to wear the comfortable, sturdy dress I've concocted on this sheet of paper on her next excursion to feed the bloody poor's children. For that, she adores the recognition, knowing the bile they must swallow in order to accept her gifts. No, this is not a dress to wear into the streets of Paris. This—and the one I will make for her daughter—is the dress she will wear to escape them.

⚜

The pace at which I create Madame's costume puts me to shame, or it would if anyone knew. Without bolts of fabric to stroll through, or even access to a dressmaker's shop, I'm reduced to spending afternoons opening closed doors, sometimes using the skeleton key Madame slipped into my hand days after our conversation. Many of the rooms are empty, save for minimal furnishings covered with yards of dust-protective gray cloth. I rifle through closets and wardrobes, finding moth-eaten remnants even the poorest of the street would recognize as decades out of fashion.

Finally, I work my way to the upper floors, the servants' rooms, and chastise myself for not thinking to start there. There is a wardrobe filled with dresses made from a serviceable light-brown wool. No bolts of material, but generous skirts, plenty to work with. I have several yards of a pleasant calico and ample linen that still smells faintly of drying in the sun. With Madame's permission, I take one of the empty upper rooms as my work space. It is high enough that the open window spares me from the sounds and smells of the life teeming below, and when my shoulders ache from painstakingly stitching the panels, I lean out and marvel at the idea that I'm not allowed to join the outside world.

The dress I make for Marie-Thérèse is sweet, simple. Something I would have longed for in the days when all I could ever hope for were Laurette's castoffs or some other garment handed down once the girl who wore it before me grew too tall or died. Working from my meticulous list of numbers, I leave generous amounts for tailoring and still find that my search yields enough material for me to fashion something for myself. Perhaps it is time for me to abandon the colorful patchwork style which has become my signature. In fact, I'm surprised my jailers have allowed me to continue wearing it, as they seem so intent on wiping out every other reminder of the monarch's reign.

I am pleased with my creations—all three, though I fold my own away. When Madame summons me to her room to see the finished product, I nearly weep at the image in front of me. Stripped of any regal accoutrement, she stands looking like nothing more, nothing less, than a woman. Middle-aged and thickened with the settling of marriage and children and years. Though the materials were scavenged, they are of good quality. The linen petticoat and stomacher are white, but not industrially so, the bodice and gown a pleasant print that might have been originally planned for drapery but works well as a summer gown. Even the servant's skirts, cut to perfection with a ruche sleeve, have transformed into a garment worthy of the middle class. I've taken lengths of my knotting work, dyed the wool to match, and stitched it into a trim for the lapels and cuffs.

"You look beautiful, Madame."

"It will do," she says, but I know she is pleased. I hand her what I've made for Marie-Thérèse, and she holds the dress out as if the girl herself were in it. "And, *couturière*—"

She is searching for something in her mind and I prompt, "Renée."

"*Oui.* Renée. I realize this might be too much to ask, but you are so very clever, and so very quick. I wonder if you might not have the means to make one more dress. Nothing so elaborate as this. Much more simple. And small."

"Small?" My heart races at the invitation. For though I am older, I am smaller even than the princess. She desires a dress for me. I am to accompany—

"Quite small. For a child, close in size to my Louis-Charles."

It is a minute before I shift my thinking. "For Louis-Charles? But surely he has suitable clothing. Some of his play clothes are quite plain." She says nothing, but understanding dawns. The king and queen have a daughter and a son. This new family which I have helped create will have two daughters.

It is early morning, sun up yet still cool, when I venture into the garden to find the boy. His routine is to gulp down bread and chocolate before heading outside to play until called in for a more formal breakfast with the family. One of the men assigned to guard us has taken a shine to him, and I come across the two battling mightily, both armed with sticks, the guard with one arm behind him and Louis-Charles poised on an empty stone planter. I call his name three times before capturing his attention, and he makes the guard promise to be there upon his return so he—my little prince—can send him off to meet his Creator once the rush of blood has drained from his throat. The guard laughs and makes his promise, catching my eye as if searching for my approval.

I grant him none.

I've worked through the night, not knowing when the family has planned its excursion. I've not spoken to Madame and do not know how she plans to convince Louis-Charles to wear the dress, but as I kept my fingers centered in the glow of candlelight, an idea grew in the shadows around me.

Though he's not plagued with the ill health that stole his brother, the boy's shoulder is bony beneath my touch as I lead him back through the courtyard toward the house. Once we are safely away from the ears of those who tend to us both inside the walls and out, I ask if he wants to hear a new adventure story.

"Yes! Please! Does it have fighting and battles?"

"It does indeed." And I tell him an English tale of a man named Robin Hood, a famed thief known for being a gifted archer. "In one of the tales, he comes to participate in a competition, the prize for which is a bag of gold, but he knows if he is recognized, he will be arrested and thrown in prison."

"Like we are?" His eyes are full of wonder, without a hint of fear or shame.

"Oh, nothing like this. He would be thrown into a pit, with no light, or food, or even a bed."

"What does he do?"

"He disguises himself as an old woman."

"Why a woman?"

"Because he couldn't afford a better disguise. No money for a knight's armor or a soldier's uniform or even a fine suit of velvet. Nobody would suspect an old woman wandering around the king's grounds, and everybody was shocked to see a crone win the prize. He had the bag of gold well in hand before anyone suspected."

Louis-Charles claps his hands. "Tell me more stories!"

I touch my hand to his play-pinked cheek. "I will, soon. But perhaps one day—you are too young to deceive anyone as an old woman—but you might want to play Robin Hood and pretend to be a girl? I could make you a costume."

"Yes! Yes, *mademoiselle*! When?"

Until this point I've held my voice low, and I summon him close to whisper. "Soon, but you must promise me to keep it a secret until then."

⚜

It is midnight when I look down from the window in my workroom and see a carriage draw into the side court. It's large—larger by far than the one that brought me to Versailles with

Madame Gisela. It is not meant for a tour through the streets of Paris but for a drive into the country. It is a conveyance easily overtaken.

While I cannot extend any overture of a farewell, I also cannot hide myself away without seeing Madame and the children one more time. Since it has always been my custom to make clothing for myself from the scraps of what I fashion for the queen, I do not worry about appearing before her wearing the dress I stitched for myself over the past week. I hope Madame will perceive in it my loyalty to her, that she will recognize the patterns and fabric and know that—no matter the present circumstances—I remain what I have always been.

Downstairs is quiet, restrained commotion. Whispered questions. *"Do you have this?" "Have we thought of that?"*

I'm standing to the side, head down, trying to assume a profile of a household servant waiting for further instruction, when I feel a hand take mine. It is Marie-Thérèse, and before I can react, she is tugging me toward her mother.

"Can *la couturière* come with us?" she asks. "So I'll have someone to talk to?"

"Her name is Renée," Madame chastises. "And of course not. This is a family outing."

"S'il te plaît, Maman," she simpers and is soon joined by her brother. I have to force myself not to startle at his appearance. Soft blond curls puddle on his shoulders, and only the mischievous twist to his smile speaks to the wooden sword–wielding boy from the garden.

Madame looks to her husband, whose poorly tailored suit befits the lopsided wig and the sheen of sweat on his lip and brow. "Might be better, *monsieur*, given that she knows . . ."

The idea that I might betray their plan brings me to a silent protest, but I say only that I wouldn't presume to be a bother.

"I'm content to keep my prayers for your safe journey hidden in my heart."

Madame eyes me, perhaps measuring the advantage of appearing to travel with a third child, knowing that my presence thwarts the calculations of anyone who might be following her movements. She glances one more time at Louis, who says, *"Eh, bien,"* with the enthusiasm of a man whose soup, while not quite hot, is warm enough for supper.

The children each give my hands a squeeze, and I grip them tight. I'm given no instruction or permission to fetch my things. What I have in my pockets is what I'll take—a needle and thread, small scissors, a handful of yarn, and the gold knotting shuttle. As I walk out to the waiting carriage, I realize not one of my fellow passengers carries even a satchel. There is one large hamper strapped to the back, which recalls Madame Gisela and the sumptuous feast she provided for our humble table.

We are joined by Louis's sister Elisabeth, who eyes me with suspicion before deciding not to consider me at all. She and I are not strangers to one another, but I cannot recollect a single word exchanged between the two of us. She is ten years younger than the king but has never married, never wanting to divide her loyalties the way her sister-in-law was forced to do. I've heard that, in her youth, she was well pursued and courted, but now it seems spinsterhood has settled upon her the way it would any woman. Her face falls into a natural frown, and her figure into its equivalent.

Quickly, Madame instructs me as to our ruse. Elisabeth has false papers that identify her as a Russian baroness, Louis is her supposed valet, and the queen governess to her daughters. Now, apparently, there are three, but only papers for two.

"All the better that the boy doesn't speak," Louis says. "We'll keep him hidden away."

For once, I feel too big for the space I take up in the world as the family crowds into the seats that must have been copious enough before the introduction of so many coats and skirts. Little Louis-Charles, at the insistence of his father, curls up at Madame's feet and is told to close his eyes and rest, saving his strength for whatever adventures might come to pass. I whisper encouragement, reminding him how all good disguises rely on the perfect timing for true adventure.

As it happens, the first adventure occurs within an hour, when we are stopped at the gates.

"Papiers." The voice is rough and uncultured, and the command is repeated three times with growing impatience as Elisabeth fumbles through her portfolio in search of the handful of crisp, folded sheets. "Baroness." At first I think he is saying the word with exaggerated disdain, but then realize the over-pronunciation of each syllable speaks more to his ability—or inability—to read. The next word frustrates him, and I hear the rustle of paper and quiet counting.

The command *"Ouvrez!"* accompanies a rap on the carriage door. Madame smooths her skirt and tucks her feet closer as Louis complies. A thick, unshaven face fills the doorway, and the man's meaty finger points at each of us—*"Un, deux, trois . . ."*

I hold my breath. Six passengers. Five papers. He sounds out the unfamiliar names, to which each responds. Elisabeth, the baroness. Louis, the valet. Marie, the governess. Thérèse and Charlotte. *Charlotte*, of course, and before the muffled squeak from within Madame's skirt can make its way to the misshapen ear of this flat-faced citizen, I blurt, *"Oui. C'est moi."*

He grunts, counts one more time, and hands the papers to Elisabeth.

"Dieu merci," she says, breaking her words to sound like those of a foreign tongue. "Finally to be free of this godforsaken country."

⚜

We drive on and on. How long, I cannot say; my two sleepless nights soon overtake me and my head is touched to Marie-Thérèse, where I fall into a deep slumber. Surely, though, hours have passed when I wake, because the sun is up, the carriage hot. A piercing hunger reminds me that I haven't eaten in more than a day, but whom to tell? I can only hope that one of the children will soon be hungry, too, and I might benefit from their indulgence.

The road is rough, but our bodies have adapted. Louis-Charles is fast asleep on his mother's breast. Across from me, Louis and his sister sit anxiously apart, eyes cast to their feet. "We will have to rest the horses soon," he says. "They can't keep this pace for much longer."

"In an open field?" Elisabeth says. "We'll be sitting targets."

"*Non,*" Madame says. "It has all been arranged."

But we do stop once, in a copse of trees hidden from the road, where at last my hunger is sated by a simple meal of bread and cheese and fruit. There is a stream nearby, where I take the children to drink and wash our faces, and here Louis-Charles is permitted to change into his little-boy clothes again, much to his delight. We play thieves in the forest, chasing each other from tree to tree, and when we are called back, Madame smiles and declares what a good thing it is to escape from being cooped up in such a small place.

We stop again, under less ideal circumstances, when a harness breaks, and the driver must spend the last hours of daylight in repair. There's plenty of food left to eat, but we dare not wander off in the growing shadows. Instead, I gather the children to me and tell them it was just such a circumstance that brought me to Versailles all those years ago.

"I've not heard that," Louis says, surprising me that he'd been listening at all, given how low his chin sank to his chest.

"It's true," I say. "My guardian, Gagnon, fixed the wheel that night."

"And where does he live?"

"Mouton Blanc."

"Ah," Louis says. "Good sheep there. Good wool."

"Yes." I touch the tips of my fingers to each other, remembering the feel of it, the tufts falling from my carding boards.

"Did you ever want to go back?" This from Louis-Charles, who is trying to fashion an arrow from a stick, a sharp rock, and a bit of string I gave him.

"Sometimes." How Bertrand would have loved the place. "But people change. Places change. I don't even know what's become of my . . . family there."

"You're free to, if you like," says Louis. "You needn't accompany us all the way to—"

"Of course she must," says Madame. "What if someone were to see her? Ask her? She could ruin everything."

"I'd never betray you, *ma Reine*," I say, and she looks uncomfortable with the title, like another gown that no longer fits as it should.

The sun has disappeared when we climb into the carriage, and darkness cloaks us so completely that, coupled with the silence, I can almost imagine I'm traveling alone. I suppose Louis, Elisabeth, and Madame assume the children and I are sleeping, because their conversation is free with details. We are to leave France entirely and cross the border to Germany. I think about the story Madame told about stopping at the border and stripping naked, and my mind dances with the farcical idea of all of us engaging in the same, which makes me picture the pale, portly Louis in a state of undress, and I am almost too late to trap my giggle beneath my hand.

When we next feel the carriage slowing to a halt, the driver says, "Sainte-Menehould, *monsieur*."

"Can we not go on?" Madame asks with a quake of unease.

"We must change the horses," says Louis. "If we can find a team tonight, we'll not tarry."

Louis-Charles is deep in sleep. I offer to wait with him so he can remain undisturbed while the others go into the public house for a late supper, but Madame won't bear to be separated from him for a minute. She holds him as Louis hands her gently down the carriage steps. Marie-Thérèse is treated with equal attention, and I am almost embarrassed to witness such a tender moment.

We've stopped outside a familiar sight. Not specifically familiar, as I'd never even heard the name of the town before hearing it uttered by the driver, but a place that—for the first time since leaving Mouton Blanc—hearkens to home. Despite the distance of space and years, I might well be standing outside Le Cochon Gros. Orange light from cheap candles beneath thick domes. The songs pouring through the open doors are new, lyrics about freedom and humanity that I could never imagine rising above the long, rough tables of Saumon's inn, but the spirit is the same. Fueled by wine and fraternity.

Madame holds the children closer with each step, and Elisabeth looks around her with utter disdain. Thankfully, the low lights and the dense crowd afford us very little attention. Now that I am inside, the lyrics to their song are far more distinctive. They sing about the Bastille, the towers falling brick by brick into the hands of their brothers. The walls of injustice crumbling in their grip. Guns and bullets useless against the thick skin of revolution. And how the royal heads will roll.

Nearly every eye in the place is turned on one man, who stands upon his chair, one boot on the table, glass raised high. He waves his hand for silence at the waning notes of the last chorus. "We look to *l'anniversaire* of our freedom!"

A thick cheer goes up, and at that moment he turns,

confirming a dreadful suspicion I've had since my first glimpse of his back, the cascade of black curls spilling from his red cap. The proud voice, the braggart's inflection, and now those glittering black eyes that would find me if an ocean stood between us.

He allows only a flicker of recognition to cross his face before resuming his pontification with even greater animation than before, protecting us by weaving a distraction with his words.

I make my way to Louis and boldly tug his sleeve. "We have to leave."

"When I've word the horses are ready."

"We should not wait." Somehow, I've become someone who contradicts a king.

At a dark table in a far corner, Marie-Thérèse and Louis hungrily take in a bowl of a surprisingly hearty stew. Madame and Elisabeth won't touch a bite, and Louis-Charles nibbles on a crust of broth-soaked bread. I pick at the vegetables, my stomach too twisted for meat. We drink an entire bottle of wine. Elisabeth wrinkles her nose at the quality, but this, too, brings a wave of nostalgia.

Marcel hasn't so much as glanced our way again, and I might consider his efforts to hold the attention of the crowd heroic if I didn't also know how much he loves an audience. It seems an eternity before one of the servers alerts Louis to our driver, waiting at the door.

"Good, good," Louis says, shaking a handful of coins from a leather pouch. It's clear he has no clue as to the amount owed for our simple meal and wine, and his performance with the currency begins to draw strange looks from the other patrons. Madame keeps Louis-Charles to her hip, plants a hand on Marie-Thérèse's shoulder, and moves like a barge through the room, Elisabeth in her wake. I know my place, though, and whisper to the king, reminding him to put the coins in the server's hand, not on the table, and to add a few extra—not too many—to show gratitude for faithful service. Too much, and we'll be targets for thieves. Or worse.

Louis walks ahead of me, and I'm just about to the door when I feel a hand grip mine, pulling me close in a shadow behind a pillar of empty casks. It happens so quickly I am hardly aware of his intent. Those around us are, though, and they hoot in appreciation.

"How have you come to be here?"

I cannot imagine how to begin to explain. Knowing any answer I give will amount to a confession to a crime, I resort instead to an appeal to his affection. "Please, Marcel. Say nothing. Let us go."

He brings his face close to mine, close enough to fool everybody, and says, "Stay."

"What? How can we?"

"Not *them*. You. Stay here. Trust me, Renée. Haven't I saved you before?"

"The last time you saved me sent me to prison."

"You are alive. And I can't promise you will be so for long if you go with them." His warning is tangible. The death threatened by the court that sent me to Tuileries was a mere sting compared to the death threatened by a crowd of rebels on a stretch of dark road. I'd seen firsthand the determined violence of women. And this establishment teemed with men drunk on equality and wine.

"It's not enough that you and your *fraternité* have destroyed our country. You would destroy the man?"

"He is a fool, Renée, to come here, to think that he has seeds of loyal subjects. He overestimates his appeal and mistakes passivity for support. You'll be overtaken by dawn."

"Not if you let us leave. Let *me* leave."

"So you can be their prisoner?"

"They'll let me go home once they are—safe."

"They'll never be safe, Renée. I'm not the only man in here. The king's face is on the coins he used to pay for his supper. How stupid is he?"

Just then a voice breaks through, and I realize it's meant for me. "Charlotte! Charlotte!" Marie-Thérèse, somehow broken free of her mother's grip, calls to me with the sweet, naive smile that tells me she still thinks of this as some great game.

Marcel cocks a dark brow.

"Say nothing," I plead. "Rescue me one last time."

"Sweet Charlotte," he says, and kisses my lips softly before whispering, "I was truly saddened to hear about your mountain."

I believe him. Whatever Marcel lacks in character, he makes up for in hearty respect for a well-matched foe. He is the first—and only—person to offer condolence, other than the soldier who brought me news of Bertrand's death with a bloodstained touch. I allow myself a moment to access the long-buried grief, and when I say, "Thank you, *mon ami*," I am sincere in my gratitude.

When I reach Marie-Thérèse, she is giggling at the sight and teasing me about kissing a strange man.

I put on a matching playful tone to swallow my sadness. "We must keep it a secret, or your mother will think me a bad influence, and I won't be able to tell you any more stories."

The threat is enough. We lock arms for the short walk to where the carriage waits with a fresh team of horses impatient to lurch us into motion within seconds of latching the door. Their vigor is promising, and Louis informs us that we will drive through the night, possibly past dawn, to a new morning in a new country. A new life.

"All is going well," Madame says. "All is going well, I think." She is speaking to herself, repeating the phrase, though occasionally Louis confirms, "Yes, yes, my love."

I can still feel Marcel's lips, taste his wine, hear his words.

"Stay. Stay. Stay." What if he'd been there to say as much the morning I drove away with Madame Gisela? What if he'd said as much to Laurette?

Stay.

Stay.

Stay.

The word lulls me with the motion of the carriage—a steady pace meant to cover ground without overtaxing the team. There is no way to watch the passing landscape. No way to measure the passage of time. In this moment I learn that the king of France snores and that his sister mumbles. I feel the weight of a prince on my lap, a princess drawn beside me. I hear the queen breathing, intermittent sobs betraying her wakefulness. Our horses' hooves, sixteen of them, work in perfect rhythm. Chains jangle predictably. These are the night sounds of a slumbering dynasty. And I am a part of it.

Stay.

Stay.

Stay.

The interruption is almost imperceptible at first. An extra beat. An odd hoof. Then another, and another, then an army. Behind us, beside us, and the carriage stops. Long before promised. Long before dawn.

Part VI

L'Automne (Autumn) 1793
et l'Éternité (Eternity)

Au nom de Dieu le Père, le Fils,
et le Saint-Esprit—je prie.

L'épisode 29

Laurette

MOUTON BLANC

Sometime during the summer, Father Pietro closed the door at l'église du Mouton Perdu, locked it, and set out on foot for his journey back to his tiny village tucked away on the other side of the Pyrénées Mountains. The revolution brought death not only to the monarchy, but to the clergy as well. *La Déclaration*, which robbed the nobility of power, also robbed the church of its fortune, leaving Father Pietro with nothing more than the generosity of the people of Mouton Blanc to put food on his table. And, while they were as generous as their own meager livings would allow, there was much whispering about the portions of bread given at the Sacrament getting smaller and smaller, and Christ's blood watered to a pale pink.

But Father Pietro was a simple man, used to hunger and prone to sacrifice, and might have remained faithfully until his death had he not been forced to choose between his loyalty to the Pope and the demands of the constitutional church. Seeing nothing holy in a church that would force him to take an oath against His Holiness, he packed up his few belongings, including the silver from the altar which, he reasoned, he'd more than earned over decades of faithful service, and spoke a farewell Mass to the few congregants who bothered to attend.

Gagnon was among them, along with his three sons—the oldest half a head taller than himself, the youngest grown into a robust golden-haired boy of eleven, the middle a thick-waisted jovial lad with eyes full of humor. Laurette sat by his side, her face a mask of detachment. Secretly, she was pleased that her treks into town for Mass, no matter how infrequent, were coming to an end. She might miss her quiet Sunday mornings at home, alone, while Gagnon and the boys attended. Even more, those mornings with Aimée-Renée, snuggling in bed for an indulgent hour. But she would not miss the cold conversation—two sentences.

"Will you come with us, Laurette?"

"Non."

He never asked why, and she never gave reason.

On this, Father Pietro's last Sunday, however, the two-sentence conversation changed. Gagnon spoke them both.

"Get dressed. You're coming with us."

It was a cold morning, requiring shoes and socks for all. Laurette wore a new cape, fished from a trunk of clothing donated by a noblewoman attempting to atone for her wealth, and Aimée-Renée was wrapped in a thick woolen shawl. Gagnon surprised them all with a wagon and team of horses waiting at the front door, borrowed from Monsieur Girard.

"It's a long walk for the little one," he said. "And an even longer walk it'll be carrying her home."

The boys settled on the straw-lined bed, Aimée-Renée tucked up beside Nicolas. He was clearly her favorite of the brothers—sweet-tempered and strong, never preoccupied like Philippe or bossy like Joseph.

"You won't have to give Confession," Gagnon said. He leaned close and spoke low, outside of the boys' range.

Laurette brought up the hood of her cape, bringing a curtain of fur between them.

"I know that's why—that you don't like the idea of going to church. You don't want to speak your Confession to the priest. And I just want you to know, you won't have to speak it to him. You never have to, if you don't want."

She had to turn her head to look at him. "You can speak for the priest now?"

He smiled. "I can protect my wife."

Father Pietro's homily was little more than an exhortation not to abandon the teachings of Christ in favor of a constitution. That they should call on the fortitude that sustained the first generation of Christians, worshiping under the heel of Rome. And he asked for prayers for his safe passage, as he would pray for all who remained to live under the new French tyranny. Then, one by one, the family of Émile Gagnon came forward for Holy Communion—the father, the three sons, and Laurette holding Aimée-Renée on her hip. She took the pinch of bread on her tongue, swallowed it whole, and drank the smallest sip from the chalice, all the while feeling like a thief.

The drive home revealed Gagnon's true reason for borrowing Girard's wagon for the journey. This time, rather than having all of the empty bed to stretch their legs, the boys contorted themselves around the pew taken from the church—with Father Pietro's permission.

"We'll have our own church next Sunday," Gagnon said, "and every one thereafter."

"But you're not a priest," Joseph piped up from the back, never one to be silent.

"That I'm not." Gagnon's response carried two meanings:

one to answer Joseph, the other delivered with a playful grin in Laurette's direction.

"Praise be for that," she said, matching his entendre. Then, at a volume meant only for him, "Or else we wouldn't be adding a seventh member to our little congregation."

It was the first she'd told him of the new life within her, and his expression proved reward enough for the sickness and fatigue she'd been masking until she felt confident in her condition.

Gagnon transferred the reins to one hand and drew her to him, bringing his face within the hood of her cloak to kiss her. Deeply, completely, as if the garment afforded all the privacy of a closed bedroom door. "My love, what joy you bring me every day."

Though Laurette had her doubts when they first loaded the pew into the wagon, Gagnon's estimations proved true once they got home. It fit perfectly against the long wall. So much had changed in the years since she and Renée tiptoed in quiet steps outside of his closed, locked room. The stone walls wouldn't easily permit an addition to the house itself, but he and the boys worked the entire summer adding a second story—a loft that spanned nearly the entire expanse of the first floor, with a narrow stairway leading up from the farthest corner behind the table. The storage trunks that once functioned as seating were moved upstairs, making room for the pew. Laurette found a bright-stitched cushion to lay upon it.

"Doesn't seem very pious to have a pillow on a pew seat," Gagnon said, his humor thinly masking disapproval.

"Then we'll take it off on Sunday mornings," Laurette said, admiring her handiwork.

Late that Sunday afternoon, after a good dinner of a savory rabbit pie, Gagnon set off to return the horses and rig to Girard.

"Don't tell them our news," Laurette said when she kissed him good-bye. "I want to keep it to ourselves for just a little while longer."

He touched his hand to her stomach—not nearly as concaved and thin as it had been the last time she was newly pregnant, but round and soft and full. "That's not a secret you'll be able to keep for very long."

The boys were dispatched to the evening chores while Laurette brushed and braided Aimée-Renée's hair. The girl was every inch Marcel. Olive skin, thick black lashes, hair a mass of onyx ringlets that would tangle themselves to a mess if left loose on a pillow at night.

Marcel's always did.

She shook the thought away.

What must it do to Gagnon, looking at the child every day, her features so obviously in conflict with his own? He loved her fiercely, dearly. He'd been the first person to touch her, to hold her. And when she hurt—when she fell and scraped an elbow, or came across a sweet dead mouse, or suffered once again an unkind word from Joseph—it was to Gagnon that she ran. He wiped her tears. He spoke blessings upon her. He hugged her tight and told her, again and again, that she was safe and good and loved.

Laurette had asked him one night, their first night entwined weeks after Aimée-Renée's birth, when his feelings had changed. When he saw her as something more than a foundling to be protected. "As a woman?"

"It dawned slowly." He'd stroked a finger the length of her naked spine, his words the same pace as the rising sun. "When I saw you with the boys, how you mothered them. Until then, I think God shielded my eyes from seeing you that way. He held my heart for so long after Denise died. I couldn't imagine another woman. Loving another woman." His voice trailed, his touch stopped. "And then—you know, I thought nothing much of it at the time, but it's just coming clear to me now—an ordinary evening, you were cleaning up after supper—"

"Wasn't much to clean up in those days . . ."

He chuckled, and she felt every vibration of it. "*C'est vrai.* But you were, and I had a passing thought that I wanted very much to take you to bed with me when you'd finished."

"Was it that winter?"

"*Non.* Spring. Had it been the winter, God would have had to send an angel to sleep between us."

She rolled over, his warmth a comfort against the reminder that she'd soon need to get out of bed to nurse the baby. "Instead of the dog?"

"Every night, I whistled to Cossette to guard you."

A memory surged—four sweet notes that had ushered in her dreams.

"And so, the night I found you with Marcel in that room at the inn, I was so ashamed of myself. Thinking that, somehow, my thoughts had taken root in your head. That I'd made you feel—"

"It wasn't you, my love."

"I wanted to be a better man than he. I didn't want you to think I desired you in the same vein, so when you came to me that night . . . You were luminous and beautiful. But I couldn't take you the same way that he—"

"It's not the same, Gagnon."

He tugged her close. "Émile."

"*Émile.*"

Now she tied the girl's wool sleeping cap and kissed each sweet cheek. "Sleep well, *ma petite*."

"Can I sleep with you and *Papa* tonight? It's c-c-c-c-cold." She said the last with exaggerated shivers. She slept in a small cot tucked in a corner of their bedroom and would have to move in summer when the new baby came.

"*Non*. But I can put another quilt on your bed. And . . ." She bopped the girl's nose, guessing the unspoken request. "I can have the boys bring in a puppy to sleep with you. Would you like that?"

Aimée-Renée clapped her hands and burst into spinning. Cossette had slung a litter of pups fathered by an unknown drifter in late September. They would most likely be useless for herding, but one had been promised to keep as a pet.

Laurette walked with her into the bedroom and pulled a quilt from the trunk at the foot of her bed. Folding it double, she laid it on top of her wiggling daughter and smoothed her hands over the surface before tucking it at Aimée-Renée's feet. She leaned over to give a final kiss when a small voice from within the covers said, "Will you pray with me tonight since *Papa* isn't here?"

"Of course." She knelt beside the bed and folded her hands. She knew the prayer Gagnon said over his daughter every night. She'd listened at the doorway, or from the fire, or from their own bed on nights when Aimée-Renée woke up from a bad dream and needed to hear it again. And she'd prayed it, too, on those rare occasions when Gagnon worked late, or was in town, or had fallen into slumber in his chair. She knew it because he'd taught the same prayer to little Laurette and Renée. She could almost feel Renée's hand within hers.

"God of heaven, see me now
'Neath stars and moon and darkest clouds,
Grant me dreams to sleep in peace,
And with the sunrise in the East,
Wake me to a glorious day.
Father, Son, and Holy Spirit—I pray,
Amen."

Laurette made the sign of the cross and smiled at the movement beneath the pile of blankets as Aimée-Renée did the same.

Back out in the front room, she stoked the fire and sat to watch the flames dance. The boys came in, arms loaded with pups, claiming it was too cold for them to sleep in the barn, but Laurette resisted their pleas. "Only your sister's. The rest have their mother, and she will keep them warm enough."

When they returned—subdued, but not sullen—they sat with her. Philippe in Gagnon's chair, Nicolas and Joseph ignoring the new pew and choosing instead to sit on the thick braided rug at her feet, playing *le jeu d'échecs*. It was full dark, but still early, and she granted permission for them to stay up until Gagnon came home. Laurette picked up her needlework—she'd become quite good over the years, and was expertly knitting a bright-red sweater for Aimée-Renée. Philippe read from Gagnon's Bible, intermittently out loud, as he liked to ponder a passage endlessly before moving on to the next.

I have too much, Laurette thought as she worked her needles. *I am too safe, too warm, too full.*

At her feet, Joseph howled when Nicolas took his queen.

"And now— " Nicolas held the wooden piece up to cast a giant shadow on the opposite wall and made a chopping gesture—"off with her head!"

"Enough of that," Philippe said. "It's nothing to joke about."

Laurette held back a smile—not at the boy's joke, but at a foundling who sounded so much like the man who found him.

"Did they really chop off the queen's head, *Maman*?" Of all the boys, only Joseph called her such.

"They did. Now, as your brother said, let's not speak of it."

He studied the board. "It's sad, because she was very kind."

Nicolas snorted. "She was *not*. And how would you know, anyway?"

"I met her once, before *Maman* and I left Paris." His voice was distracted, dreamy, as if recalling a long-forgotten memory. Perhaps a memory he never knew he had. Both of his older brothers were laughing now, and he turned to Laurette, his face pink with indignation. "Tell them, *Maman*. You know. About the lady and the gypsy. I *told* you."

She waded in cautiously. "You've never told me that the lady was the queen."

"But she was. I know she was. She must have been. And the gypsy, she looked like—"

Nicolas guffawed. "Don't tell me. She had a patch over one eye, and rings on every finger, and bells on her ankles . . ." He rose with each detail and leapt into a dancing shadow on the wall.

"Nicolas . . . ," Laurette warned, sensing Joseph's increasing frustration. "And, Joseph, you mustn't exaggerate. *Papa* says it's the same as lying."

"I'm not exaggerating. *He* is. I'm trying to tell you that the gypsy . . . she looked a little like Aimée-Renée. Only taller, but not as tall as you. And her hair not dark, like that. Her face, though, a little, reminds me of—"

He could not continue over the unrestrained laughter of his brothers, and he soon fell silent, clutching a rook in his hand, staring at it while fighting back tears.

"That's enough." Rarely did Laurette speak with a volume of authority, but tonight her heart welled with something fearful. "Philippe, Nicolas. Upstairs, both of you. And step quick or I'll have you out curled up with the pups in the barn."

Unfazed by her outburst, Nicolas pried the rook out of Joseph's hand and put the game pieces in the drawstring bag while Philippe returned the Bible to its place on the mantel. Each stopped to plant a kiss on her cheek and say, "Good night, Laurette," before heading upstairs, recounting Joseph's story in amused whispers.

"Viens, mon cher," Laurette said, laying her knitting to the side and making room for Joseph on her lap. He was far too big for this, of course, but this evening both needed the comfort.

His head barely fit in the cradle of her shoulder, and his hair smelled more of barn than of boy. Still, she breathed him deep. "Tell me about the lady and the gypsy."

"She was the queen."

"Very well. Tell me about the queen and the gypsy."

He did, reciting the familiar story in detail, though he hadn't spoken a word of it in nearly three years. This time, though, was different. There were new details of the room, the art, the carpets, the drapes. The lady—the queen—had a big face and sad eyes, like she'd been crying. And the gypsy. Still, she wore a colorful skirt and a wide belt with all kinds of pockets and interesting things. "She taught me to play cat's cradle."

"I remember. And what did she look like?"

This was when he remembered how small she was. Almost the same size as him. And her face looked like cream. And her hair was mostly dark, but maybe had a little bit of blonde in it. And she was jumpy.

"Jumpy?"

"Oui." The word came out as a yawn. "She moved so fast. Like she couldn't sit still. You would have called her a little fish on a line, *Maman*."

Laurette held her boy, feeling him grown heavy with sleep. Her arms grew numb around him, her legs ached with the weight, but she somehow knew this would be the last time she would feel this. Soon there would be a new baby—a boy, she hoped with all her heart, longing to share a son with Gagnon from his first breath.

She awoke feeling him lifted. Even her husband's strong arms and legs protested at the weight.

"Shall I put him to bed with us? I don't know that I want to carry him upstairs."

"Non." She stretched the pins and needles out of her arms. "I want you to myself tonight. Put him in the downstairs room."

Her promise seemed to renew his vigor, and he hitched the boy for a better grip before heading to the empty room—soon to be Aimée-Renée's—to tuck the boy into the waiting bed.

Laurette stood and made her way through the darkness, every inch of the house as familiar and evident as if illuminated by the brightest light. Undressed to her shift, she crawled under the covers, and later listened as Gagnon did the same. He crawled in beside her, his hand cupped protectively over the life newly revealed to him that day.

"I hope it's a boy," she whispered into the night.

"We have so many boys," he whispered to her cheek, the softness of his winter beard tickling. He began to move upon her, but she braced her hand against him.

"I've something to tell you."

"Now?"

"It's about Renée. I think our Joseph may have found her."

L'épisode 30

Renée

PARIS

There is a certain part of the day—two hours, I'd guess, based on the count I keep in my head—when the sun fills my window with light, and I can see every stitch perfectly. My hands are a blur as I move the shuttle with detailed speed, but the pattern it creates is precise. Every tiny diamond of space. Every petal and pearl. During that time of light, I can produce a trim the length of my leg, or a square the span of my back. I race against the time, ignoring the pinch between my shoulder blades, assuring my neck it will straighten itself soon, when the first bit of shadow crosses over my hands. That is when I will rest and eat.

It is the guards who keep me well supplied with yarn for all my knotting work. I make little things for their wives or lovers (or both, as one man incomprehensibly claimed). The queen's gift had been deep within a pocket, sewn just for such a treasure, at the time I was handed down from the king's carriage at Varennes. When it is not cradled in my palm, I keep it coated with soot to hide its value.

The first time, a young guard, surely not much older than I, handed me a sad little ball of red string and asked if I could somehow fashion it into a ribbon. I did, a simple pattern of rosettes which he took with reverence—as if it were equal in value to the tool used to create it.

More and more. The same request. Red ribbons. They brought me treats in exchange. Bits of chocolate, a bottle of wine with nearly a quarter left to drink. A pillow. A hairbrush. Then one day I happened to catch a glimpse of my latest happy patron—Albert, my least favorite of my guards—before the door closed behind him. He had a thick waist and thin neck around which he'd tied the ribbon. Affecting a woman's posture, he declared in a sickening falsetto all the ways "she" would show gratitude for his gift. His compatriots laughed, and a twisting came to my stomach. The work of my hands was being used to glorify the horrifying work of the new regime. All of my stitches, my perfect, pretty stitches, wrapped to emulate the torn flesh and blood of *la Guillotine*. The same that killed my king, my queen, and others I could count only by keeping track of the cheering in the street.

From that moment I would create no more red ribbons, but my hands cannot rest idle. For the promise of socks I was brought knitting needles and wool. For the promise of white lace on an infant's burial gown, I received an enormous skein of high-quality white thread. I work according to the light. Knitting in the morning, the grayness adequate to envision simple stitches. Knotting in the afternoon, my hands following the arc of the sun. Mending in the evenings—repairing the clothing of those too poor to replace a torn garment. Whenever I feel resentful of this chore, I think of the little boy, naked in his poverty. I patch a knee or repair a seat and think, *Surely this is God's child too.*

When I learned of the king's death, and that Madame would

be permitted to wear black to mourn him, I asked for a skein of fine black wool, from which I knitted one pair of black stockings for the woman in my jailer's life, and yards upon yards of beautiful lace for Madame to trim her dress, should she desire. To have it delivered safely to her hands, I promised a tricolor bonnet I'd crafted in secret and tucked away for just such a bribe.

I do not know if Madame ever received my gift, for who can trust the honesty of a rebel? I've heard she wore her mourning gown until the day she herself was taken to *la guillotine*, but that she was not permitted to wear it to her own death. For that, she wore a simple white shift—the same that had accrued such criticism in her past—and a white cap edged with lace. I knew that cap. Even without seeing it, or having any way to confirm my suspicions, I knew. That was my lace stitched to it. The thin, pale ribbon threaded through. The one she said always made her think of her babes in heaven.

It is more than two years gone since our carriage was overtaken on that dark road. Three weeks since a cheering crowd marked the end of Madame's life. For all my days here, I have awoken with some hope of freedom. At first, I thought—surely—no one would have the courage to brazenly take the life of a king. Then my naiveté transferred to my queen, thinking such barbaric measures would not be taken with a woman, no matter how reviled. But they took her head, held up the face they'd mocked.

And now I wait.

⚜

I am roused from sleep by a voice at my window.

"Renée?"

Not the window to the world outside. That is high and barred and serves as nothing more than a source of light and a means to measure the passing of one day to the next. No, this is at the narrow window cut into my door, and for all my months behind it, this is the first I've heard my name spoken aloud.

"Renée. *C'est moi.*"

He need not say his name. There is only one man in all of France who knows of my existence here. Marcel.

I'm far too short to see out the window, but I run to the door and place my cheek upon it. "Marcel? What are you doing here?"

"Why do you *think* he's here?" Albert's equally familiar voice makes his insinuation clear. "And I reckon I can take myself out of earshot for a spell, though I hate to miss out."

The key turns and the door opens. Marcel enters with a playful push to his back; then it closes again behind him. His appearance is no longer that of the lusty rebel who sang from the tabletop at the Sainte-Menehould inn, our place of betrayal. He wears a fine suit of clothing, his hair trimmed and smoothed away from his face—handsome as ever—and tied at the nape with a ribbon of black silk.

"You look . . ." He searches for words. "Better than I expected."

"And you seem to have prospered. Was the price on our heads really so high?"

"I didn't betray you, Renée. You saved me once; I saved you once. And since then our actions have been to serve only ourselves, *non*?"

"And yet I'm in prison, and you are looking like the man who discovered a rich dead uncle. Is that what happened, Marcel? Did you finally stumble across a family that would claim you?"

A tiny flicker of hurt crosses his face, but he catches it with a half-tipped smile. "The constitution is my family. It's done more for me than any uncle, or father, or god could ever do. I can help you now, Renée."

He has a cloak draped over one arm and lifts it to reveal a small basket of fruit. "Pears, your favorite. And hard to come by here." He moves the table and chair, taking the seat and gesturing that I sit across from him on my cot.

"You can help me now?"

"Yes."

"But you couldn't earlier."

He takes a knife from his breast pocket—the guard must not be aware he has such a thing—and begins to slice the fruit.

My mouth waters and my pride falters as I greedily snatch the first sliver.

"Had you listened to me that night at the inn, you could be—anywhere. An apartment in the city, rewarded for delivering the wayward monarchs into the hands of the people. Or a little château, with a houseful of servants to do your bidding. But you didn't listen, and here you are."

"Is that why you betrayed us? Because I wouldn't obey you?"

The pear is now fanned out on the table, and he takes a piece for himself. "Do you think I am the only one who recognized you? I don't know who alerted the watch, but it wasn't me. I don't particularly care—rather, *didn't* care—about Louis and Marie. I knew he was a powerless figurehead with weak support. *You*, on the other hand . . ."

"How can you help me?"

"Do you want to know more about Laurette?"

Her name—just to hear it spoken brings her full to life within me. "You said she went home. Why was she ever here?"

"She came with me, for a time. And then she left. I came home—to what we had as a home, and she was gone."

"Is she—" I cannot bring myself to ask.

"Mouton Blanc. Safe and sound."

"You've seen her?"

He chuckles at the idea. *"Moi? Non."*

"Then how can you be sure?"

"Because I'm in a position to ask people to be sure. There's more. She's actually married to the old man."

"Stop," I say almost playfully and reach for another pear now that my stomach has unclenched. I don't consider for a moment that his heart is affected in any way by her marriage to another man. "There's no more than ten years between them. And Laurette has always been an old soul."

"They have children. Three boys that they've taken in—one that came back with Laurette from Paris."

"Yours?" At one time, such a question would have been too far beyond my sense of delicacy to ask, but these times are new.

"*Non.* An older boy. They have a child together, too. A little girl."

"She's lived an entire life without me."

"As have you without her. The difference is, she will live to be an old woman. Whereas you . . ." He shrugged, as if the possible ending of my life were nothing but a trifle.

"So there's no hope for me?"

"You've been charged with treason, Renée. Conspiring against the new regime. You won't live to see the New Year."

"Unless? You said you could help me."

"Unless . . . Early this morning, hours before the sunrise, I was walking along the river. I could not sleep, you see. Always—often—my mind is so full. I passed by a man similarly plagued. He was walking very swiftly, more so than the hour and circumstances demanded, and muttering to himself, 'I am the resurrection and the life. . . . I am the resurrection and the life.'"

"As Christ is," I say, completing the verse: "'He that believeth in me, though he were dead, yet shall he live.'"

"All that is well and good." Marcel pops a slice of pear in his mouth and chews it while extracting a sheet of paper from his portfolio. "But I am here to be your resurrection, *ma petite*. And to keep you from being dead at all. At least, not anytime soon. I can come for you tomorrow with officers of the court and set a date for a new trial at which you will throw yourself on their mercy."

I laugh out loud, the sound almost foreign to my ears. "I've yet to see any mercy to fall upon."

"Mercy sent you to Tuileries after your first trial. Don't forget that." He slides the paper around so I can see the words. "It reads, in summary, that you were unduly coerced in your participation with the events leading to Louis's attempt to flee, and that you were forced to accompany them to stand in the place of their daughter, Marie-Thérèse, should they be apprehended on the road."

"But that's not true," I say, my eyes tracking the writing as he reads.

"Did Marie Antoinette ask you to help in any way?"

"I made her dress."

"At her request?"

"Yes, but—I could have refused."

"Could you? And could you have been trusted to stay behind, knowing all the details of their plans?"

"But I knew nothing, Marcel!"

"The perception of the court is far more important than the facts in the matter."

He looks and sounds like an *avocat*, but I know he has no more education than I, beyond what he's read in the newspapers and pamphlets and political journals always at his elbow at Gagnon's table. Is that another product of the revolution? That a man can step into the profession of his choosing? Yesterday a madman rushing through the home of the king, today a legal expert extracting an innocent prisoner by inventing yet another crime?

"I won't say this. Any of it."

"Nobody wants your blood on their hands."

"Then tell them to let me go."

"I don't have any real power. Nobody's going to do my bidding. I've simply worked my way into the consciousness of the court. They know me, and for some unfathomable reason, they respect my opinions. They'll listen to this argument knowing it is *my* argument. You don't have to *say* any of this. I will. Every word. They'll simply ask if it is your testimony, and you say yes. Then you sign your name to it, I hire a carriage, and you'll have supper with Gagnon and his new family the next day. If, indeed, that's what you want."

It is the first glimmer of hope I've felt since I knew I had a need to feel it. "Surely it can't be that easy."

"Justice is a fickle thing these days."

I cast down my eyes and continue where Marcel left off reading. My ears rush with blood at the words that follow. "I renounce any loyalty to the former monarchy of France. I declare Louis XVI to be a ruler corrupt in policy and person, his wife, Marie Antoinette of Austria, to be a traitorous woman of low moral character. I will support no actions that aim to establish his children into places of power. Furthermore, I pledge my loyalty to the causes of Nationalism and the citizens of France. I give my heart and my soul to my country, granting no other entity primacy in my consciousness." My voice chokes on the words, and I look at Marcel through tears. "I do not believe this. Any of it."

"It doesn't matter what you believe, Renée. On either side. Today's beliefs won't last forever. They might not last until tomorrow."

Try as I might, I cannot see Louis as anything other than a befuddled man, more suited to life as a country squire than king of a nation. If not for the laws that bound him to the throne, I think he would have spent all his days hunting. And Madame? Had these people never seen her with her children? I recall the sadness in her eyes as she recounted the stories told about her. Worse, I remember Laurette telling me those same stories, giggling over them in the loft, back when I barely understood the crude accusations. How awful for the children to hear such lies about their mother. *The children . . .*

"Marcel, where are the children?"

"The daughter, Marie-Thérèse, has been safely delivered to Austria for the time being. And I have no doubt she'll be permitted to live a long, happy life there. She holds no threat to the constitution. She's nothing."

"And Louis-Charles?"

He has no quick answer for this. "There can never be another king in France, Renée. We've changed the law."

"Where is he?"

His eyes hold mine, and with each passing breath my heart sinks with certain knowledge. "We can never have another king in France."

I feel the paper crumple beneath my hand, the fruit turn sour within me. "*Quels monstres!* He is a *child*. An innocent little boy."

"He's next in line to the throne."

"A throne that doesn't exist, by your own choice. How could you—?"

He holds up his hands as if fending off a blow. "I haven't done anything. And you greatly exaggerate my knowledge in the whole affair. I'm here for you, and you alone, and only if you want me to be."

"How could you ask me to pledge my allegiance to something so vile as this? For that matter, how could *you*?"

"I'm only asking you to say what they want to hear. To clear their conscience of taking your life. Who knows how many lives you might save? If those accused of treason will renounce their crimes, others might go free."

I know he doesn't want that any more than the monsters of this bloody revolution do. He's simply telling me what I want to hear, finding the argument that might convince me to do his bidding.

"Whose conscience are we clearing, really, Marcel? I won't sign my soul to a lie. Not to assuage your guilt or to pardon the fiends who sentenced me here. How could God ever forgive me . . . ?"

There's a subtle shift in his posture, and I look again at the final words of the statement: *I give my heart and my soul to my country, granting no other entity primacy in my consciousness.* No, I cannot sign this document. I raise my head and look directly into Marcel's eyes. "My heart and my soul belong to God alone. Never to France."

"These are only words, Renée. They don't have to mean anything if you don't want them to."

I remember a conversation just before I left Mouton Blanc, one of those dark afternoons when the storm raged outside, Marcel chastised for not bowing his head for the blessing. The words of Holy Scripture seemed so lighthearted then, but when I recall them now, I feel my eternal soul at stake.

"Jesus says whoever confesses him before men, he will confess before the Father. And whoever denies him, he will deny before the Father."

"More words. Your Scripture is as meaningless to me as these are to you." He pounds his finger on the statement.

"I will not defame the king. Or the queen. And I cannot deny my Savior."

"You're making a mistake."

"I've made many mistakes, *mon ami*. If this is one, it will be my last."

"I'm leaving this document with you. I'll be back."

"I won't change my mind."

"I'll bring Gagnon with me."

Whatever I intended as my next retort dies on my lips. This promise draws all of the air from the room. I can see the silence. "You'd go to Mouton Blanc?"

"And fetch him and bring him here, yes. Maybe he can make you listen to reason."

Half of my heart is back at Gagnon's table, the sturdy, worn wood, the seats in all stages of disrepair. Chipped dishes, pewter mugs, the smell of his pipe when the plates were empty. If he were here, sharing this sparse meal on my wobbly table, he would echo my response with his whole heart. And I tell this to Marcel.

"But you'll listen to him, regardless? You'll heed his counsel?"

"Since when have you given any credence to Gagnon's *counsel*?"

"Since it might save your life."

"How soon . . . ?" I realize what I'm truly asking. "How long, do you think? Before . . . ?"

"I'll ride for Mouton Blanc directly. We can be here in four days."

Four days. "Will you take something to Laurette for me?" I say nothing about the stack of coins I gave him all those years ago, almost certain they never found their way to Gagnon's hand.

"I will." Then remembering too, "I promise."

I reach under my thin mattress and produce the knotting shuttle. "It was a gift to me from the queen herself. If Laurette doesn't know how to use it, have her ask Elianne. She knows."

His eyes remain glued to his palm. "Gold?"

I laugh. "More than that, Marcel. I'm going to ask Gagnon if you gave it to her."

"Renée—why not give it to her yourself? When you go home?"

"Because I don't know that I'll go home, Marcel. And I know for certain I don't want her to see me here. Promise me, Marcel. Don't bring her with you."

He sends me an indulgent, knowing smile. "Trust me, nothing could entice your cousin to return to Paris. *Non*, the two of you will be reunited in Mouton Blanc."

"If God wills."

"If you choose."

He rises, leaving me with two pieces of unsliced fruit—my trade for gold, and so much more valuable in these spare days. I offer myself for his kiss, one to each cheek and a final, chaste lingering on my lips.

"I pray you will let me atone for my sins, Renée."

"I'm glad to hear you still pray, Marcel."

"To you, *ma petite*. No one else."

He shouts through the grate for the guards to open the door and steps back in surprise to find them so close by.

"You have been listening, citizens?"

The first guard, Albert, that distasteful sack of a man, closes the door and locks it. "Didn't give us much to listen to, did he, *ami*?"

"Oh, I don't know about that." I don't recognize his voice, so I bring my chair up against the door, climb upon it, and peer out the window. The second guard is a stranger, but matched to Albert in every way. "Negotiating a way to turn a traitor. Lie to the court. Seems we ought to have the prisoner's visitor arrested for treason."

"Gentlemen—" Marcel's words so smooth and refined in contrast—"bringing such charges requires proof. Witnesses. Testimony."

"I heard it, citizen."

"As did I, citizen."

"And if you can get the judge to value your word over mine, I'll gladly stand to the charges. Until then—" He attempts to pass through the wall formed by the two men.

"Wait up," says the second guard. "I know you. We fought together—"

"My fighting days are behind me, brother. I've turned to more civil pursuits."

"Like buttin' up to one of that hag's own pets." This is Albert, employing his favorite pejorative of the queen.

"No need to speak ill of the dead," Marcel says. "She can't be resurrected and killed again." Though his words chill me, I understand his intent: to strike a chord of camaraderie with these two beasts. This time, though, as he attempts to pass, his failure is evident.

"See how the judge values this." The second guard blocks him not just with his body, but with a blow so violent, Marcel doubles over, expelling a breath that sheathes a sharper cry of pain. He remains folded and peeks within his coat as if searching. Resolute, he stands, though not completely upright, wherein Albert leaps upon the exposed weakness and follows through with another blow of his own.

At this, Marcel lets forth another note of stifled pain.

I've seen enough of brawling men to know that Marcel's injury transcends that of a punch to the gut. True, Albert and his compatriot are bigger than Marcel by half, but he is younger—strong and healthy. He would have known to brace his body against a second blow. And yet, when he stands again, he is unstable and holds his hand protectively not over his stomach, but to the left where—I suddenly remember—he stashed the knife he used to cut my supper.

I cry out with the pain Marcel cannot express, but it is lost in the cruel laughter of his attackers. He turns, sees me, and tries to adjust his expression to a mask of confidence, but I am not fooled.

"Marcel—"

"Promise you will listen to Gagnon." He's walking backward, away, pursued only by the guards' mocking taunts. "Promise you will do as he says."

I grip the bars and shout my word, praying I'll have a chance to keep it.

L'épisode 31

Laurette

MOUTON BLANC

Philippe burst through the front door, his cheeks pink with exertion beneath the scattering of adolescent whiskers.

"There's a gentleman coming on horseback. He asked if you were home and well, and told me to run ahead and tell you he's on his way so he doesn't give you too big of a surprise. And to make sure you'll let him come."

Laurette paused in her chore. It was midafternoon, the warmest hour of the day, when she could let the fireplace go cold and sweep the ashes. Aimée-Renée "helped," holding the bucket as still as she could, though somehow managing to get smudges on her face and apron.

"Who is it?"

"You won't believe it when you see him. It's Marcel. He called himself Citizen Moreau, but it's Marcel. He's waiting at the top of the path for me to come back and let him know if you'll welcome him in."

Laurette took the bucket from Aimée-Renée. "Go back; tell

him to keep riding. Or to return the horse to whoever he stole it from."

Philippe laughed. "He told me you'd say exactly that. He said to tell you he has news of Renée. That she is in danger, and if you won't see him, to send Gagnon, because the message is for him."

A single word registered. *Danger.*

"He's in the barn. Take this message to him. This is his house, after all. He'll decide who has a place in it."

She went outside to empty the ash bucket just as Gagnon emerged from the barn with Philippe. His eyes found hers across the yard, and after all their years together, the conversation needed no words.

I love you.

I trust you.

Gagnon and Philippe set out to greet their visitor and escort him to the front gate, leaving less than half an hour before they arrived. She took off her apron and Aimée-Renée's, explaining that they had a guest about to arrive and needed to prepare.

When she scrubbed the soot from the little girl's face, nothing but Marcel's image remained. He would know upon first glance. What would he say? An even greater fear, one finding purchase from a place deeper than Laurette could fathom, was that Aimée-Renée would know. Would there be some quickening in her little spirit, some flicker of understanding in her unformed mind? Would she look to Gagnon, then Marcel, then back again, and *feel* the connection to the stranger at their table?

"Chérie," Laurette said, smoothing back the child's hair and plaiting it in a single, quick braid, "why don't you go into *Maman* and *Papa*'s room and lie down for a bit? You have been such a good helper today; you need some rest."

"But I'm not tired, *Maman*."

"Just go in and lie down and see if you are. Stay there until

I call for you, and then I'll let you go out to the barn and play with the puppies. Agreed?"

Her face lit up at the mention of the puppies, as Laurette knew it would, and she scampered obediently to the room. Laurette followed, tucking a warm quilt around her body once she settled in.

"Now, remember," she said, smoothing her skirt and rolling down her sleeves, "stay put until I call for you." She wrapped a green shawl, knitted only last week, over her shoulders, crossed it against her filling stomach, and tied it in the back. A few drops of water from the washbowl kept the static at bay as she ran a brush over her hair before putting on her cleanest cap. Her cheeks were pink from the wash water; only Gagnon would recognize the nervousness in her eyes. Well, Gagnon and Marcel, but only her husband would understand the reason.

In the front room, she built up a fire and put on a kettle for tea. They had no cloth for the table—never had—but she set a narrow runner down its center and laid out a plate of bread, a crock of butter, and a jar of jam. A meager offering to an uninvited guest, but one that should convey the length of his welcome. Bread. Tea. News. Go.

She was sitting with her carding boards when they walked in, Philippe presumably dispatched to feed and water the horse. The change in Marcel was outstanding. His cloak, a rich, fine cloth; his suit, well fitting and expensive; his hat an impressive tricorn—a style she'd never known him to favor. The face beneath it, however, remained unchanged, and she hated herself for the unbidden thrill the sight of it induced.

But then, next to him, Gagnon. Her Émile. Taller, as he had always been. Broader shoulders beneath the same rough wool coat he'd worn since she and Renée were children. Laurette had knit his wool cap—long before developing any real skill for the craft—and he wore the lopsided, irregularly stitched thing with pride and affection. His beard grew thick, green eyes sought her above it, and the sadness in them drew her to her feet.

She bypassed Marcel without even a hint of a greeting and went straight to Gagnon's waiting embrace. "What news, my love?"

"Not good," he said with a kiss to her forehead. "There's much to discuss."

Only then did she turn back to Marcel, who took both of her hands in his. They were surprisingly warm, given he wore no gloves in the chill of the day. "You look beautiful, Laurette. As beautiful as I've ever seen you."

"Thank you," she said, feeling the first slip in her cool reserve. "Now, come. Let me take your cloak."

He reached up to unfasten it, wincing obviously as he shrugged it from his shoulders.

"Are you all right?" How, after all this time, could she care? But his breath had been sharp, and she took note of an underlying pallor to his face.

His smile was pained. "Part of the heroic story I failed to tell your husband. There was a scuffle with the guards as I left the prison."

"Here, then," Laurette said, leading him to Gagnon's chair by the now pleasantly roaring fire. The tea and bread could wait. News of Renée could not.

"I will tell you everything, all of the truth as I know it, and I beg that you will forgive me for not doing so before. But you must understand how much I believe in the cause of our revolution. Haven't I always, *mon vieux*?"

"You have," Gagnon said with the indulgence of a father. "Long before the first drop of bloodshed."

"And I still do, but I can see how we . . . But there is danger in our digression."

"Renée," Laurette said, moved to the edge of her seat. Gagnon stood behind her, his hand on her shoulder with the weight of assurance. "Tell us about Renée."

"Right, yes. That summer, all those years ago, I did see her. That was true. And I was shackled and she did save me. Convinced the guards to let me go."

"So you said." Laurette grew impatient. So typical of Marcel to make himself the center of the tale.

"What I didn't tell you is that when I left her, I did so with money. Not a lot of money, as it turned out, but money that was meant for you."

"And you kept it," Gagnon said, stating an obvious fact.

"I knew, even then, how useless currency would be to you. You remember? Every bit of it would have been gone for just a few loaves of bread."

"But they would have been *our* loaves," Laurette said, recalling the sharp pain of hunger.

"What did you do with it?" Gagnon asked, his words patient.

"I traded it for what we would need. Guns, ammunition. Some food and safe places. I bought goodwill and trust—the same that would allow me to later buy food for your sheep. I bought my life."

"For a cause that would kill so many." This from Philippe, who had entered the house with uncharacteristic silence. His brothers flanked him on either side.

"Go upstairs," Laurette said. "This doesn't concern you."

Gagnon contradicted her. "No. You may stay; it's an important conversation. But sit and listen. Do not interrupt again. Understand?"

The boys—all three—nodded and sat along the old church pew under the window. Philippe's eyes were set like steel.

"The man," Marcel continued, "the guard who let me go. He was the head of Madame's—"

"The queen," Gagnon corrected. "Say it."

Marcel made no effort to hide his distaste. "The queen's security detail. He and Renée—they were in love. But he . . . died. The day the family was first arrested. One of our women was killed, too, and Renée was thought to have killed her."

Laurette nearly leapt from her seat. "Never! She couldn't!"

"I know." This marked a change in Marcel's demeanor. The first hint of sadness, regret. "I spoke on her behalf at her trial, hoping and failing to get her released. Though not a complete failure. Rather than execution, she was imprisoned with the family in Tuileries. She has been in prison all this time."

"And not—" Laurette felt a grip on her shoulder commensurate with the strength of Gagnon's words—"not a single word from her? Could she not write? Not a single letter to her family to know of her fate?"

"You can't possibly understand. The fear of being seen as a traitor. People—hundreds arrested every day. Who would risk their lives to deliver a letter for her?"

"Not you, apparently," Laurette said.

"No. I risked enough in court. But she was safe in Tuileries. She would be safe now if she hadn't . . ." Over the course of the conversation, his face had gone pale, his voice hoarse, and a fine sheen of sweat formed on his brow. "Could I trouble you for a drink of water?"

"Of course." Laurette looked to Joseph. "Fetch our guest a drink, would you?" Then, remembering Gagnon's propensity for hospitality, asked, "Are you hungry, Marcel?"

He shook his head. "Thirsty, though. And warm." He moved to remove his jacket, again showing signs of discomfort.

"Seems to have been quite a fight," Gagnon said, moving around to help him.

"More so than I thought at the time." He took the water from Joseph, drank, and gave a sidelong look to Laurette. "Where did he come from?"

"Paris. And not another word."

Marcel handed the cup back to the boy, thus exposing for the first time the dark stain on his vest.

"Mon Dieu!" Laurette came to his side. "You're bleeding."

"Blast," Marcel said in good humor. "And I changed the bandage not two miles up the road."

"Come," Gagnon said, taking his arm and helping him to stand. "Lie down and let me look at it."

"Not in our room," Laurette cautioned, then mouthed their daughter's name silently behind Marcel's back.

"He is a guest. We have a guest room. Walk with me. Laurette, bring bandages and soap and water. Quickly."

Joseph stood dumbly, holding the cup, his eyes round as saucers at the whole ordeal. Philippe and Nicolas, in obedience, remained seated until the two men disappeared; then Philippe leapt to his feet.

"Why are we harboring him here?"

"You can see," Laurette said, bustling to fulfill her duty. She thrust a water bucket into Nicolas's hands. "Go fetch some fresh. Philippe, pour some from the kettle into this basin, cool it with what Nicolas brings in. Joseph, go upstairs to the trunk and bring me a towel. All of you—go!"

They scrambled at once. Laurette eased open the door to her room and spied Aimée-Renée, as she suspected, sound asleep. It would mean a late night getting her to sleep again, but then it might be a late night for them all.

Minutes later, she rapped softly on the second room's door and entered with the basin of warm water, soap, and bandages. Gagnon's face looked grim. Approaching, she saw why. Marcel, stripped of his shirt, his flesh smooth and bare and familiar, save for the gaping wound under his rib. The flesh around it was swollen and red; the flesh within an unnatural color altogether.

Gagnon took the cloth and washed the wound. After, he helped Marcel sit up while Laurette wrapped a bandage clear around. No fresh blood came through. "That's better, yes?" she said, tucking in the end.

The two men looked at each other, expressions somber.

"It's still bleeding somewhere," Marcel said. "Now, with your indulgence, I'd like to rest for just a bit. *Le vieux* here knows the rest. And why I'm here. And what you need to do to save her."

His eyes closed, dark lashes fluttering before falling still. His breath shallow—had it been so while he told his tale?

Gagnon took her hand and led her out of the room to the table, inviting the boys to join them for the forgotten tea and bread. The first gray of evening darkened the window, and one of the boys brought a long stick to light the tallow candle on the table. "Can we hear the rest, *Papa*?"

"Yes, but withhold judgment." And then he told them everything. With a voice deep and somber, befitting the truthfulness of the tale, he recounted a story of a late-night escape—royalty in disguise. He dropped to a whisper as he re-created a hushed conversation in a tavern corner, Renée's opportunity to escape, and her refusal. Then his words matched the pace of a thundering carriage, overtaken by roadside rebels within miles of passing the border that would guarantee them safety. Interspersed with prayers for the dead, he shared the grisly deaths at *la guillotine*, the revenge-hungry crowds, the blood pooled inches on the ground, the baskets softened and sticky with gore. He described Renée's prison cell and her final visit with Marcel, including the testimony that might grant her freedom.

"And she could come home?" Laurette asked, bread forgotten in her hand.

"He thinks so, yes."

"What makes him think so?" Philippe's question made no attempt to mask the disdain he felt for the man.

"*Les Nationalistes* would appear to have changed the heart of someone loyal to the monarchy."

"But everyone would know that she is lying," Philippe said.

"If it would bring her home," Laurette said, "who cares if it's a lie?"

"She cares," Gagnon said. "Renée cares, very deeply. Not only does she feel an intense loyalty to the royal family, but to lie—even for this—is a sin."

"As is putting to death an innocent girl." Any attempt to control her emotions proved vain as Laurette's throat burned too hot to speak.

"I know, my love. I know." He reached for her hand, balled into a fist upon the table, and covered it with his own. "Marcel says she wants my counsel. After all these years, all this time, she wants to see me. And he says she'll do what I say."

Laurette looked at him through a veil of tears. "Will—will you go to her?"

"I'll leave at first light."

"I'll go with you," Nicolas said.

"No, my son. Paris is a dangerous place to be. Stay here, take care of Laurette and your brothers and sister. I have another errand for you boys tonight. Take Marcel's horse and ride to Girard's. Tell him Marcel has returned, and that he is gravely wounded. Stay the night—it will be too dark to walk back safely."

"Can't we take Belle and ride her back?" Philippe asked, referring to a horse they purchased after a good payout at last spring's shearing.

Gagnon stood. "No, I'll be gone with her before you're even awake in the morning. You're going to tell Girard to keep Marcel's horse as payment of a debt I owe."

He took himself to sit at Marcel's side. Laurette cooked eggs to add to the boys' supper, and as she fussed them out the front door, Aimée-Renée emerged from her nap, rubbing sleepy eyes.

"Is it morning, *Maman*?"

Laurette hugged her close. "No, sweet girl. It is evening. Come, have some supper. Stay at the table with Joseph until I return."

She filled a plate and walked into the room to find Marcel still deep in sleep and Gagnon on his knees at the bedside, hands folded, deep in prayer. He'd built a small fire in the grate, making the room pleasantly warm. Laurette set his supper plate at the bedside and eased herself down next to him. Through her own darkness, she felt his hand clasp hers as his prayers filled the room.

"Grant him peace, Holy Father, in these last days and hours."

After a few more minutes, Laurette ventured into the silence. "I've brought you supper."

"I'm not hungry."

"You should eat."

He kissed her cheek. "I promise I'll eat in the morning."

Marcel uttered a small groan and appeared to be on the verge of waking, but merely shifted.

"He's not going back with you, is he?"

"*Non.* I think he knew that. He told me everything. Where to go. Who to speak to. What to say."

"What will you say? To her, I mean?"

He put his head down on the mattress edge and left it there for a full minute before responding. "I don't know, my love. I'm praying that God will give me the right words, with the right intent."

"He will." She put her arm across his shoulder. "He always tells you just what to do."

⚜

That night, Joseph and Aimée-Renée enjoyed the rare privilege of sleeping in the big bed with their father, while Laurette sat at Marcel's bedside. His sleep was fitful, though with stretches lasting longer than wakefulness. When he slept, she sponged his fevered body and brow with cool water; when he was alert, they talked. He asked her to tell him about her life. The boys, the baby.

"What do you know about her?" she asked warily.

"Only that you have a little girl. My friend Le Rocher was here last spring and saw her with you at the market."

"She's sleeping. We also have puppies. Did Le Rocher tell you about those, too?"

Marcel laughed, despite the obvious pain. "No. That's what I get for having a spy who cannot speak."

During one bout of waking he told her about the woman killed in the charge at Versailles, the same who killed the guard. "I think Renée thought she was you. She was wearing that green vest you left in the apartment."

"How did she get it?"

"I gave it to her."

Laurette was thankful for the darkness that hid her shame at the memory of that place. "You went back there? I watched for you. I waited for you."

"You didn't wait for long, love."

No, she hadn't. He drifted to sleep again, and when he woke she told him about Joseph, finding him in the chaos of the fall of the Bastille. Taking his hand and walking him here—home. About his clothes and his story about the gypsy and the lady. Renée and the queen. "He saw her."

"He did."

"Do you know anything about his mother? Who she might be?"

She heard him shake his head. "But in Paris, for the poor? Children aren't always such a treasure to hold."

In the dark of morning she heard Gagnon stirring in the kitchen and went out to him.

"See? A man of my word. Eating now, and taking more for the road."

She pulled him down for a kiss and kept him there until she had her fill.

"I should go away more often," he said, impressed with her display.

"After this, promise me you'll never go away again. Not even for a day. Not to town, without me."

"I promise. And when it's time—send the boys to Girard. He'll come take care of . . . everything."

"You don't think he'll live to see you return? To see Renée?"

He shook his head.

"Then come. Say good-bye. I know the two of you didn't always get along, but he did admire you. I think he was jealous."

"Of me? He stole you away."

"Of your heart. Because he knew, like I knew, that you're a good man. A better man. That's why Renée values your counsel above his."

She followed him but watched from the door as Gagnon touched Marcel's face with the gentleness of a father, whispering his name. Marcel stirred, woke, and clasped his hand.

"Why are you still here?"

"I'm just leaving. Saying good-bye, and thank you. And one more thing. Listen in your heart for the sound of God's voice calling."

"He won't call to me, *mon vieux*."

"He calls to all men who have an ear to hear. Listen. Tell him of your sins. He stands ready to forgive, *mon ami*. Believe that."

"I believe in my country."

"One of your country wounded you and sent you to die. Your country wants to execute the little lamb who once ate from your same spoon. Do you remember that, Marcel? When she was so hungry, and you yourself would feed her. And now this country that you so believe in wants her to die. But even that, even *them*, Jesus will forgive. They've killed the Church and sent away the priests, but they cannot banish Christ. You will believe all of this sometime. I will pray until your last breath that you believe before you take it."

Gagnon bent and kissed each of Marcel's cheeks, prayed a blessing upon him, touched the sign of the cross to his fevered body, and left.

Laurette followed, watching from the window as he saddled Belle and rode away, the first pink line of dawn still far on the horizon. She touched her head to the cool glass, hearing all of Gagnon's words again. That Jesus would forgive even those who would wish to murder Renée. But it was she, Laurette, who put Renée in danger in the first place. Sent her away with lies, scheming to keep a man who would betray her over and over again. Would Christ forgive a sin so long hidden? One rooted too deep to put into words? She'd never spoken of it aloud—not to a priest, not in prayer. But this morning, kneeling on a pew rescued from a dying church, she did.

"It's my fault." The circle of steam from her breath clung as a witness to her confession. "I was jealous. I lied. I gave him my body as a price. I was glad when she left, happier each day she was gone until . . . I wanted *him*. I wanted him more than a holy life. More than a *good* man. More than anything you ever gave me. And yet . . ." She turned, sat, looked around at the cozy room. Two sturdy chairs by the fire, food to eat, firewood to feed the flames lovingly built by her husband before leaving. "And yet, you give me *more*. And—" she felt it, the first tiny flutter—"more."

"Maman?" Aimée-Renée's sweet face was looking at her from across the room. From the doorway, but not the door behind which she'd slept beside her *papa*. She'd taken her detested cap off during her sleep, as she often did, and her hair sprung like

wisps of curling smoke around her head. "*Maman*, the man in the bed wants you to come to him. He says he has a gift for you."

It was the first she'd noticed that she'd been crying, and she hastily wiped her tears away. Never had she imagined this moment, when her daughter would meet the man who fathered her, and if she had, she never could have imagined these circumstances.

"I'll be right there," she said, forcing normalcy to her voice. "Where is Joseph?"

"Still sleeping. Because he's lazy."

Laurette heard the faint masculine laughter coming from the room, knowing the pain it caused. She lit a candle and brought it in, thinking it all might be less frightening for Aimée-Renée in the light, but her brave little girl didn't seem frightened in the least. She did, however, tug Laurette down to whisper in her ear, "Who is he, *Maman*?"

"He is our friend," she whispered back, but loud enough for Marcel to hear.

Again, in her ear, "Is he very sick?"

To this, she only nodded.

"In my cloak." Marcel's voice sounded weaker than at any time throughout the night, and he seemed to lack the strength even to point to the hook by the door. "An inner pocket. There's something. Very fancy and pretty. Made of gold. Can you find it?"

He was speaking to Aimée-Renée, each word increasing her excitement to please him and see the pretty gold thing. She went to the cloak and carefully ran her tiny hands over every bit of it, searching first for pockets, then fishing within. Nothing at first, and she frowned in frustration, but soon her face registered triumph. She lifted to her toes to reach down into the recess, and then stood, staring at the treasure in her palm.

"Bring it here," Laurette said, and was soon holding a work of filigreed art in her hand. She turned the object over and over in the candlelight, unable to imagine what it could be. "What's this?" For the moment, though, she was content to see Aimée-Renée's reaction to the shadow the carvings cast on the wall. Then she remembered once, long ago, Renée had sketched such an object on a sheet of paper and begged Gagnon to carve it for her.

"It's a knotting shuttle," Marcel whispered. "Given to Renée by the queen herself."

"Oh, my . . ." Laurette bent close to her daughter. "Of course. See? You wrap thread around it here and pull it through to make fancy designs. Our friend Elianne knows how. I'll have her teach me."

"May I play with it, *Maman*? May I wrap my knitting thread around it?"

"Yes, but be very careful."

The little girl clutched the treasure to her and ran from the room.

Immediately after her final step over the threshold, as if sensing the shortness of time, Marcel asked, "What is your daughter's name?"

"Aimée-Renée."

"She is mine, isn't she?"

There could be no denial. "I knew before you left—before *I* left. I knew but I didn't tell you. I was afraid."

"Afraid? I never imagined *ma lionne* afraid of anything."

Lionne. "Because of what you said. Because we were so desperately poor and didn't have a real home. But that day, when I saw—*à la Bastille*. I knew I didn't want to raise a child in that world. And I don't think you would have left it."

"She is a beautiful girl, Laurette."

She laughed, sniffled. "She looks like her father. So much

like her father. And I love Gagnon, you must believe that. I do. But sometimes I look at her, and I remember and—" A new surge of confession came upon her. "I miss you."

"Gagnon knows?"

"He knew before we married. He wanted to give her his name. For there to be no question."

"Look at her. Of course there are questions. She looks for all the world like a little sister I had."

"You never told me you had a sister."

"She died. There is only me, and I've thought for so long that my family would die with me, but now—"

"He loves her, Marcel. As if she were his very own."

"She is. If I've done nothing else good in my life, I've given her to you."

She heard Joseph stirring in the kitchen and excused herself to give him the list of chores he would have in his brothers' absence, promising *pain perdu* if he worked without complaint. Aimée-Renée continued her fascination with the gold shuttle all the while Laurette brushed and plaited her hair, turning it loose only while her dress was dropped over her head.

"Perhaps I'll have Mademoiselle Elianne teach *you* how to use it," Laurette said. "You may have more of a knack for it than I."

As Laurette fastened the tie at the back of her dress and wriggled her into stockings and soft leather shoes, she answered the usual litany of the girl's questions. "*Papa* is on an errand and will be back in a few days." "Big brothers are on an errand and should be back in time for dinner." "The man, yes, is very sick and needs to rest, so we must play quietly today." She prepared breakfast and issued the same instructions to Joseph, charging him not to fuss with his sister, a charge she repeated when Aimée-Renée would not relinquish her new treasure for even a moment.

"Give it to me," Laurette finally said, dropping it into her apron pocket. "Go outside, both of you, and run the dogs through some simple commands. Maybe the pups will learn. But stay in view of the house."

Both children were delighted and tore through their breakfast while Laurette prepared a weak broth and tea and thinly sliced bread for Marcel. She took her time arranging the dishes on the tray, waiting until the children were safely outside before entering the room.

The light of day revealed a devastating change. His face had turned as pale as the linen, his mouth agape, his eyes staring straight above him, without the slightest flicker at her entrance.

"Marcel." She hastily set the tray on the side table and rushed to his side, pleading, "God have mercy," as she made the sign of the cross.

His body responded in three shallow, quick breaths. "I'm not going to ask for his mercy, you know."

"Shh. Don't talk like that. Not now, not when—"

"When I'm dying?"

"We've both much to be forgiven."

His head lolled to the side, finding her face. "If you forgive me, and Gagnon, and Renée. And even Anne, who cared nothing for any of this until I took her—" He looked away again. "Your forgiveness will bring me peace. All the peace I need for this world. This life."

Laurette took his hand and brought it to her lips, finding hope along with the bit of warmth in it. "But this isn't our only life, dear friend. There is another, after. Where all is peace. But you must seek God's forgiveness." She thought of everything Gagnon would say, bringing out words buried so deep, they must be truth. "Only ask, and God will usher you into heaven."

"I know the heaven of this world, Laurette. Here. This house, this home. All those moments I could claim this roof as my own. In the winter, cold, hungry, unwelcome." He said this with a hint of a smile that assured his spirit remained intact. "Watching you by the fire. Beautiful and content. I thought I might give something like this to you someday, when a man could be prosperous without land. When I could be his equal."

"You can leave this life his equal. My friend, my love. Only pray." Though her words were little more than tear-choked whispers, she felt the same as if she called them out across an ocean, or across the violence of the Paris streets. She both held him and called to him, a desperate beckoning. In other times, at other bedsides, she knew to call a priest. Even her own mother, drowning in the blood drawn by her father's hand, used her final breath to give confession. But there was no priest. There was no church. Only Laurette, on her knees, waiting to hear.

"Laurette." Such a soft sound.

"*Oui*, Marcel."

"Will Gagnon bury me here? On his land? So I can be near—"

"Of course, of course he will. You always have a place."

"There is a prayer—I used to hear you and Renée, nights when I stole . . ."

"God of heaven," she began, as if for the first time, "see him now . . ." But before she could speak of the stars and the moon and the darkest clouds, Marcel breathed his last.

L'épisode 32

Renée

PARIS

It begins with a pounding on my cell door—a useless act, given I've no right to grant or refuse access to the self-proclaimed official on the other side. His manner of dress is only slightly elevated from the rough clothing worn by my guards, and nowhere near as elegant as the suit worn by Marcel.

"Renée Brodeur, you have been charged with acts of high treason against *l'Assemblée nationale* in your efforts to assist in the unlawful emigration of Louis XVI, former and disgraced sovereign of France; his wife, Marie Antoinette of Austria; their children; and the former princess Elisabeth. For your crimes, you have earned a sentence of death by *la guillotine*, with a date set for tomorrow, 29 November 1793, at the first possible hour of the day. Make peace with God if you wish."

No further opportunities to plead my case, to ask for mercy, to beg just one more day. The final words ring in my ear long after the door has slammed shut, key turned, silence descended. No offer of a priest, only permission to pray.

But I need no permission. Do I not pray to my heavenly Father every night? The same prayer since my childhood, for a peaceful sleep and a new day's awakening? I've never shared that prayer—more precious to me than any other—with a priest. Only God could provide solace on nights when I lie restless with fear, and only God could grant me strength to meet each day. And here I know I have only one more chance to hold his promises. One more night. One more day. What priest could grant me more?

Four days, Marcel had promised me. Tomorrow's dawn would be the third in the promise, and the final in my life. Unless, by some miracle, he is here before the sunrise, I will not see Gagnon again. Nor Laurette—and all by my choosing. Light is fading when I pull Marcel's well-crafted confession from its place beneath my mattress. I read it again, and again, for the hundredth time since it fell into my hands. It has been folded and refolded, its edges worn, the creases soft. The neat, scrolling hand, the lies that could buy my life. Renouncing what I love, blackening my truth. Words written in the blood of a mother, a father, and a golden-haired innocent boy.

I take my stub of a candle, climb upon my chair, and thrust it through the barred window, asking for a light.

"Don't tell me you're scared of the dark, little one." It's the detestable Albert, and I know my turn of events is a result of his betrayal. "Might want to get used to it. It'll be darkness for you forever come morning."

I say nothing, only repeat my request. He obliges, for no other reason than perhaps a smidge of kindness. Or, less likely, a repayment for the pears he took from me after Marcel left. I've not taken a bite of anything since then.

After thanking him for the tiny flame returned to me, I return to my wobbly table and plant the taper on the spiked dish.

I fold the confession, hiding the words within. My resurrection, Marcel had called it. Each letter a plea for mercy, a chance for a new life. What if I'd listened? What if I had put my hand in his, saying, *"Marcel! Yes!* Merci à Dieu, *take me before the judge. I will sign! I will say it all; just grant me life to return home. To Laurette! To Gagnon!"*

Perhaps—it is not too late. I can spend the night memorizing the words. Why do I need Marcel to convey them? I'll speak them through the night until they sound like the product of my soul. I'll say them to whatever citizen officer, citizen guard, citizen executioner will hear them. They will be the prayer for my life. They will be my hope. My restoration.

And then, as clear as if he were in the room with me, I hear Gagnon's voice.

"Why would you put your faith in Marcel Moreau, of all people, when your very life is in the hands of God?"

So clear and true is the voice, I turn and look, certain to see his familiar silhouette, enormous in the light of my candle, projected on the walls of my cell.

"I am the resurrection, and the life: he that believeth in me, though he were dead, yet shall he live."

I am tempted to read the words one more time, but know the weakness of my resolve. My confession is to Christ alone. I don't even know what words to wrap around my sin. I can only say, "Forgive me, Lord." For my recklessness. For my pride. I press my hand upon the folded sheet and speak aloud the names of those I love and will never see again in this life. "Laurette. Gagnon. Marcel." Yes, even Marcel. Then I lift it and touch a corner to the flame. As it is consumed slowly, the paper turning black and curling, I see faces in its light.

Bertrand.

My mother, my aunt.

Denise Gagnon and her infant son.

My queen, my king, *les deux* dauphins, and the child I've yet to meet.

They are not dead. They live, just as I do now. Just as I will tomorrow, and for the eternity to follow. The flame burns closer and closer to my fingers. On any other night, I would drop it, save my flesh. After all, I am *la couturière*. My hands are my trade, my life. But tonight my life has ended. My hands are useless to my salvation. I delight in the initial, sharp pain. It is exquisite, indulgent. A triumph of my consciousness over instinct. When the last word is consumed, the final corner of paper burned away, the ashes fall to the table. My flesh, however, remains. Intact, with only the promise of a blister. All pain erased.

⚜

God of heaven, see me now

The whole world rumbles beneath my feet, or so it seems. In truth I know it is the motion of the tumbril, the turning of the wheels—sluggish, with thick spokes—clearly visible to all the eyes that line the road. It is a short distance, I'm told, but the throng gathered on either side makes the going slow. Their shouts surround us like a newly built wall, each word a brick.

"Liberté!"

"Fraternité!"

"Égalité!"

Within the proclamations, gleeful taunts of death. A cry for blood and damnation for the tyrants. Tyrants like me. It is an amazing, fearful thing to be so shouted down. I have never harmed a soul, never wielded power, never armed myself with anything sharper than a scissors.

There is a jolt, and I stumble forward, my fall stopped by the stranger beside me.

"Merci, Seigneur." I assume he is worthy of the title.

He responds only with a smile, and I can't remember the last time I've seen anything so gentle and beautiful. Though I am steady on my feet, he keeps hold of my hand. Until his touch, I'd no idea the depth of my fear. I have numbed myself with hunger and clouded my thoughts with a swirling, silent hope for rescue. With the exception of Marcel's visit, my solitude has been so complete, I've nearly forgotten the simple, instant warmth of humanity, and I wish to feel it one more time.

With a boldness that comes from waning time, I ask, "Will you hold my hand, sir? Will you hold it until—?"

"My child, it will be an honor."

Child. I suppose it is natural that he sees me as such. My brow does not quite reach the breadth of his shoulder, and no doubt the dirt on my face obscures my features. At any other time, I might have taken umbrage, telling him that I am no child. That I'm to turn twenty-two in the coming December. But we both know I will see no such milestone, and I merely thank him again.

'Neath stars and moon and darkest cloud

We roll to a stop, and the wagon's tailgate is open. The others who ride with me—the ones whose features I've taken no pains to notice—are unceremoniously handed down. There is a shout when it is my stranger's turn.

"Evrémonde!"

I don't recognize the name, but I've been sheltered from much of the nobility. For his part, my stranger shows no eagerness to claim it, as he does not so much as turn his head in their direction. Instead, he keeps a firm grip on my hand, and it is he who lifts me down, leaving the filthy, bloodstained guard to stand listlessly by. My stranger spins me aloft, and for a moment we could be at a dance, my feet waltzing on air. I get only a glimpse of the terrible machine, its blade hoisted high above.

When my feet touch the ground, I see only the fine wool of his coat. I tilt my head back to look at his face, all kindness and strength, with the gray blanket of sky behind it.

"Be strong," he says.

"But for you, dear stranger, I should not be so composed. I am—" Still, here, with the worst of all fates within reach, I am afraid to tell him who I am. What I know and have witnessed. "I am naturally a poor little thing. Faint of heart." If I were truly faint of heart, I suppose, I would not be living this moment. However, a tiny sprout of fear has sprung to life within me, and I long desperately for some comfort—a final embrace. In the midst of this raging sea, I feel utterly alone. Perhaps I secretly wish for one last bit of mercy, for one of these gory monsters to hear my plea, pull me from the line, and restore me to my innocence.

"I suppose I should raise my thoughts to him who was put to death, that we might have hope and comfort here today," I say to my stranger. "I think you were sent to me by heaven."

"Or you to me. Keep your eyes upon me, dear child, and mind no other object."

Grant me dreams to sleep in peace

As he speaks, the rushing sound of the blade in quick descent ends in a sickening silence, and the crowd erupts in cheers. I hear this faintly, as if on the edge of a disappearing dream, as if I'm already drifting away from this place. But I know to drift away is to drift into the crowd that calls for my blood. I remember the women in the queen's hall, their anger weapon enough to slay Bertrand. The people of Paris rising together to destroy their country with relentless, murderous rage, brick by brick. They pose a prolonged death, a personal affront to my flesh, and right now the only thing keeping me anchored is this stranger's grip.

"I mind nothing while I hold your hand, dear sir." And I grip it tighter. "I shall mind nothing when I let it go, if they are rapid."

"They will be rapid. Fear not!"

We speak as if this is a quality to be admired, this seamlessness of justice, and not a system that has now given me a life to be measured in minutes. I want to close my eyes and indulge in the luxury of memory, but I can only recall my most recent hours, my own mind protecting itself from those days before I took my first step on the path that brought me to this place.

And with the sunrise in the East

"Brave and generous friend," I say, tugging him closer, "will you let me ask you one last question? It troubles me—just a little." I sense that he needs to be a source of strength. After all, these are his final moments too. I think of Bertrand and Gagnon, knowing they would want to leave this world having helped someone.

"Tell me what it is." He sounds indulgent, welcoming, and details that I've guarded with silence until this moment pour forth.

"I have a cousin, an only relative and an orphan, like myself, whom I love very dearly. She lives in a farmer's house in the south country. Poverty parted us, and she knows nothing of my fate." I pray that Marcel has reached Mouton Blanc safely, but I cannot know for certain. And even so . . . "How should I tell her! It is better as it is."

"Yes, yes; better as it is."

I fear his attention is growing as short as our time together—our time on earth—and I pose to him the question that has plagued me since I first heard the pounding on the door.

"What I have been thinking as we came along, and what

I am still thinking now, as I look into your kind, strong face which gives me so much support, is this: If the Republic really does good to the poor, and they come to be less hungry, and in all ways to suffer less, she may live a long time, my cousin." I think about my elusive birthday. "She may even live to be old."

"What then, my gentle sister?"

My eyes fill with tears, the first since I fell to the filthy bricks on my cell floor. "Do you think that it will seem long to me, while I wait for her in the better land?"

"It cannot be, my child; there is no time there, and no trouble there."

Wake me to a glorious day

My mind flies back to such a life. Long, listless days. Sweet grass and laughter. Hard work and deep sleep and no thought of yesterday or the next day or the next. What troubles had I known, other than a little hunger? It has now been days since I have had any taste of food, and in light of what awaits, an empty stomach seems something easily endured.

I tell my stranger that his words bring comfort, and as I do, I sense an emptiness at my back, and I know my time has come.

"Am I to kiss you now?" I ask, for it seems a fitting way to end a life.

He responds, "Yes," as if we are fulfilling a lifelong promise, and not a notion newly born.

He bends to me, and suddenly his lips are soft on mine. His kiss erases the terror of the days behind me and strengthens me for the steps ahead.

I turn, forced by a viselike grip on my elbow, yanked as if I've threatened to flee. The shouts of the crowd are softened briefly as my crimes are read above the din. I don't recognize my life in the account, but it must be true, for here I am, my face upturned to capture the autumn breeze. Each ascending step brings me closer to the giant machine, but also to some promise of freedom.

"I am the Resurrection and the Life!" The voice of my stranger carries, but I don't look back. I can't. Instead, I scan the crowd, a blur of sunburned faces, and I think I see—

"À la mort!"

Father, Son, and Holy Spirit—I pray

The sea calls for my death. My blood. In the midst of all those open mouths, those fists raised in the air, there is one familiar face. Gagnon. He is motionless, his expression set with uncomprehending compassion. There's no time to marvel how he came to be here. I can only hold his gaze, pleading.

Tell her.

Tell Laurette.

Je prie.

Je prie.

Je prie.

My throat is cradled in the blood-soaked wood, my eyes forced down to see nothing but the gore below. I close them, entreating God to show me some beauty, something within this darkness to usher me to the Light.

Show her to me, Sovereign Lord. Before I embrace her in your presence, give me a glimpse of these intervening years.

And my heavenly Father complies. I see my Laurette, at this moment, at Gagnon's table, each of her hands clasped in that of a strong son. One of them holds the hand of a beautiful little girl with Marcel's face, and the other the hand of my own little lost prince. Then, in a vision beyond description, I see a new, thriving life nestled in darkness. A tiny boy, and I know he will have his day, whole and healthy and grown, sitting at this table, his brothers long gone to their own. All this is today, this hour, but God reveals tomorrow, too. Gagnon riding past a new grave, dug in ground consecrated only by a family's legacy. It is where Marcel's body will rest with the land he so desperately loved. I will never see this friend again, but the others . . .

At the first touch of the steel on my flesh, my final prayer, my final question is answered. *How long will it be?*

My mother, awash in grace, holds her arms out to catch me. I'm folded in a softness beyond any silk my hands have touched.

I feel my name, *Renée*, and turn to see Laurette, restored to the beautiful young woman I last saw through the window of a royal carriage. I know she has left generations behind—soon to follow. Bertrand awaits by a fountain. Gagnon stands off in a field. Marie, freed from the shackles of royalty, holds her children. All of us wait together, made glorious in spirit.

All of this before I exhale my final breath. Laurette's story, my story. I live every moment of both in less than the blink of a blade.

A Note from the Author

This story had its first spark of life when I was standing in front of a class of tenth-grade students, doing my due diligence as an English teacher, making them consider every nook and shadow of Charles Dickens's novel *A Tale of Two Cities*. In talking about the redemption of Sydney Carton and the role the little seamstress played, I tossed off a comment: "I would love to write the story of the seamstress." And for years, as the idea spun around in my head, more questions presented themselves. *How did she come to the guillotine? Why mention a cousin? Would anyone else even care about this?*

Then, in a flurry of Facebook messaging with my dear friend Rachel McMillan brainstorming story ideas, this idea that had been buried for years resurfaced. As usual, I feel blessed to be a part of the Tyndale House family, where acquisitions director Jan Stob caught the same enthusiasm. I am grateful for the opportunity to bring my stories to life through Tyndale House. Thank you, Kathy Olson, for not putting up with my nonsense.

Careful readers of *A Tale of Two Cities* will recognize the seamstress character immediately, and to them I apologize for a novel that is at least 50 percent spoiled. I do hope you'll appreciate how very much I love this work and have tried to be true to the world Dickens brought to life in his untouchable way. I don't consider this an homage or a retelling of that story at all, save for the final pages. And, again, I ask historians to forgive lapses in facts that result from a desire to pave the path for my characters. Specifically, you'll have to indulge my idealistic portrait of Queen Marie Antoinette. I did strive to faithfully re-create key moments of the French Revolution. The Palace of Versailles was overrun by an army of women; a guard was killed while protecting the queen; the family did attempt an ill-fated escape. However, the role that my Renée plays in all those events is purely fictitious. Hence the fun of writing this story! I also own up to placing a red cap on Marcel's head a few years too early, but he seems like the kind of guy who might have started that trend.

Readers—you have no idea how much I cherish your faithful support, how you've carried my spirit through book after book. Thank you so much for sending me an email at just the right time, for posting encouraging reviews, for welcoming me into your mind for a few hours with every page. If you don't already, please follow me on my Facebook author page, Allison Pittman Author, or on Twitter and Instagram @allisonkpittman. You can even enjoy the occasional, infrequent blog post on my website, allisonkpittman.com.

> May the God of hope fill you with all joy and peace as
> you trust in him, so that you may overflow with hope
> by the power of the Holy Spirit.
>
> ROMANS 15:13, NIV

Discussion Questions

1. *The Seamstress* was inspired by a minor character in Charles Dickens's *A Tale of Two Cities*. Have you read that novel? If so, did *The Seamstress* change anything about your view of that story? Is there another Dickens novel that is a particular favorite of yours?

2. Marie Antoinette is portrayed sympathetically throughout the story. How often do you think there is a difference between a highly visible figure's private life and public persona? What effect do you think the passage of time has on our perceptions?

3. Do you think Renée's decision to remain with the queen stemmed from compassion, or was it motivated by pride? Or some other reason?

4. Patriotism and love of country can take many forms. How would you compare and contrast Gagnon, Marcel, and Bertrand in terms of their love and dedication to their country? In what ways are patriotism and love of one's country the same thing? In what ways, if any, are they different?

5. In general, should people in positions of power choose their duty to their nation over the well-being of their family? Why or why not?

6. What do you think motivates Marcel to get involved in the revolutionary cause? What motivates him in his relationships with others? What consistent themes or attitudes do you see in his character? Is there anything about him you admire? Why or why not?

7. Despite a series of bad decisions, Laurette finds herself with a safe, blessed life. Can you think of a time when God turned a bad choice into a blessing for you or someone you care about?

8. Although Renée's role is purely fiction, the women's march on Versailles (during which the character of Bertrand is killed) actually happened. Is it ever appropriate for social reform to find its voice in anger and violence? Give reasons to support your answer and, if you can, other historical examples.

9. Suppose Renée's final "confession" could have saved her from the guillotine. Did she make the right decision in refusing this offer of help from Marcel? Why or why not? What do you think you would have done in her place?

10. Romans 13:5 says, "Therefore, it is necessary to submit to the authorities, not only because of possible punishment but also as a matter of conscience" (NIV). Do you think this holds true when authorities are in clear violation of God's Word? Should Christians ever consider disobedience to authorities a righteous act? If so, how and when?

About the Author

Award-winning author Allison Pittman left a seventeen-year teaching career in 2005 to follow the Lord's calling into the world of Christian fiction, and God continues to bless her step of faith. Her novels *For Time and Eternity*, *Forsaking All Others*, and *All for a Sister* were named as finalists for the Christy Award for excellence in Christian fiction, and her novel *Stealing Home* won the American Christian Fiction Writers' Carol Award. In 2012, she was named ACFW's Mentor of the Year. She also heads up a successful, thriving writers' group in San Antonio, where she lives with her husband, Mike, and the canine star of the family—Stella.

Chapter 1

My father always told me if I never took a sip of wine, I'd never shed a single tear. One begat the other, and only the common cup in the hands of a priest, the blessed wine of the sacrament, could offer peace. Only the blood of Christ could offer life. Any other was nothing more than ruin, a sinner's way of washing sin.

And yet he drank. Every night, the flames of our small fire danced in the cut glass of his goblet.

It seemed a silly warning, but for all of my brief childhood at home, I had only two sips of wine. The first over a year ago when, at the age of five, I begged for a taste at the grand table. The other just months ago, in the feast following Mother's funeral. Then, true to my father's prophecy, tears streamed down my face.

So, too, as I stood in his embrace, the cold wind of November whipping all around us. Ice like pinpricks upon my cheeks. Perhaps I'd taken in a sufficient amount from the constant scent of wine on his breath, and from the traces left on his lips when he kissed me.

"My Katharina." He stretched my name, and I imagined it pouring out in a stream mixed with tears and wine. He knelt before me, the patched fabric of his breeches touching the last bit of unsanctified ground.

"Papa? Where are we?"

To answer, he took me by my shoulders and turned me to look at the foreboding stone structure on the other side of the iron gate. "A church, kitten. A house of God."

That much I assumed from the tall, arched windows and the lingering echo of the bell that had been tolling upon our approach. Six rings, and the sun nearly set. A new sound emerged in the wake of the bells. Footsteps, strident and rhythmic, displacing the tiny stones on the path beyond the gate. They carried what looked like a shadow—tall and black and fluttering.

Frightened, I twisted back in my father's embrace. "Papa?"

"Be strong, my girl."

Before I could say another word, I heard the screech of metal and a voice that matched its tone in every way. "Katharina von Bora?"

"Papa?" I clung to him, even as he stood tall and away.

"*Ja.* This is my daughter."

A heavy hand fell on my shoulder. "Say good-bye to your papa, little one."

Good-bye?

Two days before, when Papa told me to pack a few things—extra stockings and my sleeping cap—into a small drawstring bag, he'd said nothing about leaving me at a church to say *good-bye*. In all our travel, the miles riding in the back of farm carts, the night spent among strangers at the small, damp inn, he answered my questions with platitudes about what a fine, strong girl I was, and how it was good to get away, just the two of us.

"Is it because of the new mama?" The woman loomed large, even with two days' distance between us. Her stern commands, her wooden spoon ever at the ready to correct a sullen temper, her furrowed brow as she counted the meager coins in the little wooden box above the stove. "I can be good, Papa. I will work harder and speak to her more sweetly. I'll be a good girl. I promise. Papa—*please!*"

I grasped his hand, repeating my promises, feeling victorious when he scooped me up off the ground. I tried to bury my face in his neck, but he jostled me and gripped my chin in his fingers.

"Ruhig sein." His voice and eyes were stern. "Hush, I say. You are Katharina von Bora. Do you know what that means?"

"*Ja,* Papa." I touched my hand against his grizzled whiskers. "Bearer of a great and proper name."

"Very old, and very great." He was whispering now, his back turned to the shadowy figure. From this height, looking down over Papa's shoulder, I could clearly see that it was only a nun. A soft, pale face peered from behind a veil, while long black sleeves fluttered around clasped hands. A tunic over a plain black dress bore an embroidered cross, and in many ways she was not unlike the nuns I knew from our church back home. So why had Papa brought me here, so far away?

"But I don't want to stay here, Papa." I had to look down into his face, and it made him seem so much smaller.

"Be a good girl." He set me back on my feet and bowed down to meet me eye to eye. "Grow up to be a strong, smart young lady. And do not cry."

"But—"

His admonishing finger, nail bitten to the quick and grimy from travel, staved off the prick of new tears. "Strong, I tell you."

"Are you coming back for me? After a time, after I've grown up a little? When I'm a lady?"

A weak smile played across his lips, and he cast a quick, nervous glace up to the nun. "Child," he said, gripping my shoulders, "I am delivering you into the hands of God, the same God who once gave you to me. Could you ask for anything better than to be in his loving care?"

I knew, instantly, how I should answer. Thinking back to our small, dark home, with rooms shut away to ward off the chill. My three older brothers crowded around the table, squabbling for the last bowl of stew, and taking mine when there wasn't enough. Now, with me gone, there would be more for everybody else. Not enough, but more. Maybe the new mama would smile a bit and not stomp through the kitchen rattling pots like a thunderstorm. Maybe my brothers would stop stealing bread and making their papa lie to the red-faced baker when he came pounding on the door. There would be one less body to soak up the heat from the fire, and more space in the crowded bed.

I stood up straight and wiped my nose on my sleeve. "I'm ready now, Papa."

"That's my good girl." He kissed my forehead, my cheeks, then briefly, my lips. One kiss, he said, for each of my brothers, and one final from Mother watching from heaven. The nun kept her own silent watch until the end, when Papa handed me the small bundle he'd been carrying over his shoulder for the last mile of our walk.

"No." The sister's sturdy hand stretched from within the long black sleeve. "She comes with nothing."

"Please, Sister—"

"Sister Odile, reverend mother of the convent of Brehna."

"It's just a nightcap," Papa said, not mentioning that it was the cap Mama—my mama—had stitched with small purple flowers. "And clean stockings and an apron."

"Nothing." Sister Odile tightened her grip and dragged me to her side.

Head low, Papa shouldered the bag once again, saying, "As it should be, I suppose."

I noticed the quiver in his chin and knew it was one of those times when I would have to be strong in his place. I needed to stand straighter, fix my eyes above, and set my mind in obedience. A pinpoint of cold pierced my shoulder where the gold band on Sister Odile's finger touched my flesh. Ignoring the growing grayness of the sky and the imminent demise of Papa's resolve, I took a deep, cleansing breath.

"You should start for home, Papa. It will be dark soon."

"Yes," he said. And that was all. In the next instant, I was turned toward the gate, then marched through it. Sister Odile's robes flapped against her, an irregular rhythm in the growing wind. For all I knew, Papa remained behind the iron bars, watching every step. Counting them, maybe, as I did. I listened for his voice, waiting for him to call me back, but if he did, the words were lost to the crunching of the stones beneath Sister Odile's bearlike feet. I myself felt each one through the thin, patched leather of my shoes. When we came to a turn in the path, one sharp enough to afford a glance out of the corner of my eye, I saw the gate, with Papa nowhere to be found.

Then came the rush of tears.

"Stop that, now."

To emphasize her command, Sister Odile stopped in the middle of the path, leaving me no choice but to do the same.

I scrunched my face, calculating the distance between the looming church and the empty gate. Both were within a few easy, running steps. And I was fast—faster than any other girl on my street, and some of the boys, too. I could outrun my brothers when I needed to avoid one of their senseless poundings, and I could cover the distance from our front door to the top of the street before Papa could finish calling out my name in the evenings when he came home before dark. In an instant I could be free, back at the gate, squeezed through, and in Papa's arms before the nun would even realize I'd escaped. Or I could fly, straight and fast, right up the path to the looming church. Surely Sister Odile's cloddish feet and flapping sleeves would make her lag in pursuit. The height and breadth of the outer stone walls promised a labyrinth of dark corridors and twisting halls within. I could run away, hide away, lose myself in the shadows until morning, when the clouds might disperse and reveal a shining sun to direct me home.

Labyrinth. It was a word Papa taught me, reading from a big book of ancient stories. A monster lived in its midst—half man, half bull. *Minotaur.* I mouthed the word, feeling the dryness of my chapped lips at the silent *m*, and reached a tentative hand out to Sister Odile's skirt, wondering if the voluminous fabric might not be hiding such a creature within.

"Hör auf." Sister Odile slapped my hand away and resumed our journey, doing nothing to allay my fear that I might well be in the custody of a monster. The size of the feet alone promised supernatural proportions, and now the woman's breath came in snorts and puffs like some great-chested beast.

"You want to run, don't you, girl?"

"No." The lie didn't bother me one bit.

Sister Odile let out a laugh deep enough to lift the cross

off her frock. "Back out the gate, wouldn't you? And what if I told you to go ahead? You're little enough to squeeze right through, aren't you? You want to chase down your papa? Do you even know which way he went? Up the road or down?"

Every word in every question climbed a scale, ending in a high, gasping wheeze.

"If I did run, you'd never catch me. I'd disappear like a shadow." It's what I did at home, on nights when Papa wasn't there. I'd fold myself into the corners, away from the reach of the new mama's spoon.

"Not even a shadow can escape the wolves," Sister Odile said, her grip softening a little. "And hear me when I tell you this, my girl. That is all that waits for you outside these walls. Wolves ready to tear little girls into scraps for their pups."

This, I knew, held some truth, as Papa had often said the same thing. Still, my trust faltered. "And what is inside the walls?"

Sister Odile laughed again, but this time the sound rumbled in her throat, like the comfort of long-off thunder. "Great mysteries and secrets. The kind that most little girls will never learn."

"Like in books?"

"In the greatest book of all. And sacred language."

Our steps fell into a common pace, with mine trotting two to every one of Sister Odile's.

"I can read a little already," I said, my words warm with pride. "Papa taught me. I can read better than my brother, and he's eleven."

"Then your father has done a very good and unselfish thing, allowing you to come here. Let your *Dummkopf* brother fend for himself."

I stopped my laughter with the back of my hand. Fabian was an idiot, by all measures. Cruel and thick and lazy. He was the closest to me in age, and therefore the most likely to deliver abuse. Clemens was thirteen, and Hans a full-grown man, almost, and I wondered if they would even notice my absence. Our sister, Maria, had been gone for nearly a year, married to a solicitor's clerk, and had rarely been mentioned since.

"You can find peace here," Sister Odile was saying, "because we work to keep the darkness of the world away."

We'd come to a heavy wooden door with an iron ring fastened so high, Sister Odile had to stretch up on her toes to reach it.

Thud. Thud. Thud.

"There is another door on the other side of the building," Sister Odile said, "open to all who seek sanctuary. This one is just for us."

Us. I repeated the word.

"The sisters. And the girls. Other little girls, just like you. And bigger, too. We don't lock the door until after supper, and then don't open it at all after dark. You got here just in time."

The mention of the word *supper* brought my stomach rumbling to life, as loud as the sound of the sliding bolt and creaking hinges. Whatever hunger I felt, however, knotted itself into pure fear at the image in the open doorway. No amount of black fabric could shroud the twisted figure of the old woman who stood, leaning heavily on a thick walking stick, on the other side. A stub of candle illuminated a face the likes of which I had never seen before. One eye clouded with blindness, thin lips mismatched to each other, and a cascade of fleshy pink-tinged boils dripping like wax down one side. In stature, she was not much taller than I, and I stood silent and still as a post under the woman's studious gaze. Then the single squinted eye was aimed up at Sister Odile, and a voice squawked, "She's too late."

"Sister Gerda." Sister Odile spoke soothingly as both greeting and introduction. "This is our newest charge, Katharina."

"Supper's over and cleaned up." Her lips moved like waves, producing a spittle that dripped unchecked down her chin. "Thought you made it clear to have her here by three o'clock."

"So are we to stay out here until morning?" Sister Odile brought me close to her side. "Or will you kindly allow us to come in?"

Sister Gerda muttered as she scuttled backward, opening the door wide enough for a full view of the entry, where another door—equally impressive—dominated the facing wall. The long, narrow room was lined with two wooden benches. Above each hung a tapestry, but the light was too dim to make out the images.

"Go and fetch her a cup of water," Sister Odile said, leading me to sit on one of the benches. "And some bread, too. I'm sure you're hungry, aren't you?"

I nodded, then said, "Yes, ma'am," in case it was too dark for a silent response. An invisible prod from Papa prompted me to add, "Thank you, ma'am."

"Kitchen's closed up," Sister Gerda said with a sniff. "Cleaned up, too. It's nearly seven."

"This wouldn't be the first time somebody crept into the kitchen for a slice of bread after dark. Would our Lord not bid us to share what we have? Does our obedience to him snuff out with the sun? You're a quick, silent little one, Sister Gerda. No doubt you can be there and back before the hour tolls. And should anyone comment, tell them you are there on my errand. *Schnell!* Before the poor girl collapses from hunger."

I listened, fascinated by the rise and fall of Sister Odile's tone. Demanding at first, then affectionate, authoritative, and almost playful at the end. Almost as if four different women spoke from within the habit, each spinning to show her face from behind the veil. This, I knew, was a woman to be respected, maybe even feared. While her size brought on a certain intimidation, a level of comfort came with it too. Stooping, she took the candle stub from Sister Gerda, touched it to a sconce on the wall, and handed it back with a sweetly whispered reminder to hurry. Then she went to one of the benches and settled her weight upon it, bringing out a creaking protest from the wood.

"Komm her." She held out her hands, gold band winking in the candlelight. It was impossible to distinguish sleeves from shadow, but the face floating in the midst of the darkness was wide and smiling.

Without another thought, I took the few steps to cross the room and climbed up into the softness of Sister Odile. Arms wrapped around me, and I was absorbed in the deepest embrace I could remember since before Mama fell ill. I pressed my face into the warm, worn wool and felt the rumbling of the sister's breath. Humming, now, a tune I did not recognize, but somehow knew to be ancient. Sacred. I closed my eyes, knowing it would be safe to cry now. The tears could flow into the wool, and as long as I did not sniffle, I could pour my fear and sadness into this woman. Instead, with each breath, I felt the block of fatigue from the journey begin to crumble, turning to little pebbles like those on the walkway, and finally to dust. I felt heavy, too heavy to cry. Too heavy to lift my head and ask where I might go to sleep. Too heavy to close my lips when I felt its pull.

The last thing I remembered was the coarseness of the cross on Sister Odile's breast pressed into my cheek, each stitch wrapped around the lullaby.

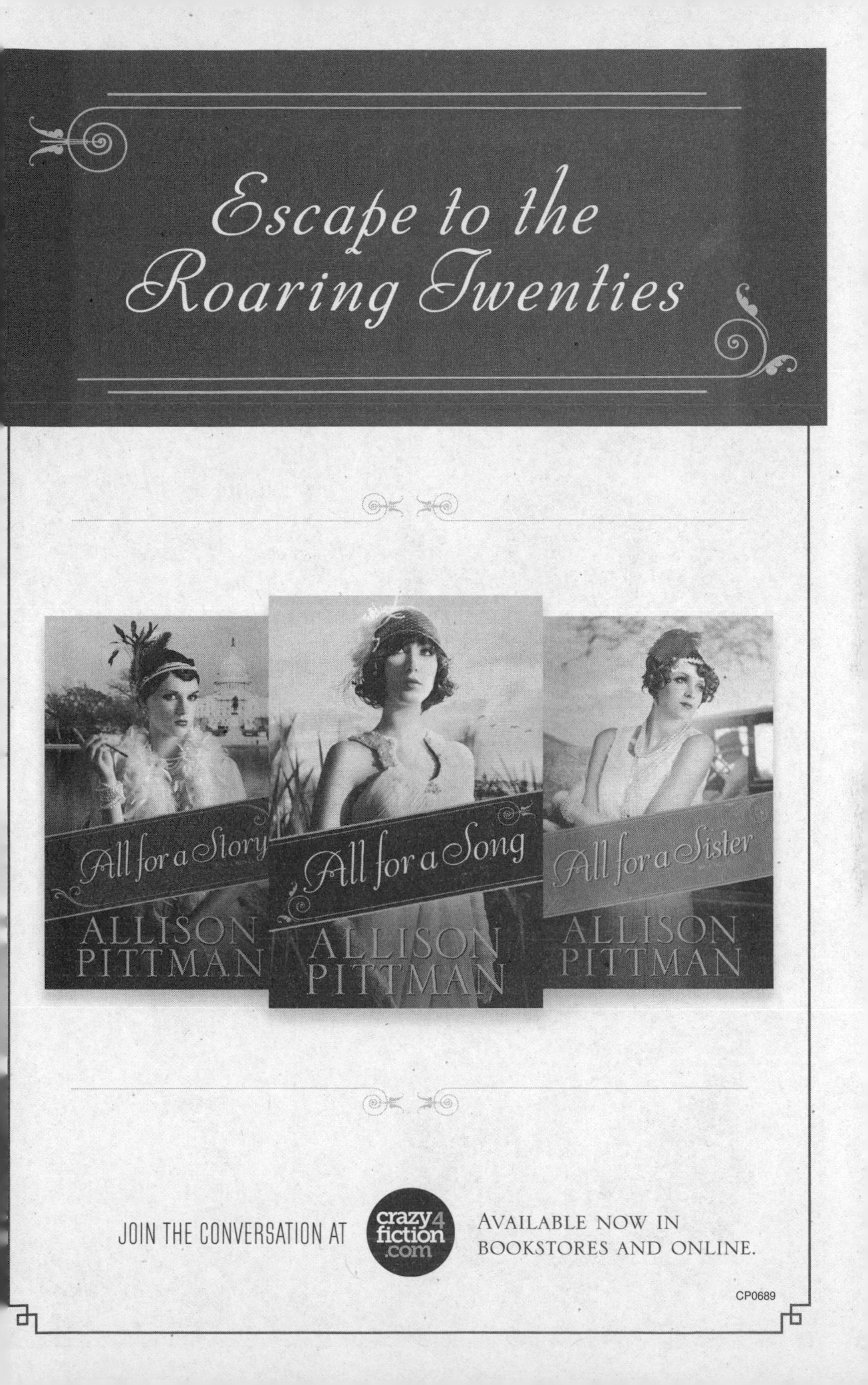
Escape to the Roaring Twenties
All for a Story
ALLISON PITTMAN
All for a Song
ALLISON PITTMAN
All for a Sister
ALLISON PITTMAN
JOIN THE CONVERSATION AT
crazy4fiction.com
AVAILABLE NOW IN BOOKSTORES AND ONLINE.
CP0689